the grumpiest billionaire

USA TODAY BESTSELLING AUTHOR
PIPPA GRANT

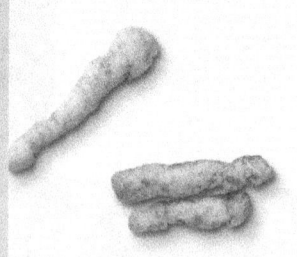

Copyright © 2025

All rights reserved. This book or any portion thereof may not be reproduced or used in any manner whatsoever, including the training of artificial intelligence, without the express written permission of the publisher except for the use of brief quotations in a book review.

This is a work of fiction. Names, characters, businesses, places, events and incidents are either the products of the author's imagination or used in a fictitious manner. Any resemblance to actual persons, living or dead, or actual events is purely coincidental. All text in this book was generated by Pippa Grant without use of artificial intelligence.

Pippa Grant®, Copper Valley Fireballs®, and Copper Valley Thrusters® are registered trademarks of Bang Laugh Love LLC.

Editing by Jessica Snyder, HEA Author Services
Proofreading by Emily Laughridge & Jodi Duggan
Cover, Edge, and Formatting Design by Qamber Designs
Edge Design embedded by Painted Wings Publishing
Cover Art Copyright © Wander Aguiar.
Illustrations by Seaj Art / James John Andres

To sisterhood in all of its forms, and to the best kind of chaos and mishaps.

1

Best laid plans

Miles William Oliver Cumberland IV, aka Oliver to his friends, aka a billionaire on the run

Of everything I expected to feel when I left my father's welcome-home party four hours ago, joy over my headlights illuminating a *Welcome to Pennsylvania* sign wasn't top on the list.

It wasn't on the list at all.

But here I am, driving into—actually, let me stop there.

I'm *driving*.

Myself.

Alone.

In the front seat.

No chauffeur. No assistant rattling off my meetings for the day. No business associate pitching a marketing partnership. No hovering security listening in to every word.

No relatives demanding to know why their exclusive, limitless credit card has been canceled or why I sold the family estate on Martha's Vineyard.

No phone calls interrupting with an emergency that needs to be dealt with.

No weight of my family's expectations squeezing my lungs and making it hard to breathe.

Just me, the pitch black of a moonless night, endless possibilities with zero expectations, enough mental preparation that driving doesn't trigger panic attacks anymore, and my road trip playlist.

This must be what peace feels like.

There's an edge to the peace—tossing my phone so it can't be used to track me and operating with cash only isn't a foolproof method of disappearing—but it's more peace than I've felt at any point in my life, and especially the past four years.

I feel around on the door for the button to roll down the window, hit it, and my seat starts to recline.

The unexpected motion startles me, and I swerve the SUV before straightening it out. No panic. Road's practically empty, and I corrected, and I'm nearly to my destination, and everything's fine.

"Wrong button," I mutter to myself.

I feel around again, and *ah, yes.*

There it is.

The right button this time. Fresh, cool air whips into the vehicle, drowning out the symphonic pop music I'm playing in honor of knowing how much my mother hates it when major symphonies cover pop songs.

And also because I love it.

It's unexpected.

It makes me smile.

And smiling has been rarer than a penguin in the desert for the past few years.

Thirty miles to go once I hit my exit, and I should—ah, yes.

There it is.

My headlights illuminate the large green sign telling me that my escape off the beaten path and into the backcountry of nowhere-land is fast approaching.

I roll my shoulders, feeling even lighter than I did with the *Welcome to Pennsylvania* sign. The exit approaches, and I swerve onto it.

Huh.

the grumpiest billionaire

Going a little fast. And that's a sharp curve. A sharp curve that keeps going.

Oh, this is one of *those* exits. The kind with a two-seventy curve. Probably need to—

"Slow down!" someone shrieks behind me.

Someone *in my car*.

I wrench the steering wheel and hit the brake.

"*Slow!*" she shrieks again. "Brake! Brake! Slow! Turn! Shoulder!"

Who the *fuck* is in my car?

Am I hallucinating?

Why isn't the road stopping? Why am I leaning against my window? Why am I going faster when I'm hitting the brake?

I—*shit*.

Gas pedal. I'm hitting the gas pedal.

I switch my foot position and slam on the brake in the middle of the off-ramp while memories of crunching metal and screams reverberate through my head.

The SUV swerves. Tires squeal. The centrifugal force has me smushed against my door, and no matter how I turn the wheel, the car doesn't go in the direction I want it to go.

It's spinning.

It's spinning out of control.

I'm spinning out of control, the laws of physics taking control of my car and my body, making breathing impossible and squishing me against the doorframe with my head leaning out the open window while I relive the reason I haven't driven myself anywhere since I was in college.

This is it.

The end.

Four hours after *freedom*, four hours after leaving the life I was stuffed into thanks to my father's greed, ego, and pride, and it's over.

Done.

Just when I thought I was finally free, it's *done*.

3

I've never eaten a fresh chocolate chip cookie straight out of the oven in my own kitchen.

I've never gone skinny-dipping.

I've never watched a rainbow from when it formed to when it faded, or seen the sun rise or set from the top of a mountain.

I've never held a baby.

I've never held a baby.

And now I never will.

News headlines flash in my vision.

"Convenience Store Heir Dies in Inconvenient Fiery Crash."

"Fitting End for Criminal's Son on the Run."

"Billionaire with Burnout Perishes in Spinout."

There's total blackness behind my eyelids as my world jerks to a sudden near-stop.

My lungs engage, and I gulp in a massive breath as I open my eyes again.

The SUV faces the pavement that was behind me a moment ago. Bouncing headlight beams illuminate fresh tire marks on the sharply curved exit ramp as the vehicle continues to rock and settle.

My fingers have gone numb. My thigh muscles quake as I push with all of my might onto the brake with one foot and into the floorboard with the other.

Dots dance in my vision.

My breath comes again in a gulp of air that's too much and not enough at the same time.

The symphony hits a crescendo that matches a rush of loud, heavy breathing.

Is that me?

No.

Not me.

I still can't get my lungs to work right.

"*Hooo,*" the person in my back seat says. "That was a trip, wasn't it?"

The person.

the grumpiest billionaire

In my back seat.

The one who yelled for me to slow down as I exited.

I finally make myself take two more breaths, more in control but still mostly fueled by adrenaline, before I shift to stare back at her.

We.

Almost.

Died.

And she thinks it was a *trip*?

"*Park!*" she shrieks as the car starts rolling. "Shoulder! Park!"

What.

The actual.

Fuck?

I slam on the brake again with a shaky foot, realizing my engine died sometime during the spin and the SUV is being guided by gravity, while I gape at the vision in my back seat.

No.

Absolutely not. This is not happening. I'm hallucinating.

I'm dreaming.

I've anticipated this day for so long that I'm dreaming, except my dream has turned into a nightmare.

Which means this—this woman I'm staring at—she's not real.

Daphne Merriweather-Brown, socialite of chaos, boundary-pusher, and my former fiancée's little sister, is not here.

Not in her tight black cocktail dress that's somehow managing to shimmer in the ambient light off the streetlamps lining the exit. Not with her blond updo half-smushed and…crooked?…and sliding off?

I shake my head.

Why is her hair sliding off?

"First donut?" she says. "Nice one, big guy. High-five. Thought we were gonna tip for a minute there, but you pulled it off. Didn't think you had it in you. But for real, how about you ease Betsy here over to the side of the road before we get murdered by a semi coming off the interstate and up this exit ramp?"

5

Oh my god.

I'm dead.

The car tipped and smashed my head, and now I'm dead.

And in hell.

Hell feels a lot like a cool Pennsylvania night, and it sounds a lot like symphonic flutes shifting into a Waverly Sweet pop tune.

Smells a bit like burnt rubber too.

I slap myself.

It hurts.

So either hell is very realistic, or I'm not dead.

But I'm definitely in a very realistic nightmare.

Daphne heaves the agitated, impatient sigh of every woman I've ever known. It's not cold enough for me to see her breath hanging between us—of course it's not, it's August—but I see a glittery, sparkly sigh float through the car's interior anyway.

Or possibly it's late and I'm tired and those are dots dancing in my vision.

Am I dead?

Am I nightmaring?

And—"*Betsy?* Who the hell is *Betsy?*"

"I named your car. She felt like a Betsy. It's very *Mercedes G-Class*, don't you think? But if you don't like it, or if she has another name, I'm happy to call her that. Or is the car a he? Or a they? I'm cool with whatever if I'm wrong about Betsy and they need a new name. So. The shoulder? Scootchy-scootchy to the sidey-sidey?"

I survived.

I had to have survived.

Even hell couldn't be this annoying.

"*Please*," she adds. "Dude, I'm all for fun, but I'm also in favor of living. Got a stuffed lobster waiting for me at home who'd be very upset if I didn't make it, you know? Plus the whole Margot thing. She'd miss me. I think."

the grumpiest billionaire

Mention of her sister—my former fiancée from a lifetime ago—has me whipping my head back around to face forward, where headlights from another car are racing the wrong way, which is actually the right way, and is also exactly toward us.

I'm backward.

The SUV ended its spinout with us facing the wrong way on the sharp off-ramp.

My heart leaps into my throat a split second before the oncoming sports car veers onto the shoulder, honks, and then flies past us and onto the highway beyond with a string of obscenities mingled with what sounds like country music following after it.

Now that I'm breathing again, my shoulders have merged with my ears. My jaw is clenched at least twice as tight as it has been at any other point since my father's driver pulled up to the house in the Hamptons three days ago, delivering him safely home from prison. And a red haze is obstructing my vision.

I restart the engine, lift my foot off the brake, and let the car roll to the edge of the road before another night owl takes the exit the way it's apparently supposed to be taken.

Fast and reckless.

But without the spinout part.

I put the engine in park and debate getting out to throw up as Daphne rolls her window down too. "Good job. Very nicely done. Quick question. Where are we?"

"Get out." The order is instinctive.

Or possibly protective.

All of my plans are unraveling because *fucking Daphne Merriweather-Brown is in my car.*

She smiles at me. "Wouldn't be the first time I've been dumped in the middle of nowhere, but hitchhiking home wasn't in my plans today. And did I see a sign that said we're in Pennsylvania when I woke up? A little far from home, yeah? You got something secret going on out here?"

"Get. Out." As the words leave my mouth a second time, even with the sentiment ringing so hard through my entire being, I know I can't leave her here.

Margot would kill me.

And while Margot and I are no longer a thing, and haven't been since my father got arrested a few years ago, and never will be again, I still care about her.

Enough that I made an excuse to go tell her goodbye last week.

In code. So she wouldn't realize it was goodbye. So she wouldn't blow this for me.

But can't a guy run away from home without his ex-fiancée's little sister stowing away?

Daphne stares at me in the dim light with that perpetual *this is fun* grin that always annoyed the shit out of me. "Getting out does seem like the safer option, but I'm good with a little excitement. Also, you and I need to have a discussion, and so unfortunately for both of us, I'll be declining your invitation. For the moment, anyway."

I stare at her while I process exactly how much control of my life I've just lost.

Again.

She shifts in the seat and pulls her hair off, then some netting, revealing more hair underneath.

It's a wig.

She was wearing a wig. That's why it was crooked. Why—never mind.

Not important why she was wearing a wig.

What's important is that I've clenched my jaw through countless boardroom meetings the past few years, not saying everything I've wanted to say to all of the people demanding I fix my father's mistake to keep the company going while he was serving his time. I've clenched my jaw through countless dinners with my mother while she pretended he was on an extended *spa vacation* so that she wouldn't have to face the reality that the company might not pull through after what he did and we might have to sell more than a few vacation homes and the artwork in three others and half of the unadulterated wine in the wine cellars to get through it.

I'm supposed to be done with my jaw-clenching days.

I'm supposed to be *free*.

But here I am, forcing words out of my mouth when my jaw is aching because the damn bite guard I'm supposed to use isn't working the way disappearing from my old life will.

"What. Are you doing. In my car?"

"I would *love* to answer that question, but I'm starting to have a few more of my own that seem a little more important. You okay? You don't look okay."

"Because *you're in my goddamn car*. Get—"

I cut myself off as crashing adrenaline battles with my rising blood pressure and makes me realize exactly how screwed I am in this escape attempt.

We're thirty miles from the little house where I have an alternate car, an alternate wardrobe, and an alternate passport and matching driver's license waiting for me so that I can shed this life and start a new one as a normal person with a normal job and maybe, *maybe*, one day make a normal family for myself.

Maybe I'll be a farmer. Or an electrician. Lumberjack. Popcorn maker at a movie theater. Bush trimmer at a theme park.

My entire life, I haven't had a choice. I'm the last in a long line of only children, raised from birth to be the next Cumberland to head up the gas station and convenience store empire that my great-grandfather built. For as long as I can remember, I've known that the only option I have is to work for and eventually run Miles2Go. That my family's wealth has given me privileges I have to pay for with my entire destiny. That I was brought into this world to serve a purpose that I don't get a say in.

But it doesn't *fit*.

It's not me.

I've been the CEO of Miles2Go for the past four years, saving it from near-certain collapse—or rather, listening to my executive assistant tell me how to save it from near-certain collapse—after my father got caught embezzling company funds to invest in a fake rare wine scheme, and I'm done.

I did my part, played the role, and now I'm done.

And until Daphne sat up in my back seat, I thought tonight would give me what I've always yearned for—the freedom to figure out who I am when I'm not living up to family expectations.

If I kick her out and she calls her father for a helicopter rescue, she'll tell everyone she was with me, and they'll know I didn't leave for the airport.

My parents think I'm headed out of the country for the next two weeks, having a well-earned vacation. By the time they get the letter telling them that I never went to the Galápagos, that I have officially resigned from the life they want me to lead and am never coming back, and that I'm endorsing Carmen Miller—my executive assistant—to be the next CEO, I'll be somewhere in a small town in a flyover state with a new identity and a new look and a made-up history.

They'll never find me.

If my family wants me back, they'll spend years searching Europe and the Caribbean and Latin American countries.

But only if Daphne doesn't fuck it all up.

If she hasn't already fucked it all up. "Give me your phone."

"What?"

"Give. Me. Your. Phone."

"Why?"

"Because I said to."

She studies me with far more intelligence than I like to give her credit for but that I know she has in her.

Margot told me once that her family's underestimation of Daphne would someday be their downfall. That everyone thought she was flaky and irresponsible and careless, but that she had a passion their parents didn't understand and the drive to burn down any obstacle in pursuit of her causes if necessary.

Margot said it with the kind of reverence usually reserved for scoring an original, previously undiscovered Picasso or for putting a nemesis out of business.

"What are you doing out here, Oliver?"

Forget the dress. Forget the chaos. Forget the number of colleges she left or was kicked out of while I was dating her sister.

This woman is dangerous. "Give me your phone, or I'm coming back there to get it."

Another car comes careening up the ramp, and my SUV shakes and my hair blows in the wind created by the other vehicle.

We need to get off the road.

But first, I need to get my hands on Daphne's phone.

2

And this is why I never go back to the city

Daphne Louise Merriweather-Brown, aka a woman who should've made an appointment to talk to Oliver instead

I've known Oliver Cumberland my entire life. He and Margot didn't start dating until they were both out of college, but our families have operated in the same sphere since before I was born.

I always thought he was a stuffy pain in the ass. Slightly dorky. Definitely boring.

So boring.

Like the *he would bore white toast* kind of boring.

Never murderous.

Until now.

Oliver's getting out of the car.

Right here. On the side of the interstate. In the middle of the night.

And he has murder in his eyes.

He wrenches my door open and holds his hand out, palm up. "Give me your phone."

On a scale of one to *I'm in deep shit and need to figure this out quickly*, I'd say this situation is a very firm *it's actually quicksand shit and there's no one here to toss me a rope.* "My phone? I don't have it."

His dark hair falls across his forehead, and the glow of the interior car lights is enough to illuminate the stress lines on his forehead and the deep purple circles beneath his eyes.

He's the same age as Margot.

Thirty-one.

In this light, he looks fifty.

At least.

"Why not?" he demands. "Where is it?"

I wave my empty fingers at him, knowing it'll aggravate him, and tell him the truth. "It fell while we were pretending the SUV was a roller coaster."

He growls low in his throat, then leans into the car.

I pull my feet up onto the seat, and he uses his own phone as a flashlight while he searches the footwells.

Not murdering me.

Yet.

My brain is in hyperdrive.

I don't know where we're going beyond *away* from New York.

I don't know why we're here.

I mean, I know why *I'm* here. I'm here because I wanted five minutes to talk to him about something important, and I made a terrible plan for the best way to see him after a few weeks of the worst insomnia of my life, and then I fell asleep in the back seat of his SUV while I was waiting for him and his driver to get in to take him home, where, I'm rapidly figuring out, he was not going.

And I don't know why.

I don't know why he's so far from his Manhattan penthouse.

Alone.

No security. No driver.

Only him.

Either he has a dark side, or there's something very, very wrong.

And considering he looks decades older than he should—"Are you ill?" I ask him.

He doesn't answer.

Craaaap.

Do I like Oliver?

Not really. Like I said, stuffy, uptight, boring, hurt my sister even if it was several years ago, blah blah, etc. etc.

But nothing about this situation is normal. He should have security with him at the very least.

And right after I woke up, as we passed the sign for Pennsylvania, he giggled.

Giggled.

The Oliver Cumberland that I've known my entire life does not *giggle*.

He's either running away to meet a woman, in which case I am *absolutely* justified in my mission here, given that I overheard him telling his father he'll be asking Margot out again next week, or he's having some kind of crisis, in which case I have to make a decision.

Do I help the twat-nugget who doesn't deserve another chance with my sister, or do I mind my own business?

That decision won't make itself, so I need more information. "Going to see a mistress?"

He lifts his head and glares at me—understandable, since I think you technically have to be married to have a mistress, and he's definitely not married, so he knows I'm baiting him—then he leans over again, peering under his driver's seat and patting around beneath it.

I scooch my butt back another inch and pull my legs tighter against my chest, trying to be smaller.

The sooner he finds my phone, the sooner I can pull up a map, figure out precisely where we are in relation to the closest city with public transportation, and make a plan to get home.

My *real* home.

The home where my friends are my family and I finally have a job I love and where I've been thinking my heart is healed enough now that maybe—*maybe*—I could get another dog.

That's exactly where I'm going, provided he's okay and not in need of some kind of crisis management help.

While I don't like the man, I *do* have a conscience.

And goddess knows there have been good people who've helped me during my own crises the past few years.

"It's pretty fair for me to ask about a mistress, given your plans with Margot," I point out.

He breathes loudly through his nose. "*What?*"

"I know you want Margot back."

"What the actual fuck are you talking about?"

"Margot. My sister. Your former fiancée. About five eight. Light brown hair. Blue eyes. Always wearing power suits. Likes tea. Eats cherry jam straight out of the jar when she thinks no one's looking. The woman you told your father tonight that you were going to propose to again now that he's out of prison."

He straightens and tries to glare at me.

He tries to speak too, but all that comes out of his mouth are unintelligible words.

Like he's trying to deny that he went to see Margot last week. For the first time in a couple years, I might add.

He said the magic words—*I wish things could've been different*—and got in her head.

Bad enough my shithead of a father had already planted the idea in Margot's head that they should get back together once Oliver's father was out of prison. As if I didn't have enough I'll never forgive *that* man for.

But after Oliver went to see her?

She's been texting me all week.

He was under so much stress when we broke up. Do you think I should've fought harder for him?

There was something in his eyes when he came to see me. I feel like he was trying to tell me something, but I don't know what. Do you think he wants to get back together? Like as a real thing again, not as a business arrangement thing?

the grumpiest billionaire

Would I be an idiot to take him back? I mean, assuming that's what he's ultimately after. He didn't cheat. We had a nice time together and never argued until he broke up with me. We understood each other. Do you know how hard it is to find someone compatible when you're at the level I'm at in business? And it's not like I'll ever give my all to a relationship, so why not marry someone I can tolerate for professional reasons?

My response to every text was the same in spirit: You deserve more than "he didn't cheat and we had a nice time together so let's get married and merge the businesses."

That's the whole reason I went to his father's welcome-home party. To find him and tell him to leave her the hell alone.

He hurt her once. He doesn't get to do it again.

The rest of my family can go to hell, but Margot—she deserves happiness. *Real* happiness. The kind that comes from being involved with someone who knows there's no sacrifice too big, no gesture too small, to show her every day that she is the reason he breathes and that their love will last beyond the existence of time.

She believed in me when the rest of our family didn't.

I believe in her too, and I want nothing but the very, very best for her heart.

Oliver finally grunts, steps back, and slams the door.

Shit, he has my phone.

My stomach catches up to the possibility that this is a step above the normal trouble I used to get myself into, and it's knotting as he shoves my phone in his back pocket, then climbs into the driver's seat.

"May I please have my phone back?" I ask.

"No."

Inconvenient, but given everything else about this situation, not too surprising. "Why not?"

He ignores me as he buckles in, then turns up the radio right as the symphony is getting to the bridge on my favorite Half-Cocked Heroes song. I lean up and watch as he fiddles with the lever on the steering wheel.

And then I'm flung back into my seat as the SUV lurches unevenly. Like he doesn't know how to drive.

Though, honestly—most of the people I grew up with learned to drive so that we could have freedom when we went on vacation, but none of us drove ourselves in the city.

In retrospect, I know it was a great situation for our parents—they always knew where we were and had total control.

Ultimately bad for me for the same reasons.

But in Oliver's case—he didn't drive himself at all.

Anywhere.

Margot said it had to do with being in a bad accident when he was in college, and since he didn't have to drive anywhere, he didn't.

I don't remember every detail she ever told me about him—see again, he's very boring—but I remember that one.

Possibly it's the least boring thing about him. The perfect Oliver Cumberlands of the world don't find themselves in car accidents.

Even when it's not his fault.

Which it apparently wasn't.

He was in the passenger seat.

Naturally.

He gets the SUV under control and manages to turn us back the right way before another car comes up the ramp.

I buckle myself in.

He can't hold my phone—or me—forever, and I'm curious where this is going.

I'm also mildly worried about Oliver, even if I don't want to be.

I spend a few minutes debating with myself about if I'm up for the challenge of talking some details out of him while he drives us past a Miles2Go gas station, a Cod Pieces fast food fish restaurant, and an Aurora Clover hotel, one of the lower-tier hotels in my family's brand of chains. He could easily drop me there—especially if he had any idea how much I'd hate staying anywhere associated with my parents—but doesn't. We leave the last bits of populated areas and drive deeper and deeper into the darkness on a gently winding country road.

This situation is so far past normal that I have my doubts he'll tell me anything, but I have to try. "For my own peace of mind, can you assure me that you're not running away from committing some kind of felony too?"

It's too dark to tell for sure, but I think his shoulders hitch at *running away*.

Not. Good.

Neither is the feeling in the pit of my gut telling me I know what's going on.

I sincerely hope I'm wrong.

He's definitely not committing a felony.

See again...too boring.

I really just wanted to see how he'd react to the *running away* part.

"How many times have you seen the inside of a jail cell?" he replies instead of answering me directly.

"Lost count." Happens when you spend your college years unsure how to channel your general rage with the state of the world and go overboard with the protests since you have unlimited access to money to bail yourself out. Oh, how the times have changed. "Out of curiosity, have *you* ever been arrested?"

He doesn't answer.

"Just saying, kidnapping is an arrestable offense..."

"I'm not kidnapping you." He glances in the rearview mirror at me, and I swear I hear him add *yet*. The car swerves a little, but he corrects it. "You did this to yourself."

"Yep. Big mistake. That's my life. A series of little mistakes that turn out to be big mistakes. Is someone extorting you?"

He mutters something that sounds like *that would be better than this*, then turns up the stereo volume.

Every time he takes his hands off the wheel, the SUV veers before straightening out.

"If it's extortion, I'm great at talking. Happy to help. You wouldn't believe the number of situations I've talked myself out of."

"It's not extortion."

He's irritated enough that I believe him.

Also, yes, I understand why he's irritated.

It's me.

I'm the problem.

But seriously—dude wouldn't be swerving all over the roads in the middle of the night if there wasn't something wrong. Even if I wasn't in the car with him.

And I'm positive he didn't know I was in the car with him.

He was too startled when I sat up for him to have known.

Relatable.

I was startled that I'd finally fallen asleep hard enough to not realize the car was moving. Probably rocked me. I do like sleeping in moving vehicles, and I haven't slept well in almost a month.

"That's a relief." If it's not a woman and it's not extortion and he's not fleeing from a crime—and legit, it's Oliver, he wouldn't crime well—then my gut is probably right, and that's *bad*. "So, since everything's on the up-and-up, what's the plan?"

"None of your business."

"Oh my god, are you on a secret government mission? Was your dad not in jail at all? *Are you a spy?*"

He makes another noise, and the car swerves slightly again. "How drunk are you?"

"Totally sober. That's why I've figured out you're a spy." He's so not a spy. I'd bet the last fifty dollars in my bank account on it.

Though since my best friend upstate adopted me when my parents disinherited me not long after Oliver broke up with Margot, I do have more than fifty dollars in my bank account. Bea grew up in a normal family with a normal household budget, and she taught me as well as she taught her brothers.

And thinking about Bea makes me feel even more guilty.

the grumpiest billionaire

I need to get my phone back.

She'll freak out if I'm not home like I told her I would be tomorrow. And she doesn't need that on top of everything else she's had going on lately.

"I'm not a spy," Oliver says through gritted teeth.

"But you're on a secret mission."

I should stop.

I should.

But one of the many lessons I've learned in my life is that when you annoy someone enough, they'll eventually spill exactly how they feel.

Or in this case, exactly what he's doing.

He'll confirm for me that I do, in fact, know exactly what's going on.

Would be nice if I still enjoyed this game. I'm honestly annoying myself too right now. Am I—dammit.

I am.

I'm getting old and tired of games.

RIP, Daphne of my youth.

"Yes," he says flatly. "I'm on a secret mission. And I can't talk about it. You can't breathe a word about this to anyone when you get home."

"Hilarious. What are you really doing?"

The car jerks yet again, and Oliver mutters something to himself.

I pinch my lips shut.

But I don't make it a full mile before my mouth is running again. "I had to learn to drive a few years ago—I mean, learn how to do it without getting speeding tickets and parking terribly—and I'm pretty damn good at it now. And contrary to popular belief, I do know how to follow directions. If you wanted to, you know, let someone competent behind the wheel."

"This is how spies drive."

Did he—oh my god.

He did.

He made a joke.

And it was surprisingly funny.

I start to laugh, try to stop it, and choke on my own spit. So now I'm coughing like my lungs and I are battling out if they're staying or going.

Oliver looks at me in the rearview mirror again. The car drives all over the lane again.

We have to be nearly to wherever he's going, don't we? He'll run out of gas before too long.

He *does* know you have to fill a car with gas, right?

He's heir to a gas station-slash-convenience store empire. He *has* to know you have to fill this car with gas.

I stifle a sigh, unbuckle myself, and lean close to him so he can hear me over the symphony performing an old Bro Code song.

"Oliver. In all seriousness—why are you running away?"

"I'm not running away."

"No security, no driver, no assistants. News flash, Tighty-Whities. I might not be Daddy's ideal daughter, and I might not be a genius, but I *am* smarter than all of you bigheaded moneybags give me credit for. I know a runaway when I see it. So what's the sitch? You do this often? Get out to the wilderness before getting back to the office on Monday? Didn't think you were the type, but then, I didn't think you'd be the type to install free electric chargers at your gas stations all over the country either."

It's a gift and a curse to be able to feel his shoulders tightening as I talk.

"Tighty-Whities?" he grits out.

"Saw you once when you stayed over at Margot's place. Want me to keep talking? Or do you want to maybe contribute to this conversation so I can help you through what you're going through? I'm a good listener, and since Daddy revoked my trust fund, I've learned how important it is to let people help you. I've gotten pretty good at solving problems too."

He turns the volume up to max.

The car lurches, I get tossed sideways, and I finally force myself to acknowledge that I can't fix this *right now*.

the grumpiest billionaire

So I strap myself back in and watch the night go by while listening to music that I won't tell Oliver I like.

He'd probably change it.

And that makes me mad.

Because Oliver Cumberland, the man who hurt my sister and gave all signs that he was ready to do it again, shouldn't have good taste in music.

Just like the man who hurt my sister shouldn't be the best CEO that the Miles2Go convenience store chain has ever had.

He shouldn't be the reason I've finally found a purpose in life.

But he is.

He made a difference in the world.

What he's done as CEO of Miles2Go made a difference in *my* world. My disinherited-and-found-my-purpose world.

And that's what makes this situation—the fact that I'm growing more convinced by the mile that what I accidentally crashed is Oliver running away from all of it—worse than him trying to get back together with Margot would be.

I grew up surrounded by billionaires and CEOs and world leaders.

These guys don't drive themselves places in the middle of the night. When they travel in the middle of the night, it's by helicopter or private jet to one of their weekend mansions, escorted by their entourages of security and advisers and assistants. And their entourages know when they have secret girlfriends or mistresses, and their entourages know when they're in legal trouble, and their entourages know when they have health issues, and their entourages keep their mouths shut because that's what they're paid to do.

To be there through everything and not tell a soul.

This?

This lone wolf stuff?

He's running away.

My suspicions that I'm right get stronger when he finally pulls to a stop on a gravel driveway at a teeny-tiny dark cabin miles and miles from the highway. There's a sedan parked in the clearing that looks a lot like my car. I peer closer and confirm for myself that yep—that's a late model Toyota Camry. Black or dark blue. Blending into the night.

Oliver parks the SUV—though *lurches it to a stop* might be a more appropriate way of putting it—and climbs out, then wrenches my door open.

He jerks a thumb, indicating I should get out of the car. "Get inside."

"Fancy digs. I like it." I'm being obnoxious and I know it. It's a defense mechanism that being around people from home brings out in me. And it's why I don't like to go back to New York City. I don't *like* this side of me. I like the side of me that lives upstate in Athena's Rest with Bea and our other friends and her brothers and my coworkers, where they're my family and I have a purpose and I'm not angry about everything all of the time. "We staying long?"

His eyelid twitches. Given that he's only lit by the interior lights of the SUV, it looks less like a twitch and more like a ghost took possession of his eyeballs for a minute there.

The tickle of fear hits behind my breastbone once more. "Or is this where you're dumping my body?"

"I'm not—Jesus. *I'm not a fucking murderer.* Even if I want to be. Tomorrow morning, first thing, I'm taking you to a hotel. I'll leave very specific instructions on what you should tell your family and mine about why you needed a pickup in the middle of nowhere, and I'll leave you with whatever cash you want to keep your mouth shut. This never happened. You didn't see me. Understand?"

He's not saying the words *yes, I'm running away*, except he is.

And while I don't want the guy anywhere near my sister, I also don't want him to disappear.

Not when I know what it would mean for my own future.

And the world, truthfully.

I nod in response to his demand for silence and slowly climb out of the SUV, but as my second Louboutin hits the ground, I lose my footing and tumble forward.

the grumpiest billionaire

I have *not* missed this kind of shoe since I got myself disinherited and quit going to fancy dinners and parties. If I could've crashed the party tonight while wearing work boots, I would've.

Oliver catches me by the arm with a low growl in the back of his throat.

When his hand connects with my skin, I suck in a breath that comes with a whiff of lemon and fresh-cut grass. Goosebumps race up my arm.

I open my mouth, but the smart-ass comment I want to give him dies in my brain before it can make it anywhere near my tongue.

He tugs and straightens me. "Walk."

I take three steps before my heel catches wrong on the gravel driveway again. My arms windmill. My ankle twists. It's so dark beyond the SUV's headlights that more anxiety makes my legs tremble, and I squeak like a mouse as I struggle to get my balance back.

How did I ever wear shoes like this regularly? "If I'd known we were going glamping, I would've packed better stilettos."

He growls once more, and then the world is upside down and cool night air is flowing up my legs and teasing my ass.

The short dress was not the smartest decision tonight. For sneaking into the party uninvited, yes. For a road trip to nowhere, Pennsylvania, no.

But also—who knew Oliver could manhandle a woman like she's no bigger than a doll?

I never saw him toss Margot over his shoulder like this. And she never talked about him having an iron grip like the hand clamped on my thigh.

Or the way being manhandled could make a girl feel things she absolutely does *not* want to feel.

Primal instinctive reaction, I tell myself.

Nothing to do with Oliver.

Which is exactly what I hope my entire life gets back to soon.

Nothing to do with Oliver.

Directly, anyway.

But unfortunately, I don't think that's in my immediate future.

Because if I'm right and he's running away—I'm screwed.

My job? My dream job?

The job I have now, working for a nonprofit that saves animal habitats?

Most of our operational costs are covered by a grant from the M2G Foundation.

A foundation that Oliver started almost as soon as he took the reins of the company as a PR stunt to immediately work on rehabilitating the corporation's image.

If Oliver's out, there's very little chance the next CEO will continue to funnel profits into charitable causes like mine.

Because while Miles2Go's reputation has turned around, stockholders are grumbling that there's no profit. And there's no profit because of the current focus on the public image, which I swear I only know because my boss was talking about it the other day.

I need my phone.

And there it is.

In his back pocket.

I reach for it, miss, and touch his ass.

His shoulders tighten beneath my stomach, and then once again, my world spins as he hefts me off his shoulder and sets me on the porch.

He eyes me, and another shiver races across my arms and down my spine.

"Don't even think about it," he mutters.

"About what?"

"You'll get your phone back when I give you your phone back. Understand?"

I smile and nod despite the way I'm suddenly uncomfortably intrigued at how bossy he's being. He was never bossy to Margot. *Ever.* "You're in charge. Whatever you say."

He sighs the heavy sigh of a man trying very hard to control his breathing.

the grumpiest billionaire

Understandable.

We both know I'm lying.

Before the night's over, I'll have my phone back.

And then I'll make a plan.

Even if it's not the plan I *want*.

Because, much as it pains me, making sure Oliver's okay before I take off is what Margot would want me to do.

And after the way Bea took care of me when I was suddenly penniless, family-less, and overall lost in the world...I think the universe would call this situation my chance at restitution for what I've been given the past few years too.

3

Can I go back to nightmares only when I'm asleep, please?

Oliver

My father is a giant hermit crab.

He's Cupholder, the giant hermit crab mascot of the Miles-2Go Corporation, and he's come all the way inland to Pennsylvania to take a gigantic hermit crab dump on my glass cabin.

Yes, my glass cabin. My see-through glass cabin, where my father, with his beady little hermit crab eyes, is watching me panicking inside as he crushes my greenhouse with his giant hermit crab excrement.

He scuttles so hard that my bed shakes.

It's a hermit crab earthquake.

I take a swing at him and he makes a weird, feminine *oomph*.

Feminine.

Pennsylvania.

Daphne.

My eyes fly open, and motherfucking fucker, there she is.

Daphne's on the ground in the small cabin bedroom, hermit crab style, legs and arms on the ground, staring at me with big brown eyes that are telegraphing *goddammit, he caught me.*

"What are you doing?" I bark. She's supposed to be sleeping on the couch in the next room.

Or sneaking out in the middle of the night to go do whatever it is she does.

Shit.

Shit. "Did I hit you?"

"As if. My reflexes can handle a sleeping man. Your snoring stopped so I thought you were dead. Glad to see you're not. I hate police paperwork."

She has a tell that she's lying.

She has to.

I have no idea what it is, but there has to be a tell.

Doesn't matter.

I know what she was doing. She was trying to get her phone.

I stare at her as it dawns on me that I can see her clearly against the wood-paneled wall, that she's still in her dress, and that her dark hair has blue and green highlights in it.

Sun's up.

Time to go.

"Unless you want to put your hands down my pants, you're not going to find it," I tell her.

"Already looked there when I thought you were dead."

I freeze, momentarily believing her.

She smirks and settles on the floor, reaching between the mattress and the box spring of this ancient bed again.

I scoot closer to the edge to squish her hand. "What's your price?"

Sleep has made everything clear.

I don't know what she's doing these days, but I know she doesn't have money. Her family cut her off after one too many public scenes, and she's living—actually, I don't know where.

Most of what I know about her situation came from my best friend, since she was disinherited after Margot and I broke up. Not long after, but after. I wasn't part of the family discussions on that one.

I know she has a real job somewhere outside the city where she's relatively anonymous and she's living like—*dammit*.

She's living like I want to.

Like a normal person.

While I have the resources to live like she used to.

Never thought I'd see the day when I'd be jealous of Daphne Merriweather-Brown, but here we are.

"Price for what?" she asks.

"For your silence."

She snorts again and pushes her arm deeper under the mattress like I weigh nothing, which is annoying. "Nothing about me is for sale."

"You don't want a pony? I thought all girls wanted a pony."

She flips me off.

Probably deserve that.

I know full well my ex-fiancée's sister has no interest in owning a pony. She'd rather set them free.

I heard about it enough times at various Merriweather-Brown family dinners while I was dating Margot.

"A donation to your favorite charity that rescues dogs from dog-fighting rings," I try again.

I don't care how late it might be in the morning, it's still too early for that kind of side-eye.

"No, thank you," she says primly.

Primly.

Daphne.

The girl who once told me to eat a bag of dicks in front of her grandparents because I'd suggested—kindly, I might add—that she suffer through not getting herself arrested for a few months so that she didn't have to listen to her family berate her about it.

"Everyone has a price. What's yours?"

"Why do you want to buy my silence?"

"Confidential spy project."

"You turned on the windshield wipers when you were trying to adjust the air conditioning in the car last night, double-oh-seven. Try again."

the grumpiest billionaire

"Because I don't trust you."

"So you pay me off and I tell the world about your super-secret serial killer lair out here in the woods anyway, which we both know I'll do. You're never going to trust me no matter how much money you give me, so why offer me money at all?"

She's had coffee.

Coffee that has given her an innate advantage over me. That has to be what's going on here.

I left my thinking brain at the M2G headquarters when I walked out of the building for the last time because I wasn't supposed to need it for anything beyond checking my itinerary every morning to plug my next destination into my GPS on this road that will eventually get me to a place that I'll know when I find it. The place where I'm supposed to begin my new life, somewhere in the middle or western states, far, far away from Manhattan.

I'm supposed to be waking up today free and clear of all obligations and responsibilities beyond making it to the next overnight stop on my road trip to explore all of the places I might consider settling.

Heading into a fresh start without the burden of generations of expectations from people who feel entitled to dictate my entire life simply because they made me.

After one good night of sleep.

Which was supposed to be last night.

I haven't slept more than four hours in a single night since my father went to jail because I was holding his company together for the shareholders and employees and franchise owners all while realizing I don't have the drive or the instincts for what I was trained to do from birth.

But here I am, with one more obligation smiling broadly as she plops onto her ass, pulling her arm out from between the mattress and box springs with her phone in hand.

It takes more effort than it should, but I snatch it from her and shove it under the covers and down my underwear.

Yes, my *tighty-whities*.

And you know what?

They'll hold the goddamn phone.

Boxers wouldn't do that.

"What. Do you. Want?" I growl as she stares at my midsection like she's seriously contemplating coming after the phone.

Her brown eyes meet mine.

Margot has blue eyes. Blue eyes and light brown hair. Sharp wit. Strong moral compass. Good sense of humor. She's a tad more slender than Daphne, though neither are the waif-thin model-types everyone expects children of the rich to be.

Daphne, on the other hand, is brown eyed and used to be brown-haired, though there are some streaks of color in it now. Her fairy-tattooed arms are on full display this morning. She was wearing a jacket over the cocktail dress last night, and the wig that's still in my SUV was hiding her half-smushed, half-wild dark hair as it falls past her chin.

She has a diamond stud in one nostril, three piercings in each lower ear, and a loop in one upper ear.

And I've never understood her.

She was born with everything.

Everything.

Same as I was.

But while Margot and I worked our asses off to give back to the families that gave so much—to pay an invisible debt that we didn't ask for but shouldered anyway—Daphne thumbed her nose at every convention and expectation.

And she actively sabotaged herself every step of the way.

Yes, yes, fine.

I'm walking away now too.

Actively self-sabotaging, some will say.

But at least I did my part to save the family's company before I left and identified the best candidate to replace me as well.

I paid my debt. And I'm not only running away—I'm *searching*.

I'm looking for the good in the world, and I'm looking for how I can *be* the good in the world.

Quietly.

In a recluse kind of way.

Daphne just—I don't even know what she does now.

She bites her lower lip and squints at me. "You know what I want?"

"I'm listening."

"I want a ride."

"To?"

"Wherever you're headed."

"This is it."

"This *isn't* it. There's getting away to a weekend hunting cabin, and then there's getting away to a secret place no one would ever expect you to go. Nice cobwebs, by the way, you totally missed my dance moves this morning. Also, there's a car outside that no one would ever expect you to drive, with fake IDs that have your picture and someone else's name, along with duffel bags stuffed with cash. You're not here to stay. You're here as a stopover on your way to somewhere else."

My mother used to say I was the only child she knew without a temper.

The past few years have changed that.

There's a boiling rage simmering beneath my skin, and Daphne's announcement that she's snooped through my getaway car is lava on the molten steel, igniting my wrath hotter.

"How—what—*the fuck*? I hid the keys."

"Just because I never got caught picking locks doesn't mean I never learned how to do it." She shrugs like it's, as she used to say, *no biggie*. "I have your passport and fake driver's license, by the way. Not telling where. The price of getting it back is giving me a ride to wherever you're going. Nice name, by the way. Tom Johnson. Very boring. Very…you. So. We're going…where again?"

This trip is full of firsts.

First time driving myself in well over a decade.

First time having a stowaway.

First time almost feeling sorry for Daphne.

First time I've ever truly wanted to murder someone.

"No," I say instead of answering her question.

"Do you know how to live in the woods, Oliver? Because I know how to live in the woods. I can pick a direction and start hiking and I'll find a road and that road will lead to a town and I'll talk someone into borrowing their phone and I'll call Margot because not only do I have her personal cell number memorized, but I also know the password to get through to her at work if I had to call the corporate number on the website. The minute I tell Margot you held me captive, I'll also be able to tell her exactly where, because I'm a genius at navigating the woods. I'll give the cops the name on your fake passport, and I'll do it all before you can reach Mexico, and you'll be the second Cumberland to go to prison in under a decade."

I am.

I'm going to have to murder her.

Shit.

This isn't how I wanted to start my new life.

She smirks at me again and leaps off the floor like she's not wrapped in a too-tight black cocktail dress that now has cobwebs stuck to the ass. "I'll fix you coffee. A little caffeine, and you'll see the bright side to this arrangement. For instance, I'm a very good driver. *Very* good. I had the best instructor ever. Re-instructor, I should say. When I learned how to park well and not speed so much. And I like the idea of how mad my father will be when he finds out you've wrecked all of his plans for merging the companies so much that you can rest assured of my silence so long as you take me where you're going and don't piss me off."

Her phone buzzes in my underwear, against my dick.

And my dick is a dick.

It's not smart enough to be horrified by Daphne's phone giving us a woody, or by the fact that she managed to turn it on before I got it back from her, potentially sending her location to someone.

the grumpiest billionaire

And on top of all of that—she's right.

She might be useful, and she might be the only person in the world who wouldn't take reward money for bringing me home.

Not if spilling the beans would mean making her parents happy. And if she hates her parents as much as the vibe she's giving off suggests she does.

Fuck me.

Just fuck me.

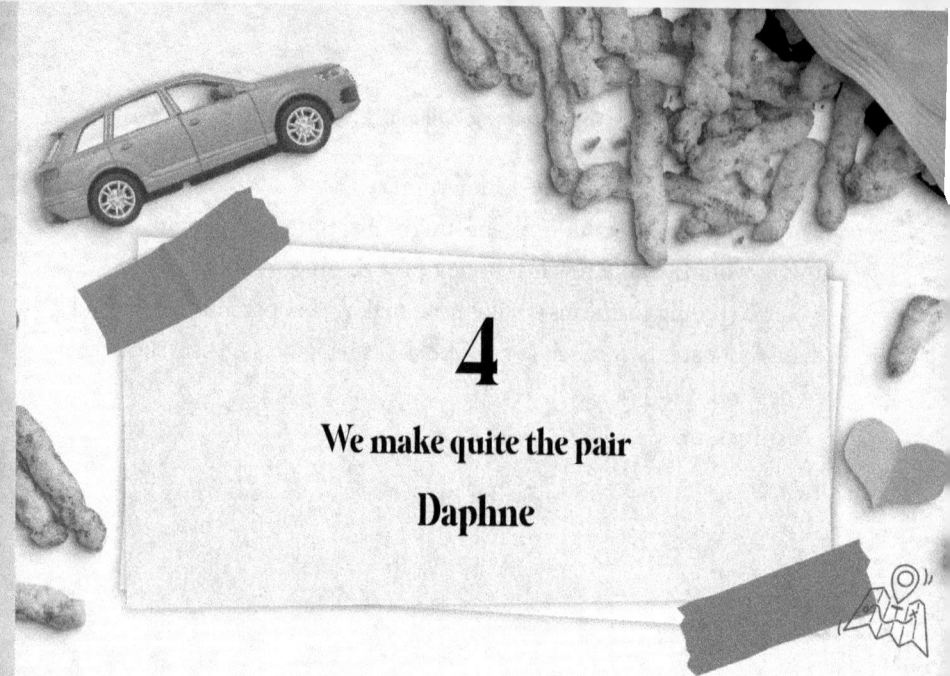

4

We make quite the pair

Daphne

Oliver is a serious killjoy on a road trip.
Not that I can blame him.
I'd be pissed at me too.

Probably crossed a line with the whole *I can survive the wilderness and foil all of your plans* thing.

Even if it's true—during daylight hours, anyway—I didn't need to rub it in his face.

And honestly?

I'm sad.

Devastated, actually.

He's running away. He's leaving the country.

People who are going to work on Monday morning to continue the good work they've been doing don't run away.

"Have you ever been on a road trip?" I ask him as he steers the Camry down the dirt road away from the cabin and the Mercedes SUV. When we got in the car, he studied the dash and all of the buttons and knobs so thoroughly, I wasn't sure we'd be leaving today.

I'm still in my cocktail dress.

the grumpiest billionaire

He's changed out of the suit he wore last night and is now in a buttoned-up red flannel, boat pants, and Carhartt boots.

Yes, boat pants. The white linen pants that stop above a guy's ankles. Super popular with the yacht crowd.

And yes, a red flannel.

In August.

Dude is a mess, and I say that as someone who's regularly been a mess herself.

I desperately want my phone.

But on top of the S. S. Lumberjack getup ruined by the boat pants, he's also wearing the scowliest scowl that has ever scowled this side of the Scowlissippi River.

I don't think the scowling is because it's too hot for a flannel shirt either. It's already eighty outside, but the air conditioning is working well.

Too well.

I'm definitely turning the temperature up in here very soon.

He sips the coffee I made him from the ancient Miles2Go to-go mug that I found in one of the cabinets and cleaned for him. The side of the cup is decorated with the original version of Cupholder, the hermit crab mascot for M2G who got a makeover at some point between my childhood and Margot starting to date Oliver, and there's a dent in one side that makes me question how long it will keep his coffee warm.

But how serendipitous that I could give him that mug.

Remind him of all the good parts of Miles2Go.

"No talking on my road trips," he says.

"Talking is half the fun of road trips."

He grunts.

"Are you going to have a no-food-in-the-car rule too?"

"Yes. Be quiet. I'm driving."

I humor him and zip my trap for a while.

Contrary to what I'm sure he believes, I'm not intentionally trying to bait him, even if his cheek twitches every time I shift in my seat, making my dress squeak against the rough cloth.

And even if I'm shifting a lot.

I don't sit still well. And that's a personality feature, not a bug, now that I've found what I'm supposed to do in life and the people who accept me for who I am.

The people who are going to be rightfully pissed if I don't figure out a way to give them a call and let them know I'm okay and slightly delayed in getting home.

I'm trying to sit as still as I can. I can't talk him into going back home and continuing to run Miles2Go if I've over-annoyed him, and I haven't yet figured out how to reverse psychology the situation.

I make it all of seven minutes. "Margot said you had electric car charging stations installed at hundreds of M2G locations around the country. So what's with the full-gas car?"

He doesn't answer.

It's like sitting with every other businessman I've ever had to be around in my entire life.

Appreciate that Oliver made it possible for the nonprofit I work for to exist and gave jobs to a dozen amazing people who are doing so much good work for the world? Not to mention the other charities and nonprofits that he funded with Miles2Go revenue?

Yes.

Want to be around him?

No.

I've played out this conversation in my head a thousand times since I snuck out of the shack last night after I was sure he was asleep and broke into both the Mercedes and the Camry to look for clues about what he was up to, and it always ends the same.

I could say, *So, Oliver, I work for Beeslieve now—yes, yes, it's a pun on the word "believe" with "bees" in it—and we're doing great work with the state department of transportation to get wildflowers planted for bees and to make better crossing routes for suburban wildlife with strategically placed natural-style fencing, and you've been funding us, so if you could return to work on Monday morning and keep doing what you're doing so that we can keep doing what we're doing, that would be great.*

And he'd say *Shove it up your ass, Daphne, you're a disaster, you've always been a disaster, you will always be a disaster, you couldn't even have a five-minute conversation with me without ruining my life, and even if I go back to work on Monday, I'd make sure that we shift money away from your company and onto someone else's to make you pay for the heartburn you've given me.*

Yep, I know what you're thinking.

But Daphne, he told you to name your price for your silence. Tell him the price for your silence is lifetime funding for Beeslieve.

Here's the thing about the uber-rich of the world: They don't get uber-rich by not stepping on the little guy, and they don't stay uber-rich by keeping their promises to the little guy.

That's me now.

I'm the little guy.

If I tell Oliver what I want is for him to fund operations for Beeslieve for the next ten years so that we can continue doing the work of saving animal habitats instead of shifting to channel three-quarters of our efforts into fundraising to spend a quarter of the time making a difference, he'll promise me he'll do it, and the minute he drops me off and disappears to wherever he's going, he'll turn into a cartoon villain, rub his hands together, laugh while lightning flashes, and then withdraw support to show me who's in charge.

Who has the power.

Who has the control.

Not because I'm continuing to annoy him now, but because I annoyed him in the first place by simply wanting five minutes of his time at the exact wrong moment in his life.

And make no mistake—yes, Oliver implemented all kinds of great initiatives and policies when he was in charge of Miles2Go. But every last change, every last donation, every last operation, gave Miles2Go great publicity in a time when the company was in crisis because of what his father did as CEO.

If there was real altruism in any of his actions, that goodwill was a side effect, not the underlying intention.

I grew up in his world. I know too many people in that world to believe anything differently.

I study his profile. "Must be nice having your old man out of the slammer."

His entire face pinches.

Not merely his lips or his eyes, but his lips and his eyes and his nose and his chin and his forehead and his cheeks and his ears.

Huh.

Wonder if that's about anyone referencing his old man being in the slammer, or if he's not happy that his father's out.

Oh, shit.

Are they forcing Oliver out? Are they firing him?

Is that why he's here? Is he running away because he's having his teenage rebellion fifteen years late after being given a toy that they're now telling him he can't have anymore?

My stomach drops.

Was he never going to continue being CEO once his dad was released?

I need more information. "Your mom seemed happy last night."

Another grunt.

"Margot always gushed about how much she loved your parents and how lucky she was to be getting good in-laws."

This time, the grunt upgrades to a grimace.

Also, I'm lying. Margot would always roll her eyes a little and say Oliver's parents were a little annoying.

The whole reason his dad ended up in prison, after all, was because he used company funds to buy a ridiculous number of bottles of rare wines for his personal collection and bought into a fake business for locating more rare wines in an attempt to impress my father and his ridiculous cellar.

It turned out the vintage wines Oliver's father bought—and the company he bought into—were phonies.

He used Miles2Go funds to buy the world's largest collection of *nothing*.

When he already *had* a nice wine cellar.

Just not as nice as my father's.

The desire to keep up with the Joneses—poorly, I might add—was Oliver's father's downfall.

Speaking of lying and cheating—"I told a friend I'd meet them for brunch today. If I don't check in, they'll worry."

"What friend?"

Like hell I'm telling him anything about Bea or her family. I don't think he'd hurt them, but he hates me enough that he'd hate them too, and Bea deserves zero hate, *ever*. She's the best of the best. "My friend Denali from work."

Distrustful hazel eyes slide my way. "Where do you work?"

"Local Cod Pieces. It's a fish restaurant. A chain."

"I know what Cod Pieces is."

"So you know how awesome their hush puppies are."

The way his eye twitches tells me he hasn't ever set foot inside a Cod Pieces, or if he has, he wasn't impressed.

Very on-brand for Oliver.

That is to say, *boring*.

With a side of poor taste.

Cod Pieces is *the best*.

Ever.

"Where do you *actually* work?" he asks.

"To the best of my knowledge, my own parents don't know that information. Why do you think I'd give it to you?"

"Because I'm not letting you out of this car until I trust that you're not going to tell everyone you saw me. And if you lie to me about where you work, you'll lie to me about what you're telling people."

"*My own parents don't know where I work.* I never talk to them. Ever. For any reason. I can keep a secret."

"You'd tell Margot you saw me."

Oliver holds the power to shut down Beeslieve. Of course I'll tell Margot and ask for her help. It's been a source of pride for me that I've refused anything other than letting her take me out to dinner and occasionally stock my fridge with good cheese since I was disinherited, but desperate times call for desperate measures.

And I don't mean asking Margot to find Aurora Gardens money to fund Beeslieve.

She'd do it.

But *I don't want it.*

Not when it's money tied to my parents. All I want is for her to talk to Oliver about it.

I'm willing to accept that the funding for Beeslieve comes from Oliver and his company because he doesn't know he was helping me. He definitely didn't give me a job on purpose. I came to Beeslieve *after* he'd arranged funding for it.

"Afraid Margot won't want you back if she finds out you kidnapped her sister?" I ask him.

"I'm not—I'm not *kidnapping* you. *You stowed away in my car.*"

"To talk to you for five minutes. I climbed into your car to talk to you for *five minutes*. How was I supposed to know you'd be running away right after the big welcome-home party?"

"I'm not running away." He swerves the car as he looks at me again, and an oncoming semi honks at us.

He overcorrects, veering across our lane, and dirt and gravel spew beneath the car while his knuckles go white and his breathing gets shallower.

"I'm a good driver," I mutter.

The car straightens out on the two-lane country highway, but I can still feel how tight he's gripping the wheel in the way the car rides over the asphalt. "I can't get good if I don't practice."

I shift in my seat—seat belt on today, seat belt very much on—and stare at his profile. "I leveled with you. I wanted to talk to you for five minutes about how it would be terrible for Margot for you to try to weasel—excuse me, for you to try to win her back. I wasn't trying to crash your road trip."

"You sure took your damn time letting me know you were in the back seat."

"Dude, I was asleep. *Hard*. Been a rough—not the point. Point is, I'm here. You won't give me my phone back. You won't tell me where you're going. You won't tell me why. Which means this has gone from an honest misunderstanding to an intentional kidnapping."

"You said you wanted to go wherever I was going."

"Hindenburg principle."

"Hindenburg—what the actual—*Stockholm syndrome?*"

"Airship disaster. Falling for your kidnapper. Same thing. It's all bad."

"There is no *Hindenburg principle*."

"Okay, Mr. Smarty-Pants Know-It-All." Yes, yes, I could've been a better student of history. But why stay in the past when I can see where the future's going if we don't save the animals? The cascade effect will be real, and humanity won't survive. "My point is still very valid. I'm at your mercy."

"You could've hiked out while I was sleeping and lived on bugs and leaves and poisonous berries while looking for an interstate and strangers. You threatened to do exactly that if I didn't let you in the car. Who's holding who hostage here?"

Dammit.

Me and my big mouth.

And me and my arrest record too.

When it comes to the CEO of a billion-dollar convenience store conglomerate and the disinherited criminal-record-holding fuckup daughter of another bajillionaire, we both know who the cops will believe.

I switch tactics. "Why are you running away?"

"No talking in my car." He hits blindly at the radio on the dashboard while swerving into the oncoming lane again.

"I love road trips, but I love road trips with safe drivers more."

The tires squeal as he slams on the brakes.

I'm flung sideways, since I'm the dummy who's turned in my seat to face him. I flail my arms, looking for something to brace against to keep myself from going into the windshield while the seat belt cuts into my neck.

"I'm done," he says.

"Can you be done on the side of the road?" I gesture in front of us and behind us. The car's stopped over the center line with a curve in the road right in front of us. "We're sitting ducks here."

He growls, hits the gas, and we stop-go-stop-go-stop-go all the way to the shoulder.

"Thanks," I say. "Appreciate your thoughtfulness here."

"Get out."

I could.

I could get out, even without my phone, and I'd be fine. Call it my superpower. I wouldn't get more than two miles before someone would pull over, pass my vibe check, and let me use their phone to call Bea, first to tell her I'm okay, second to ask if she's worked things out with the guy she's been seeing this summer, and third to promise her I'm coming home.

When I told her I was headed to the Hamptons to stop Margot from taking Oliver back—the first time I've set foot anywhere near the city since I was disinherited—there was something in the way she hugged me that told me she was worried about me leaving.

I *have* to get my phone back to call her.

She's as much my family as Margot is, and she saved my life when my parents cut me off.

She'd come get me herself because that's who Bea is. Sister of my heart. Best friend. One of only two people on the planet that I would honestly die for, the other being Margot.

I finally look Oliver square in the eye and tell him the absolute complete truth of my life instead. "I don't know what's going on in your life. I don't know why you're here. All I know is what it looks like you're doing. I also know what it's like to leave the world we grew up in. I know what it's like to not fit there but need to stay there because people like you and me aren't taught how to live in the real world. And I know what it's like to suddenly have nothing, including the skills to survive without a driver and security and a household manager and a trust fund."

He stares back at me, nostrils flaring, a hint of desperation touching his eyes as one eyelid visibly twitches.

Or maybe that's my imagination.

Maybe?

I don't know.

I suck in a deep breath and keep going.

I've told this story a handful of times, but never to people from the world I used to live in.

Only to people in the world I live in now. People who like me for me. People who know I have nothing and will continue to voluntarily have nothing for the rest of my life. People who are dedicated to causes they believe in that are bigger than their own bank accounts and wine cellars and art collections.

"But now I know how to get along on my own anywhere from the streets of New York to mountain trails miles and miles from civilization. I know how to shop on a budget in a grocery store and cook for myself. I know how to change the oil in a car. I change my own lightbulbs and communicate with my own landlord and walk around festivals without security at my back. And I can do it because very, very kind people took me in and taught me how to live in the normal world when I had absolutely nothing to give them for it and when they had absolutely nothing to gain from it."

His chest is rising and falling rapidly while he stares at me.

I keep going. "You're clearly having some kind of crisis, and you were almost my brother-in-law. I don't have to like you to have empathy for whatever it is you're going through. And watching your father go to jail and taking over his company and breaking up with the woman you were with long enough to propose to her and then your father getting out of jail and you fleeing the city with literal suitcases of cash in the back of your car? Something's wrong. I'm not getting out until I know you'll be okay. That's what Margot would want me to do. Because even if you're not right for each other, she still cares about you. And she's a good person. The best, in fact."

Shiiiiiiit.

It's not my imagination that his eyes are getting shiny.

That his Adam's apple is bobbing.

That he's gripping the steering wheel so hard with his left hand that his knuckles have gone a shade past white.

"I. Will be. Fine." His voice is thick and gritty, and I can't decide if he's trying to not hit me or trying to not absolutely lose his shit.

Dammit.

Dammit.

I'm not supposed to feel sorry for this man.

But I suddenly do.

"Yeah, I know. You'll have your money to help you in ways I didn't. But that doesn't mean you can't use my help."

He breathes.

Breathes and stares at me.

"Where are you going?" I keep my voice quiet in case he does want to hit me.

He's among the last people that I'd suspect of being capable of violence, but he's also among the last people that I'd suspect would spend a weekend driving a boring old sedan loaded with briefcases of cash and a fake passport.

The boring sedan part, yes, even if I can't talk since that's what I can afford too these days.

But the rest of it?

This isn't the Oliver I know.

"Away," he finally says.

"For how long?"

He blinks.

One blink.

Then a slow, deep inhalation through his flaring nostrils.

"Forever then." I can barely hear myself.

His eyes dip to my lips like he's reading the words. "What do you care?"

This is bad.

This is very, very bad.

It's not only *if he disappears, the new CEO will cut funding to Beeslieve*. It's also *if anyone finds out that I was the last person seen with him and all of his cash before he disappears, and disappears good, I'll be framed for murder even without a body*.

Disappearing is hard, but if anyone can do it, it's someone with the kind of money that Oliver has.

I lick my lips. "Do you have a plan?"

Oh, goodie. It's the dead-eyed look that always accompanied my father telling me not to be a fool until the day I quit talking to him.

I curl my fingers into my fists and fight the internal rage that starts swirling at the implication that I'm stupid. "There are levels of plans when you're leaving your old life behind. Clearly, you have the whole *go with cash, get the fake passport* thing under control. But your driving sucks. No offense. I get it. You don't drive much, so you're new to driving this much. Everyone sucks at first. I sucked at first. And honestly, for a long time before I suddenly couldn't afford moving violation tickets anymore."

"I don't suck at driving."

He does. But I let it go. "Have you ever been inside a ValuKart? Do you know how to use the self-checkout lanes in a grocery store? How are you going to get housing when you don't have any credit history under your new name? You can't pay for a house with cash. People ask questions. They asked me all of the questions when my father cut me off, and I didn't even need to get my own place for a while after that. Just a new phone line and bank account. They're going to ask you *so* many questions."

He's still glaring at me.

The old Oliver would roll his eyes, but he was too passive to glare.

This Oliver is telling me with his eyeballs that I have underestimated who he's become after four years of being a CEO and he doesn't need me.

So I switch tactics. "Listen, I truly don't give two craps if you want to run away."

"Don't you?"

"Nope. Not a bit. Don't care why. Don't care where you go. Don't care what you want to do. But *I've been there*, Oliver. I've started over. I know how to navigate the world. I can anticipate problems you wouldn't even dream could exist. I can help you the same way that—that people helped me when I suddenly didn't have a dime left to my name. I know you'll have your money to make it easier, but the world without security and drivers and chefs and executive assistants—that takes some adjusting. I can help you. And I'm probably the only person in the world who can."

His poker face stops pokering.

"You're wearing white linen boat pants with a flannel shirt. You've picked literally the only kind of pants in the entire world that don't go with flannel. You are not prepared for the world outside of the C-suite in Manhattan. Let me help you."

His solid jaw that's far more defined than it was the last time I saw him works back and forth while his eyes bore into me. The barest hint of dark scruff covers his cheeks and jawbone. I've never seen him with a beard. Or more than two days' worth of growth back when he was with Margot.

The man even shaved on vacation.

I wonder if he'll grow out his facial hair as part of his disguise. Or if he'll even need to.

The more I look, this Oliver is *not* the same man I knew. On top of appearing twenty years older than he is, complete with premature gray hairs dotting his scalp, the arm muscles I glimpsed when I was trying to get my phone this morning weren't there when I last saw him shortly before I was disinherited. The scowls, the grumpiness, the fury that I swear I feel simmering below his surface—he's nothing like the passive, agreeable, safe, *boring* dude that I knew when he dated Margot.

And it's unlikely he'll settle anywhere that anyone would recognize him anyway.

How much money has he shifted to offshore accounts in his new name already? Where's the next place he's going to find another suitcase of cash? Will that cash be American dollars, or will it give me a clue where he's headed next?

Will he set himself up on a beach in Mexico with a small staff? He speaks Italian, which would be a non-boring thing about him if he'd learned it so he could go live in Italy rather than because we all had to take foreign language classes in school and he was a pompous windbag who made a big deal of keeping up his education. He could pass himself off as an eccentric forty-something-year-old Italian millionaire who retired young from the banking industry.

He was good for the world as CEO of Miles2Go, but I don't think the world of being CEO was good to him.

I mean, obviously, if he's running away from it.

"And what's in this for you?" he asks. "If I take your help, what do you want?"

"One favor."

"How much?"

I do quick math, knowing full well we're both talking dollars and cents for payment now.

Yes, in fact, I can be bought. But it's for a good cause. "A number under a million."

"How much under a million?"

"Does it matter?"

"Yes."

"It's not for me."

"Who's it for?"

"I'll tell you when I cash in the favor."

He's still studying me like he can see right through me. "Why?"

"Why don't I trust you? I'd think that's pretty obvious."

"Why do you want to do this? Was this your plan all along? Is my family paying you to be here? What's in this for you?"

"Your family can eat a bag of dicks. Mine can too. Except Margot. That's all I wanted. All I wanted was to tell you to leave Margot alone, that she deserves someone who will treat her like she invented cheesecake, not someone who loves her just for her brain and her connections. Those are the least interesting things about her."

"I didn't—"

"Didn't tell your father you were going to propose to her again last night?"

"*I fucking lied and told him what he fucking wanted to*—never mind. Doesn't matter."

That would be reassuring if he hadn't made Margot think he was interested too. "You're right. It doesn't. What matters is that we're here, and part of my life is pretty good for reasons that unfortunately have to do with you, and I'd like it to stay good, and it won't if you're not at Miles2Go. That's the whole truth. You did something that gave me a purpose, and I don't want to lose that."

"What are you talking about?"

"You let me help you until I'm sure you won't get yourself murdered or kidnapped or worse, and then I'll tell you more. Right now, all you need is my offer. Once you've got the basics under control or until you get to wherever you're going where someone else is waiting to help

the grumpiest billionaire

you, you'll transfer some amount of money that's under a million dollars to where I ask you to, and I'll take the secret of where you are and anything we did here to the grave."

The only sound in the car is the buzzing of a fly that somehow got inside.

It zips between us crookedly like it's been swimming in lemon drop martinis while Oliver continues to glare at me.

I've resigned myself to having to climb out of the car in this horrid dress and no shoes—like hell I'm hiking to the next town in those Louboutins that I stole from Margot's closet the last time I saw her before the great disinheriting—when he speaks.

"Three days."

Yes.

Three days.

I can work *miracles* in three days.

I hold out a hand. "Shake on it."

His hand is clammy when he puts it in mine, and he's still staring at me like he wants to strangle me, but he shakes firmly without trying to murder my hand bones, even though I'm convinced he could. Dude must've spent a *lot* of time in the gym the past few years. "Three days."

"A sum of money under a million to be deposited into an account I name at the end of three days."

"For your silence."

"And my help."

"Mostly your silence. Get in the back seat. And be quiet."

If he's expecting me to get out of the car to get into the back seat, he's going to be very disappointed.

He can't get rid of me that easily.

I unbuckle and wiggle between the front two seats to climb into the back.

Probably flash him my ass cheeks on the way.

I do *not* miss wearing thongs now that I go to work in boots and thick denim every day, and I'd prefer to not be wearing one now.

He makes a strangled noise. "And I'm buying you new clothes."

"Perfect." I flop into the back seat beside the lone suitcase he brought out of the cabin this morning that's half-full of protein bars, turn to face forward, and strap myself in, noting that his cheeks have gone a shade of pink. He definitely saw my ass. "I'll teach you how it's done. Hand me my phone, and I'll direct you to the nearest farm goods store. You're gonna love it."

He doesn't hand me my phone.

He does heave another sigh though.

Fine.

Whatever.

I'll get it soon enough.

We've declared a truce, and I have three days.

This…might actually end okay.

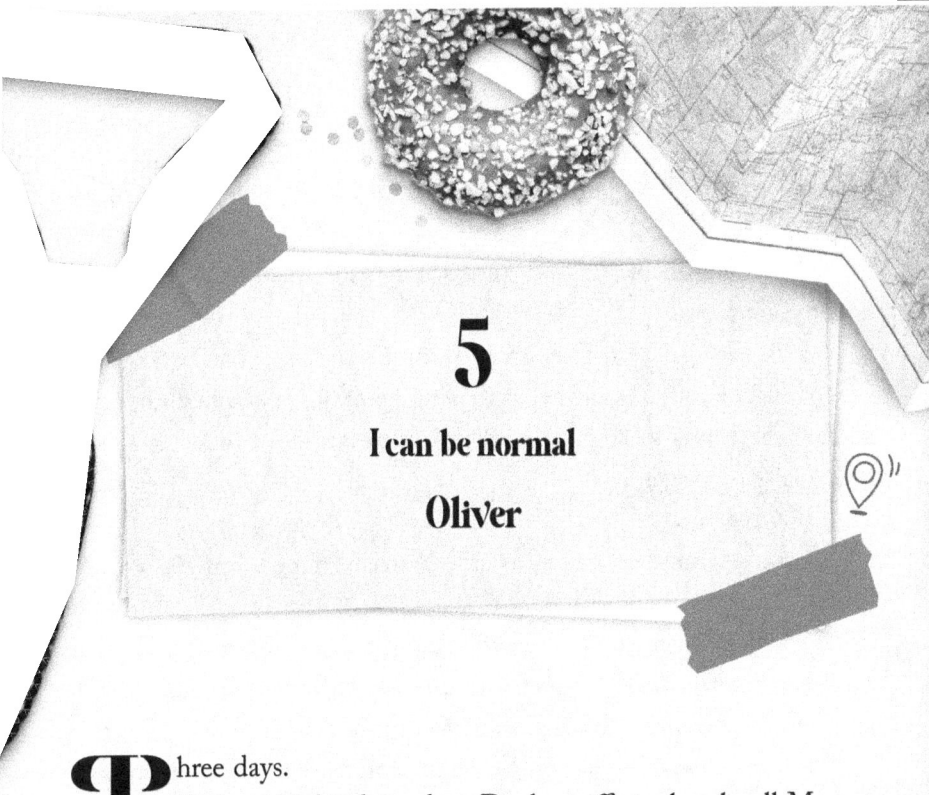

5

I can be normal

Oliver

Three days.

Or less if I decide to drop Daphne off at a hotel, call Margot, ask her to do me one final favor, and then I can truly disappear.

Not that that's a good option either.

On top of my father's insistence that I pick things back up with Margot, her father cornered me at the party last night to tell me that now that the Miles2Go reputation had been redeemed and my father had served his time, the Merriweather-Browns were looking forward to renewing discussions between us of a potential merger of some of our smaller divisions to create one-stop travel centers for road-tripping families.

As if I'd still be in control.

Still working for M2G.

Which makes me suspect Margot's recent renewed interest in him was professional instead of personal. Convenience stores and hotels are a good match, and it was a match we were supposed to make before my father went to prison.

When I hurt her by calling things off.

Why would she keep my secret that I'm running away now?

I shouldn't have gone to see her at all last week, but I felt like I needed closure.

I needed to look her in the eye, see that she's okay, that she doesn't hate me anymore.

Not because I want her back—I'm not the same man I was when we got engaged, and I can't begin to imagine finding peace with her and the life she wants to keep living now—but because I needed to tie up that one last loose end.

For me.

And one more loose end is exactly what I'm pondering as we approach the outskirts of Pittsburgh.

How do I get rid of Daphne without her alerting my family that I'm gone before I've done what I need to do with the cash in my trunk and find wherever it is that I'm supposed to start my new life?

I'm supposed to have two weeks before they know anything's wrong. So I might need to keep Daphne with me for the full two weeks.

I don't want to tip my hand to her this early though.

The minute I stop at a gas pump, she leaps out of the car. "Potty," she says. "By the way, you parked on the wrong side for the gas tank. There's this little arrow thingy on your gas gauge that points to which side your tank is on. For future reference. Don't leave without me."

She dances inside the convenience store almost before I've unfolded myself and climbed out of the car.

She finally stopped talking once she climbed into the back seat, and after I got the radio turned on, I almost forgot she was there.

Almost.

Hard to forget I have a stowaway who's somehow managed to already blackmail me.

I look at the pump, and Cupholder the hermit crab waves at me from a video screen centered above the payment display.

I blink at it.

Why did I pick a Miles2Go?

Why?

the grumpiest billionaire

I didn't have to pick a Miles2Go. There's a different store, a different brand, right across the street.

And I went immediately for the familiar.

Even though I've never driven up to one of these in my life.

It's not simply the summer heat making me sweat in my flannel now. I grunt to myself, get back in the car, crank the engine, and turn it around so the tank is on the same side as the pump.

Facing this way, I can clearly see the wildflowers blooming in the grassy area between the parking lot of this shop and the next one down. At least four butterflies flutter among the purple cornflowers and black-eyed Susans and milkweed.

My heart squeezes in my chest, but for once, it's not anxiety or fear or overwhelm or stress or anything bad.

It's pride.

Fucking *pride*. Pride that I earned.

Because I did that.

I gave bonuses to franchises that planted butterfly gardens.

But after being in crisis management mode for the past four years, this is the first time I've seen one in person.

If I were alone, I'd walk over and watch the little ecosystem in action. Take five minutes to breathe and soak in my favorite pet project.

The one my father told me I could do with some special projects funds.

The same special projects funds that he used to buy thirty million dollars' worth of useless wines.

And that's how it always was.

Of course, Oliver. Of course I want to hear your vision for the company. Oh, haha, butterflies at gas stations. Get that out of your system now because when you're CEO, you'll have bigger fish to catch. Or should I say, bigger butterflies to catch?

Of course I'm listening to you, Oliver. But what you think is important isn't what the family needs you to think is important so that you can keep our shareholders happy.

And the flip side of that reminder was always *and the family holds the majority of the shares, so keep us happy first and foremost.*

I rub my chest and blink back the heat in my eyes as I climb out of the car again.

My arms are starting to lose circulation.

Most of the wardrobe I ordered online to be delivered to the cabin didn't arrive, so my options were limited this morning.

Very, very limited.

And of what I did get, not all of it fit right.

I need to stop somewhere to get more clothes, but I've prioritized getting as far from New York as I can, as fast as I can, first.

I'm starting to reconsider that as I unbutton my flannel in the heat and study the pump.

Cupholder waves at me again from the screen and then shrinks to one corner as a video starts, featuring some newscaster behind a desk.

Fresh gossip out of New York this morning as pictures are emerging of the welcome-home party held last night for William Cumberland, beleaguered former CEO of the Miles2Go conglomerate of convenience stores and gas stations, following his release from prison earlier this week...

My jaw tightens, and I grab the nozzle to refill the gas tank as I actively ignore the video screen.

I turn to the car, remember I have to pop open the gas cap, then remember there's a button inside the car to release it.

It's *pumping gas.*

I've been around the gas industry my entire life.

I'll get this.

I'll get this before Daphne gets back out.

I angle a look inside the store and don't see her.

Should be easy to spot her, because she's Daphne.

She's never not standing out, so she must be in the bathroom.

Swear to god, if she betrays me, I'll make her life hell.

I find the button to pop open the gas tank inside the door, then unscrew the gas cap.

the grumpiest billionaire

More pictures of my father—including some in an orange jumpsuit and some with him holding up a bottle of counterfeit wine—appear on the video screen as the reporter hustles through covering that he used company funds to purchase fake vintage wine from a scam artist.

And then there's my name.

I look back at the video screen.

And there's my picture.

Fuck.

Three other people are pumping gas, including one on the other side of the pump from me.

I duck my head and shove the nozzle into the gas tank, except it won't fit.

The hell?

Why won't it fit?

I angle it differently and try to push it into the hole, but it doesn't go.

It hits the rim of the tank and stops.

I shove.

It doesn't move.

I shove harder, but not *too* hard.

A fire broke out at a pump at one of our Nevada franchises last year, and I do know a thing or two about metal-on-metal causing a spark.

So why the hell won't the damn nozzle go into the damn hole?

I look at the pump, still keeping my head down. The guy on the other side of the pump isn't looking at me, and the newscaster has gone on to talk about expected weather in the Pittsburgh area.

But I don't want to draw attention to myself.

There's a little diagram on the pump.

It shows the nozzle going into the hole for the gas tank.

It doesn't show Superman.

There's no picture with a specific diagram of how the nozzle fits in the hole.

Did I buy a defective car?

Is there something wrong with my car's goddamn gas tank?

57

What the actual—

"Problem, Captain?" Daphne says next to me.

Jesus.

I'm in flannel and boat pants, and she's in a cocktail dress.

I don't want to think about what this looks like.

"The fucking nozzle won't fit in the fucking hole," I mutter to her while I demonstrate. "It's too big."

She looks me dead in the eye. "Bet that's the first time you've heard that in your life."

Is she—

Dammit.

I walked right into that.

My molars grind together as she grins and takes the stick from me.

"This particular nozzle," she says, "is for diesel. Your car takes regular unleaded. This nozzle. This one over here on the other side of the pump."

The guy across from us lifts his eyes to look at us as my face heats even hotter.

I knew that.

I fucking knew that, but today is going so wrong that my brain is malfunctioning.

Daphne—standing there in her cocktail dress with her bedhead somewhat tamed but not enough to look normal, especially with the blue and green streaks making her look like a goth mermaid—smiles at the guy who's now watching us and gives him a little finger wave.

"We're getting into character to audition for a reality TV show. *Bros and Hoes*. Have you heard of it? It's awful. Like, truly awful. But don't we look like we belong? We're going to do this bit so my friend Spencer here looks like a complete idiot who doesn't know how to pump gas. Do you think they'll buy it?"

The guy ducks his head and mutters something while he goes back to his own business.

"*Bros and Hoes?*" I hiss at her.

the grumpiest billionaire

"I know. I hate that word. It's so demeaning to women and their sexual experience. That's why I didn't tell you sooner where we're going. But if the producers want to give me that much money to call me names, whatever. It'll pay for my astrophysics degree."

The screen on the pump cycles back to the same story about my father being released from prison and the party my mother threw him last night.

Daphne stares at the screen, then grimaces. "I hate dresses," she mutters.

I look at the screen too.

They're showing a picture that includes her as one of the many partygoers on my parents' packed patio at their Hamptons house. It's taken from the balcony, but you can see Daphne holding her head high, blonde wig on, martini glass in hand, mid-stride like she's on a mission.

Like she fits in there.

Wonder who she paid off to get in. She wasn't on the guest list. Probably why she wore a disguise too. Security would've let someone's girlfriend in.

They likely would *not* have let Daphne in, and I get the impression she didn't want to be there anyway.

The guy on the other side of the pump starts his engine.

"Also, you have to pay for the gas inside first if you're not paying by credit card or phone tap," Daphne murmurs.

Fucking fuck on a fuck-bucket. I knew that too.

Daphne has made half my brain cells scatter and refuse to work together, and now I look like an even bigger dumbass.

"So do you have phone tapping set up on your phone?" she asks.

Not a chance.

I don't even like being here when I know there are likely security cameras on the premises. Eventually, my family will hire investigators to track me. It won't matter that they'll get a letter informing them that I'm willingly opting to remove myself from life in Manhattan and I don't want them to contact me. It won't matter that I'm divesting myself of all of my shares in M2G after I use them to vote for my choice of my own successor. It won't matter that I'm not leaving a digital trail. They'll find ways to track me.

That's half of why I'm taking a circuitous route to get to wherever I decide my final destination is and the only phone in my possession—other than Daphne's—is a phone with exactly one phone number in it, to exactly one person that I trust with my life.

I pocket the keys, then shrug out of my flannel to hand it to Daphne. "Put this on and get in the car."

"It's too freaking hot for—what are you wearing?" Her gaze dips to my chest and my arms, and she makes a face that I don't want to interpret. It comes with bulging eyeballs and parted lips and then a head shake. "Oh my god. Do you still have feeling in your fingertips?"

I look down at the white T-shirt I shimmied myself into this morning.

It's brand-new.

And it's the smallest freaking size large T-shirt I've ever worn.

Order clothes online, I told myself. *Have them delivered to the Pennsylvania house. Enough to get you deep enough into the countryside that no one will look twice as you get a new wardrobe.*

Except most of the packages didn't arrive. All that was waiting for me at the cabin last night is what I'm wearing today.

So here I am, in a T-shirt so tight that my nipples are caving in and the smallest slice of my stomach is showing over my waistband.

"Get in the car," I repeat to Daphne.

"I know you come from a long line of people who'd take candy from a baby, but I didn't think you'd take their shirts too. Who did your shopping? There's no way that's an adult-size shirt."

"Get in the car," I repeat.

She rolls her eyes and circles the car to open the back door. "Tell them you need to put thirty dollars' worth in the car at pump seven."

As if I can't calculate for myself how much gas I need. Even if I've never had to pump it myself, I work in the industry.

the grumpiest billionaire

But the brain cells that aren't already on vacation are fizzing and popping and burning from the stress of my unexpected companion.

I'd handle this fine if she weren't here.

Probably.

A sigh leaks out of me.

Or possibly not. I'm not sure I've handled anything fine in the past four years.

When I walk in the building, the woman behind the counter's wearing a nametag that reads *Carol* on her red vest with Cupholder and MILES2GO printed across the front. She eyes me. "Pump seven?"

"Thirty dollars' worth," I say, shoving a hundred-dollar bill across the plexiglass countertop that's showing off small postcards with dollar, two-dollar, and five-dollar price tags on the top of each.

She looks at me.

Then down at my pants.

Then at the currency on the counter between us.

Lottery tickets.

Those are lottery tickets.

Not postcards.

"Keep the change," I add.

Maybe she'll buy lottery tickets.

Maybe she won't.

She snorts softly. "Right. *The change.*" She pulls a marker out of a drawer and swipes it across the hundred-dollar bill, then eyes me.

"It's real," I say as the doorbell jingles behind me.

She eyes me again, then slides a look outside.

She's seen Daphne.

She's seen Daphne, and I'm standing here wearing a shirt three sizes too small and linen boat pants and yellow work boots.

Dammit.

I don't look like an average Joe.

I look like the cops want to talk to me.

It takes everything inside me to keep watching Carol like I'm in complete control and not internally bracing myself in case that was a cop who walked in the door.

Why do I have my back to the door?

Why don't I have a good angle to look at my own car?

These stores need to be revamped. They need to be renovated so that I can pay for gas with cash without being blind as to who's approaching me from behind.

Dark hair with blue and green streaks appears in my peripheral vision, then a subtle heat as red flannel brushes against me too.

"These too," Daphne says beside me, dumping six bags of Lava Cheese Puffs on the counter. "We definitely need these. Oh, and two MegaHit energy drinks. Hold on a sec. I'll go grab them." She winks at the woman behind the counter. "Gotta keep him going all night, you know what I mean."

She turns, slaps my ass, making me jump, and strides barefoot to the cooler along the back wall.

Carol stares at me more.

"Thirty dollars' worth at pump seven, and whatever she wants," I say.

You still own this building, I remind myself.

Or at least the licensing to the company name.

I own a quarter of it outright with the stock shares I inherited from my grandfather.

Carol looks at the hundred-dollar bill again.

It's good. I saw her check it with the pen. Mark turned yellow.

It's good.

She knows it.

I know it.

So why am I sweating like I've done something wrong?

"*Honey,*" Daphne squeals. "*Matching T-shirts!* Your family will *die*. What size is Uncle Herman again? Oh, never mind. You never know things like that. Men, am I right? We'll get a few sizes in case." She drops a pile of black Cupholder the hermit crab T-shirts on the counter.

the grumpiest billionaire

Carol stares at both of us while she scans all of the barcodes with a little laser gun.

"My mom is gonna be so mad," Daphne says to me. "She hates matching T-shirts. But your family's Thanksgiving cards with the matching shirts are always so cute." She turns to Carol. "*Thanksgiving cards*. Isn't that the cutest?"

"One sixty-eight fourteen," Carol says.

"Give her another hundred, honey." Daphne wrinkles her nose, then reaches into her cleavage. "Or, you know what? Never mind. I've got this one. Ooh, but add three of those five-dollar Tarzan lottery tickets in too, would you?"

She drops a folded hundred-dollar bill on the counter.

I look at her cleavage.

How much of my money did she shove in her cleavage while she was searching my car last night?

She laughs and pushes me. "Save it for the car, horndog."

Carol checks Daphne's hundred, and moments later, Daphne's carrying an armful of shirts and chips and MegaHit energy drinks out to the car, with three lottery tickets sticking out where her hundred-dollar bill was a few minutes ago.

I'm horrified.

So horrified, in fact, that I get in the car, crank the engine, and I'm pulling away before I realize I forgot to put gas in the tank.

I look in the rearview mirror as another car slides into the slot I've just vacated. "*Fuck*."

Daphne grins at me from the back seat. She's discarded my flannel and is throwing a black Miles2Go T-shirt over her head. "So...Speedy Sloth across the street instead?"

Dammit.

Dammit.

She noticed I forgot to get gas too.

"I'm not going to Speedy Sloth."

"Why not? You could get a Speedy Sloth Slushie. I'll bet you've never had one."

I will never.

Ever.

Ever.

Enter a Speedy Sloth gas station or convenience store.

Ever.

Fuckers added that *Speedy Sloth Slushie* to their offerings to compete with the Miles2Go Landslide Slushy—yes, they spelled *slushy* the other way—right after my father went to prison.

The number of meetings I sat through calling that a crisis—and the number of people who felt so strongly about it that it was like I was personally insulting their babies when I declared it wasn't a crisis—just no.

Never.

"Do you want to stay in this car and continue with our deal, or do you want to see yourself out right now?" I ask Daphne.

She rolls her eyes. "Testy much? Fine. There's a Quickie-Lickie on the other side of the highway."

"Why is every gas station named something awful?" I mutter.

"Don't diss on the Lickie. They have the best squeegees for cleaning all of the bugs off your windshield—don't worry, I'll walk you through that too—and they give away a free sucker with every fill-up, and they're not flavors you can find anywhere else. Have you ever had a mango root beer sucker?"

I gape at her in the rearview mirror. *Mango root beer?*

That sounds as awful as continuing this road trip with her in tow.

"*Stop sign!*" she shrieks.

I slam on the brakes as another car honks and veers around me while I'm halfway through the intersection.

Shit.

Daphne has one arm braced on the ceiling of the car and her opposite leg pressing into my seat. "Can I *please* have a turn driving?"

I look every way I can look, breathing through the way my heart is trying to pound out of my ribs, then continue through the intersection, swinging left at the last minute to head toward the country highway and the Quickie-Lickie so that we can get gas.

I don't hear Daphne draw a full breath again until we pull into the second gas station.

She huffs out a breath, and then she laughs.

Laughs.

"Holy shit, look at this. One of the scratch-offs I got to throw her off won us ten grand."

Ten grand.

Ten grand.

I haven't even begun giving away the millions I have in the trunk, and now I have another ten grand to deal with.

I lurch the car to a stop at a pump, realize I've once again parked backward for the gas tank, and I drop my head to the steering wheel.

The car honks.

Fuck.

Just *fuck.*

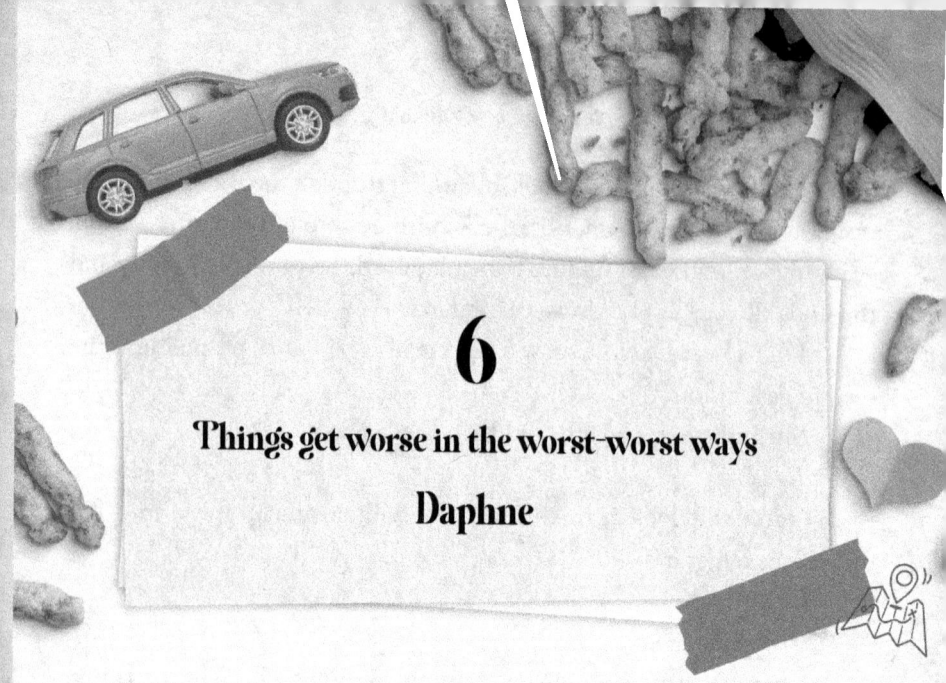

6

Things get worse in the worst-worst ways

Daphne

In the interest of not being the total asshole that I could be, when we stop at a ValuKart Goods and Groceries after getting gas, I *don't* insist Oliver try on any of the shirts with funny animal jokes on them.

It's clearly causing him enough suffering that I only bought Cupholder-themed T-shirts at that Miles2Go, one of which he's now wearing.

Voluntarily, for the record.

Kind of.

He changed into it in the car to get out of that undersized T-shirt that left nothing to my imagination when it comes to his body.

Not that seeing him shirtless helped steer my imagination away from his body.

Just—holy shit.

He's *ripped*.

That time I saw him in his tighty-whities, he was your average slender guy who was a little too cautious about everything.

Not buff like he's been training for a boxing match when he wasn't at his CEO's desk for the past few years.

Nor nearly as forceful as he's been since last night.

the grumpiest billionaire

Oliver is—

He's not *Oliver*.

And it's causing me some very distinct problems.

And that's another reason why I'm not pushing anything fashion-wise. Instead, I steer him directly to the jeans and the simplest button-downs that I can find in ValuKart's men's clothing section.

But I do tell him he has to try them on before we can leave.

So that I know what sizes to tell him to look for when he shops for his own clothes later.

Not because it's fun to watch him grimace under the watchful eye of the suspicious lady watching over the changing rooms.

That's merely an added bonus.

"Is it supposed to be itchy?" he mutters to me from behind the closed door.

"Yep."

Silence answers me, but I can sense him aiming a growly, aggravated face at me.

He is easily the grumpiest man I have ever met in my life, and Bea's brother Ryker is pretty grumpy.

I'm beginning to think Oliver's grumpies are permanent.

Probably also my fault.

"You should wash it before you wear it," I tell him.

While not imagining him without a shirt on at all.

Stop it, stop it, stop it, Daphne.

The lady watching us squints at me.

I point to the door. "Just left a nudist colony," I stage whisper. "He grew up there. It's his first time off the naked compound."

A very loud inhale from inside the dressing room tells me Oliver overheard that.

And I have now left myself thinking about Oliver completely naked, my brain filling in details about what his thighs must look like if his arms and abdomen are that buff.

This is *not* what I need.

It's not what any of us need.

What the hell is wrong with me?

The door swings open, and Oliver stares at me.

It's the darkest, growliest, most dangerous stare I've ever seen on him, and I've seen plenty of dark, growly danger from him since I woke up in the back seat of his Mercedes SUV last night.

I suppress the wince I want to make, and I step into the doorway. "Turn around."

He's in a blue short-sleeved button-down that does unexpected things for his hazel eyes and one of the pairs of jeans I grabbed for him to try on, and he does not do what I'm telling him to do.

"I need to make sure it all fits right," I mutter.

"I think I can tell if it all fits right," he mutters back.

"Did you bend over? Sit down? Test how it feels when you're moving?" You'd think the questions aren't necessary, but they are. This man is accustomed to tailor-made clothing for his entire wardrobe.

I'm completely certain he's never seen the inside of a ValuKart, much less the inside of a ValuKart fitting room.

"I know how to—do I look fucking normal or not?" he hisses.

He does.

He looks like any other guy who might be randomly walking through ValuKart.

Except for the part where his whole body is vibrating with an angry energy that I feel in my soul and his jaw is too tight and his eyes are too full of rage and if the wrong person says the wrong thing to him, I'm pretty sure it wouldn't take much for him to snap and murder them.

So basically, he still doesn't look like he fits in at ValuKart.

Mostly.

The store can be pretty aggravating sometimes, but not usually *I want to murder people* levels of aggravating.

I swallow hard. "Yes. You look like a normal human being."

He doesn't answer and instead slams the changing room door.

the grumpiest billionaire

Ten minutes later, we're strolling to the checkout with three pairs of jeans and four shirts for him, plus two sets of shorts, a pack of underwear, three bras, a pair of flip-flops, and an extra shirt for me.

Plus a bag of gummy bears and a basic toiletry kit—also for me.

We'll have to stop somewhere else for more clothes later, but for now, we won't attract too much attention. Small clothing shopping spree, paying in cash? All good.

Dropping a thousand dollars at ValuKart on complete new wardrobes and full-size toiletries?

Nope.

People talk, and Oliver's all over the news, and probably not only the news on the Miles2Go pump screens.

I point to the bathroom once he's paid and dropped the change into the charity bucket at the end of the checkout lane. "Since we paid, we can both change. Plus, I need to go to the bathroom."

"You just went to the bathroom."

"This is something else."

Oliver's eye twitches, but his sigh tells me that he's not going to argue more.

I take the bag with my clothes, cringing only a little at the thought of putting them on without washing them first, and dash for the women's room, hovering long enough to verify that he's headed to the men's room.

And then I reach into my cleavage for the secret purchase that I made at the gas station when I went in the first time, power it up, and dial Bea's number from heart.

Beatrice Best saved my life. She's been my best friend since a few months before I got disinherited, when we met in class at Austen & Lovelace College in Athena's Rest, and I won't be able to live with myself much longer if I don't call her.

She's a worrier.

I was supposed to be home by now.

I hope she answers, since she won't recognize the number on this burner phone, and—

"Hello?" she says on the other end.

Thank you, baby sea turtles. "Bea. It's me," I whisper.

"*Oh my god*, Daph, *where are you?*"

Hearing her voice makes me tear up. "I'm okay. I'm safe. I'm voluntarily doing what I'm doing."

"Why is your phone showing in Pennsylvania?"

"Shit. You weren't supposed to see that."

"*Daphne.*"

I rip the tag off one pair of my new shorts and step into them. "The reason I don't go home? I don't go home because then I'm the Daphne who was an epic fuck-up and things just *happen* that aren't supposed to happen because I have the worst timing ever, and something happened again, but *I am okay*, and I'll be home…sometime…and I just didn't want you to worry."

"There is nothing about this conversation that isn't making me worry."

My heart squeezes so hard in my chest that I almost can't breathe.

She's my age, and she worries too much about everyone. Because she's had to for the past decade since her parents died in a house fire and she left college to move home to finish raising her brothers. I hate making her worry about me.

"Remember when I moved in with you?" I say in a rush while I tear the tag off of my new bra. "When you had to teach me to drive and how to do laundry and grocery shop on a budget?"

"Yes."

"I have to do that for someone else right now."

"Who?"

"I can't tell you that."

"Daphne—"

"Bea. Listen. I love you more than I love anyone else on this planet. You saved my life, and I would literally die for you, but I cannot tell you who I'm with. It's—it's sensitive, and it's just easier if you don't know, okay? But I'm okay. I'm on a little unplanned road trip. My phone is, erm, temporarily out of commission, so I got this burner phone. I'm going to have it off a lot, but if you *need* need me, you can call me on this number or my other cell. I'm…working on getting it…working again."

"What about your job?"

"I'm calling in sick for the week. If Margot calls—if Margot calls, just tell her I got twitchy and had to go camping off-grid, and that I'll call her back in a week or two, okay?"

"Daphne—"

"Did you make up with Simon?"

"Yes, but—"

Yes! My eyes prickle with tears. The good kind. When I left, she was debating if the hot single dad she'd accidentally started dating this summer was worth a real risk after he betrayed her trust. "For real?"

"He's right here. Want to say hi?"

I do.

I want to hear Bea's British boyfriend say something normal and funny, and I want to tell him if he *ever* lies to her again about anything, I'll murder him, and then I want Bea to tell me every last detail about how they made up, but I don't have time. "No, I need to go. He's going to notice that I'm taking longer than I should in the bathroom."

"He? Who's *he*?"

"Bea, I really have to go. But quick—are you happy?"

"Other than my best friend disappearing with an unnamed *he* and being really cryptic about it? Yes. Very happy."

Best.

News.

Ever.

"I'll be home as soon as I can."

"Madame Petty told me you wouldn't come home one day," Bea blurts.

Stupid fortune teller.

Who's too right sometimes. "Fuck Madame Petty. I'm coming home, and then I'll tell you everything. I'll call you every other day or so. So you know I'm still alive. Gotta dash, Bea. I love you."

I hang up before she can stop me, and my nose gets that telltale sign that tears are on the way.

Everything I'm about to teach Oliver, Bea had to teach me.

She'd be so much better at it.

But there's zero chance I'm convincing Oliver that the best way for him to learn to live like a normal person is to turn around and head back toward New York, even upstate instead of the city.

Not with his plans.

I leave my boss a voicemail and rush through changing the rest of my clothes, and then use the toilet one more time since I have no idea if Oliver will be the type to tell me to hold it.

Oliver several years ago?

He was a pushover who did whatever Margot told him to, or whatever his parents told him to, or whatever my parents told him to.

This Oliver?

I have a feeling—

"Are you done yet? And where the hell are my car keys?"

Yeah, this Oliver has no qualms marching into the women's restroom to get me as I'm washing my hands.

This man is *not* the same man my sister was engaged to.

You know that song with the line about how the singer can't answer the phone since she's deceased?

That's what it's like looking at Oliver.

Outwardly, he has the same hazel eyes and the same shortish haircut and the same normal lips and the same ears that stick out a little too much on the sides, but everything else about him—from the more chiseled jaw to the attitude to the way he talks to me to the way he carries himself—everything else is like he's a different man.

It's like he found his spine and now uses it regularly, and it's making me wonder how else he's changed.

I shake my hands off, then pull the keys out of the bag where I've also hidden my burner phone inside the wadded-up dress from last night and dangle them between my fingers. "My former life of crime is gonna help me make sure you don't leave without me."

He growls something softly to himself, snatches the keys, and gives me the *move your ass* glare.

"Are you hungry?" I ask him. "I could go for some fried fish. It's great road trip food."

He does that thing where his chest expands as he draws a long breath through his quivering nostrils, then slides another glare at me.

Maybe he's hangry.

We haven't had much to eat today. A coffee and a protein bar apiece.

Food's a good idea.

A *very* good idea.

And then I'm convincing him to get off the road.

We stroll out of the store, and a tiny human being yells at us from a table set up in the sunshine beside the exit. "Hey! Hey, mister and miss! I'm selling discount cards to raise money for my gymnastics club so that we can get new equipment and be a lot safer when we fall on our heads! Will you support me not getting brain damage so maybe I can find the cure for cancer one day and also be a gymnast?"

I barely tuck in a laugh.

I've seen some small humans selling stuff for their clubs and teams before, but this—this is a next-level sales pitch.

"We can't *not*—" I start to say to Oliver, but I cut myself off.

Because everything about Oliver Cumberland has shifted, and he's not growly, and he's not glaring, and he's not radiating barely suppressed fury.

He's switching directions to approach the little girl with the red pigtails who can't be more than six years old, with his shoulders more relaxed than they've been at any moment since I woke up in his car last night.

He squats in front of her while the adult with her watches both of us.

"What's your favorite part of gymnastics?" he asks her.

This isn't grumpiest-of-the-grumpy Oliver.

But it's not pushover Oliver either.

This is—this is *mature* Oliver.

Confident Oliver.

Aware Oliver.

"I like the uneven bars because I can swing for *hours* and *hours*," she tells him. "But when I fall, it hurts."

He nods gravely. "It hurts when I fall too. How much money do you need to raise for better equipment?"

"Ten seventy thousand million dollars," she replies.

He smiles.

Oliver.

Oliver Cumberland.

Smiling at a little girl.

Fuck.

Fuuuuuuuuck.

"We're trying to raise five thousand," the woman I assume is the kid's mom says.

"That's a lot of money," Oliver says to the little girl.

"Good thing I'm cute," she replies.

His entire face relaxes into an even broader smile.

And then he does something even worse.

He pulls out his wallet and empties it into their donation jar. "Hope that helps."

The mom's eyes go huge.

Like, I don't think I could open my eyes that wide if I tried.

Understandable.

He must've had thirty or forty hundred-dollar bills tucked into his wallet. It was so thick it barely folded.

"Is that seventy-eleventy bajillion dollars?" the little girl asks.

"Definitely not that much."

"Here. Here, take a discount card," the mom stutters, shoving a plastic card at us while the little girl starts telling Oliver about a time when she fell off the balance beam.

If I were a good be-a-normal-person coach, I'd dive in and say thank you and take the plastic card and hustle Oliver away.

But I'm a little too stuck on the way he's smiling softly at the little girl, listening to her story about the time she did three cartwheels in a row like it's the most important thing in the world.

"Take two." The mom shoves the cards at me, and I shake myself back to reality.

To a reality where these two are going to tell their friends about the man who dropped three or four thousand dollars into their donation jar.

I take the cards, then poke Oliver. "Hey, M-dub-O, we're gonna be late for my brother's birthday party, and you know how much he'll be a pill about it."

I get a hairy eyeball of irritation at the use of his old nickname—I deserve that eyeball, because I know that's what his bullies called him in high school, which makes it about the best way I know to irritate him into moving.

And it works.

He rises and nods to the little girl. "Keep practicing and you'll fall less."

"Thank you," her mom says, still clearly a little lost for words.

He nods, and then tucks his hands in his pockets, puts his head down, and turns and heads back into the parking lot.

I jog after him.

"Shut. The hell. Up," he mutters.

I squeeze my hands into fists.

Not to keep from punching him since I haven't said a single solitary word.

No, it's to keep from hugging him.

It's absolutely nothing to him to donate a few thousand dollars here and there. It's like pennies to him.

Less than pennies.

But watching him smile at a little kid, watching him pause for them—it's shaken something loose inside me that I much prefer to not have shooken loose.

What's the word for a fuckup bigger than a fuckup?

Because I think that's exactly what I've gotten myself into.

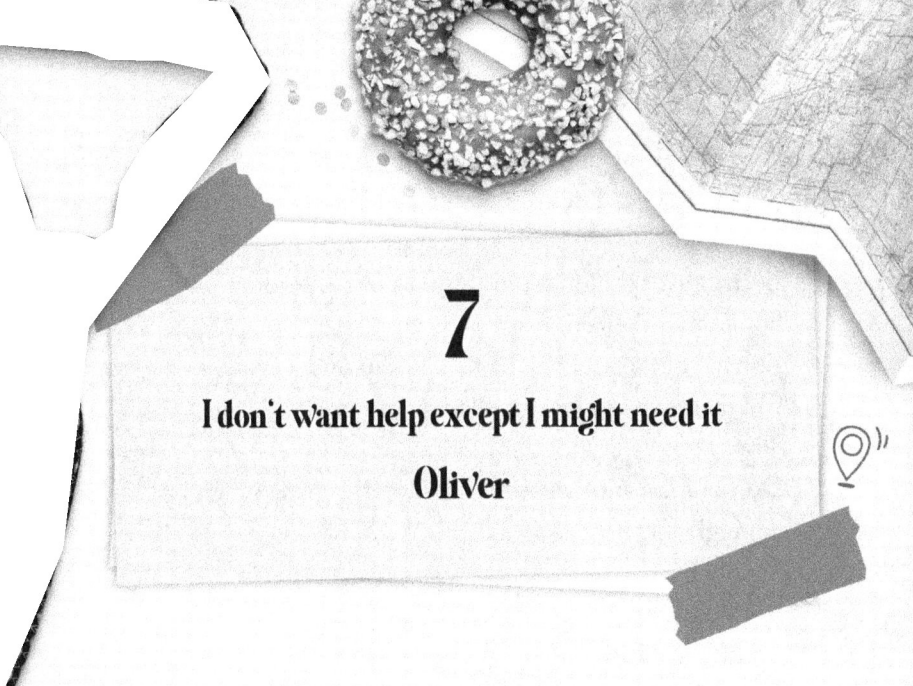

7

I don't want help except I might need it
Oliver

How is it that I spent the past four years working twelve- to fourteen-hour days, yet six hours driving a car has me completely wrecked?

And it's not a post-trauma thing.

Despite the close calls last night and this morning, I'm not worried someone's going to sideswipe me every minute anymore. Not worried that we'll end up upside down beside a river. Not concerned that a runaway train will appear out of nowhere.

I'm *beat*. Physically, mentally, and emotionally.

I slide a glance to my right as I pull off the state highway and onto a bumpier road marked with a wooden sign announcing some state park. This isn't a planned stop, but I don't have four more hours of driving in me to get to my next destination. And if I don't make day two, I'm not making day three, or day four, or day five, and just *dammit*.

Daphne pops a gummy bear into her mouth. "You sure you don't want one? That protein bar you had this morning wasn't a lot of food."

We're maybe forty minutes past the ValuKart, and she's been suspiciously quiet the entire time. Like she took me seriously when I told her to shut up. "No eating in the car."

She grins at me and pops another gummy bear into her mouth. "Won't find food in a state park either, and if you eat outside of the car, the bears will smell it and come and eat us."

"Bears don't eat humans in this part of the country."

"Sometimes they do."

"*Rarely.*" Fuck me, I need a nap. A nap, and a drink, and a steak.

And then a solid night of sleep.

Or maybe a solid month of sleep.

"Do you have another secret cabin in this park, or are you looking for something?" Daphne asks.

I ignore her.

"Are we meeting one of your friends?"

"I don't have friends."

"None? None at all?"

I have *a* friend. One that I trust with my life, and one that I'm due to check in with tonight to verify that I've survived on my own this long.

One that I probably could have called to handle the Daphne problem, but that didn't occur to me until right now, and it turns out, she might be useful, even if I hate that.

Everyone else that I've ever considered a friend?

They either dropped me as soon as my father was convicted, or they slowly fell away when I didn't have time for drinks after work anymore.

I don't trust other executives because I didn't know who was honestly being nice versus who was being cordial to get secrets out of me or who was hoping I'd fall flat on my face so they could take my job or even the company.

So what I truly have is paranoia.

All of it. I have all of the paranoia to ever exist in the entire universe.

I spot a parking lot that's relatively empty and pull in at the far end.

My shoulders relax as I shift the car into park.

My breath eases out.

My head drops back.

My eyelids droop.

And Daphne crinkles another goddamn bag.
Then crunches.
Loudly.
"Tired?" she says.
"Stop talking."
She doesn't have to say a word for me to hear what she's thinking.
I can drive if you'd like to go farther down the road.
I pry one eyelid open and glance her way.
She holds up a misshapen *thing* in an unnatural orange. "Lava Cheese Puff?"
And my shoulders are at my ears again.

The interior of my car will be glowing orange from all of the fake cheese dust coming off her fingers, and I doubt anything that unnatural comes out of the cloth seats easily.

I squeeze my eyes shut and turn my face away from her, willing myself to imagine the sounds of a burbling creek or a thunderstorm in one of those apps that never worked well enough to help me fall asleep.

"That was a nice thing you did for that little girl," Daphne says quietly.
"We're not talking."

"I helped my—someone with a carwash fundraiser a few years ago, and the town's worst person ever came through and barely gave five dollars, and then this single mom came through and dropped in a hundred bucks, and every single teenager working that car wash that day remembered her until they left town. If they had part-time jobs at the diner, they gave her a discount. She'd get tickets to the high school plays dropped in her mailbox. One day, she found homemade cupcakes right after a rumor went around that she'd had a bad day."

I suck in an uneven breath.
That.
That's what I want.

A community where people help each other and remember each other and don't care if you were born a billionaire or piss-poor. Where they remember each other and do nice things for each other because it's what you should do, not what you do to look good.

Where you can belong.

I rub my chest where the longing for a place to belong is sucking the life out of me.

I never belonged in my parents' world, and the only thing these past four years since my father was arrested have proven to me is that I never will.

Can I run a multi-billion-dollar corporation?

Apparently yes. Save it from the brink of ruination, even.

But I don't want to. And honestly, it only worked because I listened to the people around me who seemed to have better ideas than the others.

Half of what I did wasn't because I thought it was what needed to be done.

It was because my executive assistant is a genius who told me what to do, and I was smart enough to listen to her.

"That little girl will remember you for the rest of her life," Daphne adds, even softer.

My eyes flare open, and I jerk my face toward her.

Dammmmmmit.

Why didn't I think of that?

Daphne lifts a brow. "Kinda doubt she recognized you. Her mom either. If they did, they'll remember you more for this than anything else."

She flicks at my shirt with her orange-covered fingers.

I look down and spot the price tag hanging off the breast pocket. "Goddammit," I mutter.

She grins and munches on another cheese puff.

And I cave.

I fucking cave.

"If I let you drive, will you drive where I tell you to go?"

"Yep."

"Without any side trips or stops along the way?"

the grumpiest billionaire

"If we pass the world's largest pink eraser or I realize we're within five miles of any world-famous attraction involving cows, we're stopping. You're not really on a road trip if you don't."

I can't believe that's a comforting answer, but it is.

She'll go where I tell her in the hopes she can see some stupid— I shake my head.

In the hopes that she can see something *unique*.

Something that a community somewhere is proud of.

Or even a single person.

Something out of the ordinary that a single person cares about enough to try to draw visitors to it.

I pop open my door. "If you double-cross me—"

"Oliver."

"What?"

She stares at me with an intensity that's unnerving coming from her. "Our families suck, and the world they exist in sucks worse. That doesn't mean it's not hard to break away and set your own course. I still don't like you, but I respect you for what you're doing right now."

Also unnerving?

How much I relate to that last sentence.

I don't like her either, but I appreciate that she has exactly the experience I apparently need.

Travel logistics were easy to plan. A driving route to explore as much of the country as possible in two weeks, and lodging booked with prepaid credit cards and a fake name on hotel and vacation rental accounts that match my fake ID.

Check that.

Not *easy*, but at least logical.

Spontaneously finding ways to give away as much of my money as I can along the way—I can already tell that will be far more difficult. I'm seven hours in, and I've rid myself of less than five grand of the literal millions in my trunk.

Less than what Daphne won on that stupid scratch-off that's sitting in the cupholder between the seats.

I point at the wooden structure at the other end of the parking lot. "Go wash your hands. You're not getting that shit on my steering wheel."

She doesn't tell me not to leave her while she's in the bathroom.

I want to think that's weird, but I get a glimpse of myself in the side mirror, and I grimace.

There are dead people who look more alive than I do right now.

I'm so exhausted that I don't even stretch before lumbering around the car and shoving myself into the passenger seat. I'd be asleep when Daphne returns, except my knees are shoved up against the dashboard and I can't find the button to push the seat back.

She climbs into the driver's seat, takes one look at me, and reaches between my legs.

"What the *hell*—" I start, and then the seat is jerking backward.

"Lever's under the seat. No automatic buttons on the passenger side."

I pinch my nose and squeeze my eyes shut.

"There's another lever near the back of the seat if you want to recline it."

"Wasn't planning on sitting in this seat, so I didn't need to know how it worked," I grumble.

"There's a lot I wasn't planning on today."

I slide her a look.

She grins at me again.

Like *no big deal, just on an unexpected road trip to start my week, and now I'm having fun.*

She scoots the driver's seat forward, adjusts the mirrors and the steering wheel, straps in, and starts the engine.

Then she revs it. "Did Margot tell you that I'm racing cars for a living now?"

I spring straight up and slap my hand on the dash. "*Out*—"

"Kidding. I don't have my driver's license on me, so we'd be screwed if I get us pulled over. Take a nap. I've got this."

I glare at her.

Meanwhile, she's smiling so big—a real smile, a smile that holds pure joy, not a spite smile, not a smile that says she's enjoying torturing me—that something else takes hold in my gut.

Envy.

Envy that Daphne has found that magical, mystical *thing* I'm chasing.

The thing that I'm terrified I won't find no matter how far I get from my old life and no matter how hard I look for what I know is missing.

I ease back into the seat, feel around, and find the lever to recline it.

But only a little.

"You're happy," I say.

She glances at me before putting the car in gear. "My life doesn't suck."

It's more than that.

Much more than that.

Maybe I'm too tired to pick up on everything I always noticed about her before, but while there's still chaos to her, there's something else.

It's like...*peace.*

The frantic energy that went with her is gone.

She's not a tornado operating at the whims of whatever pressure system steers her next.

It's like she *is* the pressure system steering the tornado.

She can control it.

I tap the screen in the middle of the console. "Follow the GPS."

"You got it, Captain."

"Don't call me captain."

"Okey-dokey, Skipper."

I'd be annoyed, but I'm too busy letting my body melt into this seat.

It's uncomfortable as hell.

But that doesn't stop me from falling asleep.

All while hoping Daphne takes us where the car GPS is pointing.

If she doesn't—

What the hell.

In this exact moment, I'm too tired to care.

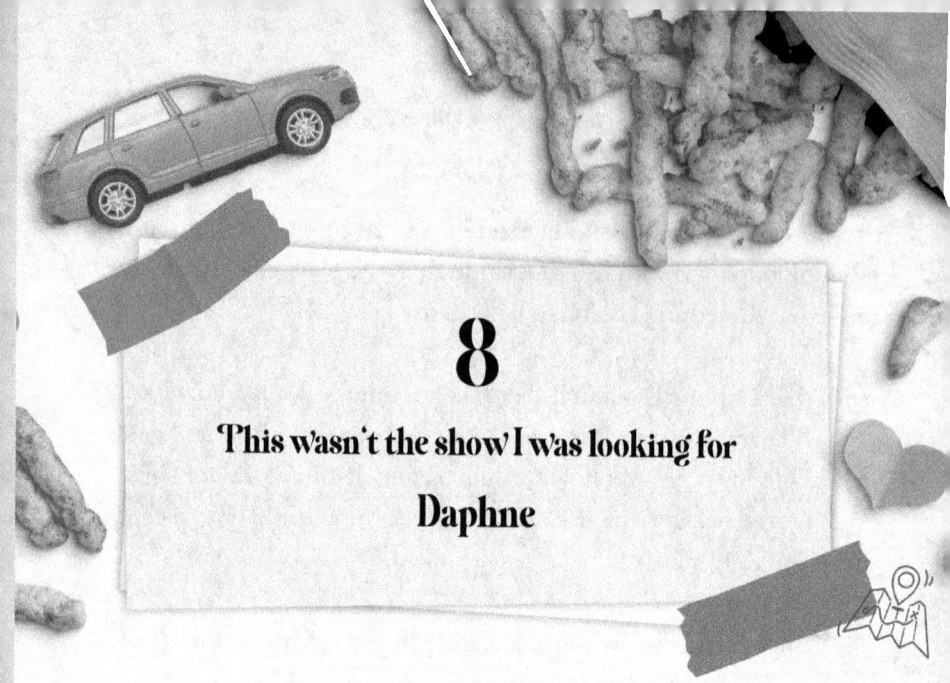

8

This wasn't the show I was looking for

Daphne

I took a road trip with Bea and her brothers about two years after my parents disinherited me.

Her youngest brother, Hudson, had gotten his driver's license a few months before, and her middle brother, Griff, was playing baseball in the minors. He had a series in Michigan, and Bea talked even her grumpy oldest little brother, Ryker, into coming with us to see Griff's baseball game.

I was between jobs at the time—it was right before I stumbled into working for Beeslieve—and feeling like a complete broke failure, which is likely why Bea insisted I go along.

She knew it would be fun and that I needed something fun.

Fun is never a bad thing in my world, and I honestly think that's why I still have a job with Beeslieve today.

I keep it fun for everyone else too while we're doing the hard work.

Hudson kept taking his shoes off and stinking up the car. Ryker kept grumbling that he shouldn't leave his farm for so long, even though he'd left it in good hands.

Bea and I, meanwhile, sat in the front seat and turned up the showtunes and sang our hearts out.

She didn't know any of the words, but that didn't stop her.

the grumpiest billionaire

By the time we got to Michigan, I'd discovered road trip food is *the best food ever*.

And that's why I'm pulling off the road right now.

Because I've passed four Cod Pieces already, and if I don't get some fish and chips at this one coming up, I'm going to die.

Okay, probably not, but also maybe.

Oliver's been asleep for three solid hours.

He's snored a few times and has drool slipping down his chin. Oliver drooling in his sleep would be adorable if he wasn't my sister's ex-fiancé, and I have to keep reminding myself that he is.

It's incredibly unfortunate that I need to keep reminding myself. But I do.

My hormones are *not* behaving themselves.

Between the sympathy I have for his situation and the way he's changed since the last time I saw him, and then his complete one-eighty from Mr. Grumpiest Billionaire Ever to Kindest Stranger in the Universe when he paused to make a donation to the little girl and her gymnastics club, I can't look at him without getting that feeling in my belly.

You know the one.

Yeah.

That feeling.

That *I think I like something about you* feeling that I absolutely, positively, *cannot* have for this man especially.

This is my hardship to bear for all of the crimes of my youth. Zero doubt.

Karma has come calling.

I turn into the Cod Pieces parking lot, intending to line up for the drive-thru, when Oliver bolts straight upright.

"Wha-bum?" he gasps.

Tell me any normal woman could resist a guy when he's disoriented and babbling nonsense while he has his own drool on his chin.

85

"We're about an hour from our destination," I tell him. "Grab the cash from the glove compartment. We're getting the best road trip food ever invented."

Not that it can hold a candle to Bea's fish and chips—her dad was a chef and taught her how to cook the most amazing food—but Bea's not here, and even if she was, she'd agree that Cod Pieces is the way to go for a road trip.

"Why are we eating at a place that's named even worse than the Quickie-Lickie?"

"Because it's delicious." I switch plans and pull into a parking spot instead of hitting the drive-thru. My bladder isn't the teeniest, but it can't handle two MegaHit energy drinks for long either. "And it's fine if you hate it, but I'm not doing my job well if I don't show you the best-worst food in existence. Although—no, never mind."

He blinks at me like he's still waking up. "Although what?"

"The real worst food ever is the Miles2Go signature corn dog. It's *really* bad. Like all the way bad. Not like so bad it's good. Just *terrible*, if I had to use a single word to describe it."

"William's dick," he mutters.

"You've seen the websites about it!" People have strong opinions about the corn dogs, and after Oliver's father, William, went to prison, they nicknamed it for him. "That's hilarious. I wasn't sure if they'd bother you with something so trivial."

"The nickname is why I made them keep it on the menu." He blinks at me again, opens his mouth, then shuts it like he didn't want to admit that to me.

I grin at him. "Daddy issues?"

"He *went to prison*. Do you know how hard it is for someone with our attorneys to actually go to prison? You have to fuck up more than anyone has ever fucked up. Ever."

"And he left you holding the company together, so you took it out on him by keeping mementos of his penis in stores across the country. Oliver Cumberland, you have a petty streak. Who would've guessed?"

the grumpiest billionaire

"Are we going inside or not?"

I unbuckle and swing open my door. "Yep. Culinary delight awaits."

Oliver refills his wallet with more cash, then joins me to cross the parking lot.

It's a little crowded, but that shouldn't be a problem.

"Cod-stravaganza?" Oliver mutters as we approach the door, where this month's special is advertised on a bright red background featuring Sir Pollock, the Knight Fryer, Cod Pieces' mascot.

I clap my hands. "We can get *seven* pieces of cod for the price of five. This is a good day."

He squeezes his eyes shut, but I think he's partially smiling.

The tiniest amount.

The itty-bittiest amount of smile that one can smile, in fact.

But it's still a smile. I swear it is.

Or possibly he has gas.

Those protein bars he has stocked in his back seat will do a number on a normal person's digestive system.

I tilt my head sideways at the other sign on the door—*Closed today.* Weird.

Clearly, the store is open.

There are people inside.

The menu is shining brightly.

Cars are moving through the drive-thru.

It's definitely open.

I grab the door handle and we stroll inside.

Cod Pieces' signature fried fish smell permeates the air. I get one good half whiff in, and then the singing starts.

"What in the hell?" Oliver mutters.

I look around wildly, and then I spot it.

The kids' fishbowl.

It's a kiddie playground that not every Cod Pieces has, but this one does. Rounded plexiglass, to simulate a fishbowl, usually holds the kids inside while they run around on underwater-themed slides and climbing thingies.

And there's clearly a birthday happening inside.

That's where the singing is coming from. I can't see the kids, but I can see the adults singing.

Looks like grandparents.

"When you have a happy Cod Piece, your happy's happy too! For your Cod Piece Birthday, your wishes will come true! Happy happy Cod Piece! Happy fish and chips! Happy happy Cod Piece! Good luck with your fish lips!"

"Oh my god," I whisper.

"That's for a *kid's birthday*?" Oliver mutters to me.

They start the song over again as I pull us toward the counter to order. "Let's get it to go," I say.

"Oh, no. I need to experience what normal people do for their birthdays."

I try to stifle an unexpected laugh and end up snorting instead.

The kid at the counter makes a face at us.

Typical teenager.

I interpret it to mean *dammit, more customers.*

Probably playing on his phone a minute ago.

"Welcome to Cod Pieces, where our pieces are lit and our chips don't drip," he says. He's wearing a giant cod head as a hat, and I can't tell if Oliver's choking noise is from the greeting or the outfit.

"A five-piece cod and two chips, plus an order of hush puppies, please," I say.

Gotta ease Oliver into this.

The grease can be a lot when you're not used to fast food.

Although this might not be easing him in.

Guess we'll see.

"Thirty-two seventy-six," the kid replies, looking behind us toward the fishbowl and not paying much attention to us at all. "You want a codpiece with that?"

Oliver makes another choking noise.

the grumpiest billionaire

I can't look at him—if he's horrified, I'll feel a little bad, and if he's laughing, I'll lose my shit and laugh with him until I can't breathe.

The Cod Pieces closest to Athena's Rest doesn't offer actual codpieces the way the diner offers kids fake diner hats so they can pretend they work there too.

This might've been a bad idea.

The chaos that I find whenever I go back to where I came from has clearly followed me out onto the road.

But a girl can only drive by so many Cod Pieces before she needs a snack.

Though I will *not* be saying that out loud to Oliver.

Probably.

It would be amusing to watch his reaction.

But maybe not yet. Maybe in another couple days.

"You got the cash, Ollie?" I say without looking at him.

He forks over a hundred-dollar bill.

The kid looks at me, then at Oliver, then pulls out the magic marker that they use to check that a dollar bill is real.

"This again?" Oliver mutters.

I pinch my lips together.

The kid makes change and hands it back to him.

He drops all of the change into the tip jar—it's a fishbowl, of course—and the kid's eyes go as round as the mom's eyes did this morning.

And then he looks down at Oliver's shirt, where I forgot to make sure he took the tag off, as someone shrieks behind us. "That's the sign! Oh my god! The stripper's here!"

I choke on a gasp.

I'm up for a lot, but— "A *stripper*? At a *kid's birthday party*?" I say to the teenager behind the counter.

He squints at me, then at the tip jar, then back to me. "So you're like…playing that you don't know?"

I give him the double eyeballs of *know what?*

He glances at Oliver, then back to me. "Dude. That's game to bring a girl to your show."

"What show?" Oliver asks the kid.

He smirks. "Okay, yeah, I'll play like you don't know what's up. They're senior citizens, and they gave us a thousand bucks to not let anyone under twenty in the door. If you're planning on shaking them down for more, can I get a cut?"

"I thought he was supposed to be in a medieval knight costume," a woman says, much closer now.

"I thought he was supposed to be Sir Pollock."

"Maybe he's the handler."

"I hope not. Look at that ass. I like looking at ass."

I finally get the courage to look up at Oliver as the kid leaves the cash register to go get our food. "I swear, I didn't know," I sputter. "I've never—this is—this doesn't happen at my usual Cod Pieces."

Although now that I think about it, it's a brilliant idea.

I'll have to ask Bea if we should do this for her next birthday. Not the stripper part, but the party at Cod Pieces part.

Her birthday's in the off-season for Griff. He could come home, and he's making the kind of money that would lend itself to renting out a fast-food fish restaurant for an afternoon. Hudson might not have to be back at college yet. Ryker will be grumpy about it, but seriously, what's new there?

And Simon—my eyes sting as I start to smile at remembering what Bea said this morning about making up with Simon.

Simon would be all in.

He'd make it fun.

In a kid-friendly way. His twin teenagers would want to be there.

And we could all go down the slides.

I never got to play in the kiddie areas at fast-food restaurants when I was little.

I mean, yes, I got to spend vacations in Europe and South America and luxury beach resorts, and there was that one trip to Japan, but shouldn't everyone know the joy of a kiddie play area at a fast-food restaurant too?

Oliver's staring at me with an expression I can't interpret.

"Come on, honey, take it off." An older woman with a tight brown bob and a shirt declaring her *world's best aunt* shakes her tits at him. "Mama needs a show."

Do I want to stand here and watch Oliver suffer?

Yes.

This is next-level hilarious.

But if I'm truly going to be a good wingwoman and not get left on the side of the road before I can convince him to turn around and go back home to continue running M2G and doing good in the world, then I need to get his cranky ass out of here. "There's been—" I start, but Oliver interrupts me.

"Is it your birthday?" he asks her.

"Aren't you precious, pretending like you don't know." She smacks his ass.

I gulp.

And also gawk a little.

"How old are you?" Oliver asks her like she didn't just assault him.

"Sixty years young, baby! My parents didn't live this long. I'm setting *records*. Go on. Take it off."

Oliver stares at her, then tugs at his collar.

Is he—is he *going along with this*?

Oh my god.

Is Oliver going to *strip*?

What is even happening right now?

Is this real?

Is this actually happening?

Or is he pranking me?

As he tugs his collar again, fresh air wooshes through the room.

"Did somebody order a *fish strip*?" a deep male voice says from the front of the restaurant.

Gasps go up among the birthday guests. The birthday girl herself freezes and stares at Oliver in horror. "You're not the stripper," she whispers.

"It was not on my calendar for today," he confirms.

"Oh my god, I slapped your ass."

"It had fallen asleep in the car. Thank you for confirming feeling has come back."

I smack a hand over my mouth and turn around, and I don't know if it's because of admiration for how Oliver is handling this or if it's horror at how much I appreciate the way he's handling this.

"Is that your girlfriend?" the birthday girl whimpers.

"All of this fish, here for the stripping," the stripper calls. "Who wants to...scale me?"

"She's my companion," Oliver tells the birthday girl.

Okay, that was low.

I know what *companion* means.

Probably payback for me using his nickname earlier. I deserve that.

"Voluntarily?" The birthday girl's voice has changed. "Is she *voluntarily* your companion, or are you holding her against her will?"

I turn back to face her, knowing exactly where she's going. "I'm good," I say as Oliver's brows furrow like he knows there's subtext happening but hasn't puzzled out what it is.

"Of course you'd say that," she says.

"No, no, I'm good. He grew up in this weird cult where they called all of their friends their companions, if you know what I mean, and he hasn't been out long enough to understand the subtleties. If anything, I'm more a danger to him than he is to me."

He slides a look at me.

"It's a *fintastic* show coming your way, ladies," the stripper croons as he pushes his way between the birthday girl and Oliver. To us, he mutters, "I don't know who the hell you are, but don't ignore closed signs around here. You messed up my entrance. And who the hell else drops the change in the fishbowl?"

"We didn't know." I jerk a thumb toward Oliver. "He was in a cult."

the grumpiest billionaire

"Who shuts a restaurant on a busy road in the middle of a Sunday afternoon?" Oliver adds. "That's bad business practice."

The kid at the counter tells me my order's up before the stripper decides to argue back about his methodologies.

I grab the bag with one hand and Oliver's hand with the other and tug him toward the door while the man in a full-fledged Sir Pollock costume grinds against the birthday girl with his codpiece.

"It's getting *cod* in here!" he crows.

I barely make it out of the door before I double over laughing. "I swear, I didn't know," I gasp out. "Didn't—wouldn't—never—*gah*."

And I didn't use the bathroom.

Didn't use the bathroom, and now I have to pee, and I'm laughing so hard I can't breathe, and this isn't gonna end well.

Oliver sighs.

He takes the bag of fish from me, then does something even worse for my bladder. Once again, he tosses me over his shoulder to head to the car.

This really will look like he's kidnapping me if any of the birthday people look out at us.

Including the part where I've gone past normal laughing and into laughing so hard that I'm crying.

Oliver deposits me next to the passenger door. "Absolute chaos," he mutters.

He doesn't sound mad.

And I swear he's smiling as he turns away from me, even if he's totally straight-faced when he strides around the hood and grabs the driver's door handle.

I scramble to open my own door as soon as he unlocks the car.

Pretty sure he'd leave me if I didn't.

Maybe.

Probably.

Or maybe not.

He reaches into the bag, pulls out a fish fillet, grimaces, and hands it to me. "You eat this regularly?"

I'm still giggling and wiping my eyes with my free hand. "The grease makes it slide right through your digestive system. You're gonna love it."

There it is again.

The hint of a smile.

Is Oliver Cumberland *having fun*?

Can't be.

Whatever I thought was a smile disappears behind a wary grimace as he pulls another fish fillet out of the bag.

He sniffs it, which has me rolling again.

Who sniffs fried fish?

But I don't say that out loud when he gives me another look before biting into the fish.

I simply watch him discover the beautiful, delicious horror that is Cod Pieces' fried fish.

He chews it slowly, frowning, and I realize we forgot to get drinks.

That's what the fast-food restaurant next door will be for.

Drinks and the bathroom.

They go together.

"This is horrendous," he says.

"Right?" I agree as I munch on my own fillet. *Mmmm*. Delicious greasy fish. "Can I have a fry? Please? And wait until you try the hush puppies. I don't know what their secret ingredient is, but I also don't think I want to know. I just want to eat it."

He takes another bite of his fish, this one larger. "Truly awful," he says with his mouth full.

Oliver Cumberland.

Talking with his mouth full.

Oh my god.

I'm enjoying this road trip.

Road trip in general? Yes. Sign me up. Sounds fun.

But with Oliver?

This is unexpected.

He hands me a french fry, then shoves three of them in his own mouth and makes a rough, low noise of pleasure in the back of his throat that has my nipples tingling.

He dives into the bag again and pulls out another piece of fish.

I eat my own fry slower, watching him inhale the food.

This isn't normal.

Definitely not for him.

Possibly not for anyone from my old life.

Two more fish fillets later—yep, he's eaten *all* but the one piece he gave to me, and I realize belatedly that not only didn't we get our bonus two fish for free, but we didn't get the full five we paid for either—he finds the hush puppies.

He doesn't even stop to give it a squinty eye before he pops the whole thing in his mouth.

There's that rumbly growl of pleasure again, this time with his head dipping back against the seat rest.

His knees are cramped under the steering wheel.

His hands are coated in grease.

And he's moaning in pleasure over fast-food hush puppies.

Once again—this is *not* the same boring man who proposed to my sister.

He's someone else entirely.

But that doesn't give me permission for my body's reaction to him.

Not in the slightest.

He's off-limits.

A project.

A chance for me to put the same good out into the world that Bea once put into me.

Nothing else.

I swallow twice before I trust myself to speak. "You gonna be okay to drive, or are you gonna be too drunk on fish and hush puppies?"

"Shut up and let me have this," he grumbles.

Whatever that means—at least he's happy.

9

Who gets the bed?
Oliver

While I check into the Carter Pillars Hotel in West Virginia's largest town, Daphne runs to the bathroom off the lobby with two ValuKart sacks dangling from her hands. She's back at my side by the time the clerk is handing me the single key card into the room.

And she hasn't said a single word about me *not* picking the Aurora Gardens hotel across the street.

I'd have to be truly dead to miss the fact that she doesn't like her parents much.

Not that she should. I don't particularly like mine either, and they didn't disinherit me and leave me unprepared for the world without money.

"One key card?" the receptionist repeats as she takes Daphne in.

I nod curtly and leave it at that.

"If you think I'm letting this guy out of my sight for one minute when we have nothing but a hotel room all to ourselves and no kids yelling for us and no parents forgetting to put clothes on before they leave their rooms since they moved in with us too, you can think again," Daphne says. "We probably only need the card to get into the room once. There's room service here, right? Oysters? Dark chocolate? Wine or—"

the grumpiest billionaire

I grab her by the arm and steer her toward the elevator bank.

"—champagne?" she finishes.

"Can you *not?*" I mutter to her.

The fish hangover has faded, and I could use another three-hour nap.

Or seven of them.

Back-to-back.

For six days in a row.

"She thinks you're kidnapping me. At best," she murmurs back.

"The more obnoxious I am, the more they'll think it's the other way around, and they're less likely to interfere. But if anyone asks you if you're okay or slips you a note while we're in public, that's why."

The elevator doors open, and I hit the button for the top floor, slightly uneasy as I realize I don't have to swipe my room card to get there.

Anyone can get anywhere inside this hotel.

Including directly to my room. *Our* room.

No security.

No layers between me and the general public.

The reality of my planned future hits me as I fully take in the idea that people who might want to hurt me could have easier access to me now.

If they figure out who I am.

Daphne eyes me. "You get used to it," she says.

"Used to what?" Am I that easy to read? Or am I having a normal, natural reaction that she had too?

"Being...alone." She shoots a look up at a globe in the corner of the elevator ceiling and doesn't say anything else.

So she's picking up on my unease and understanding the cause of it.

"How long did it take you to get used to...being alone?" I ask.

If someone overheard us, they'd think we could be discussing anything from a breakup to moving out of a roommate situation.

But I'm certain she knows what I'm thinking.

Shouldn't be comforting.

Especially not from Daphne.

But it is.

"I still had Lady Catherine Ophelia after my…breakup, but she was old and could only do so much as a…loud companion," she says.

Right.

Her dog.

Yappy little thing, though it never yapped at me.

It treated me almost like I was invisible.

Hated her father though.

"Had?" I ask.

"She only made it a few more weeks after the grand life change."

"Sorry for your loss."

For once, she doesn't immediately pop back with a grin and a smart-ass comment. Just keeps talking like I didn't say anything. "And I got some roommates. They knew about my…breakup…so they made sure I wasn't ever in a position where I felt…lonely."

This elevator is so slow that I only know it's moving because of the slight shimmy as we pass the second floor.

"It was probably six months to a year to fully adjust," she finally says. "Until I realized I couldn't remember the last time I thought about…him."

I grunt softly. Long time to adapt to not having security in your life.

Some kind of monitored security system will be a must until I feel comfortable being whoever the new me is.

I don't feel like a *Tom*, even though that's what's on my fake ID.

I should ask Daphne to call me Tom.

To get used to it.

But I don't want to.

I want to be *me*. And part of me will always be Miles William Oliver Cumberland IV.

The part that *made* me.

Colliding with who I'm meant to be.

Who I *want* to be.

the grumpiest billionaire

"It might not take that long for you," she says. "Or it might take longer. Probably depends on what direction you go now that you're...out of that relationship."

I make a noncommittal noise.

She starts to say something else but then closes her mouth.

I side-eye her.

She looks up at the camera in the ceiling corner again.

"But in my opinion, a dog can help when you're lonely."

"Did you get another one?"

"Not yet. I might be almost ready again, but...not yet."

It's been four years.

That's a long time to mourn a canine companion.

Not an observation I'll make out loud though.

I don't want to know why she hasn't gotten another dog.

What exactly she meant when she said I did something that gave her purpose.

Where she lives.

Who her roommates are.

If she finished college somewhere.

What her life is like.

We ride the rest of the way in silence, and the doors finally open to the seventh floor.

The suite I booked as *Tom* is at the end of a swampy-smelling hall, and when I push open the door, I'm startled to find it's a single room.

I wasn't expecting a penthouse—I'm well aware I'm not in New York anymore, and there was no listing for penthouse suites anywhere in this town—but the listing *did* say *suite*.

There should be at least two rooms if it's a suite, shouldn't there?

Does the hallway with the microwave and sink seriously count as a full room?

What kind of crap is this?

"Dibs on the couch," Daphne announces, breezing past the bed covered in a bleach-white comforter to drop her ValuKart bags on the

99

yellow-and-pink striped loveseat. Not a full couch. "I love sleeping on couches. I thought about getting a couch for my bedroom in my apartment, but that's not the best when I have guests over. Know what I mean?"

I give her another side-eye.

She spreads her hands. "Fine. You got me. Couches aren't my favorite. But until I look as old as you look, and until I'm paying for the hotels and the food and the gas and my own new wardrobe, fair is fair, and fair is you getting the bed."

The bed is king-size.

We could both fit.

I don't offer to share though because I don't want to.

She's not supposed to be here, but now that she's here, I can't let her go without worrying she'll blow my plans up, and the only place I can hide from her in this hotel room is in the bathroom.

Unless I get her a separate room.

Where I can't keep an eye on her.

"What do you need from the car?" I have to get out of here, and grabbing stuff from the car is my only option for a brief reprieve.

She points to the two ValuKart bags. "Got clean clothes, a toothbrush, and all of my leftover gummy bears right now. I'm good."

"I'm going to get my bags. Stay here."

"You know the first rule of hotels is that whoever grabs the TV remote first gets to pick the channels, right?"

My eye twitches.

She grins at me. "Still too easy," she murmurs.

And I'm out.

I need five minutes to myself to untangle everything I'm feeling right now.

The elevator is somehow slower going down to the car than it was going up.

You'd think gravity would help it.

I know the family who owns this chain of hotels.

I could tell them they have a hotel with an elevator problem.

And a carpet stink problem.

And a false advertising problem.

That is *not* a suite.

But then I'd have to tell someone else what I'm doing, and I don't want to.

The room we're in doesn't overlook the parking spot for the car, so I take an extra minute to fire up my secret cell phone while I debate what I want to take inside with me.

Only one bag of cash. I don't give two shits if someone steals the rest. If they need it that badly, they're welcome to it.

Fuck knows I have access to more.

Even divesting all of my M2G shares after the investor meeting next month won't come close to wiping me out.

Unlike my father, I've diversified. Into real investments that have real returns. I have more non-Miles2Go money than what my stock shares are worth.

I was proud of myself for that until I realized I don't want it anymore. And now I need to figure out how to give it all away.

Preferably to causes that will truly put it to good use.

The phone blinks at me with a text notification from Archie.

Proof of life? is all it says.

Sent this morning.

I dial him back.

It's a Sunday. He might be golfing. Might be on a date. Might be in the office catching up on paperwork.

He's due to step into his father's shoes in a few years too, but unlike me, he's excited at the prospect.

It takes five rings before he answers. "Dude. You catch that race today? Unbelievable." A door clicks, and his voice echoes more. "Hold on. Signal's bad." One more door click. And a third. "I'm at my parents," he finally says quietly. "Grandmother's doing her thing again. Talk to me. You survive so far?"

"Fucking Daphne Merriweather-Brown stowed away in my car."

Silence stretches over the miles.

So much silence.

"And yes, I've survived so far," I mutter into the continued silence.

"How the hell did she—"

"Still piecing that together. I think she fell asleep in the back seat waiting to talk to me about something, and I didn't see her until she woke up and said something when I crossed into Pennsylvania."

"Shit. You need me to send someone to get her?"

"No."

"*No?*"

I pull the pack of undershirts out of my original suitcase, spot the very large writing announcing they're *Youth Large* size—dammit, I'm a disaster—and toss them into the back seat, then throw three more pairs of boat pants next to them.

Travel plans? Success.

Internet shopping for my new wardrobe? Fail.

Need to start batting better than five hundred soon here.

"What do you know about her situation?" I ask Archie. He's her age, a couple years younger than I am, grew up with all of us, and he's the only one of the original crew of friends I hooked back up with after college who stuck after my father's sentence.

"Completely cut off from her family except Margot, living somewhere upstate, not getting arrested anymore—"

"You're sure?"

"If there's one thing her father loves, it's bitching about Daphne when she screws up. If she got arrested, I'd hear about it from one channel or another. Tell me again why I'm not immediately sending someone to get her."

"I can't keep an eye on her and make sure she doesn't blow this before I've even started if she's not here."

More silence.

the grumpiest billionaire

Archie thinks I'm a dumbass. Don't have to be in the same state as he is to feel that coming through the phone right now.

I sigh. "And she knows how to do things like pump gas and how to get in and out of ValuKart as fast as humanly possible when you need new clothes."

"Why'd you need new clothes?"

"Sizing error."

More silence.

Archie's not usually the silent type.

"You alone?" I ask him.

"Yes. I'm refraining from asking for pictures."

"I'm refraining from flipping you off."

"Have you flipped Daphne off yet?"

"No."

"Have you wanted to?"

"Is it possible to know her and not?"

"Where is she right now?"

"Hotel room. I'm in the parking lot. Getting my luggage. I have her phone so she can't call Margot or anyone else."

"Last time I was in a hotel, they still had landlines. Think she knows how to use it?"

Fuck.

Now I have a headache and indigestion, when a minute ago I merely had a pebble in my shoe.

I dump the ValuKart bags with my clothes straight into the suitcase, shut the door, grab one of the duffels from the trunk, and head for the hotel.

Then remember to lock the car.

Then double-check that I've locked the car.

And triple-check it.

"I'm sending—" Archie starts, but I cut him off.

"She's staying. We made a deal. She's…possibly…unfortunately…what I need. With me. For this part of my trip. Because…just…I've got this."

"You convincing me or yourself? You haven't been this hesitant about anything in at least three years."

I grimace.

I don't miss who I was before I was thrust into the head role at M2G, back when I'd second-guess everything and let other people order me around—but I don't want to be who I am right now either.

And it's not because the person I'm meant to be isn't somewhere inside me.

It's more that I've never had the freedom to find myself.

To find what I love enough to fight for it.

And while I haven't been at this road trip more than twenty-four hours yet, I'm already realizing Daphne's right.

I need help.

And she has something that I've *never* had.

She has *fun*.

"We stopped for fast food, and these sixty-year-old women had rented the place out and thought I was their birthday stripper," I say to Archie. "One of them slapped my ass."

"I hear the words you're saying, but they're not computing."

"And it was hilarious." I drop my voice as I approach the door. "I don't—I wouldn't have picked her, but chaos follows her, Arch. And I think—I think I need a little of that."

The silence is shorter this time. "That makes unfortunate sense."

My shoulders relax.

"Call if you change your mind and want me to pick her up. And keep her somewhere for a few weeks."

"She says she could ride squirrels home if she needs to."

He snorts with laughter. "That's Daphne."

Another bout of pride swells my chest.

That *wasn't* Daphne making a joke about squirrels.

It was me.
Look at that.
I can be funny.
And I've needed that too.
I approach the elevators. "Have to go. She doesn't know I have a phone, and I need to make sure she's not using the landline."
"Be safe."
Be safe.
That's the last thing I'm doing.
With every aspect of my life.

10

He's very inconvenient for a convenience store heir

Daphne

I'm not trying to bait Oliver by lounging on his bed and eating Lava Cheese Puffs when he returns from grabbing his bag, but it's very clear that irritating him is exactly what I'm doing.

Let's be real though.

I irritate him by breathing.

I scoot to one side and gesture to the other. "Look. I found the reality TV channel. Have you ever watched *Romance Castle?* They drop two dozen men and women into a run-down castle somewhere in Europe and see who runs out screaming first. Usually they're haunted and the electricity never works right and you never know what kind of animal will break in and freak them out."

He stares at me like he can't decide if I'm messing with him on purpose or not. "If you made any phone calls, I'll see it on the bill."

"Dude. I'm not making phone calls. I'm an irresponsible brat who's gonna love all of the attention I get when I show back up at home after everyone thinks I've gone missing and died."

Why am I like this?

Why?

the grumpiest billionaire

I don't want to be an asshole, but Oliver looks at me and issues an order, and I answer in my favorite way without thinking.

And now he's probably realizing that if I don't check in at home, someone's going to notice, and that's going to be a problem.

If I were making the face that he's making, that's exactly what I'd be thinking.

But if he is, he doesn't say it. Instead, he drops a duffel bag on the floor—one of the money bags—and turns with his suitcase in his other hand. "I'm taking a shower."

"Cool. Don't use all of the hot water."

And now his expression is exactly what you'd expect of someone who has no idea the hot water might ever run out.

"That happens in regular houses or apartments," I tell him. "My roommate has a friend who's been staying over a lot this summer"—he's her brother, but that's none of Oliver's business—"and he is such a hot-water hog."

Oliver doesn't thank me for the information.

He ignores me and carries his suitcase into the bathroom and pulls the sliding barn door shut behind him.

And then sighs very, very loudly.

It's probably the echo of the sigh against the tile in the bathroom making the sound louder as it slips between the cracks of the door.

Barn doors for the bathrooms in hotel rooms might look pretty, but they do *not* give the kind of privacy someone like Oliver would probably prefer.

It's no picnic for me either, honestly.

I have to turn the television volume up to keep from hearing the sounds of him unzipping his pants.

Tossing his clothes on the floor.

Turning on the shower.

Sliding the shower door.

Is it possible to hear water hitting naked skin?

Because I'm positive I can hear water hitting naked skin.

And now I'm thinking about Oliver completely naked.

Head arched, water hitting his neck and collarbones, sluicing down his solid chest and abs to where he—

Stop it, Daphne.

I snap my attention back to the television, where Heidi from Scranton is arguing with Todd from Portland about something to do with the plumbing in the castle.

Plumbing.

Water.

Naked Oliver.

I should've called Bea while he was gone, but I didn't know how long he'd be, I can't see the car from our windows, and I didn't want to get caught with my new burner phone. I powered it up long enough to check and make sure she hadn't texted, and then powered it off and shoved it back into my dirty laundry.

Oliver sighs again.

This one sounds like the sigh of a man who's having his first hot shower in weeks.

You know the one.

The *water is a miracle and I can't get enough and how do I get to live in times when I can turn a knob and have this magical device on the wall pound my shoulders with hot water?* sigh.

The kind of sigh that makes a woman want to join him, because if he thinks hot water in a shower is great, he should know about a few other things you can do in a shower.

I dial up the volume a little more while I fan myself.

Is the air conditioning not working in here?

Or is there steam coming from the crack between the barn door and the frame? Is that why it's getting hot?

I can't see *in* the bathroom, but I can imagine what's happening in there, and—yep.

That's the problem.

Me imagining Oliver naked is making me sweat.

I try to imagine him in the tighty-whities, and instead of the slender, almost meek frame I remember, I see tight muscles and a trim waist with a man-V sloping down from his hips, and him grabbing his own—

What the hell is wrong with me?

I shovel too many Lava Cheese Puffs into my mouth and stare at the TV again.

I've lost the plot.

Both of my life and the TV show.

I have myself under control by the time Oliver steps back out of the bathroom thirty minutes later.

But unfortunately for me, he walks out without a shirt on.

And he does, in fact, have one of those man-V's sloping down from his hips, disappearing beneath his gray cotton shorts.

Much broader shoulders than I remember him having.

Biceps of steel.

No six-pack, but he's not flexing, so I'm not writing it off.

And his thighs—the definition of his thighs over his knees, beneath the hem of his cotton shorts—if I took a picture and framed it back home in Athena's Rest, at least a half-dozen old women would call and accuse me of distributing pornography, and many, many, many more people would ask how much to buy a print for themselves.

And don't get me started on how it's undeniably obvious that he's not wearing underwear beneath those shorts.

Did the man run a multi-billion-dollar international conglomerate the past few years, or did he take up training for that obstacle course show with all of the swinging and jumping and climbing and dodging?

And to have the nerve to walk out of the bathroom with his hair still wet and his face unshaved too?

I try to eat another Lava Cheese Puff and miss my mouth.

"Stop eating on my bed," he says, sounding bored.

I snatch the cheese puff up and shove it in my face again, this time hitting my mouth. "You gonna want dinner, or was the fish enough for you?" I ask.

He stares at me.

It's a pointed stare.

A *get out of my way* stare.

I roll my eyes and lumber slowly off his bed.

He hits the button on the back of the TV to turn it off.

I hit the button on the remote to turn it back on.

We do that dance another thirty seconds or so before he lunges for me and claims the remote too.

I get a whiff of lemon and fresh-cut grass again and a brush of hot, still-damp skin against my arm.

He's traveling with his favorite body wash or shampoo or something, and it reminds me of a cold glass of lemonade after a long day working along the road, and I want to sniff him more.

Get it under control, Daphne.

Like I can help it.

This is dangerous.

Boundary-pushing.

I'm slipping into the same old habits, with the same old person who's…not the same old person I'd subtly test whenever I saw him with my sister.

He's from my past and a complete stranger at the same time.

So while I might try to act the same, his reactions are anything but.

"I'm going to sleep," he informs me. "Don't do anything you'll regret when I find out about it."

Little too late for that.

Except for the part where he doesn't have to find out I've suddenly realized he's a grown-ass man and I kind of like him bossy.

He grabs me by the shoulders and pushes me to one side, strides past me, yanks the blackout curtains shut, and then flops face-first onto the bed.

He doesn't even pull the covers back.

Simply flops down, the curve of his back and shoulders and gray-cotton-covered ass on full display.

Taking up the entire king-size bed himself.

"Yeah, I wasn't hungry either," I mutter.

"You haven't stopped eating all day. Be quiet and go to sleep."

"It's five thirty."

"It's midnight somewhere."

He slaps at the nightstand until his hand connects with the switch that turns off the wall lamp, and the room plunges into mostly darkness.

"Don't," he says to me, like he knows I was a hairsbreadth from asking him if he's going to get under the covers.

I shift to the couch—tiny couch built for two, definitely not a full-size couch—and move my bags off of it.

He audibly sighs again, like the rustle of the plastic bags is irritating him.

"I have this app on my phone—" I start.

Naturally, he doesn't let me finish. "I have *every* app in the known universe for sleep assistance and sound cancellation, and they're all shit."

"If none of the apps work, maybe the real problem is—"

He growls.

I stop talking.

Not because he growled.

More because I liked it.

He's Margot's ex, I remind myself.

Margot wouldn't recognize him if he leapt in front of her stark naked in the middle of a boardroom meeting, I retort to myself.

As if that would ever happen.

Which is part of why she wouldn't recognize him, but also, he wouldn't do it.

Or would he?

In fact, I think this Oliver might if it would get him whatever he wanted.

I test the couch to see if it's a pull-out bed, discover it's not, and stifle a sigh of my own before curling up into myself and trying to position the single throw pillow appropriately for me to rest here.

I'm hungrier than I want to admit out loud, and I'm exhausted too, but I miss my freaking stuffed lobster that I sleep with every night at home and I'm too keyed up to sleep.

So I lie there, waiting for his breathing to even out.

It doesn't.

He flops to one side.

Sighs heavily.

Wrestles with the covers until he's underneath them.

Flops to his other side.

Sits up and beats a pillow.

Flings himself back down again.

Breathes heavily, but never steadily.

It's like he can't fall asleep either.

I have that problem sometimes after a hard week whenever I let myself think too much about the uncertainty that comes with not having a trust fund anymore, with the satisfaction of building my own retirement account—slowly, *so* slowly—and the fear that I'll lose another job and have to swallow my pride and take help from Margot, who would help me in an instant if I asked, except maybe not once she hears about this road trip.

And after those worries set in, then the insomnia comes.

Followed soon thereafter by the panic attacks.

It was easier to hide them before Bea moved in with me after she had a rough breakup a few months ago, but having her in my apartment made me panic less.

Not always sleep better, but definitely panic less.

Until Margot started talking about taking Oliver back when his dad got out of prison.

And then I'd panic about why I was panicking.

And I think I've finally realized what my issue was.

I don't talk to my parents anymore. No relationship. None.

It's not that they took away money that I didn't earn.

It's that they did it in a way that left me completely vulnerable to the world because of who *they* were too. There were people who would have hurt me because of my name, and they no longer cared that *they* were part of the reason that I wasn't safe.

And then they didn't call. They didn't check in. They showed me, in no uncertain terms, that they didn't care.

I was a problem, the daughter who failed to live up to expectations, the daughter who would never add to the bottom line of the family coffers, and since I was useless, I was no longer their problem.

Margot calls. Margot visits. Margot offers to help me.

But she still works for the family company.

She still has dinner with them sometimes.

She's still in that world. In *their* world. As their good daughter.

When she started talking about taking Oliver back, now that his life would be returning to normal, it was one more thing that made me feel like she was returning to who she was before I was disinherited.

The idea made me terrified that I'll lose her too. That eventually, she'll quit straddling this line where everyone knows she sees both of us, and she'll pick them over me.

And that—that wouldn't just hurt.

That would wreck the tenderest part of my heart. The part that even Bea, in all of her amazing wisdom and freely given love, couldn't fix for me.

Dammit.

Dammit.

The panic attack is coming.

Even if she wants him, he's not getting back with her, I tell myself. *She's not going to abandon you.*

It's not enough.

But you know what I have?

I have a guy in this room who can tell me that for himself.

And it's not like I don't mind annoying him.

Far better that than letting him know I'm asking because of how much it matters to my entire life.

"Oliver?"

"What?"

"Why did you break up with Margot?"

Great.

Now I can't hear him breathing at all.

My question has murdered him, and this is where they'll find his body, with my Lava Cheese Puff fingerprints all over the crime scene.

"Don't give me that bullshit answer that you didn't want to drag her down because of what your father did either," I add. It's what she told me he told her, and neither one of us believed it. Not completely. "I want the truth."

After what feels like seven eternities, he starts breathing again.

I think that'll be my answer—him breathing—when his voice drifts through the semi-dark, too-chilly room.

"Once I was living the life we both thought we wanted—me running M2G, her running Aurora Gardens—it became rapidly clear that it wasn't what I needed, and she wasn't what I needed either."

Is it possible to feel slapped in the face on someone else's behalf at the same time that relief floods your body for yourself and worry pops up for him? What does that mean, *she wasn't what I needed?* "Did you tell her that?"

"As clearly as I could at the time."

"She told me last week she'd take you back," I whisper.

He sighs.

This one sounds defeated.

"Why are you pushing this?" he asks.

"Because I want to know what to tell her when I get back home if she ever finds out about…this."

"You won't tell her anything."

"But—"

"Would it make any difference at all if you found out your last boyfriend couldn't put into words why he didn't want you in his life anymore?"

I snort. "I'd have to date for that to be an issue."

Dammit.

He tricked that out of me. Swear he did.

"You don't date." He says it like he's repeating my assertion that the sun revolves around the moon.

"We're discussing Margot."

He thrashes about on the bed again, this time turning so he's facing me. I can see his outline. The tilt of his head toward me. The drape of the white sheet low across his stomach. "That subject is closed. Why don't you date?"

I could tell him it's none of his business.

Except—

Well, it sort of is.

If he's going to assume a brand-new identity whenever he gets where he's going, if he's going to never again claim any link to M2G, then it's kind of my job, as part of our agreement, to tell him.

Give him a heads-up on how fucked he might be.

And honestly?

I probably need to talk this out too, if I'm ever going to work through why I don't date, why I have panic attacks at the thought of my sister eventually abandoning me, and why I often have insomnia.

It's all related.

All tied together.

And no matter how much work I've done on myself in the past four years, there's more to do.

"Because the people who know I was rich only want to date me because they think I'll come back into money—it's hardly a secret that Margot would prop me up for life if I ever asked her to—and the people who don't know I was rich haven't been people I trust deeply enough to let them find out."

Silence settles thick in the room.

Oliver's not me.

He's smart.

Not that I'm not smart, we're simply…different smart.

He's the boring kind of *invest wisely and have a backup plan* smart.

I'm *know how to get yourself out of trouble when it inevitably comes calling* smart.

We're opposite smart.

Though it was definitely smart to tell him all of that.

Because my own breathing is evening out, and I'm feeling better for having said it to someone out loud.

"Are you going to tell people who you really are?" I ask.

"I don't know."

"I wish no one had known who I was."

"Why?"

"There's freedom in being nobody. No expectations to live up or down to. It took a long time for me to figure out how to accept that there will always be expectations, but that doesn't mean I can't just *be*. The only expectations that matter are my own. Not anyone else's."

It's a great sentiment that I'm still trying to put into practice, and it will never be entirely true.

Bea's expectations matter because she matters.

I asked her one time how she could tolerate me when I felt like a disaster more or less every day.

And she told me she was a disaster herself, so I made her feel less alone.

I didn't believe her. I still think I was one more stressor in her life when she didn't need so much as the toilet to flush wrong a single time or the power to flicker during a thunderstorm.

But now, now that I'm making it mostly on my own in ways I never thought I was capable of—now I get it.

It's normal to feel like a disaster even when the world tells you that you should keep your shit together.

It's normal to feel like you'll never get ahead of the issues that pop up and that you'll never handle them with the right kind of grace and humor and proficiency that social media and the world tell us we should.

We're in this together.

the grumpiest billionaire

She's my anchor, and I believe her now when she tells me I'm hers too. And that's enough for now. As enough as it can be with all of my other worries about Margot one day abandoning me too.

Oliver's staring at me in the darkness. Even if it were completely pitch black, I'd know.

He gives intense scrutiny.

He didn't use to. But he does here.

"That's unexpectedly helpful," he finally says.

He doesn't add *thank you*.

Boring old Oliver would've.

But this Oliver doesn't.

"Wouldn't be me if I wasn't full of surprises," I say.

He grunts in acknowledgment.

And three minutes later, his breathing regulates, slow and steady and deep, and I know he's out.

Hopefully for the night.

If I'm lucky, I might sleep some tonight too.

I need it if I'm going to get through the next two days.

And hopefully longer.

Until I convince him to go back home.

Back to being CEO of Miles2Go.

Back to where maybe he and Margot could have a relationship, professional or more.

To where whatever he does will continue to affect my life, good or bad.

Dammit.

Definitely not sleeping again tonight.

Because I'm certain there's not a chance in hell that I'll be successful.

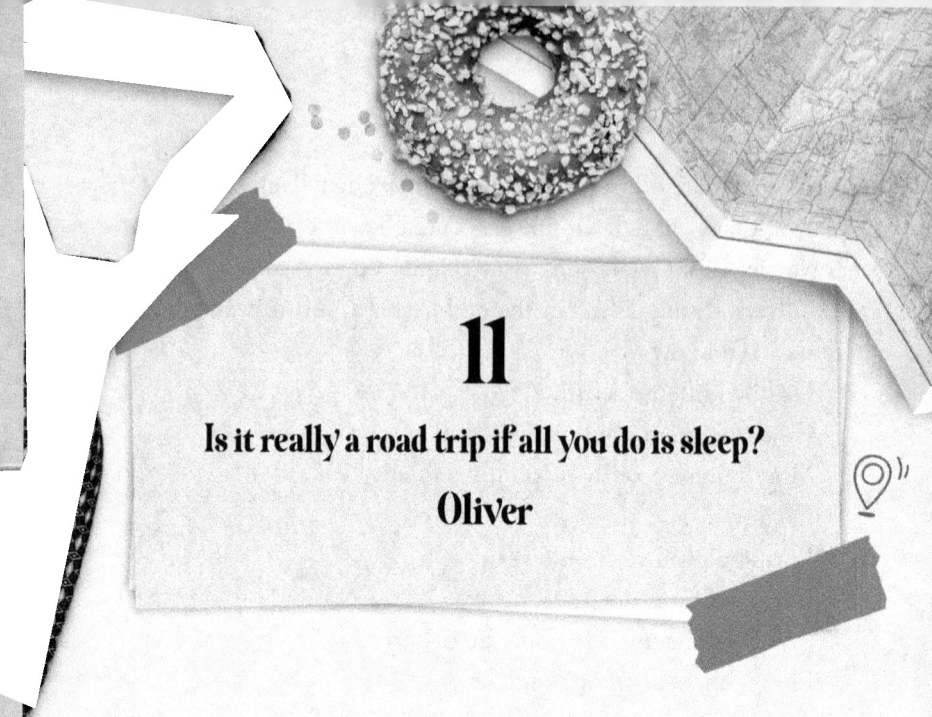

11

Is it really a road trip if all you do is sleep?
Oliver

I don't know how I sleep as well as I do Sunday night, but I wake up Monday morning feeling like I have a hangover, yet also more fully awake and less stressed.

It's odd.

Daphne's clearly crawling out of her skin—she's already showered and ready to go the minute I open my eyes, and room service lands with an impressive spread minutes later.

"Know what Aurora Gardens chain hotels don't have? Hamburgers for breakfast. They're so dumb," Daphne says while she eats.

And there is indeed a hamburger on the tray, along with pancakes, a plate of pastries, scrambled eggs, fruit, coffee, orange juice, and a pastrami sandwich.

I have some of everything.

Sleeping made me hungry.

And I slept so late that it's almost ten thirty before we hit the road, headed south.

Within half an hour—half an hour filled with an ungodly number of bugs hitting the windshield—I pull over and tell her to drive.

Most of the morning passes in a blur of me sleeping in the passenger seat, having dreams about dogs talking to each other.

She stops at some hamburger joint for lunch, more gas, and to clean the windshield—at a Miles2Go, naturally, where I sit in the car and watch the news talk about me on the little video screen on the pump. She grabs extra road food and drinks at the same time.

I pass out again as soon as she gets the car up to speed on the back country roads.

Tomorrow.

Tomorrow, I'll be awake to see the towns we're driving through. We're still in the eastern time zone, though. Too close to New York. It's fine if I miss this part of the road trip.

Daphne goes through a Cod Pieces drive-thru when we're about thirty minutes from tonight's stop, and that pulls me out of my sleep again.

It's possible the scent of fried fish is the only thing that would've done it.

Three empty MegaHit energy drinks are in the cupholders between and behind us, and she orders each of us a sweet tea to go with the fried fish.

"And extra hush puppies," I insist.

She's strangely quiet, to the point that I double-check that she didn't change the destination on the GPS while I was sleeping.

She did not, and soon, she's pulling up to the vacation rental house I booked for my second night of travel.

Pain in the ass to rent it, but I learned a lot about fake identities and prepaid credit cards while I was plotting my escape. Wish I'd booked all rental houses. This feels more secure than the hotel last night, though I'd prefer that the main house was farther away.

The listing made it sound as though there were several miles of rolling hills between the tiny house and the property's primary family residence, but the main house is clearly in view across the rolling lawn, with several other neighborhood residences dotting the surrounding hills, all close enough that I could see if another person stepped out their doors or drove down their driveways.

Apparently I underestimated the size of five acres.

"Tell me you know the code to get in, or I'm peeing in the bushes," Daphne says to me as she dances at the front door.

I move significantly slower with that greasy fish and french fries and the fried dough balls sitting heavily in my stomach for the second day in a row.

Worth it.

And disturbingly delicious.

I reach the door and pull out my burner phone—the one that only Archie has the number for—and pull up the email with the door code in it.

If Daphne wants to call me out for my electronics when I still won't give her back her own phone, she doesn't give any indication.

Possibly because as soon as I open the door, she dashes inside. "Bathroom, where are you?" she shouts.

I almost smile.

Maybe it's the sleep and the fish—or maybe it's gratitude that she was able to drive us today—but she's growing on me as a travel companion.

"I'm sure it's eager to answer you, as soon as the toilet learns how to talk," I say.

She flips me off and dashes into a room behind the entrance door that honestly shouldn't fit.

"Oh my god, the toilet is *in the shower*," she says, the delight in her voice clearly coming through what is most definitely not a solid wood bathroom door.

Very, very not solid.

I can hear everything.

My stomach gurgles, heavy with the fish and chips and hush puppies, and I squeeze my eyes shut.

She might be growing on me, but not in every way.

"Should've stopped for the restroom at that last Quickie-Lickie," she mutters as she attempts to set a record for the world's longest piss. "I'm gonna get a kidney infection."

"Unlikely from a single day of holding it," I reply.

"Whoa. It's like there's a door, but there's not, exactly like in the hotel. Is this a vacation rental, or did you buy the land and have this plopped down on the spot for the third night of your adventure?"

She's still peeing.

Still peeing, and clearly waiting for an answer, and likely has a day's worth of words bottled up because when I don't reply immediately, she adds, "Oliver? You with me? Or did you pass out in a fish-induced coma?"

I take stock of the small house. My first impression is that the pictures did it too much justice. "Do you always have conversations while you're impersonating a racehorse?"

"If someone's around to listen, yeah. Pretty different from the urinal rules, am I right?"

"Are you baiting me on purpose?"

"No, more habit. I'm working on kicking that, but no promises it'll happen fast. So. This place yours? If so, you definitely should upgrade the doors so that people who aren't as comfortable with other people hearing them pee don't have to."

"If one's here *alone*, it doesn't matter if there's a door at all." I check the fridge and find an open carton of half-and-half, a partial stick of butter, and three cans of orange fizzy water.

"That's a good point."

She's *still* peeing.

Or is she running the water in the sink and messing with me?

It's Daphne, so—

So I don't know.

I honestly don't.

The Daphne I last saw five or six years ago? She'd be messing with me.

This Daphne?

I haven't figured her out yet.

She pushes my buttons, but then she drives all day without complaint. One minute, she's telling me it'll take me a while to fully adjust to life on my own—*truly* on my own—as if she understands me better than I understand myself, and the next, she's bringing up Margot and demanding answers for why I hurt her sister four years ago.

She's contradictions and controlled chaos, and I need to stay on my toes.

But I'm so damn tired.

Again.

I check the cabinets and locate the coffee maker that was promised in the rental listing and the packets of premeasured coffee, then turn my attention to the living area beyond the kitchen.

It's a nook with a plain ivory couch adorned with throw pillows and blankets, plus a small bookshelf of—I tilt my head—romance novels. There's also a loft that should have the bed in it above the couch.

"How many nights are we staying here?" Daphne asks.

And yes, she hasn't stopped peeing.

She cannot *possibly* still be peeing.

This has to be her pranking me.

"Does it matter?" I ask back.

"Just getting a sense for what kind of road trip this is."

"What does that mean?"

"Some road trips are about the journey, and others are about the destination." She sighs, and the peeing stops. "*So* much better. So which is it? Journey or destination road trip?"

"Does it matter?" I ask again.

"It does if you're going to need me to cover a lot of driving shifts again like today. I learned the hard way that I can only survive on energy drinks for so long before I crash out, and I have too much to live for to crash out while on a road trip with you. No offense. There are other people in my life that I'd like to see again."

The toilet flushes. I brace myself, fully expecting it to break or explode, but the only other sound I hear is sink water running.

"Oh shit, are you waiting to get in here? Sorry. I'll hurry."

That.

the grumpiest billionaire

That part of her personality—the part where she's considerate to other people's needs—it's new.

To me.

Margot always insisted Daphne was more misunderstood than self-centered, that she usually put other people's needs before her own, but I didn't see it.

Or possibly I didn't want to see it.

The door swings open and Daphne grins at me. "All yours, Jeeves."

"*Jeeves?*"

"You didn't like Captain or Skipper yesterday. Jeeves is a good chauffeur name though, don't you think?"

She is *definitely* fucking with me on purpose now.

After today, I should be calling *her* Jeeves.

"We're not too far from town," she says. "Do you have a credit card loaded to your phone? We could order dinner for delivery. Unless—"

My stomach announces its current preoccupation with digesting the fish, and Daphne grins wider.

"Yeah, thought so. Don't worry. The discomfort passes way quicker than you think it will."

"I'm fine."

"Lot of hurried late-night fast-food meals the past few years?"

Of course not, and she knows it.

I had a lot of late-night meals planned and delivered by a private chef that I could hardly afford.

It's remarkable how pinched you can feel while having billions in holdings when you know your every financial move is being watched by someone waiting for you to screw up. Selling any part of my portfolio would've been seen as a signal that M2G's financial crisis was getting worse, and taking anything beyond the barest salary would've been seen as out-of-touch and selfish.

Or possibly I was over-paranoid.

Overworked, over-stressed, over-paranoid.

Daphne waves a hand in front of my face. "Earth to Oliver. You okay, bud?"

I scowl at her. "Can you *not* talk for a while?"

She's still smiling. "Unlikely, but I can try. It was a long day of not talking. Sometimes I need to get all of my words out, and I haven't yet."

"You're sleeping on the couch."

"Again? That's…weirdly poetic."

I squint at her.

"I've had a couch crasher myself all summer. He'll be thrilled to hear I got a taste of my own medicine two nights in a row."

Of course she's had a couch crasher.

She smirks. "Not what you think, but I don't care if you think what you're thinking."

"And what am I thinking?"

"That I'm an irresponsible party girl who's had a crappy rock band camping out—huh. Actually—no, never mind. I can absolutely frame this in my mind so that it's exactly what you're thinking. *Ooh*, look. Scrabble. We could play a game."

I don't have to use the bathroom, but I stride into it anyway and shut the door.

"I'm gonna go grab a few things from the car," Daphne says. "You need anything from out there?"

"No." I scowl again, this time to myself, then add, "Thank you."

"No problem, big guy."

The door shuts, and I heave a whole-body sigh and let my shoulders sag.

She's right.

The toilet's in the shower.

I do business that I don't need to do and am checking out the bed when she gets back.

You'd think that sleeping basically the entire day in the car would've helped with some of the bone-deep exhaustion, but as soon as I'm flat on the bed, instinct takes over and everything inside me starts to relax.

the grumpiest billionaire

I barely manage to pull my phone out of my pocket long enough to text Archie. *Made it to N3. Much obliged for your assistance. The problem we discussed yesterday is still present but unexpectedly clearing itself up in odd ways. Situation remains fine. For now.*

I shut the phone back off and shove it into the pocket of my new jeans, then roll over onto my stomach, my limbs and head getting heavier.

Daphne pokes her head up over the side of the bed from the stairs. "Seriously? *Again?* Are you sick? Are you contagious? Or do you look like you're seventy-five because you need to catch up on a few years' worth of sleep?"

"*Couch*," I order.

"You out for the night?"

"I don't know."

"I'm gonna turn on the TV. Let me know if it's too much noise, and I'll shut it off."

I squint at her.

"I've had roommates, my dude, and I've learned the art of living with another person."

"You didn't act like it last night."

She smiles. "When I talked in my sleep, when I turned the TV back on after I thought you were asleep, or when I annoyed you by dropping Lava Cheese Puff dust on your bed?"

I don't stop squinting at her, even though my brain is telling me it's time to shut up and go to sleep, because she'll keep talking as long as I let her.

I like her hair.

It's fun.

She's fun.

That's what's different.

Me.

I'm different.

I want *fun*.

I want Daphne to teach me how to have fun.

Maybe not put streaks in my hair, but they work on her.

Wait.

Wait.

I had this realization already. Yesterday.

If I'm having it two days in a row—fuck.

Fucking *dammit*.

We agreed on three nights, but I've slept one of the days completely away, and yesterday was…something.

I need to convince her to stick with me longer.

"I don't like how you're staring at me," she whispers.

For one split second, I picture myself pulling her into the bed with me.

Asking her to teach me to have fun.

Holding her hips.

Studying her breasts.

Showing me how to completely let loose and destroy this bed in ways that'll make it necessary for me to pay for damages here.

I wonder if she tastes like those gummy bears she was eating in the car yesterday.

Sweet.

Maybe cherry-flavored. Maybe lime.

Maybe—

No.

No, no, *no*.

Maybe *nothing*.

I'm disappearing. Starting a new life. Taking on a whole new identity, with *nothing* from my past to draw me back.

Especially my ex-fiancée's unpredictable, chaotic little sister.

Who is *not* attractive.

She's trouble.

And shouldn't I experience trouble? Especially fun trouble?

I lift my groggy head and turn it so I'm facing the other wall, ordering my brain to get a handle on itself. "Go away, Daphne."

She doesn't answer.

But I swear she stays there staring at me long after I should be asleep.

I can feel it.

And when I start to think I'm being paranoid, that of course she's not staring at me and my overactive imagination is fucking with me because of how close I am to freedom and also how far away it feels at the same time—that's when I hear the ladder creak.

"Sleep well, Oliver," she whispers. "I'll see you in the morning."

My brain betrays me again, this time with a memory of her crawling into the back seat of the Camry in that short dress yesterday morning, showing ass cheek—*all* of her ass cheeks, in fact—and now I have a goddamn boner.

Over *Daphne*.

I'd punch the pillows and roll around, except she'd hear me.

And offer to help put you to sleep, some moronic asshole in my head suggests.

Forget three days.

I'll find someone else to teach me how to have fun, and I'll send her home tomorrow.

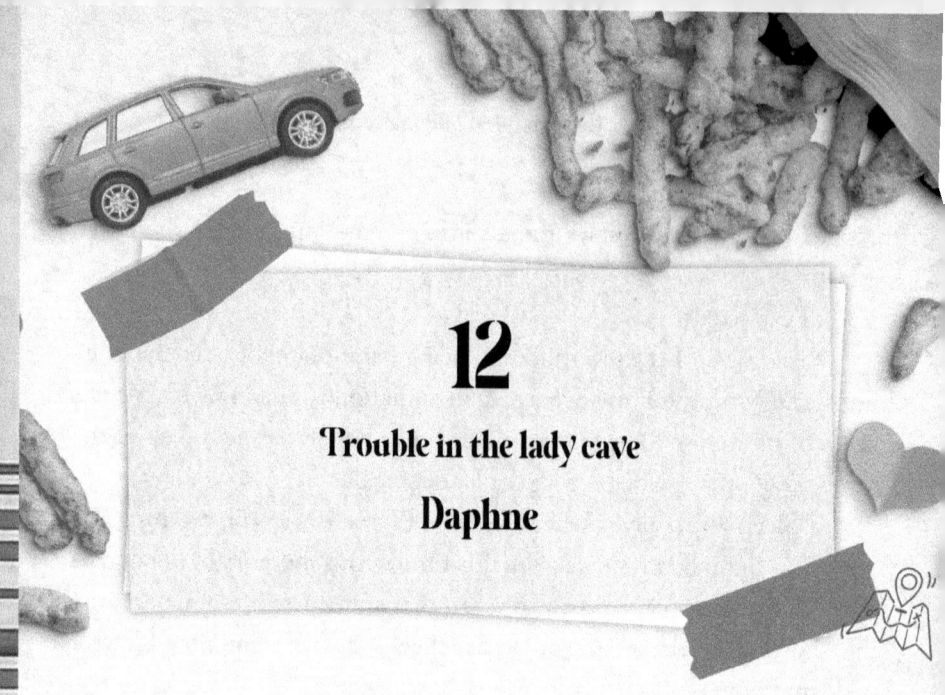

12

Trouble in the lady cave

Daphne

Oh god, oh god, oh god, oh god, oh god.
He looked at me.
I mean, yes, of *course* he looked at me. We're traveling together. He's going to look at me.

But he looked at me like he was *seeing* me for the first time, and I am freaking the hell out.

Oliver Cumberland is no more supposed to look at me as though he recognizes that I'm a woman who is something more than Margot's little sister than I'm supposed to spend the day driving him farther and farther from New York while trying to find *any* distraction from remembering how he looks when he's sleeping practically naked.

And I'm wrong.

That's the answer.

I'm completely wrong about how he was looking at me and—

And I want Bea.

I want my best friend.

Since Oliver slept all day, we made good time, but we started late, so darkness is falling outside. If Simon has his kids today, I likely won't be interrupting private time if I call now because the boys will be up for another hour.

At least.

Teenagers keep late hours.

If he doesn't have the twins and Bea and Simon are busy, she won't answer.

Probably.

Maybe.

I pace the very small pace-able area in the tiny house.

I could go outside. I *should* go outside. Get fresh air. Stretch my legs.

But Bea would murder me if I was attacked by wild dogs or dragged off by some chainsaw murderer lurking in the shadows.

Neither of those are appealing to me either, and contrary to popular belief when I was younger, and contrary to what I told Oliver our first night on the road too, I don't generally have a basic disregard for my own health and safety.

I only disregard my own health and safety when I have a cause more important than myself.

It's never been *generally*.

I'm on my sixty-eighth pacing pass, listening to the sound of Oliver's steady breathing overhead, debating dashing out to the car with my burner phone to call Bea, when I notice an unusual, seemingly useless lever beside the cabinets.

And then the outline of a trap door in the wood floor.

No. Way.

I've lowered all of the lights so that Oliver can sleep better, so I half think I'm imagining things with the subtle outline in the floor. I'm also wary of doing anything that will make noise.

See also, I didn't even turn on the TV when I came down here, even though it would be a *fabulous* distraction.

But when I tug—carefully—on the lever, the trap door glides open silently, revealing a set of stairs.

Go outside in the dark in a strange place all alone?

No. I do prefer camping in groups. More fun with other people, and the wild animals are less likely to take on a whole pack of us. Yes, I'm a walking contradiction. I want to save the animals while being terrified of them.

But I'm not afraid of checking out a hidden basement in a tiny house by myself.

I drop to my belly and peer inside, smiling with glee as I realize the lower level is fully lit up, so I can see *everything*.

There's a pink chair that they had to have lowered in there before putting the floor in, with what looks like a chenille blanket tossed on it and an end table with an extra lamp.

I twist my head, and—*yes*.

There's another TV down there.

I push up off the floor and scurry down the stairs.

So. Fucking. Cool.

If I ever move out of my apartment and get a real house, I want *this* one.

It's small.

It's cozy.

And it has a lady cave, which is *exactly* what this deserves to be called.

I don't shut the trap door until I'm sure I understand how it works so I don't get trapped inside here—Oliver would seriously think I ran away in the middle of the night like I threatened to two nights ago—and I inspect all of the soft pink-painted walls to make sure there aren't any other secret doors into or out of this room too before plopping down into the plush pink chair.

After I turn on the TV, I wait long enough to see if the noise prompts any response from Oliver, and then I dig my burner phone out of my bra.

Bea answers almost before the first ring has finished ringing. "Daphne?"

The sound of her voice instantly makes me feel at home. "Yeah. It's me. What's up?"

"*What's up?* Are you for real right now? Where. Are. You?" she demands.

Bea's my age, but she left college the spring of her freshman year to finish raising her three younger brothers when their parents died in a tragic house fire, so she often seems much, much older.

I'm practically on the border of North Carolina and Tennessee, according to the GPS. "I don't know, but I'm safe, I had Cod Pieces yesterday *and* today, and things are going…erm…well."

Silence lingers on the other end of the phone.

Not hard to picture my best friend squeezing her green eyes tightly shut and breathing slowly while she grabs a fistful of her curly brown hair.

"Shall I call Butch's friend?" I hear Simon say in the background in his British accent. "I'm certain we can locate her without much trouble."

"No! No." I shake my head, even though they can't see it. "I have everything under control. No issues. No worries. I'm safe. I'm here on purpose. Bea, tell him I'm here on purpose. And that I'm having fun. And then tell me about you. I want to know absolutely everything Simon did to deserve you again. Spare no detail. I think I have five hundred minutes to talk on the burner phone, so we have time."

"Remind me again why you're calling from a different phone?" Bea says.

"Mine fell out of my dress because it didn't have pockets so I was storing it in my bra except I forgot I wasn't wearing a bra and it got busted and I don't have my ID or credit cards on me so even if we could stop at a store to get a new one, I can't," I lie.

Bea breathes on the other end of the phone.

I've heard that breathing before.

It's the same breathing she did when her youngest brother would lie about why he was out too late or when her middle brother would lie about how badly he was injured—he's a professional baseball player now—or when her oldest brother would—actually, when Ryker would do nearly anything because he's a grumpy-grump monster, as she says, and it's often annoying that he can't find *anything* to be happy about.

Huh.

I wonder if Oliver's taking us past any of the cities Griff might be playing in.

We could catch a—

No.

No, we couldn't, because if Oliver was recognized in the stands, or if I was—unlikely as that is, since I'm pretty much irrelevant to the gossip world now—Oliver's whole *I'm running away in secret* thing would be blown.

"You were wearing a dress *again*?" Bea says.

"It was another costume party." We did one together a week before I left for the Hamptons.

"Who are you with again?"

"You wouldn't know them."

"*Them*? You said *he* yesterday. Are you with multiple people, or is this someone finding themselves who wants to use they/them pronouns now, or are you hiding something from me?"

"You remember that time before my parents kicked me out of the family when I tried to talk you into going to a frat party with me to get signatures on a petition to save that old tree down Haysmith Road, and you told me you were too old for frat parties, so I went without you and then I realized someone slipped something into my drink and I called you and you came and got me and everything was fine?"

Honestly, I don't fully remember it, but I remember the story.

It still makes me want to throw up, and it probably always will.

But I had enough training in my youth to know when something's wrong, and I knew to call Bea, and she got there and shut the whole party down before anything worse happened.

She's a badass mama bear, and she'd figure out how to teleport to get me out of here if she thought she needed to.

"*Daphne.*"

"There is absolutely zero chance anything bad will happen like that here."

"Not feeling reassured."

"It's someone I've known most of my life. Someone very boring. Like, someone who's so far the opposite of me that it's weird to realize that the thing we have in common is that we didn't fit into the world we grew up in. *I'm safe*, okay? Like extra mega super boring safe. *Oh my god*. Hudson went back to college, didn't he?"

"He did, but we're not talking about Hudson."

"He's not mad that I missed it, is he?"

"Daph. He's nineteen. If you're not his guitar, a girl he's interested in, or food, he'll be okay with a text wishing him a good semester."

"Good point. I'll text him. When I get my phone fixed. Now tell me Simon's treating you like a queen."

"Pardon me, I am treating her *far* better than one would treat a queen," Simon says with a sniff.

I break out into a case of the smiles, and my heart sighs in happiness.

"Daphne—" Bea starts again.

And I know where this is going.

It's not her fault.

She had to become a parent the wrong way many years before she would've chosen it herself, and she can't turn it off sometimes. "Bea. This thing I'm doing? It passes the rocking chair test. I already have stories. Like, not even kidding, we got in a situation yesterday where someone thought my companion was a stripper. And I'm sitting in a lady cave right now. *A lady cave*. It's a secret room in the…place we're at."

"In the interest of my deepest desire to make Daphne stop saying *lady cave*, may I ask what's a *rocking chair test* and how, exactly, does it relate to Daphne's situation?" Simon asks.

"It's how we decide if we're doing something stupid," Bea tells him.

I grin wider. "Like you going on your first date with him."

"I'm sorry, what? Our first date was a *rocking chair test*?" he asks.

"You passed," she says.

"Had I known, I certainly would've tried harder to fail."

I can hear him smiling—he's *always* smiling—and that helps me feel a little more normal too.

"Tell him I don't think he passed," I tell Bea.

"He can hear you," she assures me.

"I know. I just wanted him to know that I give him failing grades. That thing in your bus after dinner that night was *not* prime keeper material."

She laughs, and I relax deeper into the pink chair.

If I can make her laugh, she's loosening up enough that she'll still be worried about me, but not so much that she'll ask Simon's security detail to call in favors to find me.

"Please relay to Daphne that I delight in disappointing people," Simon says, "so I'm rather more likely to find excuses to fail to meet expectations if she insists upon setting them so high."

Yep.

Still hear him smiling as he says it.

He's hilarious. Sometimes odd but always hilarious.

"Really? You're going to intentionally fail to meet expectations now?" Bea asks him, and I can hear her smile too.

"Only when it doesn't put me in danger of provoking your ire."

Dammit.

Now I'm smiling so hard myself that my cheeks hurt and my eyes are burning.

I hate that I'm missing seeing them happy together. Bea deserves this so much.

"You two are adorable," I say, but my voice drops on the last syllable, because something isn't right.

I look up. Was that footsteps on the floorboards above?

"Daph?" Bea says.

The trap door.

Shit.

Shit, shit, shit.

The trap door is open.

the grumpiest billionaire

"Gotta go, love you, bye," I blurt.

I hang up the phone and shove it into my bra a split second before Oliver pokes his head down the stairs.

His hair is disheveled.

The bags beneath his tired hazel eyes have their own bags too.

And his lips are drawn down in a pouty, scowly, angry frown that has my nipples tingling even as apprehension slithers up my neck.

"Who were you talking to?" he says.

I gesture to the TV. "No one. You must've heard this."

His head disappears, and a moment later, his denim-clad legs appear on the ladder.

Then his crotch, which I try to pretend doesn't exist.

Then his trim torso in a white undershirt. One that fits.

Broader shoulders than Oliver Cumberland should legally be allowed to have.

Thicker neck than Oliver Cumberland should legally be allowed to have too.

And then—there it is.

The scowly, irritated, grumpy face. "You're watching a nature documentary with a male Australian narrator."

"Are you sure it's Australian? I was thinking English. Scottish, maybe?"

He ignores my attempts at deflecting this conversation and stalks to my chair. "What the hell is a *rocking chair test*?"

Fuuuuuuck.

He heard my whole conversation.

Did he hear me call him boring too?

"And who where you talking to?" He's full-on growling now.

I hate it and like it entirely too much at the same time. "You never have conversations with yourself to rationalize the crazy shit you're doing?"

He leans over me and pokes his hands between the cushions, his face close enough for me to see the individual whiskers making up his five-o'clock shadow and a scar over his left eyebrow that's so thin, it's barely perceptible.

Are his eyes hazel? Or are they green?

Why have I never noticed before how much green is sprinkled in his irises?

"What are you doing?" I ask boldly, to try to fool both of us into believing I have any control in this situation.

"Where'd you get a phone?" he replies.

"*I was talking to myself.*"

His fascinating eyes meet mine, and I realize he has unbelievably thick lashes. They're not long enough to be the kind that I'd envy, but they are *stupid* thick. He smells like sleep and salt and my kind of danger, which is the very, very, very last thing he should smell like.

And the very last thing I should be thinking about now is how much control he must have to be breathing like that, right in my face, and not strangling me. "Our agreement includes you not telling anyone about our agreement. Give me the phone or I'm getting it myself."

"I don't have a phone, and no one knows what we're doing."

"Who's *Bea*?"

He has a phone. He's used it. And it's undoubtedly one he bought with cash or his fake ID so that no one who'd want to track him could track him.

He could look me up and find out who Bea is in a heartbeat.

And that makes *my* heartbeat stutter.

He wouldn't hurt her.

I don't think.

"Give. Me. The. Fucking. Phone."

"Why don't you trust me?"

"Because you're *you* and you have an agenda and you won't tell me what it is. And that's only the first reason."

"People change when their whole life is ripped out from beneath them. You don't know me. You don't know me *at all*."

"And that makes me trust you even less."

He's still in my face.

Still breathing heavily, nostrils flaring, the honey parts of the hazel in his eyes flickering like a candle fighting for its flame.

"So kick me out," I tell him. "If you don't trust me, kick me out. Take me to town and drop me off at a hotel. Then I'm not your problem anymore."

I'd still be his problem, and we both know it.

But I'm enjoying the hell out of watching his nostrils quiver harder and his Adam's apple bob and his lips tighten into a grim line while he has his hands on the arms of this chair, trapping me here.

I'm so damn messed up in my head right now.

Messed up enough that I don't respond the right way when he sticks his fingers down my shirt and finds my phone in my bra for himself.

Because I *like it*.

I *like* his fingers on my chest.

I *want* him to touch me.

I *want* to work out this issue between us by grabbing him by the collar and pulling him the last few inches so that I can taste his lips, feel his stubble against my cheeks, and find out if this thing I'm feeling is mutual or if I'm truly, completely, and in all other ways fucking up my life one more time.

But as quickly as he touched me, he's gone.

Standing straight up.

Powering the phone off.

Shooting me injured looks like it's my fault he had to touch me and now he's disgusted with both of us.

I shimmy back in the chair and pull my legs to my chest, wishing it didn't suddenly feel cold as an iceberg in here. "Some of us have jobs that we'll get fired from and then be unable to afford rent if we don't call in and take vacation time."

A muscle clenches in his jaw.

"And I didn't tell anyone who you are, where we are, or why we're here." Goddammit.

Why do I suddenly feel like crying?

I hate crying.

Hate it.

The number of times I got yelled at for crying when I was little—and then the way I was accused of weaponizing my feelings to get my way—and then the time I overheard my mother telling one of my friends' mothers that I was *sooo* overdramatic and then both of them laughed about how much my friend and I both cried...

Yeah.

Crying makes me feel like an asshole and then reminds me that everyone in my life for the first twenty-four or twenty-five years of it were all assholes too for making me feel like that.

Bea was the first person in my life to hug me when I cried and tell me to let it all out, that crying was the body's natural response to stress and it was okay to cry.

The first person.

How was that even possible?

"Fine," I spit out. "Fine. You win. You're in charge. Happy now? Get out of here and let me sleep. I'm tired of your ugly face."

It takes every ounce of control I possess to not let him see how angry and hurt and desperate I feel right now, and honestly?

I'm probably doing a shitty job even with every ounce of control I possess because let's be real here.

I might not be the Daphne who gets kicked out of colleges and regularly arrested for going overboard at protests anymore, but I'm still impulsive and I still love to have fun and I want to know that I'm lovable despite my flaws.

And Oliver's making it incredibly clear that I'm not.

Not to him.

"Ungrateful asshole," I add.

the grumpiest billionaire

He flinches, and then he's gone, striding up the ladder so quickly that I barely register him leaving.

I grab the blanket and shove it over my head, in case he comes back.

He's gotten all of the satisfaction out of my discomfort that I'm willing to give him tonight.

And if he leaves without me in the morning—well, I hope he does.

Because then he's not my problem anymore.

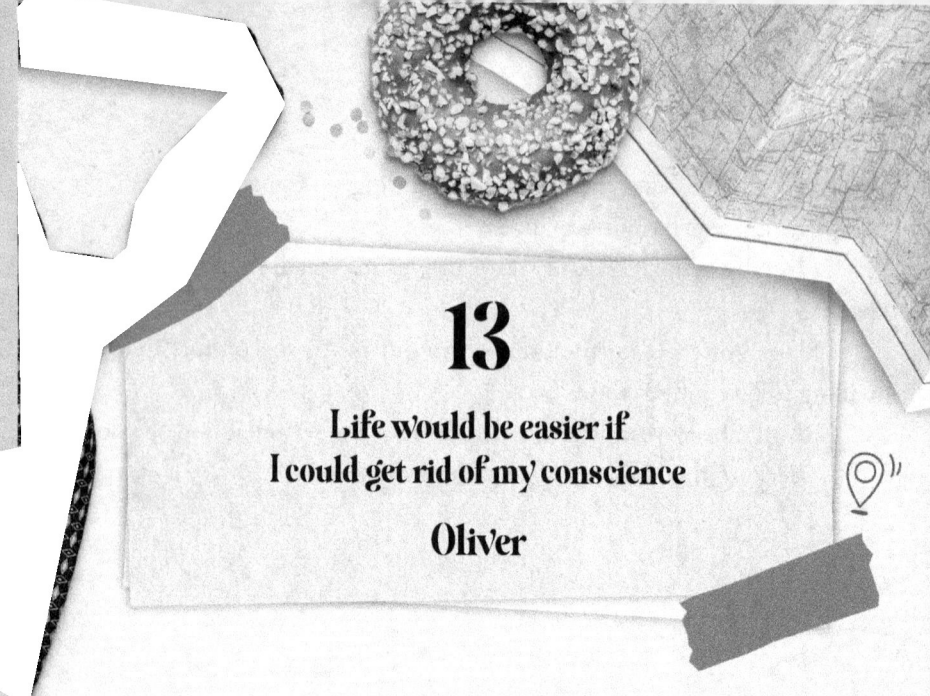

13

Life would be easier if I could get rid of my conscience

Oliver

When I was suddenly elevated into my father's role as CEO of Miles2Go after he was ordered to prison, one of the hardest early lessons I had to learn is that when you're the boss, you regularly have to do things that make people mad or that they disagree with. And then on top of it, I was regularly choosing the option that my executive assistant advised me to pick, so I had to be the shield between her and people's opinions of her opinions too.

There's never an option of making everyone happy.

There's often no meeting in the middle.

There's just the knowledge, day after day, that you probably fucked something up while trying to fix something else, and you're going to hear about it, and then you're going to lose sleep over it, and there's only so much stress that can be alleviated by working out your frustrations in the gym.

I fucked up with Daphne last night.

I fucked up hard, and I'm pissed at myself for it, but I'm also rightfully pissed at her.

There's no good answer, and I don't have a set of weights and I can't go for a run or a swim or a bike ride to push it away because I have a schedule to keep if I'm going to see everything I want to see and do everything I want to do and find where I want to live before these two weeks are up.

This road trip is possibly the dumbest idea I've ever had, no matter how good it feels to put miles and miles between me and Manhattan, and no matter how good it felt to spread some of my wealth to random people the day before yesterday.

That was always the plan.

To give away as much as possible on my escape to a life of being a normal person.

Though it might never be possible.

Daphne and I are both in bad spots.

I don't know what Daphne does for a job, but I know when people don't show up without calling, they get fired, and I'm sure that would suck for her.

Her.

The woman who's asking for *some figure under a million* to be sent someplace she refuses to say in exchange for her services in helping me get a wardrobe and learning how much you can toss in a donation jar without drawing too much attention to yourself.

And meanwhile, she's had access to a secret phone where she could be feeding her sister or god only knows who else information about where we are.

She doesn't tell me good morning or make me coffee when we both get up in the tiny house.

I don't tell her good morning or share any thoughts on breakfast plans, nor do I ask for her help when I can't figure out the damn coffee machine.

She uses all of the hot water in the shower and walks out in one of those Miles2Go T-shirts she bought at the gas station Sunday.

The shirt with Cupholder the crab on it.

I refuse to let her see me twitch about it, and I take a cold shower without bitching to her about that too.

Fuck if I'll let her see she's annoyed me.

Or that I'm sorry I grabbed her chest.

Even if that's eating me alive.

I don't do that.

I don't manhandle women.

I'm also not an ungrateful asshole, regardless of what she or my parents think.

Yeah, that last jab of hers last night—*ungrateful asshole*—that landed.

You've been given the position of a lifetime, Oliver, and all you do is glare at me as if your father and I have put you in prison instead of him being there. Could you be grateful for something for once?

My mother said it over and over.

My father repeated his own version of it on the rare instances when I'd visit him in prison.

Maybe I *am* ungrateful.

Maybe I *have* been an asshole.

Maybe I *am* selfish.

Maybe I *don't* deserve to be able to use my money to disappear from my old life.

Maybe I won't be happy with anything, and running away won't solve what I think it will.

Daphne doesn't tell me she's going to wait in the car for me.

I don't ask her if she's strapped in before I fire up the engine and point my car toward tonight's destination while taking vicious bites out of a protein bar. We're staying on backcountry roads the whole day again today.

She turns the satellite radio on to some god-awful country music station.

I switch it to the symphonic pop station.

She changes it to a polka station.

I switch it to a talk news station.

"*Trevor, it's interesting to see how Miles2Go's stock is performing. They haven't turned a profit since William Cumberland was sent to prison, but in* the past two years, they've grown three times as fast as their nearest competitor, gaining more and more franchises across the whole of the North American continent, and even without profits, we're seeing the stock price steadily rise."

"Well, Emma, I think that speaks to how positively the public has responded to Oliver Cumberland's emphasis on investing what would've been profits into environmental and diversity charities. They've been in a growth phase as a direct result of public relations initiatives that benefit communities, and—"

I switch the radio back to the polka station.

Daphne switches it to the news again.

I switch it back to symphonic pop.

She huffs and slouches back in her seat.

When we stop for gas, I follow her into the store to make sure she doesn't buy another burner phone before pumping gas.

She grabs six taquitos, four donuts, three energy drinks, an egg burrito, a Quickie-Lickie T-shirt, and four bags of Flaming Finger Lickies, which I deduce are Quickie-Lickie's version of the Lava Cheese Puffs that Miles2Go sells.

She balances all of that in her arms until she dumps it on the counter as I'm paying for gas. "He's got this too," she tells the clerk.

I don't twitch a single facial muscle while I pay for it all.

Or while she adds a canvas bag with Quickie-Lickie's tongue logo and the phrase *Get Licked* on it.

When we get back to the car, I direct her to fill it with gas while I clean the stupid bug-splattered windshield, which will be bug-splattered again before we get another five miles down the road.

And that's how it goes the rest of the day.

When I want her to drive, I order her to drive. When I want her to pump gas, I order her to pump gas. When I want her to clean the windshield, I order her to clean the windshield.

Before my time as CEO at M2G, I would've added a *please* and a *thank you* after asking if she felt up to it.

Today, I just order.

She pulls over to gape at the world's largest metal cricket—yes, the insect—and mutters, "Gosh, I wish I could take a picture to remember this amazing road trip," before getting back in the car and driving us another thirty miles before stopping for a taco craving, despite the breakfast she bought herself at Quickie-Lickie still stinking up the car.

I don't give a damn what road trip protocol is.

When we finally reach tonight's vacation rental house, I'm cleaning out the car.

If she didn't eat it, it goes in the trash.

But there's one issue I forgot about.

Tonight's vacation rental is even smaller than last night's.

It's a true one-room hunting lodge in northern Mississippi.

One bathroom.

One single bed.

A chair—not even a couch—and a kitchenette.

We arrive shortly before five, and once again, Daphne pushes me out of the way to run to the bathroom as soon as I've opened the door.

She doesn't talk at me as she pees this time.

And I get even more pissed when I realize I've missed her talking today while I was awake.

She should be asking me if I have a thing for staying in places that axe murderers would like. Or if I know how to sleep in a bed that narrow. Or if I know how to cook for myself on a stove like this.

Instead, she takes the lone pillow from the bed, along with the quilt, and makes herself a nest on the floor, and goes immediately to sleep.

Or feigns it.

Either way, she's clearly telegraphing that she's not available for me this evening.

I clean the car out, twitching when I find the lottery ticket, which I shove into the glove compartment. I can't throw it away, but I can't cash it in here either.

Should've dropped it in that kid's donation jar outside ValuKart on Sunday.

the grumpiest billionaire

Dinner for me is a leftover glazed donut—it's wrong how delicious this thing is—and two of the three leftover bags of Flaming Finger Lickies for dinner.

They're also stupidly delicious.

Two weeks ago, I was having chicken marsala with a side salad and fresh-made dressing delivered to my office for dinner, and tonight I'm eating a donut and hot cheese puffs.

Fairly certain this is what's meant by *girl dinner*. Which is a phrase I only know because three separate people demanded meetings with me over how much they didn't like that the M2G social media accounts used it as part of a sales campaign for the snack foods available at our convenience stores.

My stomach rumbles in protest, but I'm suddenly unexpectedly happy.

Even with Daphne tagging along—I'm *free*.

I *can* eat a donut and two bags of chips for dinner. I can have *girl dinner* and screw those assholes who wasted my time whining about it being a thing.

I don't have to listen to them anymore, and no one needs me to keep my arteries in good shape so I can continue saving the company that my great-grandfather founded.

I pause to stare toward the setting sun. I can't fully see it through the canopy of leaves on the trees all around me, and I realize I spent all day being so mad at Daphne for somehow acquiring and using a phone that I didn't pause to appreciate the very thing I'm supposed to be appreciating.

Freedom.

The world I've never seen before.

Everyday people doing everyday things the way I've longed to since well before I was willing to admit to myself that that's what those internal cravings have been.

A desire to connect with the world instead of living in a gilded tower above it.

And now I'm a thousand miles from New York, and between sleeping all day yesterday and being pissed all day today, I haven't experienced this trip the way I should at all.

I haven't given away more than a few thousand dollars of the millions I intended to leave in my wake.

I'm failing.

I'm failing *myself*.

I stay outside, leaning against my car, watching the leaves shimmer with the waning sunlight as they rustle in the evening breeze, until everything's dusky-dark.

When I reenter the cabin, Daphne's curled up under the quilt, one hand tucked under her chin and clutching the fabric at the same time, as if she's afraid I'll try to take it from her.

I stifle a sigh and open up my suitcase, realizing I either need to do laundry soon or buy more clothes.

More clothes that fit as well as these that Daphne helped me pick.

Because she knew.

She knew the wardrobe I left behind consisted of tailor-made clothes and that I couldn't tell you my own size.

I can run away from my life, but I can't run away from myself, and I need some degree of organization.

Especially if we can make that large of a mess in the car in only three days.

Daphne doesn't move as I get myself ready for bed.

She's breathing so softly I almost can't hear it, and I don't know if she's asleep or if she's faking it, but I know I can't go another day like today.

Today sucked.

And tomorrow's supposed to be the day that we negotiate how she's leaving while also keeping my secret.

I have to talk her into riding along with me for another week instead of putting her on a plane back to...wherever she lives now.

So tomorrow, I have to apologize to her.

But not only for my sake.

the grumpiest billionaire

For hers too.

Quiet, injured Daphne isn't right.

She might've annoyed me when I dated her sister, and she might be pushing and poking me on purpose now, but she *is* fun.

I took that from her today as well.

Tomorrow—tomorrow, I truly will be a new man.

Tomorrow, I'll be the man that I *want* to be.

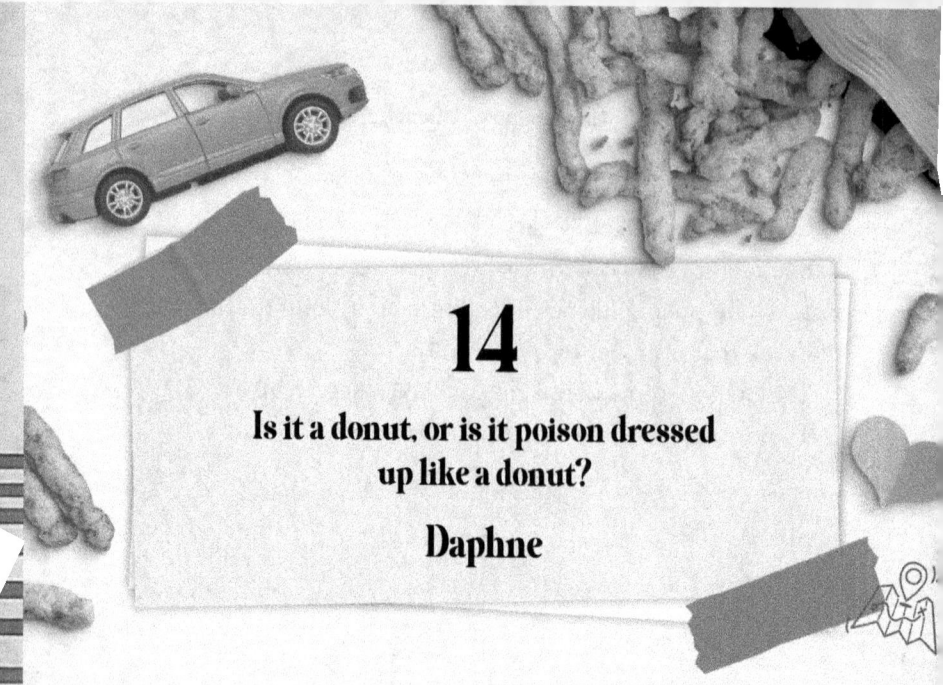

14

Is it a donut, or is it poison dressed up like a donut?

Daphne

I sleep like absolute shit, but I clearly *do* sleep, because when I wake up, Oliver's making coffee and there's a fresh box of donuts on the counter. He must've left *and* come back when I was unconscious.

As I sit up on the hard-ass floor, rubbing my eyes, my shoulder hitching right where it meets my neck, I become convinced I've been transported to another dimension.

Because he's holding out my phone to me.

My real phone.

"What's this?" I ask, my voice groggy with sleep and heavy with suspicion.

"Peace offering."

"Why?"

"I don't like being an ass."

I stare at him.

He stares back.

It's like a challenge. *Will you accept this as an apology, or are you going to make me say more? And are you willing to take the risk that I tell you to fuck off when you demand more?*

I take the phone, still squinting at him.

the grumpiest billionaire

I power it up, and he only flinches the tiniest bit.

"Margot can't track me on this," I tell him.

He flinches harder.

Like he's not comfortable with me knowing what he was thinking. Or maybe like he's not comfortable with the mention of my sister.

The woman he was engaged to a few years ago.

The woman he hurt when he broke up with her.

The woman I feel like I'm betraying every time I look at Oliver's ass.

And that's when it hits me.

I leap to my feet, almost tripping over the quilt, but saving myself as I ignore Oliver lunging for me. "*Oh my god*, you're leaving me here."

His eyes flare wide, his hands inches from my hips. "No."

"Then what's all of this? Donuts? Coffee? *My phone?* You are. You're leaving me here."

"I—no."

I glare at him.

"I want—I'm sorry." He says the words as if he's never tasted anything worse in his life, which should be utterly hilarious.

Oliver wasn't a complete pushover when he was dating Margot—only mostly a pushover—but I remember her telling him once at some family dinner that he'd have to apologize less whenever he took over for his father after he apologized for someone else bumping the table wrong.

At the time, we all assumed he'd have a couple decades to break the habit.

Clearly, four years was *plenty* of time.

I cross my arms over my chest. "Sorry for what?"

He scowls. "For being an asshole."

"With making me drive for a full day? Or the radio thing? Maybe for continually issuing orders without saying please? Or is this about you refusing to stop for a bathroom?"

He purses his lips together and keeps glaring at me, though it's the kind of frustrated glare that could mean he's irritated with me or he's irritated with himself and doesn't know how to handle that.

"For leaving me alone last night?" I press, partially to see how far I can go, and partially because he was an ass over a lot of things. "For not offering me the bed like a gentleman? For making faces at me when I ate in the car yesterday, *which is a human necessity*, Oliver."

"For taking your phone," he spits out. "For the way I took your other phone. And for—yes. For all of that. Will you take a damn donut with sprinkles and get ready to go? Ten hours in the car today. Shouldn't waste time."

I tilt my head. "Sprinkles?"

The exasperation rolling off him is so thick it could suffocate a lesser woman. "Yes."

"Chocolate frosting?"

"It's blue and green. Like your hair."

It's my turn to blink.

He got me a donut that reminded him of my hair?

That's—huh.

I think that qualifies as sweet.

Maybe?

Or is this more psychological warfare?

I step around him and lift the lid on the donut box.

Five round donuts with swirly blue-green frosting under glittery gold sprinkles stare up at me.

He didn't merely find donuts.

He found fancy donuts that remind him of me and my hair.

"Do they taste good?" I ask.

"How should I know?"

"One's missing."

"I don't expect you to have the same opinion or standards for donuts that I have."

That's the strangest answer I've ever heard. I'm intrigued.

I poke at the coffee on the counter. "Did you make this?"

"Yes."

"Did you poison it?"

"Drink the goddamn coffee, Daphne."

"I can't help you drive if I'm dead. Or unconscious. And you should definitely *not* drive ten hours yourself. You're getting better, but you're still not very good."

"Noted."

"And I get to control the radio today."

"I retain the right to three vetoes that will last the rest of the trip."

Either he's serious, he feels bad because yesterday was so shitty, or he's plotting a way to dump my body before noon.

There's no way anyone who's known me for more than forty-five minutes would ever let me control the radio while only asking for three vetoes.

And speaking of three—our three days are up. He *should* be trying to get rid of me.

I ponder that while I bite into a donut.

And holy fuck.

This donut.

Oh my god.

A moan rolls out of my throat before I can stop it.

It's the perfect combination of yeasty and doughy and rich and sweet and sprinkly. Almost as good as the homemade donuts Bea made when I couldn't stop crying after I moved in with her. Those are the donuts that I judge every other donut against, ever.

I should talk her into having donuts as her secret menu item in her burger bus soon.

After I get back.

I take another bite and sigh in bone-deep satisfaction. "Okay, that's a good donut," I say with my mouth full.

My parents would have a conniption fit at my lack of manners.

Oliver doesn't.

My eyes are still a little crossed, but I think he's staring at me—in the uncomfortable way.

Like he doesn't want to watch me have an orgasm over a donut.

Or maybe like he doesn't want to admit he's enjoying watching me have an orgasm over a donut.

Stop it, dumbass, I order myself.

He's still Oliver and he doesn't like me.

I'm still Daphne and I need to not like him.

We're on this road trip until he dumps me at a bus station or something.

I need to figure out how to negotiate staying with him longer because I didn't make any progress at all in talking him into going back to Miles2Go yesterday.

As the CEO, clearly.

Not as a customer who needed to pump gas at one of their stores. Even knowing I'm fighting a losing battle, I owe it to myself to fight it.

I grab the coffee and sniff it, then take a hesitant sip.

Not bad.

Not great—nowhere near as amazing as this donut—but not bad.

I set it down, finish my donut, and grab another one while I open my phone.

An unsurprising number of text messages need to be answered, but I prioritize the one from my boss—*yes, family emergency, I'll be back next week*, I tell her in response to her question about if I'm okay—and several from Bea that were clearly sent before I called her on Sunday afternoon.

Phone back, you should do donuts for your next secret menu item, I text her.

Oliver doesn't attempt to look at my phone, but he does start to twitch in the face again.

I sniff my pits, decide I can go a day without a shower, and finish off the second donut. "Let me brush my teeth and I'll be ready to go."

And then—then we'll see if his change in attitude is real or if it's all a ploy.

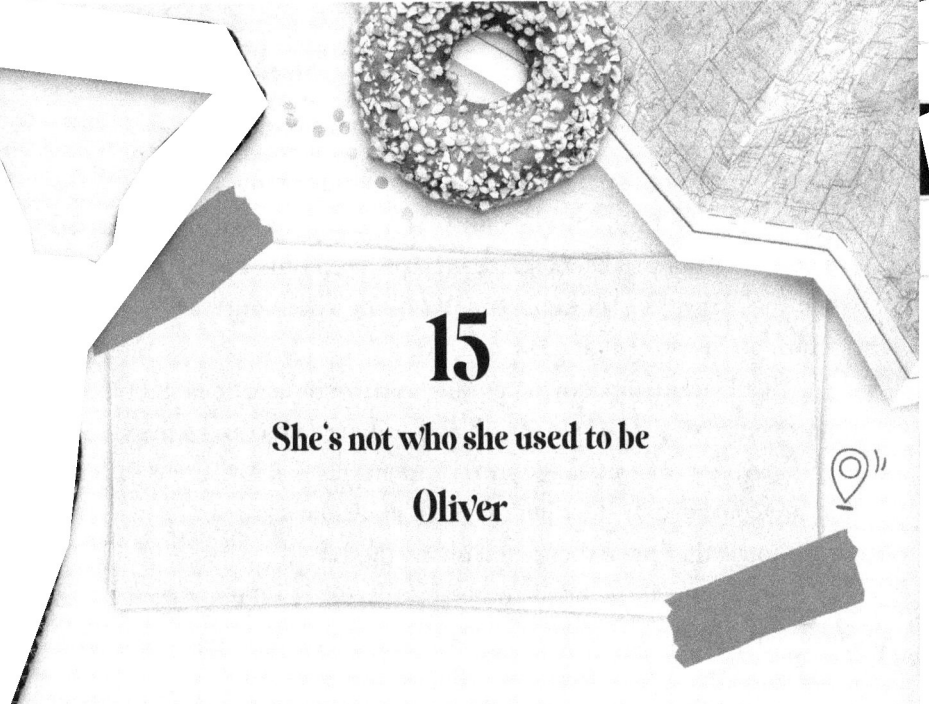

15

She's not who she used to be
Oliver

Despite the havoc watching Daphne eat those donuts played on my hormones, it's easier to breathe on the road today without the crushing weight of her pissed silence yesterday.

I've made a peace offering.

It's been accepted.

Honestly, it was accepted easier than I expected it to be.

She could've—*should've*—held out for more than donuts and coffee and me fumbling through trying to apologize after four years of having it hammered into me that CEOs don't apologize for anything.

And now I have to figure out how to convince her she wants to stay in the car with me for another few days without making her suspicious about my intentions or angry that I'm keeping her from her regularly scheduled life or provoking any other unpleasant reaction she might have.

That was another hard thing about being CEO of M2G.

How I *felt* about letting someone down or making someone mad.

Those radio talk show hosts yesterday—they thought I had some master plan with the charities and initiatives I invested profits into.

I didn't.

It was the only part of my plans that I didn't fully consult with my executive assistant for, and the only part of my plans that she cautioned me could turn out to be a bad idea. Throwing profits away is one thing when you're investing in expansion. It's dicier when you're not expecting a return on investment at all.

But I needed to do something worthwhile and meaningful at a time when all of the bad was crushing me. I needed to know there was a bigger purpose than making as much money as possible through gasoline and convenience store junk food and knickknacks.

Bonus that my father hated my methods.

Unfortunately, a lot of other people did too, and they had no qualms in telling me I was fucking up. Even when they didn't tell me, I could sense it.

That they thought I was a dumbass nepo baby who was only in the role because my family has the majority share of the company's stock.

I roll my shoulders and try to let it go. It doesn't matter anymore.

I'm free.

In the middle of nowhere.

With an unexpected travel companion whom I'd like to have fun with today.

"You can change the station," I tell Daphne after we've stopped at another ValuKart to get more essentials for both of us, including another pair of jeans and three more relaxed shirts for me, and for her, more underwear that I'm actively not thinking about, two pairs of shorts, a package of socks, three T-shirts with jokes I don't fully understand, a hairbrush, shampoo, conditioner, a bag of Halloween candy—hell if I know why it's in stores in August—and two gossip magazines from the checkout counter, plus a root beer from the fast-food restaurant inside the ValuKart.

And I don't know if she needed all of that because she wants to stay on the road with me or because she's screwing with me.

Screwing with people always seemed like one of Daphne's favorite pastimes.

Case in point?

She's grinning at me as she points to the radio. "Nah. This is my favorite station."

We're still on symphonic pop, and I veer a little on the road as I whip my head toward her, but I correct faster than I would've two days ago and have much less of a panicked reaction to my own poor driving.

Sleep's helping my driving skills. This is the first time I've veered all day.

"You're a little easy to manipulate." She punctuates the statement with a loud slurp as she finishes the root beer.

She follows it with a soft burp, then chuckles. "Can you imagine if I did that in front of my parents? They'd shit a brick."

My upbringing has me appalled.

My freedom has me smiling.

At all of it.

Her lack of basic drinking manners. Her fucking with me. Her saying *shit a brick*.

But mostly—I'm grateful for the opening to talk about her family.

Talking about her family will definitely take my mind off the way she looked when she was eating that donut.

Wait.

Was she screwing with me then too?

Goddammit.

She probably was.

Still, I push ahead. In case she wasn't. "I thought you didn't see your parents."

She snorts softly. "I don't."

I cut another glance at her before turning my attention back to the road.

Pretty outside today. We're driving through a hilly area with green trees surrounding us. The sky is a deep blue with a few nonthreatening clouds floating along without a care in the world.

I'm close.

I'm close to not a care in the world.

But not quite there.

"Ever?" I ask.

"Don't see them. Don't text them. Don't talk to them."

My pulse rattles unevenly.

I don't know if I ever want to see my own parents again.

Definitely not for several months.

They're not bad people.

Yes, yes, my father went to prison. They are actually *that* kind of bad people.

I meant that they're not the worst parents in the world.

They just never saw me as anything other than a person to train to take over the family business. A person who should be grateful for the opportunities I had, even if they don't fit the personality that I was born into.

Walking away like this—it's not something anyone would expect of me.

"Was that ultimately your decision or theirs?" I ask. She said something about them not calling or checking on her, but she didn't say if she tried to contact them.

Did she?

She might've.

I can't remember, but I know my brain feels more awake today than it has been. I probably missed a lot of subtext the past few days.

She slides me a look like we've been over this, but answers anyway. "Mine."

"But you're still tight with Margot."

"Yes."

I fully recognize the discomfort in my stomach that was a result of donuts for breakfast.

It's sitting next to the discomfort that came with thinking too much about the bras and panties Daphne threw into the cart at ValuKart not half an hour ago.

And the discomfort that's come from remembering her ass cheeks when she climbed into the back seat two days ago and the memory of how badly I wanted to kiss her as much as I wanted to throttle her when I caught her with that phone. That wasn't something I was able to acknowledge to even myself until this morning when I watched her eating that donut.

Probably time to call Archie and check in and get some much-needed perspective and a reminder of what I'm doing this for.

I subtly clear my throat. "Does she play go-between?"

"Like, so I stay in touch with my parents without having to talk to them? No. She tells me things about them occasionally—she *does* work for the family business, so it's part of her life, and I like to know what she's doing—but as far as I'm concerned, they're dead."

"Harsh."

"It's not because they cut me off, if you're thinking I'm some spoiled rich girl who—okay, yes, I was a spoiled rich girl who always thought I'd have my trust fund. But that didn't make me a bad person."

I cut another look at her.

This one's very pointed.

She grins. "Lighten up, Tighty-Whities. I'm saving the world on a regular basis now, so I have to balance that out with annoying the shit out of some people."

"I suddenly understand why they would've revoked your trust fund."

She snorts softly, clearly not offended at all. "Yeah, they weren't the assholes at all with how and why they did it. But you better believe if I ever have kids, I'll pay attention to who they are and what they need and not worry about the box I want them to fit into to make sure I look good and that they do what I want them to do. And even if Aunt Margot leaves them each ten billion dollars, they'll know how to survive in the world without it. You know?"

I steal another glance at her.

She's frowning at the windshield, clutching her empty cup so hard it's caving in.

Maybe I haven't offended her, but I've hit a nerve.

"Why'd they cut you off?"

She looks at me, then down at her cup. "Three months before I would've fully come into my trust fund outright, I started a protest at my college over their policies around emotional support animals, but it turned out I'd misread the policy, and I made the college look terrible when they weren't at fault, and they kicked me out."

I wince.

She laughs softly, but it's not an amused laugh. "Yeah. So with one more failed college experience under my belt, my parents sent their family manager to tell me that I would no longer be financially supported by the Merriweather-Brown fortune. Effective immediately. No money except what I had in my purse. They took my security team and chef and stopped payment on my rental house and disconnected my phone from the family plan. I didn't know how to cook. I didn't have any credit cards that weren't tied to them, and they stopped those too. I should've set myself up to take care of myself in basic ways already—I was old enough. But I was still in college and I'd never had to learn. They used their money and my own ignorance to try to control me, and when they realized it wouldn't work, they cut me off with no idea how to get by in the real world."

I rub my chest.

I'm running away. I've put plans in motion to give away a significant portion of the fortune I was born into, and I'm developing plans to give away most of the rest of my money as well.

But I'll keep enough to live a comfortable life—more than a comfortable life, honestly—so that no one else ever has to take care of me. So that I can invest in learning how to be a normal person with normal hobbies and interests and goals without worrying about paying my bills for the rest of my life.

Shit. I'm boring.

"That's—" I cut myself off, uncertain what word is right to describe what her parents did.

"Like turning a ten-year-old loose in the world for all that I knew about how to manage the critical everyday parts of life, with the added bonus that the entire world knew I was suddenly on my own," she says. "They thought I'd come running back to them and promise that I'd quit protesting and that I'd finally finish the next college degree program and that I'd go work for the company like Margot did so that they could look like the big, happy, money-making family that we were."

"But you didn't."

"Fuck them. If they didn't want me, then I could want me enough to be my own whole family."

It's not lost on me how much more I have in common with Daphne than I ever would've dreamed.

I didn't lead protests to… I don't even know what all she's protested in her lifetime. Can't begin to guess, in fact.

But I know this trip, my life, my future—this is a big *fuck you* to my parents.

"What did you— How did you get through it?" I ask.

"I'd made a friend in a couple classes. She let me move in with her. She taught me how to drive—better, I mean, when I didn't have money to pay for those speeding tickets—and how to cook the most basic stuff ever. She helped me find a job. She taught me about money management and paying bills and how to clean up after myself, and she didn't make a fuss about the fact that my aging dog kept crapping all over the carpet when she had enough else to worry about in her life. She saved my life."

"She sounds like a good person."

"The. Absolute. Best." She giggles softly.

I slide another look her way.

She shakes her head like whatever's funny, she's not sharing. "I realized about two years ago—my parents cutting me off was the best thing they could've done for me. I still don't want anything to do with them, but it's not because I'm mad anymore. I mean, no more angry than anyone would be over parents dumping a kid they hadn't prepared for the real world. Maybe I'd feel differently if I had to see them regularly, but I don't sit around fuming about what they did anymore. I've realized they don't deserve me, and that's a good thing."

"Healthy attitude," I murmur.

"Or incredibly egotistical and self-centered."

She's wrong, but I don't correct her. I'm already feeling too close for comfort with her today. "Margot didn't help you at all?"

"She offered. Tried to insist on it, in fact. I told her no. Because once it was all gone, it was—well, terrifying and horrible for a little bit, but *after* that, I realized I was stronger and smarter than I'd ever given myself credit for. Making it on my own—it's—I can't fully describe the satisfaction that comes with knowing that everything I do in my life, every change I make in the world, every personal interaction I have that makes someone else happy—it's like I finally understand why I was born. What I'm supposed to do. And it's—it's magic to know that it's *me*. Powerful, I think, might be the right word. I was never supposed to be able to take care of myself, and here I am, operating a budget and holding down a real job and having real friends who like me for me, goddess only knows why some days, but they do."

Dammit.

I shouldn't have asked.

Shouldn't have brought it up.

Because now I'm sweating.

I'm sweating and heading toward a panic attack because Daphne Merriweather-Brown, my ex-fiancée's chaos-loving, criminal-record-holding, tattooed, multicolored-hair sister, is not only living the life I want, but she's *owning* it.

And that's sexy as hell.

It's like my entire libido has been asleep since my father was arrested, and it's now awake and remembering women exist, and Daphne is the only woman on the planet.

the grumpiest billionaire

"You wanna lighten your grip on the steering wheel? Feels like you're trying to drive the car into the ground."

My fingers flex instinctively at her suggestions, but my knuckles are stiff.

"Your parents put you in a box too?" she says.

I don't answer.

Not because she wouldn't understand. She clearly would.

But I'm not ready to say it out loud yet. Even a simple *yes* is too much.

Especially to Daphne.

I can't be like her.

I *cannot* have more in common with her right now.

Not when feeling like we have so much in common is dangerous on a level I don't want to analyze.

"Sounds like you did a bang-up job filling in for your dad when he was in the slammer."

My eye twitches.

Good.

Good.

Reminders of what I did every day for the past few years is helpful.

She clears her throat. "Sorry. It's habit to irritate you."

"After three days?"

"No, mostly after how I grew up. I never go back to the city because I don't like who I was before. And bad things happen when I go back to the city. Like thinking I'm going to talk to someone for five minutes in their back seat when their driver shows up and instead falling asleep while I'm waiting, only to wake up in Pennsylvania because I have shitty timing."

This is helping. Breathing is getting easier. "And shitty assumptions."

"Like you wouldn't get back together with Margot."

I grimace and start to sweat again. "Once again—I have no interest in getting back together with your sister."

"Why not?"

"Our lives aren't compatible anymore."

"How?"

I glance at her again. "Are you serious?"

"It's not like you've told me your life plan. All I know is we're driving ten hours today, possibly deeper into the South, and you don't want anyone to know where you are. Where *do* they think you are, by the way?"

"Vacation."

"Without security."

"I gave my security team large bonuses to not ask questions when I left."

"So what's after...vacation?"

We enter a charming little town with old-fashioned storefronts lining the main street. I debate how much I want to say as we approach what appears to be the lone stop sign in this village.

Two days ago, it would've been absolutely nothing.

I wouldn't have wanted to tell Daphne a single word about my plans.

But now—she'd get it.

She'd get it more than Archie could get it.

She's lived it.

She's thriving in it.

"Stop stop *stop!*" she screeches.

I slam on the brakes, sending both of us thrusting forward into our seat belts about three car lengths from the stop sign.

My heart hammers in my throat.

Two people outside a diner to our left openly gawk at me.

Someone behind me honks.

"Oh my god, pull over! We have to go in." She tugs on my arm and points to something on the right.

I ease off the brake and let the car roll into one of the angled parking spots lining the road in front of an old brick building with giant metal flowers and an ancient wooden rocking chair sitting in front of the large glass picture windows.

"What are we stopping for?" I almost get the sentence out without gasping for air.

Daphne unbuckles her seat belt and flings the door open. "I can't believe I almost didn't see it!"

She's squealing like we're about to find the holy grail.

Actually, she wouldn't squeal about that.

She'd squeal about—

"*Look*, Oliver! Just look. Isn't she beautiful?"

A brass statue of a polar bear on an iceberg.

She'd squeal about a brass bear in an antique shop off a rural highway somewhere in northern Mississippi.

Her brown eyes sparkle up at me. The blue and green highlights in her hair shimmer in the summer sunlight. And pure joy radiates off her.

Joy over a nine-inch statue in an antique shop.

"Every road trip needs a mascot," she says.

I get it now.

I get why Margot used to say Daphne wasn't the troublemaker everyone thought she was.

She simply had her own way of looking at life that didn't line up with what was expected. Her own ways of finding joy that came from different places than where the rest of us looked for it.

I don't know exactly what I'm feeling right now.

Jealousy at how much she's clearly thrived in her life.

Or bone-deep attraction to it.

Rather than dig deep on that, I do the only thing I can do.

I walk into the antique store.

Because I'm buying that polar bear for her.

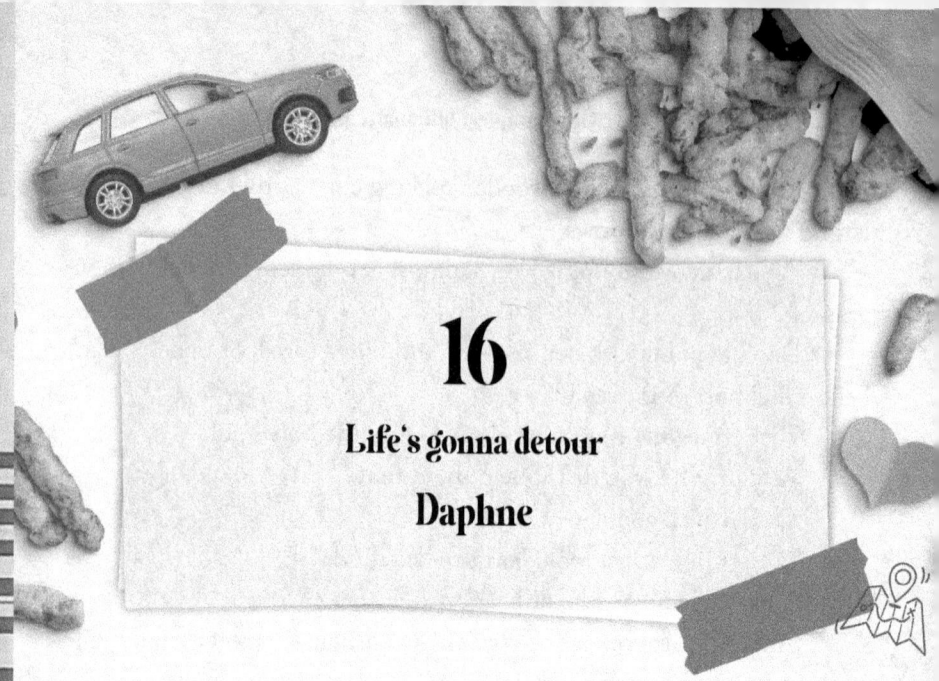

16

Life's gonna detour

Daphne

Even with the perpetual crimp in my neck and shoulder from how I've slept the past three nights, I can't stop smiling as we hit the road again, this time with me in the driver's seat and Angelina Juliana Priestly, the twenty-five-pound brass polar bear, perched behind us in the middle of the back seat, strapped in atop a box to give her a clear view of the road.

We're almost to the edge of town—so maybe three or four blocks down—when I stop again.

"Ten hours today, Daphne," Oliver says.

He doesn't sound exasperated or irritated though.

It's odd.

Not the part where he'd tell me we have a schedule, but the part where he's very patient about it.

And while I appreciate the patience, the man has something to learn here. "The fourteenth rule of road trips is that you always stop for little kids doing a lemonade stand."

"Fourteenth? How many road trip rules are there?"

"As many as you want there to be."

"Fuck rules," he mutters.

the grumpiest billionaire

He's the last person on earth I ever would've expected to say something so simple and yet so very, very right, and it has me smiling even bigger as I climb out of the car, reaching across myself to rub absently at my neck and shoulder.

I have about seven hundred dollars stuffed in my bra, so even if— Nope, Oliver's getting out too.

There are two kids running the lemonade stand. The boy's wearing the same grumpypants expression Oliver sported the first few days of our trip, and the girl is a lot younger, maybe six or seven, with a big gap where her front two teeth should be.

"Y'all want some lemonade and cookies?" she asks in a soft Southern accent.

"Heck, yeah," I say. "How much?"

"Five dollars."

"Each?"

She grins wider. "Yep!"

"No one's gonna pay that much for lemonade and Oreos, Tilda," her brother grumbles.

"Shut your big ol' mouth, Sammy," she replies. "Mama says you have to be nice."

"Not nice to say *shut your big ol' mouth*," the preteen says.

"Two lemonades and four Oreos, please," Oliver interrupts.

Tilda snorts an *I told you so* snort at her brother, who rolls his eyes.

I can't stop smiling.

Donuts.

Angelina Juliana Priestly the polar bear.

And highway robbery lemonade and cookies, where my thus far extremely grumpy companion is totally stuffing five or six hundred-dollar bills into the payment cup.

Best. Day. Ever.

Maybe not the *best* day, but all things considered, it's a very fine day.

"You trying to give us fake money?" the preteen says to Oliver.

"Are you for fuc—" He catches himself and clears his throat.

"We won a scratch-off lottery ticket and decided to take a road trip with the winnings and feel like rich people," I tell Sammy as I take my lemonade from Tilda. "It's fun. But don't waste your money on lottery tickets. It's much more reliable to get a real job and be responsible."

"I'm fixin' to put my money in my college fund," Tilda announces.

"What do you want to go to college for?" I ask her.

"I'mma be a famous actor or a vetrineenian or a baker."

"It's *veterinarian*, Tilda," Sammy mutters.

"You're a fart face," she replies.

"This lemonade is delicious," I interrupt. "I hope it makes you a ton of money for your college fund."

Oliver sips his lemonade, almost chokes, and then gives her the most forced smile I've ever seen. "So good," he lies.

I haven't tasted mine yet.

Neither kid notices that though.

Tilda hands me four Oreos. "Don't share with him," she whispers to me. "He makes weird faces, and weird faces don't deserve cookies."

"Thanks for the tip," I whisper back. "Gotta run. We're hoping to hit Dollywood tonight."

Are we? I have no idea. I think we're headed away from the Dollywood area, but who knows? I haven't figured out where Oliver's going yet.

"*Oh my god, I love Dolly!*" Tilda yells.

"Same, kiddo."

Sammy rolls his eyes again.

Oliver gives me a look.

I grin at everyone, and then I grin wider at the trees and the grass and the sky and the flowers lining the walk to the small little house behind them because it's quaint and perfect and I'm happy today.

In this moment.

Who knows what the next will bring, since I'm now headed back to the car.

the grumpiest billionaire

"Do *not* drink that," Oliver mutters to me as he buckles into the passenger seat again. "I think they got into their parents' whiskey cabinet. And it's not good whiskey."

"Best road trip ever."

"Probably shouldn't eat the cookies either."

I roll the window down as we leave town. The wind overpowers the radio so I can't hear the symphonic pop, but it's so freaking pretty today.

A little warm, but we won't die.

Oliver makes me pull over in the next little town for us to dump the lemonade and stale Oreos in a trash can, and then we're back on the road.

After a while, I roll my window back up. My hair's probably imitating a cartoon villain's favorite style, and the sugar high from breakfast is fading.

"So where are you dumping me tonight?" I ask Oliver. Might as well address it and get it over with.

Out of the corner of my eye, I watch him watch me for what feels like a moderate eternity. "Your friend taught you to cook?" he finally says.

"I can make a phenomenal mac 'n' cheese out of a box and semi-homemade spaghetti, but the grill is where I truly excel. Well, the grill and oatmeal. I make a mean oatmeal."

"You make…a mean…oatmeal."

"Yes."

"The world's most *boring* food?"

"Don't mock the world's most *versatile* food."

He's totally mocking oatmeal. And me.

And honestly, I don't know if it's the world's most versatile food. Bea sometimes puts it in cookies, and you can add practically anything to oatmeal to ramp up the flavor profile.

I shrug. "I'd show you, but despite being the world's most versatile food, oatmeal doesn't work for dinner, and our three days are up today, so…"

He sighs.

I know that sigh.

It's the universal sigh of *she's going to make me ask her to stay longer.*

If I were by myself, I'd do a happy butt wiggle.

But I restrain it while he grinds out the words. "I could use a little more help adjusting to the real world."

"Don't tell anyone I told you this, but you *can* learn to cook from the internet."

"Cooking isn't everything I need to figure out."

"You did pretty good back there at the lemonade stand."

"Every last person I've handed a hundred-dollar bill has treated me like it's fake."

"Not *every* last person."

"I'm going to get arrested for suspicion of counterfeiting before I—before I'm done with what I need to do."

Dammit.

He almost spilled the beans. Almost clued me in on what he's doing.

But he caught himself.

"You know I'm using vacation time to be here?" I say.

"I can pay you for your—"

"I don't want your money. For me. I still want what we agreed on earlier, but I don't want it *for me.*"

"What do you want it for?"

"You are not yet inside that circle of trust."

"How do I get there?"

"You tell me the truth—the *whole*, real truth—about what you're doing on this trip."

I swear I can hear him grinding his teeth over the violins and cellos and flutes on the radio.

"You can't let me go because you still don't trust me to not tell anyone I was with you and what car you're driving and that there's clearly something wrong," I say. "If not wrong, then not normal. We both know

the grumpiest billionaire

it. So if you want me to continue to ride along with you, then you owe me the truth."

"Says the woman who won't tell me what she wants *some number under a million* for."

"I'll survive if you bail on our agreement, if only out of spite to prove that I don't need it. I've thrived making a point the past four years. I can keep doing it. But also, I get to keep Angelina Juliana Priestly. No negotiating."

"You get to keep *who*?"

"Angelina Juliana Priestly. The polar bear. Our road trip mascot."

"You named the statue."

"I named your car too. We've been riding in Mabel. Fits her, don't you think?"

Oliver of yesterday would've snarled something at me.

This Oliver, however, simply sighs softly.

This trip has clearly been good for him.

Even with me along.

I brake as I spot a line of cars stopped ahead of me and realize I'm rubbing at my neck again.

"Why are they stopped?" Oliver asks. "We've hardly seen any traffic today."

"Probably road construction. It's pretty miraculous that we haven't hit any yet. Peak road construction season."

"Can't you go around them?"

I do my best to not laugh at him.

I really, really do.

But honestly—*go around them*? Who wouldn't chuckle a little at that? "Sure, Mr. Big Shot CEO. I'll let them know you're important so we can go around everyone else waiting in line."

There it is.

The deep nasal inhale that says I've annoyed him now.

Which is probably better anyway.

There's this line where I can be friends with Oliver, but I can't find it.

I either hate him with everything inside me to the point that I start fantasizing about suffocating him with a pillow filled with all of the things about him that annoy me, or I can't stop thinking about how good his ass looks in his jeans and how amazing he smells when he's up close and what he must've done to hone all of his muscles for the past few years and how much I wouldn't mind being the next person to bite his sharp hips.

There's no *we can be friends* in between.

So hating him is basically my only option.

I owe my sister that much.

And myself, honestly. I don't need anything else from my past sneaking back into my life.

"I meant there has to be a side road we can take," he grumbles. "A detour around whatever this is."

I poke at the GPS in the dash, moving the map, but don't see any alternate options in the immediate vicinity. "Nothing close."

"How long will we be stuck?"

"No telling. It's usually no more than a few minutes in rural areas like this."

Now he glances at his watch.

"Something big waiting tonight?" I ask him.

"I have a schedule."

"For…?"

Silence.

Right.

I get to stay to teach him to cook—or at least spot which videos and recipes on the internet are likely to kill you and which ones might taste good—but he doesn't trust me enough to know how long he's on this trip.

"Does *anyone* in your life know what you're doing?" I ask.

More silence.

I'm about to reach for the radio volume when he replies.

"One person."

"Girlfriend?"

"Best friend."

"They couldn't go on a trip with you?"

I'm not surprised when he doesn't answer.

Or when his knee starts bouncing.

He notices as well immediately.

I can tell because he clamps a hand down on his own leg to stop it.

The cars inch along.

I rub my shoulder a little more.

"If you plugged in the map app on your phone instead, we'd get better traffic updates." I tap the screen in the dash. "This is out of date, or it would be showing traffic. A phone map app would tell us how long we'll be stuck here. Or if there's an alternate route without traffic."

I don't look at him, but I can feel him staring at me.

Because it was stupid of me to explain map apps to him?

After our experience at that first gas station, it's a legitimate thing to wonder.

Somehow, he's far more competent and in charge than he was while he was dating and engaged to Margot, but also a hot mess in several parts of his life.

Emphasis on *mess*.

Clearly.

Because I'm ignoring all of the hot parts except the part that goes in *hot mess*.

"I know how map apps work," he mutters.

I pull my phone out of my bra, flip it open, and touch my favorite map app, then hand it to him. "Here. Put the address in here."

He does it from memory.

From memory.

He's clearly put a lot of time into thinking about this trip.

But some of the little details in his preparation are lacking, and that has me wondering how much is because of the ways his family might have sheltered him, or how much stress he was under at work that his brain couldn't reach all the way to filling in some of the blanks on how road trips work.

Or if any of it has to do with that accident that had him not driving himself, even on the weekend or at vacation houses, basically for his entire adult existence.

The mechanical Australian dude's voice that I set as my default for my map app announces that we'll be in traffic for the next fifty minutes.

"Did he say *fifty*? Five zero? Or fifteen?" Oliver says.

"Five zero," I confirm.

We inch along a little more, then stop.

I make the *hand it over* gesture, and he gives me back my phone. Three taps later, I'm wincing. "We can detour, but the detour road isn't for another fifteen minutes, and it adds an hour to the trip."

"How the fuck is that even possible?"

I don't think he's expecting an answer, but I give him one anyway. "Rural areas, my dude. There are fewer roads."

He stares at me.

Then at my phone.

And then Oliver Cumberland, the man I would've called the most buttoned-up man on the entire planet, huffs, slides his shoes off, and reaches into the back seat for the last bag of Flaming Finger Lickies.

17

If it's always wrong, maybe it's actually right

Oliver

I thought I'd wanted to crawl out of my skin about a dozen different times every week since I was thrust into the role of Miles2Go's CEO, but that's nothing compared to how today is going.

It started fine.

Good, even.

Finally embracing the journey, apologizing to Daphne, even the antique store and the lemonade stand were good.

But the road construction?

It's putting us behind schedule, and I'm tightening up again. Once we finally make it to the other side, after well over an hour of Daphne challenging me to an alphabet game, then a sing-off, all while switching the temperature in the car to mess with me—or more likely distract me—we can't keep flying down the road because now we need gas.

Miles2Go is the only option.

Fantastic.

"Their Lava Cheese Puffs are better than the Flaming Finger Lickies," Daphne tells me as she pulls up to the pump. "And you haven't lived until you've had a cherry Landslide."

She's been grabbing at her neck half the morning, and she does it once again as she unbuckles.

Because she's been sleeping on floors and couches, dumbass, a little voice in the back of my brain says loud enough for me to hear over my irritation at how far behind schedule we are now.

"I'll pump," I tell her as we both climb out of the car.

"Cool. I'll go pay. You want a Landslide? I'd offer you a corn dog, but they're seriously awful. Plus, Bea made corn dogs last week, and there's *zero* chance I'm ruining the memory of her corn dog by eating one of M2G's monstrosities."

Bea. That's who she was talking to Monday night. I remember her saying the name.

"She makes good corn dogs?" I ask.

She grins at me over the car. "Almost as good as today's donuts."

Not thinking about the donut. *Not* thinking about the donut. Or how she ate it. The way her eyes slid shut. The length of her neck when she tilted her head back. The—*stop thinking about the donut.*

"Do you need money?"

"Nope. Still have about seven hundred from what I snuck out of your suitcase the other day."

I'm too twitchy already to care.

I stretch, breathe, turn in a slow circle, and—*there*.

There it is again.

One of my butterfly gardens at the side of the parking lot, the wildflowers healthy and bright with their multicolored blooms over dark green stalks.

A slice of paradise at a gas station that has my shoulders relaxing a little more on their own.

Good job, I tell myself.

Fuck knows my father wouldn't.

You don't get credit for doing what's expected.

And if the board's recommendation for the new CEO doesn't go my way in two weeks—and I don't mean *my way* as in still being CEO,

the grumpiest billionaire

I mean *my way* as in the board supporting my executive assistant for the role because she's earned it—if they give my father another shot at running the company, he'll probably end the program.

Probably do something stupid like start charging for the electric charging stations too.

Every store in the nation—*every last one*—saw a rise in profits from products inside the convenience stores. Because people spend money while they're waiting for their electric vehicles to charge, and none of our competitors saw an advantage to offering the service for free so we currently have a large advantage with electric car owners.

But dear ol' dad would probably change that too. Assume they'll stick with us when he makes them pay.

That has my hands clenching inside my pockets.

"All good to fill her up," Daphne calls to me from the door.

And just like that, I start breathing again.

Because Daphne took care of paying cash to get the pump started, and hearing her voice reminds me where I am.

Namely, in a place where it doesn't matter anymore what happens to Miles2Go.

I did my part, and I can't control the rest.

Not if I want to live my life for me instead of for my family's legacy.

I fill the car, lock it, and head inside for the restroom and snacks.

Daphne's balancing two quart-size cups with rounded plastic lids and a canvas tote bag that she's filling with more or less every item from the chip aisle.

"Save some for everyone else," I say as I join her.

"They have a truck around back right now getting more." She tilts her head toward the counter, winces, rolls her shoulder, and then looks back at me. "Driver was stuck in the same traffic we were."

She finishes grabbing the last of the Lava Cheese Puffs, then circles the aisle and heads toward the checkout counter, pausing briefly to stare at the display of stuffed Cupholders.

The hermit crab.

Miles2Go's mascot.

"Don't even think about it," I mutter to her.

"I miss my lobster." She shrugs, then winces again. "She's soft."

It takes a second, but then— "You have an emotional support stuffed lobster?"

"Better to sleep with than a brass polar bear."

She heads to the counter.

I hesitate, then grab one of the stupid stuffed crabs, even though I know it'll give me nightmares. As I'm heading to the counter too, I spot a display next to the door full of products I recognize all too well.

Wasn't often my executive assistant outright ordered me around—normally she'd bring me a problem, I'd ask her opinion, she'd give it to me, and I'd do what she suggested—but a few months ago, she marched into my office and informed me that every M2G location on the planet needed to sell these.

I grab two and trail after Daphne.

She's emptying the cloth tote on the counter next to the two Landslides.

Chips, nut bars, pistachios, meat sticks, gum, and more random items tumble out of the tote.

The clerk eyes her, then me, then gets busy scanning it all.

I wait until most of Daphne's selections are back in the bag before adding my purchases.

Daphne glances at the crab, then me, then the crab again.

My ears get hot.

I'm not bribing her with an emotional support crustacean.

I'm—hell.

I don't know what I'm doing.

Giving her another peace offering?

I don't think she needs one, but I'm strung so tight after the road construction that I might.

the grumpiest billionaire

I fork over two hundred-dollar bills. "Take it all out to the car," I tell Daphne. "I'll drive."

She stares at me for one more long minute, her brown eyes studying me like she wants to know the catch, like she doesn't know who I am, like I've passed some kind of test that I didn't know I was taking.

The scrutiny makes my heart beat erratically.

Four days ago, I'd forgotten Daphne even existed.

Today, she eats donuts and shrieks in glee over polar bears and watches me with all of the intelligence she's hidden—or that I've never noticed—and I break out in a sweat over how innately attractive it is to watch someone enjoy the little things in life.

I expect she would've been happy simply knowing that brass polar bear existed. That it would've made her happy even if I hadn't bought it for her.

She breaks eye contact, swinging the tote over her shoulder. She tucks the crab into the top of her shirt, grabs the two Landslide drinks, and turns away to head to the car.

I retrieve one of the buckwheat pouches though. "Out in a minute."

Fuck me.

My voice is hoarse.

My voice is hoarse because my body is having another unwelcome reaction to this woman.

I shake my head, pushing the thoughts away.

There are more important things to think about.

Like that the store has a microwave.

I use it to heat the pouch, and I'm back in control of myself by the time I carry it to the car.

Daphne makes a face at me as I open her door. "You said you'd drive."

I shove the buckwheat pouch at her. "Put it on your neck."

She blinks at me slowly like she doesn't understand, but she takes the pouch and does as she's told.

I shut her door, cross around the front of the car, and climb into the driver's seat without remembering to push it back first.

Daphne's staring at me again, the heating pad laid across her shoulder and neck, the crab sticking up out of the neck of her T-shirt.

She doesn't say anything.

Again.

And I don't know if that makes it better or worse.

I hit the button to start the car, grip the steering wheel, realize I'm already gripping it too tightly, and let my hands drop back into my lap. "I'm disappearing."

"Oh my god, Oliver! No! I can still see you! You're not disappearing! Don't go! Don't go into the ether!"

My lips get into a battle between wanting to huff at her outlandishness, growl and scowl at her, and freaking smile at the same time.

And the smile is winning. Dammit, she's funny.

"Not *literally*, you pain in the ass."

"Oh. You meant like…" She waves her hand vaguely as if that means something. "From your old life."

"Yes."

"I suppose that makes more logical sense."

I shift to look at her again.

Her eyes crinkle in the corners as she smiles at me, and I swear the fairies tattooed on her arms are smiling at me too. "Yeah, I guessed as much. Wanna tell me why though?"

My fingers curl into fists again, and once more, I force them to relax. "Because I hate my life, and I don't owe anyone anything anymore. By all outward appearances, I saved the goddamn company. I did my part. It's my turn to do something for me."

A shadow drifts over the car.

Or possibly that's me picking up on whatever Daphne's feeling about my plans.

It's so silent in here that I can hear her swallow.

"You did an amazing job." Her voice is oddly thick. "You deserve to find what'll make you happy."

That's not what she wants to say.

That's not at *all* what she wants to say.
I slide another look at her.
She squeezes her eyes shut and looks away.
"What?" I say, and then I understand.
I understand all too well.
Fuck me.
Fuck. Me.
I scrub a hand over my face. "You want me to go back for Margot. This—this has all been some kind of reverse psychology game."
"*No.*"
"Of course. This tracks."
"Fuck off, Oliver. You don't deserve Margot. You two were so damn *boring* together. Perfect little heirs to your perfect little family empires doing perfect little things like going boating and picnicking and golfing for dates in your perfect little clothes with your perfect little entourages and your perfect little hair with absolutely no personalities, no real convictions, absolutely no thinking for yourself, and *zero* soul to any of it."
I rear back. "Tell me how you really feel."
She huffs. "You know what else? Margot didn't deserve you either. You held each other back. You were *safe* for each other. You never fought. Ever. You agreed on everything from your favorite color to your preferred brand of towels to your boring taste in artwork. You both said you wanted the exact same things and you would've had two or three perfectly boring children who would've needed me in their life to teach them how to scrape their knees and play hide-and-seek and eat ice cream until they puked at least once. Don't you want to *live*, Oliver? Don't you want to have to *fight* for something or someone? Don't you want to know that the person you've chosen for all eternity looked at your flaws and your talents and your fears and your desires and chose you on purpose and wants to be by your side through the ups and downs because they love you beyond all reason?"
My jaw is clenched so tight I want to hit something.

But my heart—my heart is hammering like I'm either three beats from a heart attack or a massive breakthrough.

And I don't like either option. "Why the ever-loving hell do you think I'm running away?"

She turns in her seat and stares out the window at the store, then sucks in a breath like she hurt her neck again, which she more or less confirms for me when she grabs the hot pack and holds it steady. "Never mind. Ignore me."

I want to throttle her and rub the ache out of her neck at the same time, and that confounding contradiction has me cranky as hell. "You're mad at me because I don't want your sister anymore when you didn't want me to want your sister?"

"Sure. Let's go with that."

I growl.

She sucks in an unsteady breath.

I throw the car into gear and make myself carefully look all around us before putting my foot to the accelerator and pulling out of the gas station with far more restraint than I think I have in me.

And then I take the turn onto the highway too fast, and the damn brass polar bear falls right into the bags of chips.

Daphne sighs, turns the volume up on the radio, and goes back to staring out the window.

I remind myself every ten seconds to not grip the steering wheel so hard.

I order myself to not be angry.

To not care what Daphne thinks of me.

To not wonder what Daphne would say my flaws and fears and hopes and dreams and purpose are.

To not daydream about smothering her in her sleep.

I don't want to smother her in her sleep.

And that's the biggest problem.

I want—I want what she has.

I want freedom and joy and thrills and purpose.

I want to *live*.

She didn't fit into my old life.

I don't fit into my old life.

So there's a slice of this life where we're the same.

Where we fit together.

And that—that thought, more than the unexpectedness of her being here, more than the annoyance when she pushes my buttons, more than the inconvenience of realizing that she *does* know things I need to know—that thought more than anything is what has my teeth on edge and my pulse racing erratically and my dick doing what dicks do.

This road trip? Being here with Daphne?

This is a disaster.

And an hour down the road, everything goes even more to hell.

Again.

18

Nothing's the same after the rain

Daphne

I feel like the world's biggest asshole.

All I have to do is say one little sentence—*your initiatives at Miles-2Go gave me my favorite job of my life and I'm scared I'll lose it when your dad takes back over*—but I can't.

And I don't know why.

Pride?

Fear that if Oliver knows what I truly want, he'll call back to the office and cancel the contract that keeps us afloat anyway?

General contrariness that I was born with and haven't fully shaken no matter how much of a good influence Bea's been on me for the past four years?

Or possibly I've convinced myself that I can still convince him to go back to M2G without having to confess why it matters.

He's still my old world.

He's still the people who'll take away your toys to teach you a lesson and laugh while they do it.

Except he bought me a hermit crab to replace my lobster and this magical heating pad that made the pain in my neck feel better before it lost all of its heat.

the grumpiest billionaire

He got me donuts for breakfast.

He stopped at the antique store and hasn't once yelled that it put us behind schedule.

And now we're in the middle of a downpour so thick that we've had to pull over to the side of the road because we can't *see* the road.

Lightning flashes, and thunder booms so close that the car shakes.

"It should pass in fifteen minutes or so." I'm muttering because I can't bring myself to say anything nice when I know I've been an asshole, and I don't want to apologize even though I need to.

I shouldn't have yelled at him.

I shouldn't be mad about who he used to be when it's clear he's someone else now, when he's already told me he doesn't want to get back together with Margot, when he's been so kind.

But I cannot—*cannot*—handle how much I like him right now.

Knowing he definitely couldn't ever like me back—it makes me feel like I'm the old Daphne.

Like I'm a fuckup all over again. Like I don't fit.

And I want to fit. I *do* fit.

Until I start arguing with him.

"I checked the weather app myself," he replies stiffly.

I don't congratulate him on doing something obvious the way I would if he were one of Bea's brothers. They're fun to annoy on occasion, and they regularly throw the sarcasm right back at me. It makes me feel like they're my brothers too.

But when I blow out a heavy breath and my window fogs up as another bolt of lightning hits entirely too close, the rattle of the car around us shakes me enough to prompt the regrets.

"I'm sorry I called you boring."

He doesn't reply.

And he shouldn't.

I'm so confused about how much I like him right now that I can't behave like a normal, rational, kind person would, and even if he's boring, he doesn't deserve to be yelled at about it.

"You're right."

I'd jerk my head around fast if I could move my neck that quickly without pain.

And if I wanted to see his face.

But I honestly kind of don't.

His stubble and the scowls and the small kindnesses—the man is stupidly attractive in ways he has no right to be and in ways that I have no right to notice.

"I'm never right," I tell him. "It's one of the perks of being me. I'm forever wrong."

"I'm boring."

"So what? The world needs boring people to balance out interesting people." Lightning tries to strike me dead in that exact moment.

No, seriously.

It hits somewhere close enough to the car that we shake and rattle while the thunder booms simultaneously around us.

My heart is permanently residing in my throat while I squeeze the ever-loving hell out of the stuffed hermit crab, waiting for the thunder-induced earthquake in the car to pass.

"You're not boring," I gasp. "Okay? *Okay*, Mother Nature? He's not boring!"

Oliver snorts.

And it's not a derisive snort, or a mocking snort, or a *stop lying* snort.

I swear on my stuffed lobster back home, it's a completely amused snort.

The kind of snort that leads to rolling laughter.

Not necessarily funny laughter.

Possibly hyperventilating, *everything's wrong* laughter, but one minute, I'm begging the universe to forgive me for being an asshole, and the next, Oliver's laughing so hard the car's shaking again, but this time from *him*.

the grumpiest billionaire

I finally get up the guts to look at him, and find him hunched over the steering wheel, absolutely losing what might very well be the last of his sanity.

Lightning flashes and thunder cracks on top of us once again.

I squeeze the stuffed crab harder, watching while he laughs himself out, because I need to hold on to something so that I don't reach over and touch him.

His smile.

The crinkles in his cheeks from the smile.

The lines in his forehead that are probably stress, likely from me.

Rain pelts the windows in a downfall so thick that I can't identify individual drops of rain.

It's a sheet of water accompanying nature's temper tantrum.

I stare down at my lap so I stop looking at him, wincing at one more boom of blinding-white thunder.

We are in the absolute center of this storm, and there's no separating the lightning and the thunder here. It's all smushed together.

My Landslide has melted. It's flavored water now.

I don't want chips. I don't want music. I don't want to be in this Camry, and I don't want to be out of it either.

I want the rain and the thunder and the lightning to stop and for Oliver to quit laughing like a madman.

In fact, I want him to be boring again.

Could use a little bit of predictability here.

Wind buffets the vehicle.

I squeeze the crab impossibly harder and bury my face in it.

Thunderstorms don't usually rattle me.

But everything since we got back in the car after getting gas has rattled me, to include the part where this isn't a nice distant summer thunderstorm.

It's a squall directly on top of us while we're huddled inside a metal frame.

Lightning crashes on top of us again.

I stifle a shriek.

Oliver twists his neck to look at me.

His smile is dopey but so happy it's charming, showing off his white teeth against his dark stubble. His hazel eyes are flickering with warmth and something else.

Something that looks like happiness.

Like he's thrilled that I'm freaking out over a thunderstorm.

"You look like I felt after Kurt wrecked his dad's Maserati," he muses, still chuckling.

"*That's not fucking funny, Oliver.*"

Please note, lightning and thunder don't attempt to murder us when *he's* being an asshole, comparing our being stuck in a thunderstorm to the accident that led to him driving himself nowhere, ever, until now.

It's probably karma.

"Hey." He shifts in his seat, a giant mass of muscle and intelligence and boring predictability, but there's nothing boring *or* predictable about him squeezing my thigh. "We're fine. Just a storm. It'll pass."

I squint at him.

Is he being literal or is he talking about us fighting too?

I should call Bea and ask her to send someone to pick me up.

Not that I'm using *any* electronics until this storm has passed.

"Daphne."

"What?"

His hand is still on my thigh. Bare skin to bare skin.

Check that.

His bare palm to my goosebumps.

"We're okay," he says.

Lightning streaks through the car again, but the thunder isn't immediate this time.

As if Oliver's declaration that we're okay is enough to chase the storm away.

"Define okay," I tell him.

The man's still smiling.

Smiling and squeezing my thigh and brushing his thumb over my skin. "We're not dead, and we're almost not annoying the shit out of each other by breathing, and we have food, and our parents aren't here."

"*Our parents aren't here?*" I repeat.

"Best part, yeah? Even better than the rain doing all the work of cleaning the bugs off the windshield."

I don't know this man.

He's goofy and a little sarcastic and his hand is warm and his eyes—his eyes are lit up with what I'd call joy in any other person.

I don't know this man, but I *want* to.

And I can't.

I just can't.

But what if I could?

Thunder rolls through the car again as the rain continues its attempt to drown us.

Oliver leans against his headrest and closes his eyes, smile still playing on his lips, hand still resting on my thigh.

It's definitely not the thunderstorm that has my pulse trying to outrun itself.

It's Oliver.

19

There it is—exactly what I've been looking for
Oliver

I never knew laughing could make me happy.

Not that it was happy laughing.

Not at first.

But by the time the storm has died down enough that it's safe to drive again, I'm not pissed anymore.

I'm just—I'm *happy*.

There's no chance we're making it to New Orleans tonight. I'd wanted to see the city one last time—good memories from a college trip happened down there, even if I know in my bones it's not where I want to live forever—but we wouldn't arrive until after dark, and I set up my schedule for six to ten hours on the road every day. We'd have to leave early to stay on track.

My plans are wrecked. The reservations at random hotels and rental homes along the way, completely not happening now.

I need to recalculate how to get back on track, and tonight, it doesn't matter.

Screw it all.

I don't need to go to New Orleans.

In fact, I planned this entire road trip wrong.

the grumpiest billionaire

I can't find magic, I can't find my future, if I've planned every stop with eight or ten hours on the road between stops every day, the same way I lived the life I'm leaving behind.

I thought seeing everything, covering the most miles possible, was the best way to find where I'm supposed to settle into a new life. But it's not. I'm not seeing the potential in any town for how little time I have to explore, given the schedule I set for myself.

Magic requires spontaneity and trust in the process.

It's something I've forgotten in the past four years, but that I know I need to lean in to now.

So I turn off the GPS, take a right on the first state highway we come across, and I drive.

Watching the sunshine come back out over rolling green fields.

Rolling down the windows to breathe in the scent of the rain.

Stopping on a whim at a farmer's market for fresh peaches and local cheese, and to take a picture with a ridiculously large cow statue.

Daphne's been quiet.

That's the only unsettling part.

The storm seemed to upset her, and she's not bouncing back quickly.

So when she tells me she's done sitting in the car for the day about an hour after the farmer's market, I pull over in the first town we come to.

There's a single motel with a single vacancy tonight. Apparently the next town over is a big college town, and it's freshman move-in weekend.

I check into it with my fake driver's license and pay cash.

We drop our bags in the room, and Daphne points out the window at a diner. "Real food."

"We have peaches and cheese."

"Save it for tomorrow."

And that's how we end up in a run-down little diner where Daphne is telling the server to bring us one of everything.

"One of—*what?*" I interrupt, not because I care, but more because it's the first opening I've had to give her crap since the thunderstorm, and I want the old Daphne back. "We can't eat that much food."

"I've never been to this diner before, and I probably won't ever be back in this diner again, and I'd like to sample everything and see what's best," she replies.

She's wearing lipstick that she picked up at our last ValuKart run, but no other makeup. Her hair's a disaster—she made a comment about the humidity, so I assume that's why it's frizzy and a little wavy in unpredictable ways—and she's back in a Miles2Go Cupholder T-shirt, either because she wants to torture me or because she's found a theme for the day.

I'm choosing to believe it's a theme and that it's helping.

Based on how tightly she was gripping the stuffed Cupholder during the rainstorm, it's not outside the realm of possibility. Even with Daphne.

"Gonna need to move y'all to a bigger table," the server says.

"Bring us your six favorite dishes instead of one of everything," I tell her.

"Plus all of the sides. Sides are my favorite," Daphne says.

The only other couple in the diner is staring at us.

That part makes me uneasy, but I have to get used to it.

"And one of all of the sides," I agree.

"But two of the tater tots," Daphne says. "One of everything else, two of the tater tots. And do you have cheese dip for them?"

"Yep," the server says.

"Fabulous. Thank you."

The older lady doesn't act like our request was weird, but then, she has to be seventy-three if she's a day.

She's probably seen things.

Especially if she's worked here long.

Daphne and I are in a booth with brown faux-leather seats beneath an ancient photograph of a sports team that apparently won some kind of championship in the fifties. The photo and frame itself almost feel older than the time it was taken.

The other diners are at a white-topped table that clearly has something wrong with its legs, because there's a *thump* every time one of them leans on it.

The lighting is dim, which fits with the rainclouds that have come up again and are sprinkling outside.

I lean toward Daphne. "Are you trying to attract attention?"

She fiddles with a saltshaker and shakes her head. "The first rule of eating at diners after being used to Michelin star restaurants is that you have to be brave with your choices."

She's still annoyingly subdued.

So I do what Daphne would do.

I make a snarky comment. "Thank you for explaining that I'm not in Michelin territory anymore. I couldn't possibly have figured that out on my own."

"Would you have ordered chicken-fried steak?"

Dammit. She has me there. "Probably not."

"Chicken-fried steak is to diners what Cod Pieces is to fast food." She kisses her fingertips. "And I'll bet you a hundred bucks we get a plate of chicken-fried steak among her top six favorites."

"You're betting me my own money."

"If you'd stopped at my car on our way out of town, I could've grabbed my wallet and credit card, but nooooooo, you had to get us four hours down the road before I realized the car was moving."

I swipe my hand over my mouth.

She truly is funny once I'm not annoyed with her.

The idea that I would've grabbed her wallet and ID for her and not kicked her out of the car—

Her eyes twinkle, and that same feeling that I had in the thunderstorm hits me again.

I've lived an incredibly boring existence.

All of the money in the world, every opportunity right at my fingertips, and every choice I've made has been safe and convenient and for the good of everyone around me.

It was always easier than figuring out who I wanted to be.

What I wanted to do.

And I don't have to be that person letting others steer my ship anymore.

I don't *want* to be.

I sip from the mason jar of water that our server set down before taking our order. "Protest anything lately?"

She lights up more. It makes my heart thump oddly in my chest again.

"*Yes*," she says. "Last week, in fact."

"Mistreatment of a barn cat?"

"I told you how my best friend's dad was a chef? He wanted to open a restaurant in this cool old Victorian house in town, but he died about ten years ago—Bea's mom too, that's why Bea had to leave college, to move home and finish raising her brothers. So he never got to open his restaurant, but Bea told her ex-boyfriend all about it. While they were dating, I mean. Not after they broke up."

"As one would assume."

She wrinkles her nose at me. "So Jake promised Bea they'd open the restaurant together, but he was the one putting down all of the money for everything while Bea was giving him all of the ideas for how to make it great and getting all of the socials going and getting the community excited about it, and then—guess. Guess what happened."

I'm cringing, and only partially because I suspect doom while Daphne's still smiling. "He broke up with her?"

"Ding ding ding! He dumped her like a week after signing the papers on the building, and then he took the name her dad was going to use and totally bastardized it, *and* she'd moved in with him, so she needed a place to stay, which was nice in a way because I got to pay her back for when she took me in when I needed a place to—why are you smiling?"

I sip my water again. "Your storytelling skills remain unmatched. Please continue."

Her eyes narrow. "So I was protesting his restaurant last week."

"Was it working?"

That smile pops out again, the rainbow after the storm. "Oh, hell yeah."

"Did you get arrested?"

"Bea's ex's brother is a local cop who's a total terror, and he would've loved to arrest me, but I think he has very direct orders from the chief not to. Everyone's afraid I'll call in a favor from some bigshot attorney in the city and sue the town all to hell if they piss me off. I still might, since he arrested Bea a few weeks back for absolutely no good reason."

That has my brows lifting. "Your best friend and roommate is also a jailbird? Why did I picture her as the opposite of you?"

"She is—and was—*innocent*, Oliver. Keep up. When Jake dumped her, she bought a bus and converted it to a food truck to prove she could be more successful than him when she didn't even have a real building, and Simon—" She drops her voice and leans closer, not directly cutting a glance at the other couple, but I can sense that's what she's worried about.

"Simon?" I prompt.

"You know Simon Luckwood?" she whispers.

I scan my memory banks and shake my head. "The name is unfamiliar."

"He's an actor in *In the Weeds*—that horrible TV show?"

I suddenly realize I haven't asked where she's living. And that feels vitally important to figure out quickly.

Someone will notice she's gone. Possibly someone regularly stalked by the media. Which means maybe the media will notice she's gone.

But didn't she say her friend didn't have any money? I'm confused. "You're hanging out with actors?"

Her nose wrinkles. "Not like that. He has twin boys, and their mom is from my hometown. My town. The town where I live. The one I claim now as my home. Anyway, Simon's ex, his boys' mom, had to move home to take care of *her* mom this summer, so he got a house there to be close to the boys and help out too, and his boys—they're thirteen—booked Bea's bus for a party without telling him, so when she rolled up to the estate and got through the gate with a code the grown-ups didn't think she was supposed to have, security freaked out and had her arrested for trespassing. Even though she was supposed to be there."

My lips part, but I don't have a quick response this time.

Daph grins again. "Bea made Simon take her on a date to apologize."

"Because he's her favorite actor?"

"No, she hates the show he's famous for. Her ex, Jake, loved it so much that he made her watch it all the time, and it truly is kind of awful. I think that's why it's popular. The train wreck effect. But anyway—Bea made Simon take her on a date where they crashed Jake's restaurant's grand opening. And it. Was. So. Epic. Like, waaaay better than I could've expected. Simon's lactose intolerant, and the whole tasting menu was basically cheese, and then Bea got stuck in the bathroom and Simon broke the door down and carried her out, and—"

She sighs happily. "It was so romantic. And Simon got a crush on Bea and spent the whole summer talking her into dating him. And kind of talking himself into it too. He's the most unexpected celebrity you'd ever meet, and the two of them together are perfect."

"Is this another one of your stories like the one about being put in third-grade jail?"

"Excuse you, *that story is real*."

Our server appears with an overflowing tray and deposits eight plates on the table while we watch. Good thing too, because I'm enjoying Daphne's stories entirely too much now, and I need a little distraction to get myself back on even ground.

Wait.

Did I say eight plates?

Make that five plates and three bowls, plus smaller bowls with dipping sauces.

"Fried okra, french fries, cheese grits, chitlins, coleslaw, collard greens, and two tater tots," the older lady says. Then she adds dryly, "Save room for dessert."

"We should probably order one of every dessert to go right now," Daphne replies.

The older woman gives us a look I'm beginning to recognize well. It's the *you got money to pay for this?* look.

"And thank you," Daphne says.

Our server strides away.

"You're gonna have to pay for the whole restaurant," Daph whispers to me while she takes a tater tot right off the plate and dips it in cheese.

"After they check and make sure my money isn't counterfeit."

"Yeah, they'll do that too." She giggles, making me momentarily forget I ever disliked her for how happy I am that she seems like herself again.

Is this what relaxing feels like? What being a normal, anonymous person in a small town in the middle of nowhere feels like?

If so, I think I like it.

"So where's home?" I ask.

She eyes me, almost like the question is startling, while she chews her food.

Or possibly like she doesn't know if it's safe to answer.

"You ever hear of Austen & Lovelace College?" she finally says.

I nod. I don't know it well, but it's not an unfamiliar name.

"It's in a little town upstate called Athena's Rest. Bea's mom taught there, so Bea got free classes. That's where we met. It was my last school before—well, *before*."

"You're happy there? In the town? Truly happy?"

"I made a new family there after they kicked me out and my parents did what they did," she says around another tater tot.

I reach for my glass but sit there with my hand resting on it instead of taking a drink. "I—my ultimate goal when I left on Saturday was to eventually settle in a small town and find a boring wife and have boring children and do boring things."

She cringes a little, but she doesn't apologize again for calling me boring.

Not Daphne.

She takes a different route. "Hate to break it to you, but there's rarely anything boring about small towns. At least, in my experience. Honestly, I'm not sure there's anyplace that's truly boring unless you let it be."

"When you start your life going to third-grade jail…"

She nods very seriously. "I definitely took the more adventurous path. Here. Try the okra."

She leans across the table with a small fried nugget in hand and holds it to my lips.

My stupid cock decides having a woman holding food to my mouth is the most erotic thing I've ever experienced, and he springs to full-mast without warning.

And not for the first time today.

Maybe I don't like this part of relaxing.

"Or feed yourself, whatever," Daphne mutters.

Probably because I'm grimacing at the pull in my gut from popping a boner so fast.

"I've never had fried okra." Pitiful attempt at giving a lame excuse as I snatch it from her fingers.

I pop it in my mouth, and—

Once again, I'm a little lost on how I feel.

But I know I need a gulp of water.

Daphne's smile is half-powered. "Try it with ranch next."

"Is it supposed to be slimy?"

"Yep." She drags another tater tot through the melted orange goo that I've been assuming is cheese. "You should try one with ranch dressing. Or cheese. Or hot sauce. Or plain ketchup."

"Why aren't you eating the okra?"

"I'm having a clandestine love affair with tater tots first."

Clandestine love affair does nothing to cool the blood pumping through my dick.

Did I get struck by lightning?

Is that why everything looks different on this side of the road trip?

Or was shutting off the GPS and saying *forget the plans* what I needed?

Freedom doesn't come with plans. Maybe that's what's making it all click into place.

"If you don't want more okra, try the fries. Those are my favorite kind of fries *ever*. Shoestrings are unmatched, and I won't hear otherwise. The grits have to be amazing too. No one does grits like the South does grits."

"You've spent time in the South?"

"Vanderbilt was the first university I was kicked out of."

She says it so easily, so nonchalantly, that I frown.

No one can honestly feel that carefree about being kicked out of a college, can they?

"It wasn't a big deal." She unwraps silverware from a white paper napkin and dips her spoon into the bowl of grits. "Just part of my story to get where I am today. Here. Try these."

She holds the spoon to my mouth, my dick throws a party, and this time, I lean in and taste the food she's offering.

Like this is normal.

Like it's not making me sweat to let Daphne feed me as if we're—something.

But then the flavor of the grits takes over, and my eyes slide shut, and a rumble of pure happiness takes over.

They're creamy and buttery and cheesy, and it's like tasting fast-food fried fish all over again.

My shoulders sag in utter bliss.

If this is what's hiding in a nondescript diner somewhere in—actually, I don't know what state we're in—then what else do I still have to discover?

I blink my eyes open and find Daphne staring at me with darkened eyes, her bottom lip caught between her teeth.

She visibly swallows and drops the spoon, then turns her attention back to the tater tots. "Bowl's all yours, big guy."

She doesn't have to offer twice.

In no small part because I appreciate the opportunity to distract myself with my face over a bowl of food so I don't have to look at her.

It's not how I was raised to eat, but again—screw how I was raised.

I want to be more like Daphne.

Relaxed.

Owning my life.

Talking with my mouth full.

Trying things I never would've considered off a menu in a strange place where I don't have an assistant or life manager calling ahead to order for me so that I don't have to waste energy making one more decision in the day.

And it was like that even before I took over as CEO.

I was trained from an early age on how to channel my focus on what mattered and pay other people—or let my parents pay other people—to take care of the minute details that didn't matter.

It's why I was able to complete a double bachelor's degree program in four years and then finish my master's in a year.

How I was able to dig in so deeply at M2G when my father assigned me the dual roles of senior logistics director and assistant to the chief of staff, and also have time left in the day to date Margot, who was also basically hand-selected for me without me having to make any decisions.

My father's ego might have been his downfall, but the man knows how to squeeze the most out of every day.

For work and appearances.

Not for *living*.

Though Margot was a good choice.

We were happy together.

Until I was thrust headfirst into the deep end of a situation that rapidly demonstrated for me that I wasn't living the right life for me.

I've finished the grits and am discovering the okra grows on you when you have it with ranch dressing, that collard greens are not my thing, and that this coleslaw is magical, when our server arrives with the rest of our dinner.

Meatloaf and chicken-fried steak and a cheeseburger and fried chicken legs and shrimp and grits—*yes*, more grits—and fried catfish.

"That must be one hell of a cheeseburger if it's in her top favorites," Daphne murmurs after our server has departed again with a request for two sweet teas. "I expected the chicken and dumplings."

I grab the shrimp and grits without offering to share.

She laughs at me. "I'll call Bea and ask if her dad had a secret recipe for grits. Kinda doubt it, but I'll ask."

"We need salads tomorrow. And more farmer stands with fruit."

She smiles at me again.

My already full stomach flips over, and my dick strains harder again.

Hindenburg—*fuck*.

I'd say I'm suffering from *Stockholm* syndrome, but I don't think I'm suffering.

I think I'm glad for the company.

And glad my company is Daphne.

Two days ago—hell, even yesterday—that would've been the worst thought I could've possibly had.

Today?

Today, I'm glad that she's here.

20

That's not where I was supposed to land when I fell

Daphne

Oliver's so stuffed he can barely walk across the parking lot to the motel after dinner.

And yes, he paid for the other couple's meal and also left a very large tip.

And yes again, they checked that his money wasn't counterfeit. It was so on-brand for this trip that I had to excuse myself to the bathroom so they wouldn't see me laughing.

Laughing is never a good sign that you're not trying to pass off fake cash.

We've already checked into our room for the night, but it was light when we got here and now it's dark outside—mostly due to another storm, this one thankfully lighter on the thunder.

Tonight's digs are a dinky little room that keeps glowing intermittently red because we're facing the flashing motel sign. The nightstand feels sticky, and the bathroom door doesn't fully shut, probably because of good ol' Southern humidity.

"I'll take the floor tonight," Oliver says as he collapses into the roller chair at the rickety table, which wobbles precariously.

He grabs the table, clearly trying to steady himself, then leaps to his feet as the chair topples, then grabs his stomach and moans.

"You sure you can handle the floor? Not too unstable for you?"

The look he gives me isn't irritated enough.

It's tolerant.

Heavy on amused.

And an amused Oliver is unfortunately hot.

I reach for the knot in my neck, then drop my hand quickly as he notices. "Dumb for both of us to sleep shitty," I say quickly. "Take the bed. It's fine."

"Why would you sleep shitty in the bed?"

"I don't sleep well a lot."

He stares at me expectantly.

As if he honestly expects I'd confess about my panic attacks over the idea of going broke and losing Margot.

I've made such a point of insisting that I can take care of myself that I sometimes can't breathe when I think about what would happen if I lost my job and couldn't find another one.

I know there are good people in the world—like Bea—who want to lend a helping hand when they can, and she'd help me out, but it isn't her job to be my backup plan, even if we do have plans to live together forever so that we can be badass old ladies in our custom rocking chairs on our porch, telling stories someday about all of the fun we had to our great-nieces and great-nephews.

I suspect with Simon tagging along now. I'm pretty sure he's Bea's forever.

Maybe we'll tell his grandkids stories someday too.

But I also know I have to be responsible, which isn't something I was born with a natural inclination to understand.

I didn't have to be responsible, and my parents assumed I'd be a cookie cutter of Margot, so they never bothered to figure out I needed a little help figuring out how to be a truly functional member of normal society.

And the deeper I get into this road trip with Oliver, the more I'm afraid I'm going to do something that makes Margot never want to talk to me again.

Even as I'm recognizing that this Oliver?

Margot wouldn't like him.

Not like *that*.

And he doesn't want her.

Her lifestyle actively wouldn't agree with him.

It's ironic—I'm here because I wanted to tell him to leave her alone, that he wasn't good for her, that she deserved better—but I'm finding I can't convince myself that I want him to leave *me* alone, that he's not good for *me*, that *I* deserve better.

This Oliver?

I like him.

I feel for him. I respect what he's doing. Even when he's been grumpy and mad at me, I get it.

I understand.

I don't hold it against him.

Plus the fact that he can get mad at me but still tell me he wants me to stay with him? That we're able to work through the conflict and have a fun dinner and that he notices when I want a stuffed crab and he buys me a microwavable heating pad for my neck?

Then insists that I take the bed because of it?

"It's a new bed thing," I tell Oliver, switching my story and earning a flat stare from him. "It always takes me a night or two to warm up to sleeping well in a new bed, and I'm used to sleeping on a floor now since they all feel the same."

"That's working well for your neck."

It's wrong to get a little fluttery in the heart when a guy who was almost my brother-in-law wants to take care of me in some ways, right?

That's definitely wrong.

He's simply showing me basic human compassion.

the grumpiest billionaire

Compassion wasn't exactly in abundance when I was growing up. Definitely not the way I've found it in Athena's Rest.

And watching him visibly relax and turn off his GPS and get us *lost* lost, without freaking out, while seeming to enjoy himself today—yeah, that hasn't messed with my head and possibly other parts of me at all lately.

"My neck's all better," I lie.

He snorts, clearly amused, clearly *not* annoyed.

"I'm gonna sit on the bed and watch TV for a couple hours though," I tell him. "Not sleep in it. Just *sit* on it."

He makes a *help yourself* gesture and disappears into the bathroom. The door won't shut all the way, but he tries to make it, tugging it and banging it harder and harder until he gives up, apparently deciding it's stuck enough, even if it's not *truly* shut.

In any case, I can't hear him inside, so the door's better than a lot of the other doors have been this trip.

I settle my bags in a corner of the room, then plop into the middle of the bed and turn on the TV.

One channel's having an *In the Weeds* marathon, which makes me both grimace and smile.

The show truly is awful. Even Simon will tell you so, though privately.

But seeing a familiar face—even when he's in character and scowling, which is now utterly hilarious considering I learned this summer that he smiles nonstop in real life—makes me happy in a homesick kind of way.

I flip the channel and grimace again.

Margot loves these home improvement and cooking shows that are on every single one of the next four channels. She keeps refusing to try true crime podcasts instead.

She's more interested in fixing things than in worrying about all of the ways someone might murder her someday.

That's probably healthiest for her. She does have a lot of that older sister *what if something terrible happens* in her personality already.

No need to give her other ideas beyond *what if the wood beneath the carpet is rotted and we can't use it?*

I click and click and click, until I've flipped through two hundred channels three different times.

Oliver's still in the bathroom.

Maybe he's working out all of his dinner.

Or maybe he's scrolling his phone.

Could be either. Or both.

I'm just grateful for having a break from him.

Some breathing room.

He was different Saturday night from what I remember of him when he was engaged to Margot.

He was different again from Saturday to Sunday.

More so Monday, kind of. Sleeping the whole day in the car was worrisome, but given that he still looks like he's in his forties, I can only imagine how much stress he's recovering from and how much sleep he might need.

And then yesterday—yesterday, he was different all over again in his anger about the phone.

But today was something else entirely.

Today, it feels like something snapped inside of him, and now he's—I don't know what he is.

Not the old Oliver.

Not grumpy Oliver.

Not angry Oliver.

More like *found his peace* Oliver.

Got far enough away Oliver.

Let go of everything and wants to live Oliver.

Still far more confident than he was four years ago, but without the edge he's had the past few days.

And goddess help me, I like it.

the grumpiest billionaire

I'm still searching mindlessly on the television, pretending he's not hiding from me in the bathroom. I click past something that appears to be local news, and then instantly flip back as my brain catches up to what I saw.

Those kids look familiar.

Actually, they look like—"Oh, fuck."

This is bad.

This is very, very bad.

"Oliver? Oliver, are you using the toilet or are you scrolling on your phone? Because you need to see this."

There's a beat of silence, then the bathroom door opens and Oliver looks out at me. "What?"

I point to the TV and turn the volume up. "Recognize them?"

"This man and this lady was driving by and they stopped to get my fancy lemonade, and they left me with *five hundred real dollars*," a little girl is telling the news reporter.

"We're smart, so we called the sheriff to get it checked and make sure it's not fake," her older brother says.

"I got me the start of a college fund," Tilda crows. "And I ain't sharing. Because I did all of the work. I made the lemonade and I pulled the Oreos out of the cabinet and I even found my daddy's special extra ingredient to fix up the lemonade all special all by myself."

"Did you get a picture of the people who gave you all of that money?" the reporter asks, clearly holding back a smile.

"No, Sammy was being a fart-butt about letting me use his phone," the little girl replies.

"They said they won the lottery," her older brother adds. "They said this was their way of sharing. But I feel like it was a trick."

"Trick or not, this little girl has the start of her college fund with five hundred real dollars from a stranger, checked over by the sheriff and everything. And there you have it, Ella-Mae," the reporter onscreen says. "Today's good news story, right here in Farnsworth."

The scene switches back to the news studio, and I glance over at Oliver.

His eyes meet mine, half panicked, half something I can't entirely read, and then he turns his back on me and disappears into the bathroom again.

"Did we go backwards?" he mutters to himself while he shuts the door.

I pull up my phone and check the map. "No, but we're still in Mississippi. We're probably on the very edge of the viewing area for this channel. We could leave and get a little farther down the road, but this is the kind of thing the internet and social media could pick up."

He grunts in response.

It's not so much an irritated grunt—not like I'd expect—as it is a simple acknowledgment.

I glance at the duffel bag that's still packed with hundred-dollar bills that he brought up from the car. He left the other two in the car, like he did the first night.

Bags of money—it's pennies to him, but I think he very much understands that several hundred dollars isn't pennies to the people we've met so far along the way.

"Are you planning on giving all of this money away before you reach your final destination?" I call. "Like, *all* of it?"

A grumbled answer that I'm pretty sure is a *yes* comes from the bathroom.

"Do you have an actual plan besides leaving tips everywhere we go and paying for other people's dinners when we stop at real restaurants?"

Silence.

I'm gonna assume silence means *no*.

And that makes my heart hug itself.

Some parts of Oliver's plan to escape seem so well laid out—or did, until today. Then the other parts...

He's an irresistible mess.

"You want some ideas of how to give it all away without getting made and having your face plastered all over everywhere?" I ask.

The door cracks open.

Thuds open, really. I didn't know doors could thud when they opened, but I think that's the effect of the humidity. It's not *hot* hot in here, but the air conditioner clearly isn't keeping up with the moisture in the air either.

Makes me glad I'm in a T-shirt and shorts. He has to be dying in jeans.

Especially considering how much food he ate.

"One of the last things I did with my trust fund before I lost access to it was to donate almost a million dollars to a zoo that needed to upgrade its giraffe facilities," I tell him. "Well, that and setting up a trust fund for a video game at my favorite pizza parlor in Athena's Rest after having it fixed. I know how to make good use of large sums of money. Well, what normal people consider to be large sums of money."

The bathroom door creaks wider open, showing me that he's sitting on the edge of the tub, looking at his phone. His brow is wrinkled, but his voice is wary rather than irritated. "The kid at that ValuKart on Sunday is talking about it too."

"Unless one of them has prodigy-level skills with drawing people and a large internet following to share something like that, I don't think you need to worry about being made. But seriously, if you want some ideas of how to do bigger good more anonymously, I can help."

"We do reverse hold-ups where we go in with masks and throw cash around?"

"That'll get you arrested for being a public nuisance. It's the reason I had to leave my second college."

"I can never tell when you're serious."

I'm serious, but despite how much more relaxed he's seemed this afternoon, I don't want to push it by annoying him right now. "Do you have any money on gift cards, or just cash?"

"Cash was relatively easy to get."

"That's the weirdest thing I've ever heard."

"My grandfather used to hoard it," he mutters.

"He hoarded it."

"Character quirk."

"And your parents never thought to put it in a bank after he died?"

"It was pocket change."

I don't remember when the hundred-dollar bill was last updated, but I'm relatively certain his grandfather didn't live long enough to add a significant number of them to his collection. "So you're carrying around a bunch of old money? Literally old money?"

"Archie's in banking. He said it'll be fine."

"Archie? *Archie Westmore? He* knows what you're doing?"

"He's not an asshole."

"*He's the reason*—no, wait, let me reprocess this… Yep. Still a little mad, but also it's funny now."

"What's funny?"

"He's the reason I had to go to third-grade jail. My father *hated* his family. And that's what makes it funny."

Oliver smiles again.

A real smile.

A friendly smile.

Not a pushover smile, not a manipulative smile, not a reluctant smile, just a normal old smile that makes my heart pitter-patter again.

Freaking heart.

"He didn't suggest Visa or American Express gift cards?" I say.

"Maybe he's a little bit of an asshole."

"He was an absolute asshole in third grade."

Oliver gives me the single brow lift of *tell the story or quit talking about it*.

"Do you remember Mrs. Zingle reading a story to you when you were in third grade about the melting polar ice caps?"

"No."

I swallow back the *of course you don't*. He and Margot were in third grade a few years before I was. Maybe Mrs. Zingle didn't read it to them. But she probably did. She was old and set in her ways. "Well, *I* do, and I decided to do something about it."

It would be nice if he'd roll his eyes and mutter a sarcastic *of course you did* here, but that's not what Oliver does.

Oh, no.

The man smiles bigger at me, his eyes crinkling and his perfect teeth flashing and that thing he's doing with rubbing his hand over his scruffy jaw finishing up the look of a man who wants to hear more.

Like he's encouraging me.

Like he wants to know my story of triumph with a happy ending, even though he knows it ended with me in third-grade jail.

My first public activism that got me locked up.

"What does Archie have to do with you saving the polar ice caps?" he asks.

"Third grade—Mrs. Zingle reading us that book—that's when I decided to save the polar bears."

His eyes crinkle tighter at the edges as his smile grows. "All by yourself at third-grade years old."

"Eight. You're generally about eight in third grade. And yes. Of course I was."

"Did Archie talk you into stealing Mrs. Zingle's car to sell for the cause?"

"*No.* My parents laughed at me when I asked them for a jillion dollars to save the polar bears and the ice caps, so I took matters into my own hands and raided their closets, then started selling what I'd procured to my classmates."

The man smiles even bigger. "They clearly left you no choice."

"Damn right. I started small, like the shoes in the back of my mom's closet and my dad's cuff links that he never wore, and when I didn't get caught for a week or so, I started pilfering their watches and diamonds too. They had so many. It's not like they were going to notice."

He shakes his head.

I wonder what he's doing with his own cuff links and watches and designer wardrobe. He didn't bring any of it with him, but I suppose he could've had what he wanted to keep shipped to his final destination.

My former wardrobe all went to a consignment shop to set me up with the tiniest of nest eggs. Comparatively speaking.

And that was after I paid off my speeding tickets.

"So Archie ratted you out," Oliver says.

"No, I got caught when I walked into an appliance store with $38,000 in cash and asked how many air conditioners we could send to the North Pole. That was about the same time other parents started calling the school to ask questions about why their kids were coming home with used Manolos and Piguet watches. So I ended up in the principal's office in third-grade jail for a straight week so they could monitor my every breath. And *then* my father had the biggest shit fit of his life when he found out I sold his grandfather's cuff links to Percival Westmore's son."

"Not exactly Archie's fault."

"Technically not. But Archie called my shoes ugly and said I had a giant mole when I got my first pimple at school that year, so I charged him one hundred percent sales tax, and *that* had ol' Percy calling up my father to yell about ridiculous pricing and fees, which got me an extra week of being grounded at home too."

"You were grounded for an extra week for price gouging your father's least favorite person's son? Would've thought he'd take you out to ice cream for that."

"My father never took me out for ice cream, and Archie wouldn't give me the cuff links back even at double what he paid for them, and also, my parents are assholes. To the best of my knowledge, my mother still hasn't noticed she's short three pearl necklaces and a brooch that I sold from her jewelry closet."

Oliver's smile slips, and he looks down at his phone again while his leg bounces under the harsh bathroom lights. "Did you charge Archie enough to buy new safety equipment for a gymnastics group?"

"Close."

"Didn't save the polar bears and ice caps though."

"Not yet. If I'd known my parents were going to revoke my trust fund, I would've done what Margot's done and filtered money out of it into a separate fund with a good money manager so I could've kept on doing bigger good in the world without being so dependent on the family. Of course, she's like you. Fully owns her own trust fund and got it early because she was so responsible."

His smile has fully disappeared now. "I want to live a life where I feel like I'm rich because of who I'm with and the satisfaction I get from what I do. Not because I was born with a billion-dollar trust fund."

"Being CEO wasn't satisfying?"

He lifts his head and stares at me, and I see it again.

The way he looks so much older than his thirty-one years.

The random gray hairs. The bags under his eyes. The slump of his shoulders. Even his skin seems old and worn, though less than it was when we started this trip.

"Yeah. Zero sleep and massive stress and second-guessing myself becoming my primary occupation and constantly having my mother whining that I wouldn't let her sell any of her stock to keep up appearances with her wardrobe and her parties and her cars was so bone-deep satisfying."

I wince. This man is *not* going back into that role. And that's a shame for all of the nonprofits he funded. "At least you know you did a good job."

"Kept the lights on and made the stock price go up," he mutters. "Way to go, Oliver. Way to set your family up to make more money that they don't need and definitely don't deserve."

I should've expected him to be this self-aware by now, but it still takes me by surprise. "You don't think they deserve it?"

"It wasn't only the wine scam, Daphne. My father almost ran the company into the ground, and it's a sheer miracle that the right people were already on staff to steer me to do any better than he did. He's a shitty businessman and a shitty CEO who's never once looked himself in the mirror and asked *why was I the one chosen to live an easy life with more money than god?"*

I shift on the bed. "I used to think about that all of the time. I finally decided it was because the universe knew that once I had full access to my trust fund, I'd invest in the world's animals and forests and oceans. Like, that was how I'd balance it. By using what I didn't earn for the good of the entire world."

His green-dotted hazel eyes study me, and for the first time in my life, I don't feel judged by someone from back home about it.

Not that everyone was an asshole.

It's more that I was incredibly single-minded about it at the expense of everything else.

Annoying is what it was most often called.

But Oliver—warmth floods my chest as I realize it's respect coming out of his expression.

Appreciation.

Validation glows inside of me. *Someone* gets it. Someone I'd expected to judge me, but instead, he gets it.

"The only time Margot and I ever had a fight, it was about trickle-down economics." He waves a hand, like he's saying, *yes, yes, it's boring, I'm boring, we've covered that.* "She'd never stopped to consider that maybe it didn't work the way our parents said it did. That *we* were supposed to trickle it down—not other rich people, but *us*—and we didn't, but we told ourselves we did."

I unfortunately understand what he's talking about because economics and business and tax breaks for the rich funding better paychecks for the poor was a regular topic of conversation at my dinner table growing up.

"Did you trickle it down when you were in charge?" I ask him.

"Of fucking course I did." He smiles, but this isn't a nice smile.

This is—oh my god.

It's a *petty* smile.

the grumpiest billionaire

I like his petty side.

"I cut my mother's salary first to do it," he tells me.

I stare at him for the briefest of moments before I crack up. "*No.*"

"She didn't do any real work for the company. She didn't need a salary. I cut my own too."

"You might be my favorite CEO ever."

He sighs and shakes his head.

"You think your dad will give her back the, erm, job?" I ask.

He stares at me a beat too long, as if there's something I'm clearly missing. But then he shakes his head. "If he notices."

"Wouldn't *she* notice?"

"No. She never knew she was getting a salary in the first place. She has zero understanding of how any of the family finances work and very little money of her own. My father screwed her too, and she doesn't even know it."

I open my mouth, then shut it again.

That would've been me if I'd married into a family in our zip code instead of getting disinherited and deciding to give my family the middle finger by thriving on next to nothing, so I shouldn't judge.

Not because I don't understand money.

More because I would've been too distracted spending it on good causes to notice if it was mine, his, or ours.

I care less about the specifics and more about the end goal.

"Did you correct that too?" I ask.

"Yep."

"That sounds ominous."

"The optics of anyone in the family selling M2G shares the past few years were awful, so instead, I sold several vacation homes and artwork and the rarest dinnerware we possessed to get her set up with money of her own since she insisted on paying for appeal after appeal after appeal the minute he surrendered to prison."

"My mother would've died," I whisper.

"Mine claimed she was going to. She was counting the seconds until my father got out of prison so he'd fund her shopping sprees again and her friends would quit judging her for wearing fashion that's four years out of date. He'll have to sell stock to do it because that's about all he has left." He grins. "Especially since I took all of Grandpa's cash with me when I left."

"Your family will still have enough shares to keep majority control in the family?"

I don't know much, but I know that always mattered to my father.

Keep fifty-one percent in the family. Always keep a majority share in the family.

We were born with it, and it was our obligation to die with it.

Or so he wanted us to believe.

I'm sometimes still blown away that in this day and age, he also wants to use Margot's marriageability to further the goals of the company, but he does.

Easier to keep it than get it back, he always said. *So marry people who already have it.*

I knew that was part of Margot's relationship with Oliver, but she seemed to like him too, and she *was* hurt when he broke up with her.

"I don't care who has a controlling share in the company," he tells me. "I'm dead serious about giving everything of mine away. Seeing it go to good use. Making a difference in the world instead of holding on to it."

I'm not smiling anymore.

My job is definitely toast. I can't imagine there's another executive in the world who'd continue to put goodwill over profits.

And this Oliver?

The guy who's doing everything I ever wanted to do, in his own way, but for the same reason?

He's making my heart pound in ways that it hasn't pounded for anyone in years, and it's both terrifying and thrilling.

He and I—we see eye to eye on things I never expected. He's doing what I *wanted* to do.

the grumpiest billionaire

What I screwed up for myself but he was smart enough to pull off. *Because* he was boring for so long.

But he's not boring anymore.

Not even close.

I rub my temples. My neck is aching again, and now my whole chest is too.

Can't fix that, but I can work on something else.

There have to be millions in Oliver's suitcases, and there's no chance he's giving away this much cash before he's supposedly due back from his vacation. That's a lot to give away in under two weeks.

"Did you *actually* have a plan for giving this all away?" I gesture to the bags.

"Do you even know what plans are?" he teases back.

I ignore the barb because he's not far off base with the question, plus, there's no heat in his voice. Only playfulness. "You could use this to pay cash for your groceries for the rest of your life and still die with your mattress stuffed full."

He shoves off the edge of the tub, closes the small distance between the bathroom and the bed and sits beside me on the edge. "I had exactly enough time to plan an escape route. Not enough time to plan day-to-day logistics. I just—I assumed I'd find the way to give it all away in the moment. Once I had moments. And now—we haven't even gone through twenty thousand, have we?"

I run a hand through his hair.

It's natural and easy to want to comfort him in his feeling of failure, and I don't even think about it. I just scratch his scalp through his thick hair.

"Don't worry about a thing, Ollie. I'm on the job now. I'll have you down a million by this time tomorrow."

He turns his head so he's staring at me.

Eyes dark.

Unreadable.

Breath shallow.

My hand stills in his hair as I realize I shouldn't be touching him. Not at all.

Not for any reason.

"You will, won't you?" he says softly.

Reverently.

I don't snatch my hand back. I don't *want* to.

His hair is thick with more silver strands than there should be, and I want to keep touching it.

I want to keep touching him while he's so blatantly admiring me for wanting to do the same kind of good in the world that he wants to do.

"I'm very determined when I set my mind to something."

"I never thought to like that about you until right now."

"You shouldn't like anything about me."

"Am I your polar bear?"

"What?"

"Your cause. Your mission. Right now. You being here. Am I your polar bear? Am I your melting ice caps?"

I shake my head.

One of his brows arches up again. I want to trace it with my finger. And lick it.

Hoooo boy, I'm in trouble.

"I can't figure out your tell," he says, "but this time, I know you're lying."

I can't make my voice work normally. It's uneven and throaty and I should absolutely not be talking. "You're not my melting polar ice caps. You—you've needed a friend. This week."

"You've changed."

"So have you."

He holds my gaze, and it feels like a lifetime hanging between us.

He *has* changed. He's bossy and grumpy and short-tempered, but he's also kind and thoughtful and patient and funny.

Sometimes all at once, which shouldn't be possible, but it is.

I bite my lip. I need to pull my hand out of his hair, but instead, I seem to be pulling his head closer to mine. "You're not boring," I whisper when I should tell him to back up, even though, again, I'm the one steering this dumpster fire of a ship.

His lips quirk up once more, and I'm done.

Gone.

Completely smitten with zero chance of a rescue.

"You're not a complete disaster," he murmurs back.

He's wrong, but I'm still smiling as our lips touch.

This is a complete disaster.

And if there's one thing I do in the face of disaster, it's lean in even more.

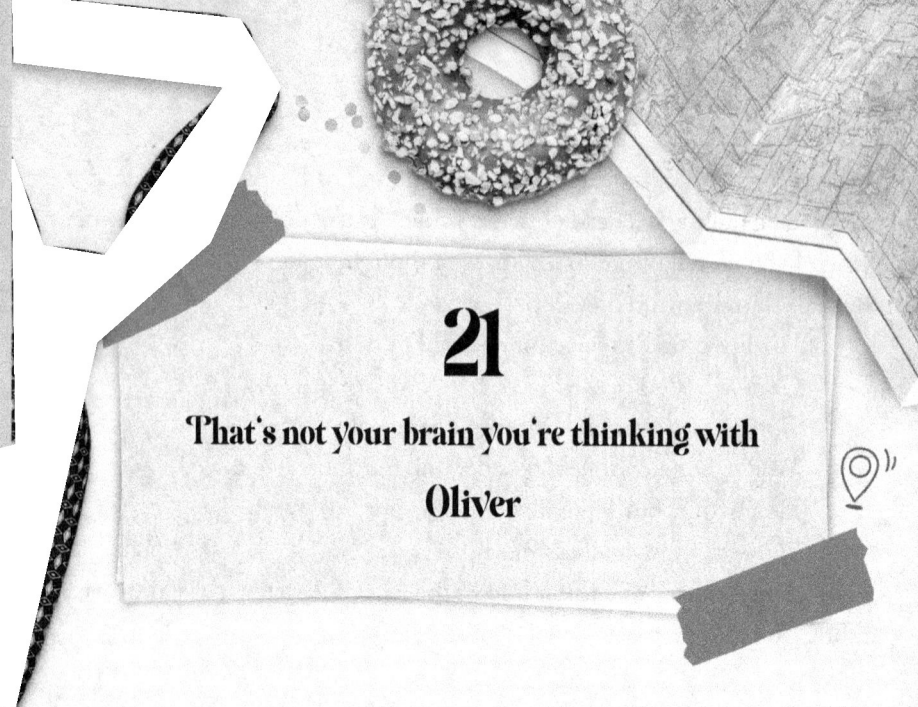

21

That's not your brain you're thinking with

Oliver

S*top kissing her.*
It's the order my head is giving my mouth, but my mouth doesn't want to listen.

She still tastes like pecan pie.

And that pecan pie was the craziest, sugariest, most terrible, most delicious thing I've ever tasted in my life.

In the sweets category.

Don't ask me to compare it to fast-food fried fish.

"You're out of practice," she says in a wispy breath against my lips.

"Clearly need so much help."

"For the future."

"Yes."

This isn't practice for some future concept of a woman.

I don't need *practice*, though I'm happy to play the part if it gets me what I want.

And what I want is to kiss Daphne because I'm drunk on pecan pie and grits and anxiety born of tasting freedom and peace this afternoon before realizing that I'm doing my escape wrong, and kissing Daphne is settling everything that's wrong.

the grumpiest billionaire

Even though kissing Daphne is inherently wrong.

Stop. Kissing. Her.

I hear the order again, and once again, I ignore it.

Because she's threading her fingers deeper into my hair, adding her other hand to hold me in place while she sucks at my lower lip and scrapes her teeth over it, and the only thing to do when a willing woman is kissing you is to kiss her back.

It's a rule.

Or something.

And when you're kissing a woman back, you're morally obligated to run your fingers through her hair too.

Scoot closer.

Lose yourself.

And that's what I'm doing.

I'm losing myself. Letting myself go.

The way I've wanted to for years.

But I never knew I'd want to lose myself with her.

That she could be the answer to all of my worries and inadequacies and questions about if I belong.

"This isn't personal," she murmurs through the kiss.

"Practice," I agree.

She tugs, and I follow her down onto the bed, deepening the kiss until our tongues are teasing each other.

I'm hard as steel, my cock pressing against her thigh while she holds me closer and slants her mouth to kiss me more thoroughly.

This is wrong.

But also right.

Forbidden.

Necessary at the same time.

I need—I need to do something bad.

Something wrong.

Something that finally makes me feel free of the shackles of my old life.

With someone who can show me how to live.

"If anyone asks, this didn't happen," I say.

"We're not actually here."

"I'm stopping right now."

I'm not stopping.

She's not stopping.

She doesn't push me away.

That leg looping around my hips is definitely not her pushing me away.

Nor is the way she's sucking on my tongue.

Fuck me sideways, is this what euphoria feels like?

No.

No, simply kissing her isn't euphoria.

Sliding my hand under her shirt and following her hot, silky skin from her waist to her bra is euphoria.

Is a woman's skin supposed to feel this good beneath my fingers?

Or is this still the pecan pie and the grits and the aftereffects of anxiety?

"You should definitely practice taking my bra off," she gasps against my mouth while her hands stroke my neck and over my shoulders and down my back to my ass.

"Good skill."

"You have a lot to learn."

"Terrible teacher."

"Best teacher."

"Bossy. No real instructions."

"Practice—best way."

I would like to continue playing at practicing whatever this is that we're doing—the kissing and the stroking and the teasing and the lying to each other—for an eternity.

Clearly I need practice at *something*, given the way I'm fumbling through trying to get Daphne's bra unhooked.

the grumpiest billionaire

"Try harder." She slaps me lightly on the ass, making my cock throb in new and unexpected ways.

But she's not being an asshole.

She's being hilarious and sexy and fun and inspiring and everything that I've been starved for my entire life.

I straighten on the bed, grab her shirt by the hem, and tug it over her head, getting it stuck when she doesn't move her arm right.

So I leave it like that.

With it shoved over her head, one arm stuck with her elbow bent, and I roll her onto her side so that I can see what I'm doing.

Her belly shakes with laughter. "Oh my god, Oliver, I'm *stuck*."

"I prefer you this way."

She laughs harder.

Until I touch the fairy dust sprinkles tattooed across her belly, tracing the little dots up over her chest, to her shoulder, where the first tattooed fairy is touching her wand to Daphne's collarbone, making all of the sprinkles fall down.

Now she's sucking in a breath, goosebumps rising across her chest and abdomen.

I bend and lick a path of them between her breasts.

"Oh my gaaa," she whimpers.

"Is that a good *oh my gaaa*, or a bad *oh my gaaa*?" I rub my stubbled chin between her breasts. "I need context to properly learn anything."

I'd like to say I'm better than adequate in the bedroom, but I've had maybe a half-dozen one-night stands in the past few years, generally at someone else's urging and insistence that it would relieve some of my stress. It never did.

My life and I didn't get along.

Probably still don't, but this—this is fun.

It is.

It's *fun*.

She fights with her shirt and finally gets it over her head, then slides her bra all the way off too, lying there with nothing on top but a smile and two pillowy mounds that I want to squeeze while she runs her fingers through my hair again and I nibble at the side of her breast.

"You're terrible at undressing a woman," she tells me, but her words don't match the irregular hitches in her breathy voice.

I slide a hand up her ribs and indulge in flicking a thumb over the tight pink nub at the tip of her breast.

"Clearly awful," I agree while her eyes cross and then her lashes flicker shut.

"The worst." She finishes the word with a gasp when I scrape my teeth over her nipple, and when I glance up at her, she's smiling.

Belly quivering.

Breath coming quickly.

Nipples pebbled.

And still smiling while I tease her breasts with my mouth and my hand.

Fun.

Easy.

No pressure.

I trace the line of fairy dust on her tattoo again. "Am I doing this right, or am I supposed to be playing with your elbows or your belly button too?"

"My *elbows*?" She cracks up, and I glow inside.

I made her laugh.

She shoves my shoulder and pushes me to my side, then tackles the buttons on my shirt.

I kiss her collarbones. "Aren't you supposed to rip it off?"

"Not when you're poor and don't know how to sew."

It has clearly been too long since I've seen a naked woman because I can't stop drinking in the sight of her breasts as they sway between us and the fairy tattoos all over her skin. "I'll save a few million for myself so I can afford new shirts when women rip them off me."

She giggles.

Giggles.

I nip at her neck, and the giggles disappear behind another catch of her breath.

She shoves one side of my shirt off my shoulder, her fingernails trailing down my bicep, and I go cross-eyed.

From a woman touching my *arm*.

Am I oversensitive, or is this—

"Less thinking, more touching." She shoves me onto my back.

I arch one brow at her and roll so she's beneath me again, her neck under my lips, her legs hooked around my hips again.

Her skin is addictive.

It's—

I snort with laughter as I suck harder at her neck.

"You gonna share with the—*ooooh, right there*—class?" she asks.

"No."

Even when I'm losing my mind, I'm absolutely not telling her that her skin tastes like coffee and pecan pie.

My two favorite things in the world.

One old, one new.

Like—like whatever this is.

Old me, new me.

Old her, new her.

Old—holy fuck, that's a good angle with her pussy.

My eyes cross again while she tightens her legs around my hips and rocks her center against my cock.

Why are pants?

Sincerely, why do humans wear pants?

Tremendously inconvenient.

Need to go.

All of the layers.

When did I start kissing her mouth again? How—what—where did she learn to—just *whoa*.

Her tongue is my new favorite toy.

Her tongue, and her arms, and her breasts—god, her *breasts*—and that whimpery little noise in the back of her throat when I squeeze them and tease her nipples.

"Pants—" she gasps.

"Why pants are?" I agree.

Can't talk straight.

She giggles again, but then she's moaning as I drop my head to her chest and suck on her nipple while I tug at her waistband.

"Oliver—"

"Be useful," I tell her breast.

Why does it make me harder to swirl my tongue around this tight pink nub?

Oh. Right.

Pecan pie, anxiety, and—

I forgot the last one.

Freedom.

That's it.

That has to be it.

She wiggles beneath me, and my pants slide away.

She wiggles again, and her pants are gone.

"Magician," I whisper against her breast.

Those fingers thread through my hair again. "Are you drunk?"

"Happy."

She grins at me, and yeah.

This?

This is all good things.

Naked.

Kissing.

Touching.

Daphne.

New life.

New start.

Freedom.

No going back after this.
It's a line.
I'm crossing it.
For the first time in my life, I'm being bad.
I'm off course. I'm off schedule. I'm *lost*. I'm happy.
I'm—"Condoms?"
Fuck.
Fuck fuck *fuck*.
Her eyes are dancing. "All out."
"*Fuuuuuuuck.*"
"IUD," she says.
I stare at her a minute while the letters sink in.
Her grin gets grinnier. "It's birth control."
"*I know that*, you little pain in the ass."
She wiggles beneath me, teasing my cock, but now with her bare pussy, and *fuck me fuck me fuck me*, what's control again?

"This is where you confess if you have any STIs that I need to worry about," she says while she glides her fingernails over my shoulders again.

I shake my head into her breasts. "No fooling around for—I'm clear."

"Who would've thought we'd have *that* in common," she murmurs.
And it's the freaking funniest thing in the world.
Grits.
The grits were spiked.
That's the only explanation for my mood.
Other than—
Nope.
Doesn't matter.

Daphne tightens her legs around me and scrapes her nails up my neck, and absolutely nothing else matters.

Nothing but her sweet pussy and my raging hard-on and kissing her pecan pie coffee skin and breathing in the scent of freedom and new beginnings and her arousal while listening to the sound of her sucking in another breath as I scrape my teeth over her nipple.

"Good," she gasps. "A-plus."

I want to bite a path down the fairy dust on her soft belly too.

Next time.

"I must be a natural."

Her laugh is far more breathy this time.

More breathy.

More turned on.

Aroused.

By *me*.

Boring, simple, plain ol' *me*.

I flex my hips, and my cock sinks into her hot, wet core.

"Oh, fuck," she whispers.

I pause. "Good fuck?"

"Good fuck." She pulls me tighter, taking me deeper with a soft moan. "Keep good fucking."

"Good fucking," I agree.

I inch deeper.

My brain melts.

My hips buck.

Her pussy squeezes me.

I can't breathe.

Can't think.

Can't do anything but exist right here, thrusting deep inside Daphne with her gasps and moans and cries guiding me, switching angles, rotating my hips, my balls getting tighter with every thrust and gasp and moan.

I catch her lips with my mouth again, bucking completely out of control, desperate to keep going.

Make it last.

Live in this feeling forever.

Her hands—her tongue—her pussy—her legs—her breasts—every bit of her.

I want to soak it in.

Revel in her.

Imprint this on my soul.

Carry it with me forever.

"More—there—practice—good fucking," she gasps as I rock into her.

"I'm—best—student—ever," I gasp back.

I'm not wild in bed.

Not usually.

But I feel completely out of control and absolutely as I should be while I slam into her over and over, deeper and harder, straining to hold myself back so I can live here, in her pussy, in this bed, in anonymity but where I'm welcome.

Where she's suddenly arching her back and tightening her legs around my hips, her pussy clenching around my cock so hard that my last ounce of control slips away.

"Oliver, I'm—*oh my god*," she gasps.

Yeah.

Hell yeah.

She's coming, her strong legs holding me tight, deep inside her, my eyes crossing while I come too, harder and faster and more out of control than I've ever come in my life.

My cock jerks inside her, coming and still needing to be deeper.

Can't stop.

Can't end.

Can't stop.

I strain into my release, into her, groaning and grabbing the sheets on either side of her in my fists.

"Daph—"

I cut myself off.

Can't talk through catching my breath.

Through the tremors in my legs and ass.

Through the overwhelming mix of emotions crashing together in my chest.

Because *shiiiiiiit*.

We did that.

And it was— I swallow.

Good.

Better than good.

Fucking fantastic. Life-altering. Reality-shattering.

Perfect.

Is it Daphne?

Or is it freedom?

Or am I feeling the freedom to make a massive, massive, *massive* mistake with Daphne and realizing freedom still comes with consequences?

Because not all of this is full-on post-coital glow.

There's some panic.

Panic, and—

A siren blares in the stillness, cutting off all thoughts and sending me scrambling off her and away from the bed.

"What the hell?" I yell over the noise that probably should've come a few minutes ago.

She blinks at me like she's forgotten what reality is, and then she cracks up.

"Fire alarm," she yells back. "This would *never* happen in an Aurora Gardens brand hotel."

I stare at her a moment longer while the blaring continues murdering my eardrums.

She grins while she throws my shirt at me. "So much more exciting here, isn't it? If it doesn't stop in the next minute, we have to go outside."

Or the world is telling me that we made a mistake.

A horrific mistake that we can't take back.

Daph has her back to me while she hops into her shorts and pulls her shirt on, but I can see her in the foggy mirror over the wobbly desk, and her grin isn't without regrets too.

Awesome.

This is gonna get awkward.

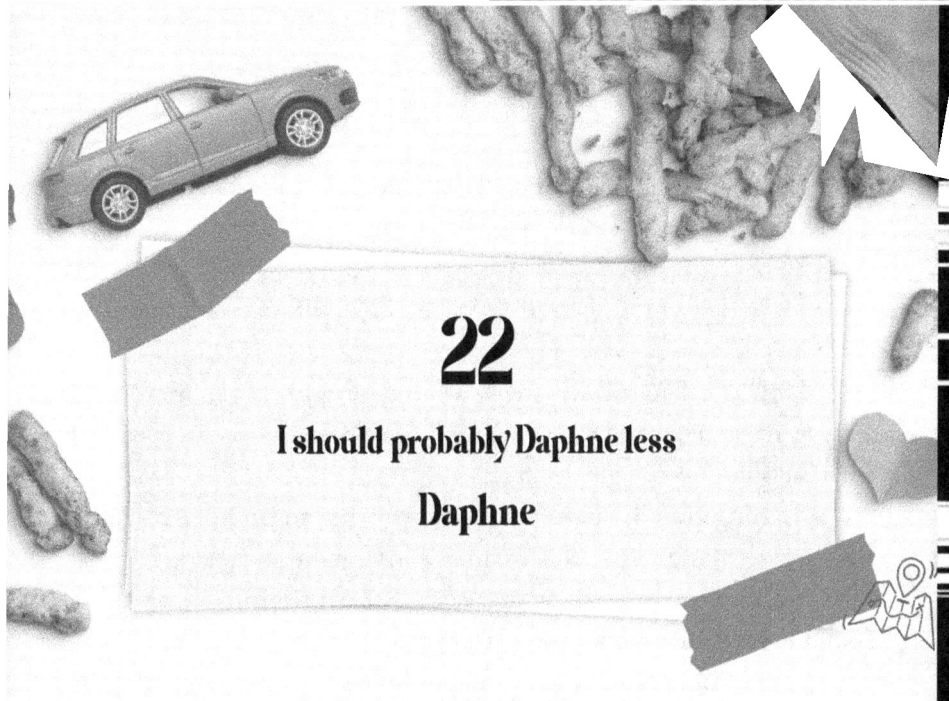

22

I should probably Daphne less

Daphne

Oooooh, shit.

I have a crush on my sister's ex-fiancé.

She's going to murder me.

Or maybe she won't.

Maybe she'll smile and be like, *well, Daphne, if you're happy, I'm happy*, but then she'll go home and cry about it and pretend she's not upset and she won't want to see me ever again, which sucks because she's the only blood relative I have left who'll talk to me.

And she matters.

When I was cut off, long-time friends abandoned me. My parents abandoned me. My living grandparents abandoned me.

Even my dog abandoned me—not truly her fault, she was super old—but she did. She died right when I needed her most.

Everyone but Margot abandoned me.

You can tell me until you're blue in the face that I chose being abandoned when I went no-contact, but they didn't make any effort to find my new number—*which Margot has*—and get in touch with me either.

They showed me in no uncertain terms that they were done with me.

And now I've gone and done something I can't take back, and if Oliver weren't Margot's ex, I wouldn't have a single regret.

I like him.

He's shown me every possible side of himself this week, and even when he's being an asshole, *I get it*, and I like him.

How can I not like a guy who wants to give his entire fortune away to make the world a better place? That's the mission I've lived and breathed since I was eight years old.

Starting over is hard. Starting over with an unexpected stowaway—the *worst* unexpected stowaway—is far more complicated.

And starting over after what's clearly been a terrible few years is bound to leave his emotions whacked up all over the place.

"How common are fire alarms in hotels?" Oliver asks me while we huddle against the side of the diner across the parking lot as the rain shower that was threatening earlier passes over us.

Like we're two people who didn't strip naked and ride each other in the name of *teaching him how*.

He's thirty-one years old.

He knows *how*.

Very, very clearly knows *how*, and I'll have the sore body to prove it tomorrow.

Holy fuck.

That's the only explanation for what that was.

It was a holy fuck. I was possessed by something otherworldly.

Except I wasn't.

This is what I do.

I mess everything up.

"They happen sometimes." Firetrucks are here, so clearly, the siren wasn't a *nothing* thing. "I know I said this wouldn't happen in my family's chains, but they do. I remember my dad shut a property completely down once because they couldn't figure out why the smoke alarms kept going off. It was getting terrible reviews, so he razed the whole building and put a new one in its place."

the grumpiest billionaire

He shoots me a quick look, then looks back through the rain at the motel. Most of the other guests have gone into the diner to hide from the rain.

Given how much Oliver tipped the staff, we didn't want to go in and be recognized.

Not after seeing the news with the kids from the lemonade stand this morning, which feels like a lifetime ago now.

"He didn't talk about individual buildings very much," I add.

As if that's necessary.

Oliver surely knows. Doubt he was spending much time on individual M2G stations the past few years unless they had specific, super-bad issues or were significantly outperforming expectations.

It's never anything in between if the guy at the top knows about it.

Oliver's chest rises as he pulls in a deep breath.

He grabbed a T-shirt—it was faster than buttons—and he has it on backward and inside out, and I don't think he realizes it.

"Does rain always smell like this?" he asks.

And my heart melts for this man a little more.

Why?

Why?

I haven't dated—not really—since I was disinherited. At first, I was too much of a mess and found myself in toxic situations more than not, and yes, sometimes it was me being the more toxic one.

I've watched Bea have a few disasters, and then there was the time working on myself, learning how to be part of a family in a healthier way, then finding my job, so dating has never taken priority.

Not to say I didn't scratch an itch here or there, but I should not have scratched an itch with Oliver.

Not when I was already starting to fall for him.

And now—has he truly never stopped to smell a rain shower?

How is that even possible?

"Rain smells different in spring than it does in summer and in fall," I tell him.

"How so?"

"In spring, it smells like the world is waking up from a long, cold slumber after the longest night of the year. Like flowers and sunshine are coming, even if they aren't here yet. In the summer, it smells like relief from the heat. Like the earth needed to jump into a swimming pool to cool down. In fall, it smells like nature is taking a shower to get ready for bed. Winding down. Putting all of its leaves away and letting the grass turn brown like I'd take off my makeup and soak in the tub for a while before going to sleep."

He's watching me without looking straight at me, like he too is realizing we've made our lives a lot more difficult.

Like I need to leave this road trip and go back to Athena's Rest and keep my freaking mouth shut, and he needs to go on without me.

That would be best.

To pretend this never happened.

"So this is summer cool-off scent?" he says.

"You've never stopped to smell the rain? I know you've *seen* rain. Everyone's seen rain."

He shakes his head and looks back across the parking lot. "When your life is one day after another after another of living up to expectations, with boxes to check and priorities set for you before you're born..."

I wrap my arms tighter around myself so I don't hug him.

That wasn't my life, but it could've been.

If Margot hadn't so firmly taken the role in our family that Oliver filled in his.

Oldest or only child.

Expectations from birth.

Trained for this.

Made for this.

And so very proficient that I didn't have to be the backup.

You can't tell me my parents and his parents didn't talk more about having an heir than they did about having a baby when they decided it was time. I know my parents. I know his parents. I wouldn't believe you if you told me they wanted to have a baby for normal instinctual reasons.

They wanted to see their family lineage and empires continue to grow under the next generation and the generation after and the generation after that too.

They didn't have us so that we could take flight and be whoever that magical little spark that made us who we are christened us to be.

He takes another deep breath, like he's trying to imprint the smell of summer evening rain onto his soul.

I hold my hand out under the overhang to feel the cool drops that are pattering softly over the parking lots. "Have you ever won a giant stuffed animal at a carnival game?"

"I can hear my father asking why I'd waste my time on a game rigged against me when I have the money to buy the damn stuffed animal."

Mine would ask the same. "What about getting your fortune told?"

"Waste of time when you can make your own fortune." He snorts softly. "Or be the lucky bastard who's born into it."

"Ever eat at a food truck?"

"Hot dog carts are for plebeians."

I know he's quoting his parents, and it's less the sarcasm dripping from his words and more that I've heard my parents say the same thing.

"Bea makes a corn dog that'll change your life."

He smiles softly. "Spoken like someone who's never had grits."

"But I *have* had tater tots dipped in very bad melted cheese, so I think I know what I'm talking about."

He makes a face like he's gagging without putting his heart into it.

It's freaking adorable.

"What else?" he asks.

"What else what?"

"What else do I need to know how to do to…to live. To be normal. To—to enjoy life on a daily basis. What normal, everyday things have I missed that I can—that I can experience now?"

Yep.

I'm a goner.

Have to leave. First thing tomorrow. No question. No doubt.

So I have tonight to tell him everything he needs to know. "Water parks. Sometimes you need to spend an afternoon floating on a lazy river through a water park while kids yell and shriek and play all around you. And if you don't have a favorite sledding hill in winter, you're missing the opportunity to feel like you're eight all over again. And apple picking. It is a moral imperative that you go apple picking in the fall with a hayride and then tease the kids around you about the apple cider having crushed worms in it."

"That's terrible."

"I didn't do it. Bea's brother did it. He's working on being the new *get off my lawn* old man."

"You laughed when he did it."

I grin. "Maybe a little. But in my defense, Bea's boyfriend that year had slipped spiced rum into my apple cider, and I was tipsy before the hayride ever started, and I think Ryker was too. Ryker doesn't get tipsy very often. He's very serious. And grumpy. You'd like him. While Bea and I are sitting on our porch someday, telling our great-nieces and great-nephews all of the stories of the trouble we got into, you and Ryker could be on the porch next door, grunting and scowling and yelling at all of us to get off your lawn."

"Wouldn't it be your lawn?"

"No, no, I have a new plan taking shape. Bea's going to guilt Ryker into letting us build our retirement home on his farm so that we're definitely on his land, and he'll let us because that's what brothers do. We'll annoy him until the day we all croak. Probably it'll be a mass casualty event when he gets fed up with us and drives a tractor into our porch."

"*Jesus.*"

"Live epic, die epic."

He stares at me.

I giggle.

Just a little.

The teensiest amount.

And then the very worst thing ever happens, and he smiles again. At me.

Like I'm funny, and he's finally realized it, and he likes it.

"Daphne—" He cuts himself off, shaking his head.

"Yes, Mr. Grumpiest Billionaire?"

That thing about him smiling being the very worst thing ever?

I was wrong.

Not unusual. I'm wrong regularly.

But this wrong makes my heart stutter in my chest, because now he's doing something even more wrong, and he's hugging me.

Hugging me, hugging me.

Tight.

Both arms wrapped hard around my ribs, his head buried in my neck while he breathes like he's now imprinting the scent of *me* on his soul, the same way he was imprinting the smell of the rain.

"Are you trying to suffocate me?" I ask in the delectable lemon-and-sex-scented heat of his hug. "Because if you are, you're doing it wrong."

"I like you."

It's eighty degrees outside, and the rain's not doing as much to cool down the parking lot as it is to increase the humidity levels, but a full-body chill passes through me. "That's a bad idea," I whisper.

"Why?"

"Margot—"

"Margot and I are over. *Over* over. Forever. And I think she'd tell you the same."

I shiver again. "Look, Oliver, tonight's been fun—"

"I *need* fun, Daph. I don't want to sit on a porch yelling at you to get off my lawn. I want to be the guy being yelled at to get off someone else's lawn. I want to live. I want to feel things. I want to have fun. I want—I want to know how to be more like you."

Good thing I already don't talk to my parents.

Pretty sure they'd disinherit me all over again if they could if they ever found out I was teaching their dream son-in-law how to be more like *me*.

He tightens the hug even harder. "I'll buy you all of the brass polar bears you want. But don't—please don't run away because of—because of what we did tonight. I'm not ready to let you go. I have too much to learn."

I close my eyes and do the same thing I've watched him do tonight, and I suck in a big breath full of the scent of him.

He's a disaster.

But he's *my* disaster.

Temporarily.

For now.

It's not like Archie Westmore's going to step into my shoes and help Oliver figure out all the little ways he can enjoy a simpler life. Archie would have him on golf courses and yachts and private jets.

Not road trips through small-town America with diners and Lava Cheese Puffs and weird souvenirs.

"Have you done your own laundry yet?" I ask.

"Never."

"I can definitely teach you how to do that wrong. You haven't lived until you've turned all of your underwear pink."

His breath shudders out of him like he's been afraid I'd tell him no.

That I'm abandoning him.

As if I could.

Most of my family abandoned me. Most of my friends too.

I won't do that to another soul who needs me.

Even Oliver, who's the last person I should be helping, for so many reasons.

I'm not fooling myself. I know when he says *I like you*, what he means is *my life is a mess and you're helping me and there are too many big feelings for me to sort through all of them and understand the difference between liking you and appreciating the help from anyone who'd be in your shoes.*

Even if I know I *do* like him.

That I'm setting myself up for complete and total wreckage of my heart.

But Bea saved me once. She took in a friend and showed me how to survive when she already had her brothers and a lot of other things on her plate.

And I believe in nothing if not the karmic balance of the universe.

So it doesn't matter that my toes are still tingling from that orgasm and my recently dormant vagina is hoping this hug goes somewhere else, a clear sign that I need to leave.

Oliver still needs me.

Oliver still *wants* me.

And so I'll stay.

23

I think it's you
Oliver

Daphne talks in her sleep.

Not all night—just in the morning, as the sunlight slowly seeps in through the curtains that I didn't close all of the way last night.

"Bear cave turned the car inside out," she mumbles.

I'm barely breathing as I lie beside her on the bed, watching her facial muscles twitch and her eyelids flutter.

We agreed to share the bed last night.

She put a pillow wall between us, because *sex lessons are over for tonight*, which I interpreted to mean that I shouldn't have told her that I like her.

Even though I hate it, the pillow wall is still there.

My cock is painfully hard.

Staring at her isn't helping. Not when I'm noticing things I never did before.

Like how thick her lashes are. Long, too.

The way she has tiny ears that make her simple stud earrings—all four of them in the ear that I can see—seem bigger than they are.

The sparkle of her nose ring in her nostril.

Why have I never thought nose rings were attractive before?

The ring there is so *Daphne*.

Today Daphne.

Not any Daphne that I've ever known in the past.

She's not chaos. She's controlled.

Mature.

Still something of a whirlwind, but not overwhelming. Still fun, but no longer full of poor choices.

She's intentional. She understands her power, and she wields it instead of letting it wield her.

I used to think Daphne was angry all the time. You could feel it radiating off her, and you knew it would inevitably lead to something big and terrible, but it was anyone's guess what would finally set her off and send her down a path she couldn't come back from.

Margot said she was misunderstood.

And that finally makes sense.

Daphne wanted to stop the polar ice caps from melting and she couldn't. But not only could she not, trying to on her own got her in trouble.

No one ever taught her how to steer her activism. How to accept the limits of what one person could do. How to find the people already doing the work to help them, instead of feeling like no one else cared while trying to do it all herself.

Her family wrote her off as the problem child instead of finding an outlet for her big feelings, and so her big feelings eventually turned into rage.

Like my family didn't understand my fascination with bugs and worms and dirt, and told me to focus on gasoline and convenience store profit and loss statements instead.

It took my father going to jail and me being thrust into the CEO position at M2G too early, too unprepared, and with too much of the wrong personality type for the job for those childhood dismissals to turn from quiet bruises to my psyche into my own rage.

But I got there too.

And now I can't stop wondering what else Daphne and I have in common that I never could've suspected.

I catch myself reaching for her hair and tell myself to quit projecting.

Maybe I'm completely wrong about who she is and how she feels and what she wants.

But it's the first time she's made logical sense to me.

And it explains why she's still here. Why she tolerated my bad moods and my pissy behavior at the beginning of the week.

Because Daphne has something very few others in our families have.

Compassion. Empathy. And a soul-deep understanding of what it means to not fit.

"Scupplenutter bought the big dick energy," she mutters.

Goddamn pillow wall.

The way she's talking in her sleep makes me want to hug her again.

Line our bodies up.

Kiss her awake.

I should get up. Shower before she's awake. Get breakfast and load the car.

"Wait, wait, wait, wait," she whimpers.

I freeze. "Daphne?"

"Don't drown the butterfly," she cries.

"Daph—" I put a hand to her shoulder. "Hey. Wake up. You're having—"

"*Snniiiiiccckkkkkeerrrrdoooooooodle*," she yells.

Then she snorts once.

Her eyes fly open.

She stares at me, pupils dilated and unfocused, and then she does the most Daphne thing ever, and she screams, flings an arm straight up in the air, and tumbles off the side of the bed.

She *thuds*.

I scramble across the bed. "Daph?"

the grumpiest billionaire

"Fucking fuckity fuck-bucket *fuck*," she pants. "I thought I was in Candelabra. Where is Candelabra? It's not even real, is it? Why do I name places in my dreams?"

She's irresistible, and I need to stop smiling, but I can't quite get there. "You okay?"

She rubs her head, winces, and flops onto her back, then grabs her neck. "Peachy. Why does the carpet smell like dog grease?"

"What's dog grease?"

She blinks at me again. "Don't talk to me until I've had three cups of coffee."

"Will dog grease make sense then?"

"Stupid dreams," she mutters. "I haven't slept that hard in weeks. Is it time to go?"

"It's barely after seven."

"*I slept all day?*"

"In the morning."

"*I'm on vacation and I was finally sleeping and now I'm awake before ten?*"

"Maybe next time, don't put the pillow wall on your side of a double bed."

She squeezes her eyes shut and flips me off with both hands.

Shouldn't make me happy, but it does.

I like her unfiltered. Unguarded.

Unafraid to flip me off.

Unafraid to be honestly, completely, fearlessly herself.

"Stop smiling," she orders without opening her eyes.

"What kind of coffee do you like? I haven't asked you that yet."

One eye barely squints open. "The kind with caffeine."

"Black? Cream? Sugar? I'd ask dark or light roast and Peruvian or Colombian beans, but I don't know if I can be that picky here."

"You definitely cannot be that picky here."

I high-five myself. "Look at me figuring things out."

She sighs. "Look, Oliver, if you're in a good mood because we had sex—"

"Sex puts me in a terrible mood. I hate it. It's so...*sexy*."

Now I'm getting a double-eyed blink. "What the actual hell is wrong with you today?"

"You've inspired me to be obnoxious, and it turns out, it's fun."

She pushes to sitting and groans softly.

I swing around to her side of the bed and climb onto the floor next to her, then press my thumb into the spot she keeps grabbing on her neck. "Sleep on it wrong again?"

"It'll be fine."

"You can go back to bed if you want more rest."

"Mm." She sways into me as I stroke the muscle harder.

"Suppose I'll miss my normal massage therapist," I murmur.

"That part was the worst," she mumbles.

"Was it?"

Her shoulders droop the barest amount. "No. It wasn't. Losing my phone was the worst. The absolute worst of the worst. I had to get a new number and most of my old friends wouldn't take my calls anymore, even when I left them voicemails telling them it was me."

"Shitty friends."

She sighs and mumbles something under her breath that I can't understand.

"What was that?"

"I said *thank you, that feels good*."

"Had chronic neck pain the first year I took over for my father."

"Lucky if that's all you had."

"Wasn't, but antacids and extra-strength painkillers handled the worst of the headaches and stomach problems."

"Do they know they were lucky to have you?"

I pause in rubbing her neck.

She whimpers.

It's a soft, pathetic little noise of *please don't stop touching me* that speaks directly to that muscle hiding behind my sternum.

"No idea," I tell her.

I dig deeper into that muscle between her shoulder and neck, and she makes another noise, this one an unholy groan that has my cock pulsing harder again.

I like it when she likes how I touch her.

"Why haven't you been sleeping well?" I ask her.

"Because Margot was talking about taking you back, and that was a terrible idea because you hurt her and you weren't right for each other," she whispers.

I stifle a sigh. I don't want to sigh. I want to be happy.

"Daph?"

"Yeah?"

"I've been thinking about that—whoa, don't tense up. Listen. Margot's cutthroat in business. Your father wanted us to merge companies before. He's been quietly buying up M2G stock himself. I think any interest she's had in me was for professional reasons and professional reasons only."

Her eyes slide open, and she angles a look at me.

"No judgment against Margot. She likes the business game, and she's gonna be a kick-ass CEO someday. But that makes the most sense. Far more sense than your sister wanting to set herself up to make the same mistake twice."

After one long, unreadable stare at me, she turns her face away, sighing as I keep massaging her tight muscles.

And once again, I'm hit with a glimmer of recognition that this is what life should be.

Not the part where we're camped out in a cheap motel with no idea where I'm headed today once the rest of the day gets started, but sitting with someone who's rapidly becoming important to me, taking care of her physical needs while she lets me be a little lost, a little broken, and a lot more sure by the day that I'm on the right path to finding my new way in life.

"Daphne?"

"Hmm?"

"I'm glad you're accidentally here with me. I— No one else could understand. Or do what you're doing."

She leans back fully onto me. "I'm glad you got to choose it for yourself. Instead of being kicked out. That—that has to be a little easier. I hope."

I loop my arms around her and kiss her hair.

"You know this isn't real, right?" she says quietly. "It's adrenaline and anxiety and the mirage of possibilities because of being out of normal routines."

She doesn't push me away when I lean my head on hers. "I will still appreciate what you've done for me for the rest of my life."

"Don't fool yourself. I'm only in it for the money."

"If that were true, you would've disappeared with one of my duffel bags of cash two days ago."

Her sigh ripples through her, vibrating against me.

"What do you want it for?" I ask.

"You can't ask me that before coffee."

"Because you'll tell me?"

Once more, she falls silent.

I've given up on the idea that she'll ever answer me when she shifts in my arms, twisting to hug me back. "You're not going back for anything, are you?"

"To New York?"

"To Miles2Go."

My breath sits heavy in my lungs while I absently run my hand over her hair. "No."

"When I was little, I wanted to save the world. I didn't. I couldn't. But you—Oliver, you've been saving the world. You've been *doing it*. All of that money you funneled into nonprofits? I work for one. I have a job—I have a *purpose*, I have a direction, I'm finally making a difference every day—because of what you did at Miles2Go. You—you did so much good. I hope you know that. Because it matters. It matters to me, and it matters to the world."

I swallow hard while I drop my head against hers. My skin is too tight and my lungs are shrinking and my pulse is hitting those zones that used to result in my executive assistant calling for the in-house doctor to come check me out. "Daph, I'm *not* going back. It would—it would literally kill me."

"I know," she whispers. "You look like a really, really, really old man."

This freaking woman.

One minute, she has me on the verge of a nervous breakdown, and the next, she's insulting me so poorly that I'm snorting in amusement.

While still hovering at the edge of a panic attack.

"Oliver, listen—you deserve the life you want to live. But I—I need you to know that no matter what anyone said about stock prices and profit margins and brand loyalty and all of that other bullshit corporate stuff—the choices you made changed the world for the better in a million tiny little ways. And I'll forever be grateful to *you* for that. Not to Miles2Go. To you. Because no one else in your seat would've done it."

My eyes sting.

If people sent thank-you cards for the revenue I funneled into charities, I didn't see them.

The day-to-day of saving M2G from the brink of bankruptcy kept me chained to my desk and not out in the world to see the impact. The marketing and PR departments wanted me out at fundraiser dinners every weekend, but after the first six months, I was so burned out that I refused to go anymore. I didn't even have regular interactions with people outside of normal work hours unless it was my mother harping on me or Archie showing up to occasionally force me to go golfing or out to dinner on the days that he didn't meet me in the gym to spar in an attempt to work off the stress.

I hadn't even seen my own pet project—the butterfly gardens—until a few days ago.

Everything I did—I had no idea how it was being received or if it was making a difference.

"It was half spite," I confess. "My father hated how low I kept the profit margins, so I kept pushing them lower and lower and lower with more and more donations and investments in various causes that I kept making my staff find for me. Just to piss him off."

She turns to look up at me. "Do you know the first memory I have of you?"

"If there's one thing I've learned in the past five days, it's to not answer questions like that."

"You should've learned that five seconds after meeting me."

I shouldn't be smiling.

I shouldn't.

Yet here I am. "Fair enough."

"My first memory that I have of you was you telling me that I should quit getting myself arrested if I wanted to ever have peace in my family."

I blink at her.

Then blink again. "When's the first time you were arrested? Not third-grade jail. Honestly arrested."

"Maybe eight or nine years ago? I was in college."

"So your first memory of me isn't until after I started dating your sister?"

"Yep."

"We went to grade school together."

"But not the same year group. You were in Margot's class."

"We were in the same school for half of high school too."

"Yeah, and I don't remember you. You must've been even more boring than I thought you were."

My eyes cross, but this one isn't nearly as enjoyable as when they crossed last night.

She grins at me. "Fucking up your father's profits isn't boring though. That gets high marks in my book. Good job. A-plus again."

I don't know how she does it, but she has me smiling again. "You're obnoxious."

"Defense mechanism that goes with abandonment issues." She sighs happily and leans back on me. "Do you think there are dried bodily fluids in this carpet that we shouldn't be sitting in?"

I shudder.

She grins wider.

"Goddammit, was that a test?"

Her laughter is all the answer I need.

It's music.

It's happiness.

It's inspiration.

And that inspiration has me picking her up off the floor, tossing her over my shoulder, and carrying her into the bathroom.

"*Oliver!*" she shrieks. "What are you doing?"

"Showering other people's dried bodily fluids off of us."

"I can shower myself."

"Sorry, don't trust you to not stuff a soaked rag down your pants to slap me with when I fall asleep waiting for you to be ready to go get coffee and breakfast."

"Who are you, and how have you figured out all of my tricks?"

It's my turn to grin, and I'm grinning harder than I've ever grinned in my life as I deposit her in the bathtub. "Clothes on or off? Three seconds to decide before I'm turning the water on."

"Don't you dare, you—*ahhhhhh!*"

It's the spark of a challenge in her dark brown eyes that makes me do it.

The tilt of her lips.

The fists on her hips.

The dare.

She's *daring* me to.

And so I do.

I turn the shower on at full blast.

24

Whoops, we did it again

Daphne

I shriek as the freezing water spikes into my hair and shoulders. Oliver stands at the side of the tub, preening, clearly proud of himself.

So I grab him by the T-shirt and yank, pulling him under the cold spray of water too.

He coughs and sputters, then climbs into the bathtub with me, stripping off his shirt, then his sleeping shorts, then his tighty-whities.

Oh, fuck.

Fuck, fuck, fuck.

I mean, yes, good fuck, but also, we shouldn't—

He cuts off my internal screaming by tossing his clothes over the shower curtain rod, one by one, and with every *plop* of wet clothes, I cannot help the giggles that come out of me.

"You can't be in here," I tell him while I struggle out of my own wet T-shirt. "We don't both fit."

This is a remarkably small bathtub.

It's maybe large enough to bathe a Pomeranian.

Maybe.

"We fit fine," he informs me.

I point at his morning boner, and my vagina tingles with the memory of what he can do with that thing. "We're not doing anything in here."

"We're conserving water."

"Who are you, and what have you done with Oliver?"

"He doesn't exist anymore." He traces the waistline of my panties with one finger.

They're soaked.

And the shower water isn't the only reason.

He has the best hands. I don't know why I never noticed before, but he does.

Large.

Capable. With thick veins running over the backs of them.

His nails are short and well-kept.

I wonder if they'll stay that way now that he's out of the boardroom.

The thought of him working with me, digging up weeds, planting new native greenery, fixing fences—I shiver.

He'd look good working outside in the sun.

His fingers follow the path of fairy sprinkle tattoos up my belly again, like they did last night, lighting my skin up in goosebumps that are only partially from the initial cold blast of the shower.

"Oliver—" Shit.

That was a breathy, needy, *take me now* way of saying his name.

"Are all normal showers this small? How am I supposed to ask a woman to wash my back if we can't both fit in here?" he asks.

A throbbing need pulses low in my abdomen at the thought of washing his back. "No, not all normal showers are this small."

"Although it's not terrible. Turn sideways. For science. So I can see if we fit."

I'm stupidly turned on and smiling at the same time.

If he weren't my sister's ex, on a runaway mission from his life, I'd have him pushed against the shower wall while I tasted every inch of his wet skin so fast. "You're ridiculous."

"High praise coming from the fairy princess of chaos." He makes a spinning motion with his hand. "Go on. Turn sideways, or I'll eat all of your cheese puff things and only stop at stores where they're sold out for the rest of the trip."

I mock gasp. *God*, this is fun. "You wouldn't."

"I would, *and* I could. Don't test my methods of tracking inventory in every store in the country."

He's staring at my breasts like he's thinking the same thing about that wall and tasting my skin.

"I can always hit the Lickie for more cheese puffs."

His eyes darken when I say *Lickie*.

I'm still in my panties.

I could lose them and let him rail me against the shower wall.

And hope we don't fall out.

This is the tiniest tub I've ever seen, even smaller than the tub in the tiny house. It's a very tight squeeze with both of us in here.

And don't get me started on how much room his woody is taking.

"We should shower and hit the road." I cannot believe I'm being the responsible one, but someone has to be, and clearly today, that someone is me. "I need to teach you to do laundry."

He pulls a face like I'm the meanest teacher in the world. "Boring."

God, who would've thought he could make me laugh so easily? "What's with you today? You're—"

I don't know how to describe him.

Happy?

That seems lame.

He's—

His face breaks into the widest smile I've ever seen. "Free. I'm free."

And there goes my heart again.

Thudding in happiness for him.

"Stop being so attractive," I whisper.

"No."

I crack up again.

He tugs at my panties. "C'mon, Daphne. I have to learn how to have shower sex."

"*Oh my god*, you have to already know how to have shower sex."

"Nope. That's not something boring people do. Clearly. I need lessons."

The man is entirely too funny this morning. "Maybe you have to learn how to earn it."

He grips my chin and tilts my head back, directly into the stream of now-hot water. "Is it true women like having someone else wash their hair?"

"Some women."

"Are you among those?"

I hesitate.

Yes means we're having sex in this tiny tub.

No means I deprive myself of having someone else wash my hair.

There's no good option here.

It's lose-lose.

Except for the orgasm part.

Unless he sucks at shower sex.

Which seems unlikely despite his insistence that he doesn't know how.

"Have you ever thought this hard in your entire life?" he murmurs.

"No, and it's rude of you to make me do it before coffee."

He's still holding my head under the hot water, face tilted up so that it's not sluicing down into my eyes.

His other hand brushes the underside of my breast, and his boner pokes me in the belly.

There's not a single solitary part of me that doesn't want to grip his cock and stroke it and ask him to lather up and wash me all over, except for that one little brain cell screaming that he's my sister's ex.

But we already had sex last night.

And his confidence that Margot wouldn't want him back for anything more than professional reasons now—that makes sense.

She's not generally one to set herself up for the same mistake twice.

So what's one more round in the shower before we leave?

Screw it. "I can't let you wash my hair while I'm still in my panties."

He has them at my ankles practically before I'm done with the word *panties*.

When he straightens, he's closer. His hard-on drags up my leg, brushing my pussy.

My clit aches at the barest hint of attention.

But he tilts my head back into the water again, running his fingers through it, getting it fully damp.

I wrap my hands around his cock and stroke it.

His eyes cross.

Honestly, mine almost do too.

He's thick and long and hot, and gripping him, stroking him, studying him in my hands, is making me hungry for more.

"Shampoo?" he grits out.

"Sink counter."

He grunts, pulls back, fights with the shower curtain, almost falls out of the tub, but then he's back with the bottle, shaking it impatiently.

I wrap my hands around his cock again.

Take my time stroking up and down. Tracing his thick head. Dipping my hand lower to cup his balls and roll them gently.

His fingers jerk in my hair as he massages the shampoo in.

I sigh in utter bliss and close my eyes.

He grunts out a soft *fuck me*, and then his mouth seals over mine.

He swipes at my lips with his tongue, and I open for him, our tongues tangling, breath mingling, bodies pressing harder together.

He hasn't stopped scratching my scalp.

I haven't stopped stroking his cock.

But he drops his hands from my head and grips me behind my thighs, turning us until I'm against the wall, shower water falling on half of me while he lifts me.

I wrap my legs around his hips, and his cock finds my entrance, and *oh my god*.

I whimper in the good way and tilt my hips to take him deeper.

"Christ, Daphne," he groans, and then he's kissing me again, wild and uninhibited while he bucks into me, thrusting harder and deeper and faster.

Uncontrolled.

Unrestrained.

And I love it.

Love it.

"More," I gasp. "Harder."

He grunts and pumps faster.

Deeper.

Harder.

Almost to the point of pain, but with a tight, hot, delicious curl winding up deep inside me, building with every thrust, every stroke of his tongue against mine, every slight shift in angle as I slip against the wall.

I love being wanted.

I love being wanted desperately so much more.

It's temporary.

He'll come. I'll come.

This will all be over.

But in this moment, I'm his world, and he wants—no, he *needs* me.

In this moment, I'm worthy.

I have value.

I won't be abandoned.

I won't be left behind.

He lifts one hand to squeeze my breast, then pinches my nipple while he thrusts even deeper, and that's it.

I'm done.

No, *undone*.

My toes curl.

My thighs strain.

My head drops back.

And I orgasm in a blinding flash of exquisite bliss, my pussy clenching around the steel rod of his cock while I scream his name.

He strains into me, moaning out a soft, "*Fuuuuuck*, so good."

My inner walls beat out an erratic pulse, squeezing him and spasming and drowning me in a steamy fog of nothing but endless pleasure.

Just me.

And Oliver.

And this place.

Nothing else exists.

Nothing but the ecstasy of coming all over his cock while he's coming inside of me.

Coming inside me and panting and groaning and pinning me to the wall as my thigh muscles begin to quake and my orgasm slowly fades away.

I can't catch my breath.

Can't feel my feet.

Don't know if I can stand.

Or why I'd ever need to.

Oliver drops his head to the crook of my shoulder, panting.

I don't know when I looped my arms around his shoulders, but it's the only thing I have to hang on to.

And I don't want to let go.

When I let go, the rest of the world is real.

He's still on a mission to disappear.

I'm still with him only as long as I'm useful.

"Daph?" he pants.

I make a gargled noise that he seems to understand means I'm listening.

"I'm glad it's you."

Dammit.

Dammit.

Heat invades my eyes and my nose gets that telltale tickle that says tears are coming. "Shampoo," I gasp. "Shampoo in my eye."

It's not.

But it's a lot better than letting him see me cry.

Over sex.

Over being wanted.

Over knowing that he doesn't truly want me.

That I'm merely what's convenient today.

Yep.

Having him stumble into action to rinse my eyes out is way better than admitting how much I like him and how much it's going to hurt when he gets wherever he's going and sends me back home.

25

Chaos is the best teacher

Oliver

After our shower, Daphne tells me she needs to get something from the front desk for her mission of helping me give away piles of cash.

As soon as she slips out of the door, I call Archie.

"Talk to me, Stevenson," he says, throwing me for half a second before I realize he's using a fake name so that no one knows it's me.

He's breathing like he's on a treadmill, and I hear the steady *thump thump thump* of his footsteps.

"You on an earbud?" I ask.

"Stupid question."

Good. I can talk freely. "I either had a mental breakdown or I've left the stress behind."

"Pick one. Can't be both."

"Don't have a clue where I am, don't care, might lose track of time and not find where I want to settle before my two weeks are up, again don't care, having fun."

"Shit. It *is* both."

It's also the sex.

I don't know how sex with the most chaotic person I know is both grounding me and giving me wings, but there you have it.

"Snapped yesterday. Hit a thunderstorm, Daphne freaked out, thought for a minute we wouldn't get out alive, she called me boring, and the next thing I knew, I was shutting off the GPS and driving wherever I felt like going."

"Things are okay with your new assistant then?" he says.

That coded question is loaded with the subtext of at least a dozen other very direct questions. "Yeah."

He's quiet for a minute.

I'm quiet for a minute.

Then— "Fuck, Oli— Stevenson. You slept with her."

"Is there really a Stevenson? Is your assistant listening in? Are you going to bring about another man's divorce right now?"

"What the hell were you thinking?"

"That she's single, I'm single, she's never going back to Manhattan, I'm never going back to New York, and she's…fun."

"I'm all in favor of fun, but dude, there are lines."

"I'm not getting back together with Margot. Actually—can you do some snooping for me? Find out if her father's plotting some kind of takeover of M2G? Don't care for my sake. I think it'd make Daphne feel better to know Margot only wants me now for my company."

"Lines and *bad ideas*."

"Daph doesn't want my money."

He snorts.

I growl.

"Bad. Ideas," he repeats.

I'm aware he's trying to look out for me. Dude's been the best friend I desperately needed.

But this subject is off-limits.

"You see my parents?" I ask him.

The grunt that comes through the phone isn't exactly what I want to hear either. "Hold on." The treadmill stops. A door shuts.

Then another door.

"Not in person, but I know they were at Kenniston's last night. Rumor has it your dad's expecting you to back his bid to get back into the CEO spot."

"You still ready?"

"Cannot wait. Though I think you need to give Carmen a heads-up."

He's standing in for me at the board of directors meeting in a week and a half. Acting as my proxy to hand over my resignation and pass along my recommendation for the next CEO, and then he'll be my proxy again at the subsequent shareholder meeting to confirm the board's choice for the next CEO.

And then he's helping me divest my M2G shares once I no longer need them to vote.

"She'll be in. She's said as much without saying as much."

"You're all the way off your itinerary now?" he asks me.

"Completely."

"The end goal…"

"Still the same."

"Solo?"

"Yes." It's what he wants to hear, even if I'm hesitating in my mind. Stupid, I know.

Daphne's not wrong about this thing between us—whatever it is—being a side effect of our close quarters the past few days.

But I like her.

This woman that she's become—she's still Daphne, but she's *more*.

She gets me. She understands not fitting. She has people in her life—*normal* people, people she loves, people who are her new family—who have taught her to live the way I want to live.

She's making me feel like *I'm* family.

Like I have a place to belong, just as I am, while I'm discovering who I'm meant to be.

"Gotta go," I murmur as I hear the door opening.

the grumpiest billionaire

I hang up and tuck the phone into my pocket as she strolls into the room with a stack of envelopes. Her hair's damp, though the light's all wrong to catch the blue and green streaks right, and she's in a pair of cotton shorts and a T-shirt with a unicorn on it suggesting that I have a nice day. No makeup today.

Not even her lipstick.

But she smiles at me as if all is perfect in the world, easing that little blip that's been sitting in my heart since she told me she had soap in her eye in the shower.

"You wanna bet control of the TV remote tonight on if I can get rid of this whole bag of cash today?" she says.

Bold and confident. Eyes sparkling like she's excited for the challenge.

She's so damn pretty.

"That's it? All you want to bet is control of the TV remote?"

"I'm not betting you dinner when I don't have cash myself, and sexual favors are completely off the table once we leave this room."

"Completely?"

"*Completely*, Oliver."

"*Boring*, Daphne."

"Don't make me go through two bags of your money."

I grin at her. "Is it hard? Being the adult for once?"

"It's annoying as hell. You ready to go? You're driving. I need to watch my phone to keep an eye out for opportunities. Also, I have to text Bea, which I know I don't have to tell you, but I am in the spirit of complete honesty. She rebranded her burger bus, and I need this full story. I've missed a lot at home."

Home.

I want a home.

But I don't say it, and instead, we load up and hit the road, leaving behind ten thousand dollars in a tip for the housecleaning crew and a note asking them to someday pay it forward.

259

An hour later, we're on a road following a river somewhere in Arkansas. Daphne's sitting in the back seat with the cash, doing something with the envelopes and her phone.

"We're coming up to a town in about three miles," she tells me. "Take a right at the stoplight."

I follow her directions, and soon, we're pulling up to a shopping center anchored around a Purple Donkey grocery store.

"We need small bills," Daphne informs me. "So we're each going into the grocery store, then into the dollar store next door, then into the gas station at the other end of the parking lot. Get something like gum, and *do not give the change away*. Not yet. We need smaller bills."

"Is this change for laundry?"

"No. Laundromats all take some form of credit cards now." She shoves three hundred-dollar bills at me. "Meet me back here when you're done."

She pretends like she doesn't know me, walking three or four steps ahead of me into the grocery store.

While I'm debating if I want breath mints, a pack of gum, or a random tabloid magazine like the one she grabbed the other day, I listen in as she chats with the clerk in her lane.

"My grandma is so ridiculous. I love her. She keeps sending me hundred-dollar bills, and I'm like, *Grandma*. No one uses cash anymore. Can't support my online shopping addiction with cash, you know? I'm forever like, 'Grandma, get me a digital gift card,' but she thinks the internet's for recipes and gossip, not for, you know, buying quirky custom T-shirts."

"Oh, I hear ya, honey," the clerk says. "Grannies are something, aren't they? Mine's memory is slipping, and I keep getting twenty-dollar bills in birthday cards. My birthday's in March. The last one came yesterday."

"I seriously love grandmas, but I'm sorry about her memory issues. Happy…five months after your birthday?"

"Thanks. Best five months after my birthday ever." The clerk laughs.

the grumpiest billionaire

Daphne laughs.

The guy behind me asks if I'm going to pick something or hold up the line, so I grab a candy bar, pay for it with a hundred-dollar bill that the clerk checks to make sure it's not fake, and I pocket my change.

Daphne's already in the dollar store next door, at the checkout counter.

I grab a random Halloween bucket and get in line behind her.

"No, seriously, I've been looking all over everywhere for these sticky notes," she's telling the cashier. "Why doesn't every store carry cute sticky notes anymore?"

The employee doesn't check Daphne's hundred for authenticity, but when I put my Halloween bucket on the conveyor and hand her my hundred, I get the look and the counterfeit test.

And then it strikes me that two people cashing in hundred-dollar bills in a row probably looks weird.

So I stop at the car and have a short conversation with Angelina Juliana Priestly, then realize I can drive myself across the parking lot, so I do.

Daphne spots me as she's leaving the market attached to the gas station.

I nod to her as I'm passing her on my way in.

This time, I grab an apple.

Just feel like it.

And the clerk checks my hundred-dollar bill before making change for me.

"They all think I'm passing fake money," I tell Daphne when I get into the car.

She cracks up. "You look so suspicious, Oliver. *So* suspicious."

We go three more blocks before she directs me along a set of turns that lead to a small pet shelter.

"Are we giving money away, or are we getting another road trip mascot?" I ask her.

She blinks at me.

It's one long, slow blink that asks if I'd let her get a pet.

"How many years has it been since Lady Catherine Ophelia passed?" I ask her.

"Four. She died right after I moved in with Bea."

"You haven't wanted another dog?"

Another blink.

This one goes with a visible swallow. "I don't want my heart to ever break like that again."

I don't know if my heart has ever broken.

There were high school and college girlfriends, but they were who I was supposed to date whether my heart was in it or not.

Even Margot was who I was supposed to date.

Safe.

Easy.

I loved her the only way I knew how to love her—the safe, easy, nonconfrontational, agree-about-everything way.

The *boring* way, as Daphne would say.

I've never thrown my entire heart into something I loved so much that I couldn't walk away from it, that I'd fight for it, that I'd bend all rules of time and space and reality to hold on to it.

Talk about feeling inadequate.

I don't know if I even know *how* to love someone.

Not the way Daphne loved her dog.

She pats Angelina Juliana Priestly on the head, then holds up a stack of cash. "Here's the deal. Whenever you want to donate a small fortune in cash, put the small bills on the outside of the wad so that they think it's a bunch of ones and fives. Garage sales are good cover stories. Had a garage sale, wanted some of it to go to a good cause. People are tipping servers less and less in cash these days, but that's still a reasonable cover, especially in more rural areas, like where I live. Bea gets a handful of cash at her burger bus every week. It's believable."

"So we're long gone by the time they realize it's more than fifty bucks."

"Exactly."

"How much is that?"

"No idea. I didn't count. I'm hoping there's a donation jar inside. If there's not, we'll pet the animals for a few minutes, then shove an envelope of cash in their mailbox on our way out. Just—let me do the talking."

I let her think I agree to let her do the talking.

But I'm making plans to insist she gets a chance to pet the animals when she reaches the door, tugs on it, and then sighs.

"Closed," she mutters.

"Mailbox?"

"Yep."

We leave somewhere between fifteen and twenty thousand dollars in the mailbox, straight up hundred-dollar bills, with a note asking them to give the animals an extra hug from two animal lovers.

It's almost the truth.

Daphne has clearly loved a dog or two in her lifetime.

My family had pets, but the staff took care of them. And in the case of my mother's cats, whoever could handle their hissing dealt with them.

"I should get a pet when I'm settled," I murmur, almost to myself, as I put the car in gear again.

"A big, fluffy, happy golden retriever," she agrees. "You'd love that."

We stop at a second grocery store in town, where she easily buys a thousand dollars' worth of Visa gift cards with ten hundred-dollar bills, and management is asked to check my two hundred-dollar bills when I attempt to use them in a different checkout lane to pay for restaurant gift cards.

Back in the car, she takes one look at me, and she cracks up laughing so hard that she nearly can't breathe.

"I give up." I toss my hands in the air. "I can't even *spend* cash, much less give it away."

I know that's why she's converting it into credit card gift cards—so that I can give away money online or with cards—but she's giggling too hard to tell me so herself.

We make one final stop in town to grab a late breakfast—the peaches and cheese from yesterday's farmer's stand were delicious, but not enough food—and I practice her method of putting a few small bills on top of the tip I leave on the table after we're done eating.

She tosses a few coins on too.

And when we're finally back on the highway, I'm twenty-five thousand dollars lighter.

Still nowhere close to giving away even a million, but we're making progress.

Together.

And it's fun. Freeing.

Right.

For the first time in my life, I'm doing what I know I'm supposed to do.

Unexpectedly with exactly the right person too.

26

A little of your life, a little of mine

Daphne

I am my own worst enemy.
And that's why I'll have no control over the TV remote at the hotel we stop at somewhere in southeast Missouri the first evening after I failed to give away the entire bag of money in one day.

Not having control over the TV remote is why I end up breaking my own rule and having sex with Oliver again.
Swear it's only that I need a distraction from his terrible television choices.

The next day, different bet, different states, but same results. We refill the bag of money from the other bags in the trunk, and when I fail to find ways to empty it entirely through giant tips and random donation drop-offs and trading the cash in for gift cards that we can use online or mail to various places, like nursing homes and hospitals and schools for the staff, I lose control of the air conditioner for the last-minute vacation rental that Oliver books somewhere in Iowa.

I teach him to boil water for mac 'n' cheese—yes, yes, he already knew how to boil water, but he humors my attempt at playing teacher so well that we have sex on the kitchen floor.

Then again in the creepy basement.
No cool lady cave there.

Except mine.

My lady cave gets thoroughly banged into ecstasy by the wonder cock in Oliver's pants while I sit on the washing machine during the spin cycle.

And I tell myself this was a necessary lesson since he did not, in fact, already know how to operate a washing machine, though he could've looked it up on the internet.

Saturday—today—it's the same thing all over again.

Except this time, I bet him a night of sleeping in a tent if I give away all of the money.

And I do it.

So now we're setting up camp at a secluded spot in a wooded state park somewhere so far northwest in Iowa that we could probably see both Minnesota and South Dakota if we climbed a tree and peered off into the distance.

"How's it feel to be down a couple million?" I ask Oliver as he watches me setting up the tent I insisted we get. It's proving to be smaller than I anticipated a four-person tent would be.

Damn.

We'll have to cuddle or something.

Horrors.

I'll probably have to fall on his dick for us to fit.

Fuck me, I have issues.

He smiles at me from his spot on a picnic blanket on the ground, where he's splayed out on his ass with his legs spread and his elbows behind him, propping himself up under the shade of the trees. My stupid heart does the same thing it's been doing all day long and starts singing songs about rainbows and stars and frolicking in meadows made of marshmallows and cotton candy.

Bea told me once that her vagina is a hopeless romantic.

Mine's apparently stuck in a fairy-tale world.

"Lighter," he tells me. "It feels—*I* feel lighter."

the grumpiest billionaire

"It doesn't bother you that literally no one realized how much cash you were handing or leaving them the past few days?"

He shakes his head. "Don't want the thanks. That part—it's awkward. I don't like it."

"You're not awkward."

I get a raised eyebrow of doubt.

"You're different. From when—from who you were when we were younger."

"When you don't have any memories of me?"

I grin. "Clearly. Now you're memorable."

He jerks his chin toward the tent. "That's built for four people?"

I study the small domed shelter. "I think they put the wrong tent in the box."

He snickers.

Oliver.

Snickering over getting a half-size four-person tent.

"Have you always had a sense of humor?" I ask him when I shouldn't be asking him anything besides *please gather sticks so we can make a fire to make dinner.*

And then he does something even worse, and he answers me with a heavy sigh and a soft, "No."

"I was kidding. Being obnoxious. Poking at you. Ignore me."

"One of my earliest memories was meeting the cast of *Les Mis* in Paris."

I plop back on my own butt next to him. "I know we grew up special, but that's *special* special."

"My mother wanted me to be cultured, and the best way to do that was to do cultured things. Not *fun* things."

"No *Panda Bananda on Ice* for you, huh?"

His brows furrow, wrinkling his forehead, and I realize he looks younger today.

Not as young as he is, but far younger than he did a week ago.

"Kids' cartoon show," I explain.

He shakes his head. "Definitely not then."

"Clearly. *Panda Bananda* didn't start until a few years ago, and you're seventy-eight, so…"

He smiles again.

This one's a soft smile.

Filled with affection.

Shiiiiiit.

I need to tell myself this is a one-sided crush on my sister's ex who happens to need a lot of sex right now.

That when I go home, I'll realize this was all for fun and not emotional at all. That I'm not honestly attracted to Oliver, and he's been humoring me because he feels bad that I will never see as much money as he's had in his trunk ever again in my entire life, and possibly never experience another penis as good as his either.

"What's your earliest memory?" he asks me.

"My grandma had this parakeet that would recite Shakespeare. It pecked me on the arm and I got sent to the kitchen to sit with her cook, who was this terrifying woman even older than my grandma, but she gave me fresh chocolate chip cookies after she patched up my arm."

He shifts on the ground and skims his fingers over my biceps. "Is that why you got tattoos? To hide the scars of all the birds that have pecked you after you annoyed them?"

Oh my god, he's funny.

I'm grinning while I nod at him. "Yep. First it was parakeets, then it was ravens, then this fat robin one time, and then a hawk…"

Dammit.

His smile's growing too. So is the warmth in his eyes. And he's leaning closer to me. "If you didn't walk around wearing squirrel pelts, I'm sure the hawks would leave you alone."

My hand flutters to my heart. "I would *never*."

"But the robins… What did you do to piss off a robin? Steal its worms?"

"I found its nest and wore it as a hat."

Again, I truly would never. I'm making up stories. He's making up stories.

This is the easy kind of fun that I have with Bea's brothers too. Each of us trying to get more outrageous than the other, telling tales of things that never happened, occasionally slipping in something real.

But Oliver isn't one of Bea's brothers.

"Daphne?"

"Yes, Oliver?"

His gaze flickers over me, warm and friendly and affectionate, and I realize he's about to say something profound.

Something intelligent and kind, probably about our trip, how much he's needed it, how glad he is that I've been with him.

My pulse kicks up again, sending the barest wisp of *I have it so bad for him* adrenaline faster through my veins while I watch him watching me, like he's weighing the exact right words to use.

His chest rises on a large inhale, and then—"Are you sure I can trust you to cook me dinner over a fire tonight?"

I deflate like a freaking balloon.

I know I'm something more to him than his ex's little sister—you don't bang a guy senseless every night on a road trip without graduating above that title, and he *did* tell me he likes me, even if I'm not sure he meant it the way I want to take it—but I hoped I'd be more than *chef and tent-keeper* too.

"That depends on how much more crap you give me about all of the birds that have attacked me over the years."

His smile pauses halfway. "There—there *haven't* been other birds, right?"

"Only people who help build a fire to cook dinner get answers to that question."

"You're so mean."

If you'd told me two weeks ago I'd feel like the luckiest woman in the world when Oliver Cumberland teased me about being mean, I would've laughed until I choked.

But the glint in his hazel eyes and the curve of his lips and the way smiling makes him almost look his own age—this isn't a road trip effect.

This is just Oliver.

Being who he's free to be when it's the two of us, alone, in the middle of nowhere.

No family expectations. No job expectations. No worries about anything at all.

Goddess knows he wouldn't put on airs for me. Pretend he's happy when he's not. Bend over backward to put my comfort ahead of his own.

And that—that knowledge that I like him, this man that he's becoming, the man he's always had inside of him, the man he's finally free to be, coupled with the knowledge that this can't last—means as much as I'm happy for him, I'm sad for me too.

My smile back is forced as I push up off the ground and head to the car for the rest of the supplies we picked up at ValuKart, and yes, I'm running away from my own feelings. "If you have any energy left, go gather some sticks for kindling. We need smaller stuff if we're going to make this firewood work."

I hear rustling behind me, and I know he's following directions.

"You make fires often?" he asks me.

"When I go camping."

"You camp often?"

"I got into it maybe a year after my parents cut me off. Some of my coworkers invited me. I try to go with them a few times every summer now. It can make your neck hurt, but also, there's nothing like sleeping in the fresh air under the stars to put your life in perspective when things are shitty."

"Are things shitty now?"

"No. Just a general observation. And things don't have to be shitty for camping to be amazing. Tonight, for instance. Tonight, camping will be amazing because we're doing it because *I won*."

"Only because you left fifty grand at that pinecone museum. They won't know what to do with fifty grand."

the grumpiest billionaire

"They figured out how to do enough with pinecones to make a museum. I think they'll figure out how to efficiently use fifty grand."

I move things around in the trunk to give myself space to spread out a tablecloth and prep dinner here instead of on the ground, *oof*ing when I attempt to move the last and biggest duffel of cash.

"Why is this last bag heavier than the other two?" I call to Oliver.

A noise that sounds like a snort of laughter answers me, so I glance back at him.

He's gathered a good pile of sticks that he's holding in both hands, and he's laughing.

Giggling, really.

Full-on snort-giggling.

That's as much permission as I need, as far as I'm concerned.

I unzip the hard-sided case and pop it open.

Half of it is cash.

The other half, though, buried underneath the cash—

I tilt my head as I start combing through the bubble-wrapped items, peeling back the tape and unwrapping enough bubble wrap to identify what's inside.

"That was my grandmother's favorite music box," Oliver says over my shoulder. "She got it on her first trip to Italy. And that one"—he points to a long, skinny thing wrapped in bubble wrap—"that one's my father's favorite Maurice Bellitano."

"Will he notice it's missing?"

"Eventually." He grins broader. "Like he'll notice this too."

He reaches past me to grab a wine-bottle-shaped bubble-wrapped object. I choke on my own tongue when he unrolls it and shows me the label.

"Is that real?" I whisper.

"High probability."

"What does that mean, *high probability?*"

"If this is what I think it is, this came from my grandfather's cellar, like most of what we had before my father's misguided foray into showing up your father's wine cellar."

"But you're not sure?"

"One way to find out."

"Find an expert?"

"Drink it."

Spoken like a true billionaire.

He giggles again. "How do you think it'll pair with hot dogs?"

Spoken like a true billionaire having a mental breakdown. As if that'll stop me from smiling back at him. "Only one way to find out."

I don't drink much that costs more than twelve bucks a bottle these days, but I've had good wine.

Good wine.

This bottle?

If it's truly a 1947 Chateau Cheval Blanc, my father would absolutely die at the idea of us drinking it with campfire hot dogs. His father probably would too.

"What else did you take?" I ask him.

"Sentimental things and a few things that can be used as blackmail in the event they try anything to get me to come back."

"Oliver Cumberland, you are *devious*."

He grins at me. "Bad to the bone, baby."

I can't explain why that makes me desperately need to kiss him, but it does.

Oliver is *not* bad.

He's utterly perfect.

And I have at least one or two more days before I need to think about reality again.

Home. Job. Him not being mine.

Maybe three or four days.

I can wait three or four days to contemplate having to get back to the real world.

Especially if he keeps kissing me back like this in the meantime.

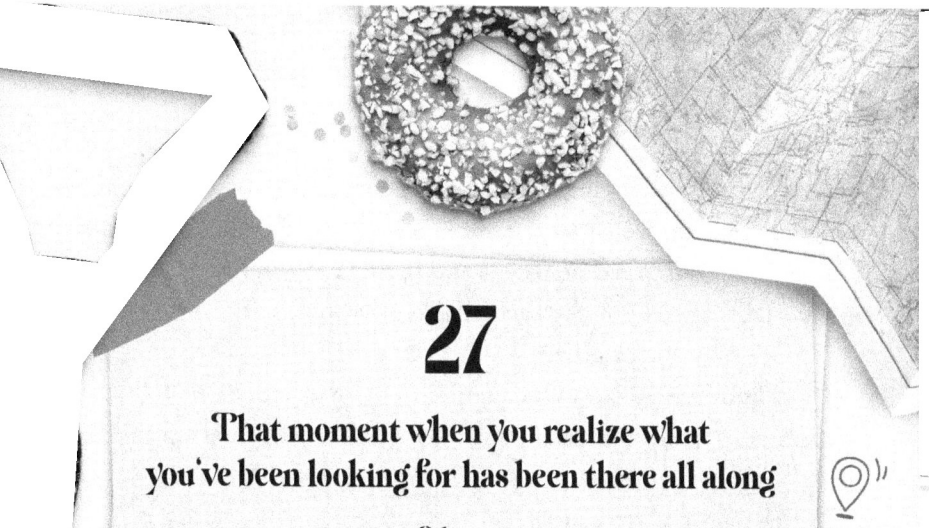

27

That moment when you realize what you've been looking for has been there all along

Oliver

Of everything I expected when I planned my road trip to find where I wanted to settle, not wanting it to end wasn't a possibility that crossed my mind.

But I don't know if another week will be enough.

We'll run out of cash to give away, but I can get more.

I'd want to upgrade my car to something electric, or at least hybrid.

We might plan to stay in the same place for two nights instead of being in this much of a rush to see as much as I can of the country.

I keep falling asleep in the car regularly when Daphne's been driving for the two- or three-hour stretches between our giveaway sprees the past couple days, which isn't surprising.

Now that I'm getting more than four or five hours of sleep a night, my body's craving sleep in a way I've never felt before.

Making up for what I missed.

From the small bit of research I've done, I expect it'll take me a year or more to fully be normal again.

But tonight, I'm in my happy place. It's a happy place I didn't even know existed, yet here we are.

Daphne's telling me stories about her adopted hometown and her adopted family as we sit by the fire, sipping the rich, decadent Chateau Cheval Blanc out of red Solo cups and roasting marshmallows after eating our fire-roasted hot dogs and corn on the cob.

Crickets are chirping.

A light breeze fans our campfire.

Stars sparkle overhead with only a half-moon interrupting their glow.

It's a near-perfect night.

"—so Simon's kids got skunked out when he was supposed to be taking Bea out for tea, and it reminded me of the time I was out supervising a job and a whole family of raccoons got into my lunch."

"What do you do?" I ask her. "Your job. What do you do?"

"Whatever they need me to do."

"Who, though?"

There's the barest hesitation before she peers at me in the firelight. "My nonprofit is called *Beeslieve*. We do some animal habitat restoration, like in places where there are abandoned buildings or where we could restore wrecked habitats for bees and butterflies, and we also do some work with the state department of transportation, making the roadways safer for animals and cars alike with natural boundaries to direct wildlife to better crossings."

"I feel like I've heard of this."

"You're our major donor. Through Miles2Go." She looks down at her marshmallow. "That's what I want money for. To make sure that even when your father revokes our funding, we can keep going the way we have been."

I rub at my chest.

"I was hired with those funds," she adds quietly. "And it's—working at Beeslieve has been—it's been everything I needed. It gave me a focus for my energy where I can see for myself, every day, that we're doing good. That we're improving the world. You know. In ways that sending a bunch of air conditioners to the North Pole wouldn't have."

the grumpiest billionaire

My heart thumps erratically.

She has a life she needs to get back to. I can't keep her on the road with me indefinitely.

I mean, I *could*.

But I'd have to ask her to give up her job to come with me.

I'd have to be enough all by myself.

Daph would be happy seeing the world, but we *haven't* seen the results of our efforts the past few days.

We've dropped bucketloads of cash into random communities along the way, anonymously supporting fundraisers for playgrounds and kids' sports teams and fire station upgrades and museum expansions and pet shelter support. We've left large tips at small family restaurants and dropped ridiculous amounts of change into charity donation jars at grocery stores and a few other ValuKarts.

And we've dashed off quickly everywhere before anyone could realize how much we'd donated or left behind.

I know she doesn't need the credit, but I think she needs something more concrete than holding onto empty suitcases that used to be filled with money.

Her heart has always belonged to animals. To the environment and the world.

The donation we made at the only open pet shelter we've stopped at was the hardest.

I could tell she wanted to pet the dogs, but she faked an allergy attack as soon as we were in the door.

It's the first time I've wondered how much she still hides of herself.

How much she'll bend over backward to protect her own heart.

When I first heard she'd been disinherited, I didn't think much of it. Couldn't, really—not with the situation my father was in and the subsequent situation he'd thrust me into at M2G.

But now—now I think it was far more than a simple disinheritance.

Her parents abandoned her.

They left her to survive on her own without any resources because they never understood her.

Never understood what she loved and cared about.

How deeply she felt about her causes.

Something new flickers to life deep in my chest.

Anger.

Fury.

Rage.

Not at Daphne.

At her parents.

Somewhat at Margot too.

She stayed. She stayed at the family company. Stayed working for people who probably don't care about her interests outside of work either. Unless it aligns with their own.

If my father hadn't been sent to prison, if I hadn't broken up with Margot because I couldn't handle the obligations of maintaining a relationship on top of the expectations from Miles2Go, if I hadn't learned so quickly that I wasn't built for the life I'd been trained for, would I have been one more person carrying on like normal when my sister-in-law was abandoned?

All they had to do was listen.

Listen and try to understand.

Instead, they wrote her off like she was the problem.

Daphne stirs beside me, pulling her marshmallow off the fire and sliding it onto a graham cracker already loaded up with a Reese's peanut butter cup. "I know enough about fundraising at this point that I know Beeslieve will be fine. And I'm good at it. I could shift to fundraising full-time. But when you can put your efforts into the work itself instead of into asking for donations—it makes such a difference on what you can accomplish for the animals and the environment. And I'd—I'd miss being outside and seeing the work as much as I do now too."

"Is a million enough?"

"I could ask Margot for funding too. I've been letting my pride stand in my way, and I need to stop that. I've made my point, you know?"

"Daphne."

"The world doesn't work the way we're raised to think it works. But the world I'm in now—I like it better. Even if it's harder. It's worth it."

"*Daphne.*"

"I'm telling you that I don't need your money, okay? This trip—this adventure—it's been reward enough, and I've learned enough the past few years to appreciate it for what it is."

I grip her wrist, noticing for the first time how small it is.

Delicate.

Nothing about Daphne has ever struck me as delicate, but I think I never looked closely enough.

"Are we friends?" I ask her.

She eyes me while she takes a giant bite of her s'more.

"Because I think we're friends." At least. At the very, very least.

Regardless of where I end up and how long she's with me on this road trip, she's become my friend.

Something more than my friend.

Something much, much more.

She licks at the marshmallow oozing out of her s'more and continues to not answer me.

I'm still holding her other wrist. "Daph, friends don't abandon friends."

That gets me a lot of blinks that come with quivering nostrils and an uneven inhale. "I don't use my friends for money either."

"You're not using if it's being offered."

"You offered it before we were friends. If we're...staying friends... then I don't want it anymore."

"What about your coworkers? The whole organization? Can I help them?"

She shoves the last bite of s'more into her mouth without answering me.

I let her wrist go and take another sip of wine.

Contemplate roasting another marshmallow.

Eye Daphne while she actively avoids looking at me.

Enjoy the crackle of the fire.

Panic in my own head that I'm missing some kind of subtle clue that I'm supposed to pick up on beyond the obvious, which is that she has a very different relationship with people and with money now, and this isn't about me.

Except maybe it is?

And if it is, what do I do about it?

This Daphne? This woman who's been with me this past week?

I like her.

I more than like her.

And I don't know what to do about it because this road trip will come to an end, and she has a day job that she clearly loves, and this can't last forever.

Eventually, she sighs. "My parents used their money to try to control me," she grumbles.

"I know."

"You're from that world."

"Was. Not anymore."

"Oliver. We're drinking a bottle of wine that probably costs half my annual salary. With hot dogs and s'mores."

"I might keep some parts of the old world."

Her lips tip up, but she's also half scowling at me.

"I'm not expecting anything from anyone that we've left cash with the past few days," I tell her.

"I know."

"Maybe I'll get a list of all of the nonprofits M2G donated to in the past few years and use the rest of my fortune keeping all of them going."

She stares at me.

Not blinking.

the grumpiest billionaire

Possibly not even breathing.

"You'd do that?" she whispers.

The reverence in her voice—like I've proposed a way to save the polar bears—it makes me squirm even as the answer—the only answer, the absolute truth—comes out of my mouth.

"Yes. Of course."

"You'd keep funding going for every nonprofit Miles2Go contributed to on your own if they cut it off?"

The math isn't hard.

M2G wasn't very profitable when I took it over, and though profits—and thus charitable donations—grew significantly in the past two years especially, I can afford to make sure none of the nonprofits suffer if things don't go my way when my resignation and recommendation are formally submitted to the board of directors in a little over a week.

"I don't want or need that much money, Daph. If it makes you feel better about me donating to Beeslieve for me to donate to all of the rest of the nonprofits that the M2G Foundation funded too, then it's an easy yes. I picked all of them for a reason, and I hadn't considered the potential that they'd have their funding cut without me there to oversee things. I hadn't—you've helped me see through the fog I was living in. See the difference I made. The difference I want to keep making."

She's staring at me in the firelight, and maybe it's the wine making everything seem softer, or maybe it's the crackle of the fire mixed with night insects setting the mood beneath the half-moon and the stars, but in this moment, everything feels perfect.

Exactly as it's supposed to be.

I'm who I'm supposed to be. I'm *with* who I'm supposed to be with. We're exactly where the universe wants us, and this is right and good and everything.

Daph moves her red Solo cup further from her body.

She turns to me, takes my cup, and sets it aside too.

And then she cradles my face in her hands while she shifts her legs to cradle my hips, and she presses the softest kiss to my lips.

It's a *thank you* kiss.

A *you see me* kiss.

An *everything has changed* kiss.

Even when she deepens the kiss, when slow strokes of her hand under my shirt become frantic movements with both of us rushing through stripping each other's clothes off—it's different.

Deeper.

More.

Everything.

She's my old world and my new world clashing together into the *right* world.

Chaos and fun with conviction and drive.

She pushes me back onto the blanket, hovers over me, and then takes me into her hot, slick heat, and I know.

I have to change my plans.

I have to find a way to keep her.

Not because I want to make love to a woman in the moonlight.

Because I want to make love to *Daphne* in the moonlight.

Not because I know all the answers of who I want to be and how to get there.

Because I want her with me while I sort it out.

I want her laugh. I want her smiles. I want to pick her brain and I want her to tell me when I'm wrong and I want to bask in the exquisite joy of her enthusiasm for finding and doing what's right.

She rides me like we're in the final, desperate stretches headed for home, kissing me as if I'm her oxygen, and when her inner walls squeeze me and I let myself go inside of her, I feel her heartbeat as if it's my own, feel the breath in her lungs as if it's my own, and I know.

I am head over heels in love with Daphne Merriweather-Brown.

This is the last thing I ever expected at any point in my life, but the peace—the peace that comes as she sags against me, the last of her orgasm leaving her, mine still pulsing out of me—the peace and the happiness and the freedom—this is it.

She's the one.

The one who's been there my whole life without me ever knowing she was exactly what I would need.

Exactly what I'd want.

Everything.

She pants against my chest and presses a kiss to my neck. "Thank you for being you," she whispers.

My eyes sting while I wrap my arms around her and hold her tight. "Thank *you* for being you."

28

That stupid L-word

Daphne

It's official.

I'm in love with Oliver.

It's Sunday morning. A full week since I tried to get my phone back from under the mattress in his secret serial killer cabin, when he'd glare at me for breathing, and today couldn't be more different.

I'm playing the role of the little spoon in the tent while a light rain falls on the canvas. He's sleeping, his hand curled around my belly, and he's breathing peacefully in my hair, the warmth of his breath in direct contrast to the cool morning air tickling my nose. The sun's up, but with the rain, it's a muted light coming through the tent.

I close my eyes and let myself breathe peacefully too.

It's not hard to imagine staying here forever. Camping for eternity. The lure of how easy it would be to fall into old habits and tell myself things like *he can afford for us to live like this forever, we don't have to work, we could do good things with his money*—but the thought sends anxiety swirling through my belly at the same time.

As it should.

He's taking his life in a new direction, and I'm only along for the journey between destinations.

But I don't know how I can end this journey without my life changing because of the experience too.

I can't go back to what life was before either. Life without Oliver.

The thought makes me sad.

He inhales a deeper breath, one of those waking-up breaths, and his fingers stretch across my belly before he pulls me closer.

"Morning," I whisper.

"I love sleep," he mumbles back.

I smile even as my heart dips.

For a hot second there, I thought he was about to tell me he loved *me*.

But there's a big leap from him telling me he liked me in the hotel the other day to loving me.

A lot of people like me.

It takes someone special to love me though.

"Sleep seems to like you too." I trace the veins on the back of his hand. "You almost could pass for thirty-seven now."

His amused snort tickles my ear. "I almost feel forty-five."

"So, is that your plan? To run away somewhere and pull a sleeping beauty for a few years?"

"Yes."

It's so easy to picture myself in a little cabin with him, making him pancakes for a late brunch after he wakes up, going on a hike, donating to charities for an hour or so, and then making grilled cheeses for an early dinner before we collapse into bed again.

Making love to him.

Slipping out of bed once he's asleep to call Bea or watch TV or take care of a garden.

No stress.

No anxiety.

And not actually my future or my reality because I can't *ever* let myself depend on someone else to provide for me again.

Even Oliver.

Who's provided my job for me for the past few years anyway, and who says he'll continue providing for my job.

And everyone else's too.

So that it's not just for me. Even when it *is* all for me.

A sigh slips out of me.

He wraps me tighter. "I like the rain. How it smells. How it sounds. Don't want to leave."

Same, Oliver. Same. To all of it. "Do we have to?"

"Nuh-uh." He tenses. "Unless—do you have to get back? For work?"

"I can tell my boss I'm wooing a donor."

The man has the nerve to relax.

Like it's no big deal that I can tell my boss I'm using him.

He doesn't even ask if this is how I woo all of my big donors.

"That'll work?"

"If not, Bea's on track to have a whole burger bus empire, so I could go work for her forever."

"Hmm."

"Hmm, what?"

"That would make you happy?"

Not the way my current job does. "Working with Bea? Yes."

"Saving the world through burgers?"

"Don't underestimate Bea's burgers. They're more life-changing than Cod Pieces."

He's smiling.

I can feel it.

The rain picks up, buffeting the tent along with another gust of wind.

I wiggle my ass back into Oliver.

He kisses my shoulder.

And we lie there, him stroking my body, me stroking his hands and arms while he strokes my body. "Why fairies?" he murmurs against my skin as he traces one of my tattoos.

"It's what I want to be in my next life."

"You'd make a very good fairy."

"I totally would."

His low laugh vibrates against me, and I almost don't realize there's another vibration coming from somewhere else cutting through the morning.

"Your phone?" he says.

I slap around the tent until I find it, glance at the readout, and smile. "It's Bea."

"Wanna take it?"

"You don't mind?"

"Nuh-uh."

He sounds like he could fall back asleep.

And that would be good for him.

"I'll be quiet," I whisper.

"I like your voice," he mumbles back.

I'm smiling through emotions flooding my sinuses while I swipe to answer the call. "Hey," I say to Bea.

There's a pause, and then her sentence comes out in a rush. "I've been trying very, very hard to not look at where you're at because I have plausible deniability that way, but I started seeing some things on social media when I was updating my pages this morning, and Daph—are you…have you…did you give away millions of dollars from Mississippi up through Iowa?"

Oliver tenses behind me.

Understandable.

I'm tensing in front of him.

"That's a very specific question," I finally force out.

"Oh my god, Daph," she whispers.

Shit.

Shit.

Oliver's grip tightens around me. "So we lay low for a few days," he murmurs.

"How—" I swallow. Then try again. "How likely do you think it is that anyone else would think that's what I'm doing?" I ask Bea. "Not saying I am or that I'm not. Just asking...do you think anyone else would suspect it?"

"Margot called a little bit ago."

I put Bea on speaker and check my missed calls.

Four from Margot. The first at a reasonable, if early hour, then three in rapid succession about half an hour ago.

I took her off my emergency contact list so that her calls wouldn't ring through the way Bea's do while I'm traveling.

"What did you tell her?" I whisper.

"Exactly what you asked. That you said you needed to disconnect and go camping for a while."

"She gave a marvelous performance," Simon says in the background. "I believed every word."

"Did she believe you?" I ask Bea.

"Daphne, I love you, and I will continue to always love you, but in the spirit of honesty, I have to tell you that I checked your location this morning, even though I really, really didn't want to look... It's just that, when the reports started saying a woman with fairy tattoos and blue and green highlights in her hair, wearing a unicorn T-shirt, was with a guy—and I know you—and I...can you maybe please tell me you're okay and I don't need to worry that you're into something you can't handle?"

I blow a soft breath out of my nose.

This is okay.

Bea and Margot are the only two people from my past who would know what I've done with my hair recently, and I'm not the only person in the world with fairy tattoos.

"I'm good," I tell Bea. "Everything's good."

"If you need anything—"

"No. No, I'm good. Totally under control here."

"Daph?"

"Yeah?"

the grumpiest billionaire

"Margot sent me a picture of her ex and asked if I'd seen him too."

I stifle a good *fuck*.

Oliver presses his face into my shoulder, and I'm pretty sure he's doing the same.

"Why do you think she would do that?" I ask Bea.

"There was a partial picture of a man in one of the news stories about...the people giving away money in the Midwest. She sent that to me first. To see if I thought there was a similarity between him and her ex."

I can't talk.

Can't breathe.

Can't think.

Oliver's partial picture made the news.

He's frozen behind me too.

"Oh my god, Daphne," Bea whispers.

And I can tell by her voice that she knows.

She knows I'm with Oliver.

It's not like he has any distinctive moles or tattoos or unusual features. To anyone else, he'd be your everyday brown-haired, hazel-eyed, scruffy-jawed guy.

"Bea, everything is okay. I swear," I tell her when I can make myself talk again.

"This doesn't sound like the boring guy you described."

Oliver relaxes a bit as he snorts behind me.

"Um...he can hear you," I whisper loudly to Bea.

"Well, isn't this is a delightful plot twist?" Simon says cheerfully.

And Oliver—oh my god.

Oliver laughs harder.

"And it passes the rocking chair test," Bea says. "Daph, what do you need? Seriously, what can I do? Do you have security with you? Simon's guys are freaking a little at the idea that you're doing this without help. And what do you want me to tell Margot? I can call her back for you."

I need to do it.

I need to tell Margot.

"No, you've done enough, thank you," I tell Bea.

"Are you sure?" she asks.

"Happy to send someone along to trail you at a safe distance and pretend they're not there," Simon adds.

If we've been made, we've been made.

And if Margot suspects where Oliver is—then I need to talk to her.

We need to talk to her.

"Not necessary, but thank you," Oliver says.

"You still know how to use your manners?" I ask him.

"With other people."

A brief silence lingers on the other end of the phone.

I cringe to myself.

Bea knows me. She *knows* me.

She has to have heard so much more in my voice that I'm not saying, and my face is getting hot because I *did* tell her Oliver's boring, and she knows I hate him.

Hated him.

Who he used to be.

Not who he is now.

This guy?

This Oliver?

"Don't worry about us, Bea," I say in a rush as she says, "Okay, then, let us know if you change your mind or think of anything else we can do."

We both fall silent for a minute, and then Bea cracks up. "Miss you, Daph. Be safe, okay?"

"Of course. And I'll be home soon. I miss you too."

We hang up, and silence—other than the pitter-patter of rain on the tent—surrounds Oliver and me again.

"They seem nice," Oliver says.

"Absolute best," I whisper back.

He hugs me tighter. "Daph—"

"I need to call Margot."

"*Daphne.*"

I fall silent.

"Your sister adores you," Oliver says softly. "And she and I have been over for a long, long time."

I swallow hard.

I know both of those things.

I know Oliver doesn't want her back.

I know she was willing to take him back for all of the wrong reasons.

And I don't know what I'll do if she decides she wants nothing more to do with me after this.

Be grateful for Bea, I remind myself.

Except it's not enough. I want both of them, both Bea and Margot, sister of my heart and sister my whole life.

I don't *want* to sacrifice my relationship with my sister.

I don't *want* her to move on from tolerating me too.

Margot was there my entire childhood.

She's held my hand through relationship heartbreak. She's stood between our parents and me when I messed up. She's bailed me out of jail.

She's always been there for me.

And here I am, sleeping with her ex on a road trip after she was making noise about wanting him back.

My eyes sting and my lungs burn.

Oliver's grip on me stays tight. Like he's trying to hold me together.

I take one deep breath.

Then another.

And another, and another, until I've put myself in the right frame of mind to dial Margot's number.

29

This is going to get awkward
Oliver

It's killing me that I can't do this for Daphne. I've known her most of my life on a surface level. This week, I feel like I've finally seen her for who she is.

She's a fighter. No, a warrior. A warrior intent on saving the world and supporting the people she loves with that enormous heart of hers.

Impulsive, but not reckless.

At least, I hadn't considered her reckless until right now.

And that's on me.

I wanted her, and she dove right in without hesitation.

Until this exact moment.

"Don't say anything," she says before she hits Margot's number.

I nod against her shoulder.

Three rings in, I hear a familiar voice. A familiar, worried voice. "Daph? Where are you?"

"Hey," Daph says, her voice light and carefree in a way that belies the tension of her body against me. "I've been out camping. Got into an area with signal and saw I missed your calls. What's up? Everything okay?"

There's a small pause, and then—"You're camping?"

"Yep. In a tent as we speak." The wind buffets the tent with soft raindrops, backing up her story.

"With your work friends?"

Daphne's body tenses even more. "You know I don't go alone. Hey, did you hear Bea and Simon are official? I'm gonna have to start knocking before I walk into my own apartment."

"Daphne."

I want to grab the phone, tell Margot she's with me, and that if anyone has a problem with it, to blame me.

But I also know Daph wants to handle this herself.

For now.

"Yeah?" Daph says.

"Are you okay?"

Daphne's chest wavers like she's having a hard time keeping her breathing steady. "Yeah, why? What's going on? Did something happen?"

Margot's sigh stretches across the country. "Mom thought she saw you at William Cumberland's welcome-home party last week."

Shit.

Now I'm tensing even more too.

"Ew, fancy people parties," Daphne says.

This woman.

Even when my jaw's getting tight and I'm feeling that pull back into my old life—hearing Margot's voice and my father's name aren't good for me—Daph can still make me smile.

"And my assistant called to tell me there's a woman matching your description who's been spotted all over the Midwest with a guy who looks like Oliver," Margot says.

"Wow, that's weird."

"Daph?"

"I'm camping. Want a picture of my tent?"

"Are you okay?"

Daphne's chest wobbles again, and she holds the phone away from her ear for a second while she sucks in a loud breath.

"If you're not okay, if you need me, you know I'll be there as fast as humanly possible," Margot continues. "Just say the word. You know the word."

"I know the word," Daph says quietly. "And I'm okay. I'm camping."

There's a long stretch of silence on Margot's end.

"Margot?" Daphne whispers.

"Yes?"

"You're the best sister I could've ever asked for."

"Daph—"

"No, I need to tell you. You are. You stuck up for me when we were little, when our parents were total dicks because I wasn't what they wanted, and you supported me in my dreams when they didn't, and you could write me off like they did, but you haven't. You never make me feel like I'm a fuckup, even when I am, and I love you and I always want to be your sister. I just—I needed you to know."

"Where are you?" Margot says.

"I'm where I want to be," Daphne whispers.

"Are you?"

"If you'd told me four years ago that I'd like camping this much, I would've laughed my ass off, but I am. I'm where I want to be. Even if—even if maybe you don't like me camping."

"Daph, you know there's literally nothing—*nothing*—you could do to make me not love you back?"

"Nothing?"

"*Nothing.*"

"I'm having a really good time camping," she whispers.

"Camping," Margot repeats.

"Camping," Daphne agrees.

They are definitely not talking about camping.

"Okay then," Margot replies. "Call me if camping goes sideways and you need anything. I'll…take care of…those bad weather reports."

"Bad weather—*oh*. Oh. Yes. The *bad weather* reports. Thank you."

I bury my face in her back as Margot huffs out a frustrated breath.

"Because I can control that," Margot mutters. "Right. But Daph, more important—don't let your stupid pride get in the way. This isn't like not having money. Camping is…bigger."

Daphne laughs softly.

Margot snorts, which you wouldn't believe Margot Merriweather-Brown would be capable of unless you'd ever seen her with her sister.

"*Call me*," Margot says.

"No news is good news," Daphne replies.

"I can't wait to hear about this camping trip."

"It's been…unexpected."

"If your camping companions need anything, I'm happy to throw up a few distractions. Like changing that weather report."

I'm assuming she's trying to say she'll take care of the news article with my face attached, which is, in fact, something she can likely do.

"Um, thank you?" Daphne says.

"Provided *camping* is being good for you," Margot adds. "If it's not, I will murder camping without a moment's hesitation."

That was definitely aimed at me.

Daph wiggles her butt back into my crotch like she knows it too. "Margot?"

"Yes?"

"This isn't how I expected you to respond to me…camping. Because I'm kind of…doing something very different than I thought I would…when I decided to go camping. And I don't want to have regrets about camping. Camping is…good."

I bury my face in Daphne's shoulder while Margot sighs again. "When you're home, there are a lot of things I need to tell you that I should've told you a long time ago."

"About…camping?"

"No. I mean, yes, but no. About you. And me. And our family. And projects I'm working on that aren't exactly what they look like. Everything's almost in place, and I—I can't say any more right now. Know that I love you and I want you to be happy, and if anyone ever makes me have to pick sides, I'm picking yours over anyone else's. Over *anyone* else's. No matter what."

"Don't make me cry," Daphne whispers.

"You'd look good as a flaming redhead. And get some long-sleeved shirts."

"Love you, Margot."

"Love you too. Go have fun…camping. We'll talk more soon. *Call me if you need me.* Day or night. For anything. I know how…*camping*…can get."

"Erm, yes. Understood."

They disconnect, and Daphne lets out the longest, loudest, most shuddery breath I've ever heard or felt.

Relatable.

I've been holding my own breath.

"We *are* camping," I murmur into her shoulder.

"*Oh my god*, Oliver, she knows everything," she says on a laugh.

A mildly panicked laugh, but a laugh.

"I wasn't sure she was picking up on everything," she says, "but now—if she's not, she's not as smart as I've always thought she was."

I shift under the light sleeping bag and tug her until she's on her back so I can see her face. After brushing away the tears that have managed to leak out of her eyeballs, I watch her until I know I have her full attention.

"Your sister is a cutthroat badass, and I could never do what she's doing."

"Forgiving us for this?" she whispers.

I start to smile.

Could I do what I think Margot's doing after hearing that whole conversation?

Absolutely not. The past few years proved to me that I don't have it in me.

But I respect the hell out of anyone else who can pull it off.

"She's playing the long game," I tell Daphne.

Her brow wrinkles. "The long game?"

"She has always—*always*—loved you more than anything."

Daph's eyes get shinier.

"Bet you a brass polar bear that she's planning a hostile takeover to push your parents out of the company for what they did to you."

She gasps. "*No.*"

I laugh.

Cackle a little, to be honest. "She has the intelligence, the experience, and the resources to do anything she wants. *Anything.* Step into a CEO role at a competing hotel company. Start her own business. Head up a venture capital fund. You don't think it's weird that she stayed with your parents after what they did to you?"

Daph sniffles. "It's what she was trained to do."

"She was trained to win at all costs in business. But that's more than who she is, and that's something your father has never understood. That part of her that loves you unconditionally makes all the difference."

"She kept saying she was going to take you back."

I try to stop smiling, and I can't. "You heard her. Everything's almost in place. There are things she's been keeping from you. Your sister's about to rock Manhattan. She doesn't want me, Daph. She wants your father to think she's still playing by his rules for what he wants."

"Oh my god," she breathes.

I arch my brows and wait.

And after a long minute of watching her brain work, I get the satisfaction of hearing her deep belly laugh. "*Oh my god.*"

I settle my head on the terrible camping pillow and watch her laugh herself out.

Eventually, she rolls to face me and presses a fast, hard kiss to my mouth. "Can we stay here for another day or two? And can I send you to the store for hair dye and a couple new shirts?"

"Yes." It doesn't matter if I figure out where I want to call home before the board meeting in a week. It'll be easier if I use my real identification after I've told my family—through Archie—to fuck all the way off.

Daphne's smile goes watery again. "I thought she'd be mad. I thought she'd finally—that she'd finally pick their side."

"If she did—which she won't—she wouldn't deserve you."

"Doesn't mean it wouldn't hurt."

I tug her tighter into a hug.

She hugs me back until hugging turns to stroking and stroking turns to kissing and kissing turns to making love while the rain falls on the tent above us.

This is peace.

This is happiness.

This is love.

And I'm going to find a way to keep it all.

I might not be cutthroat, but this—this I'll fight for.

30

Happiness is a side of queso

Daphne

Everything about today is the best.

The best.

After hiding out for a few days in the woods, with Oliver learning how to dye my hair and me drawing all over his arms to show him what a good idea tattoos would be in his new life, and us hiking and talking and napping and laughing, we're back on the road.

He got a new car while he was in town picking up hair dye and my new wardrobe—paying extra for the used car salesperson to not ask any questions about him paying in literal cash—so we're riding in style in a small hybrid SUV with Angelina Juliana Priestly strapped into a booster seat in the middle of the bench behind us and our winning lottery ticket from back in Pennsylvania in the cupholder between us.

I made Oliver a side bet involving shower sex that I could sneak it into the first car we find with Pennsylvania license plates so that they can redeem it when they get home, so we're on the lookout for Pennsylvania cars too.

He's in a *Get Cocked* T-shirt in honor of our favorite rock band. He's also wearing a baseball cap for some microbrewery called *Brew Dudes*, both of which I snagged for him at a thrift shop early this morning.

I'm in a long-sleeved, summer-weight flannel that hides my tattoos, with my now flaming-red hair tied up in a ponytail. My new dye job isn't bad—Oliver says I'd look good no matter what color I made my hair—and I wish I'd brought my wig.

We have the radio dialed in to the symphonic pop station, and we're both singing at the top of our lungs, though he's getting half the words wrong. When I realize he's doing it on purpose, I laugh until I cry.

He's excellent at getting words wrong.

Truly, it's a talent.

The skies are blue, the road's flat, and we're headed toward Colorado.

Oliver wants to see a sunrise and a sunset from the top of a mountain, so that's what we're going to do. Camp on top of a mountain.

Every time we stop, we both pay cash for gift cards. We're not giving any money away today—we want to not be recognized—but I have plans for distributing the rest of what Oliver has in the trunk.

"Can I ask you a question?" I ask over a taco lunch that we picked up at a food truck in one of the little towns we drove through. We're at a picnic table in a park a little farther down the road. Our tip wasn't *that* big comparatively, but it was big enough that we didn't want to stay in the taco truck's parking lot.

He lifts a brow that's accompanied by a smile. "Now you're asking if you can ask? This should be good."

"Prepare for disappointment."

He laughs and gestures with his taco for me to ask my question.

"You weren't driving when Kurt flipped his dad's Maserati, right?"

"I was not," he confirms before taking a big bite.

"So…why didn't you drive for so long?"

An old Oliver look, this one straitlaced with narrowed eyes, makes a rare appearance while he chews.

"I'm not going to make fun of you," I tell him.

"Yes, you are."

I drag a finger over my left boob. "Cross my heart."

He's shaking his head as he wipes his mouth with a napkin, then swallows. "If you laugh, you have to sing whatever song I pick for you tonight at karaoke."

That's the other part of our plan.

I found a bar that has a mechanical bull and karaoke.

I'm teaching Oliver to live today.

Or possibly how to crush his balls. But hopefully not.

"Deal," I say.

He grabs a chip and dips it in the takeout queso container we've been sharing. "Did you know the human brain doesn't fully develop until you're about twenty-five?"

I blink slowly at him because he's right.

I do want to giggle a little.

This is turning out to be the most Oliver answer ever.

"I did," I tell him while my face definitely does some gymnastics moves. "Bea's always talking about it with her brothers. She only has one with a fully developed prefrontal cortex so far, and he's kind of a caveman in other ways, so we're not sure he's done. The other two, definitely not."

"Yeah. That's why," he says, then he crunches into his chip.

"Because your own brain wasn't fully developed?"

"Wouldn't take a driver who was under thirty either."

I open my mouth.

Then close it.

"Go on," he says, sounding more bored and irritated than the smile on his lips and the twinkle in his eyes suggest he is. "Ask it."

"You never let Margot drive you either?"

"Nope."

"*Never?*"

"Never."

"Even though girls are smarter than boys?"

Another smile. "Yes."

"But your brain's been fully developed for a few years now. You could've been driving yourself sooner."

"Every last ounce of brainpower went into saving M2G from bankruptcy."

"*Bankruptcy?*"

"It was bad, Daph. It was very, very bad. We weren't imminently at bankruptcy, but we were close."

I munch into my own taco while I mull that over. "No wonder you look so old."

He laughs again, then throws a napkin at me.

"Boring," I tease. "If you really want to throw something, throw a chip covered in queso."

He stares at me, his face doing that thing I've come to recognize as him consciously fighting his instinctive first reaction. It's like he's actively suppressing the urge to tell me to grow up.

But I think he's doing that for himself.

Not because I called him boring. More likely because he's spent a lifetime training himself to suppress his lighthearted side, and he recognizes it, and he's trying to override habit to get back to who he's supposed to be.

And that makes my heart hurt for him.

He should've always been free to be who he is.

He shakes his head, looking off into the distance, and then he frowns. "What—" he starts.

I turn to look at what has him distracted, and that, my friends, is my fatal mistake.

The giggle hits my ear a nanosecond before Oliver's finger lands in my ear.

His wet, sticky—"*Did you just put queso in my ear?*"

I spin back and find him dancing away from the picnic table, laughing so hard he can barely bolt in a straight line.

I grab napkins and rub at my ear—oh my god, I need a shower—and take off after him, laughing too. "I know where you sleep, you jerk!"

"Not if I leave you here." He dodges around a tree, his entire face split in the widest, happiest smile I've ever seen. Eyes glowing.

Having fun.

I chase him all over the picnic area and finally dive into him when I leap over the picnic table.

He *oof*s as we both tumble to the ground, but when he rolls so he's on top of me, he's still smiling.

He brushes a loose strand of hair back from my face, and then he lowers his lips to mine and kisses me until I can't breathe.

"Forgive me?" he murmurs against my neck after he pulls out of the kiss.

"I'm so proud of you," I murmur back. "And you owe me a thorough ear-cleaning."

He snickers.

I crack up too.

Who would've guessed that he had this in him?

Certainly not me.

But I'm thrilled to be the one with him as he discovers his playful side.

31

Happiness always has a price
Oliver

This road trip has changed my life in ways I never could've seen coming.

Having Daphne along has been the gift I didn't know I needed, and now, as I'm waiting for her to return from the shower facilities at the state park where we're camping tonight near the mountains somewhere in North Central Colorado, I've firmly decided I'm changing my plans.

I won't find a home in any town we travel through between now and the end of my two weeks. Absolutely positive.

There's a frizzy-edged panic around my heart at the idea of where I want to go—it's too close to my family—but I also know panic doesn't mean it's wrong.

It means this is complicated and I have some work to do.

But if this is what Daphne's regular life is like—weekend camping trips to disconnect and soak in the world that she wants to save, days spent making a difference and seeing the family she's made with her friend Bea, trying new things, diving into the unknown while having a safe place to go home to—how could I not want to be there with her?

Not because she has the life I want.

Lots of people have the life I want.

It's that I want to experience it *with her*.

And only her.

I'm shaking my head as I lie on my back and stare up at the wide-open sky when she returns.

"My ears are cheeseless, and now I'm hungry," she announces. "What's with the face? I'm not looking where you're looking again. Never let it be said I don't occasionally learn from my mistakes."

Smiling has never been this easy. "That shirt too warm?"

She's in a long-sleeved white blouse that hides her tattoos and short jean shorts that show off her legs, and I suddenly wonder if we can order takeout to a campsite.

"No, you did good," she tells me. "It's nice and lightweight. You ready for dinner? I could eat as much as Simon's boys usually do combined. And if you don't know anything about thirteen-year-old boys, trust me when I say it's a lot."

I hold out a hand.

She grabs it and pulls me up, and I accidentally-on-purpose stop too close to her so I can sniff her shampoo and slip my arms around her waist and hug her tightly. "You smell amazing."

"You feel amazing."

Yeah.

I'm absolutely not letting her go. I don't care how close she lives to Manhattan. I don't care that my parents will be able to track me down and yell at me after the board meeting next week.

Daph's worth it.

Her stomach growls loudly. "Take me to food."

"Okay, okay. Food for you."

She drives, grinning the whole way. "I found the best place," she tells me as we pull into the parking lot of what looks like an Old West saloon in a strip mall in the middle of the nearest town. "They have a mechanical bull *and* karaoke."

"Are you—of course you're serious." I knew about the karaoke.

I did not know about the mechanical bull.

She giggles. "Excited?"

"Hell, yes."

I'll strip her naked in the tent later.

For now—yeah.

This is epic.

It's not quite seven, so the sun's still out, but inside, you wouldn't guess. No windows. Wanted posters are intermixed with dollar bills stapled to the walls and ceiling. The bar itself looks like it hasn't been fully cleaned in several decades. The floor longer. Our table wobbles more than the drunk guy at the end of the bar, and our server is in a cowboy hat.

"How did you find this place?" I ask Daphne over the sounds of someone singing karaoke so badly that I suddenly have far more faith in my ability to do the same.

"The magic of the internet."

"If I searched *fun place to go for dinner*, my phone would've steered me to a chain restaurant."

"We are definitely training your search results better. Now. What song are you singing first? And don't tell me that Waverly Sweet one we were singing in the car earlier. I don't want you to ever find out what the real lyrics are. I like yours better."

I lean across the table and kiss her.

Can't help myself.

Especially when kissing her earns me one of those broad, wide, uninhibited smiles that makes me feel like life truly can be simple.

Easy.

Experienced through the joy of the little things like the smile of the woman you love.

"Or we can try out the mechanical bull first," she says.

I raise a brow. "That won't…hurt things…will it?"

She leans closer to me and props her chin on her fist. "Oliver. Do you honestly think I'd put your wonder stick in danger?"

God, I love her.

I do.

She's hilarious and fun and underneath it all, she has the kind of heart that's willing to put her entire life on hold to help a guy she's never liked.

"Maybe," I tell her. "You could still be mad about the queso."

She laughs at that.

We order buffalo burgers and fries—hers with a side of cheese dip—along with milkshakes—chocolate for me, cookies and cream for her—and while we're waiting for our food, Daph gets us both onto the mechanical bull.

"Better before we're stuffed," she says as my name's called.

My *other* name.

My Tom name. The name that she has to remind me is mine.

I make it four seconds, which has her rolling. But I'm happy to report there's no damage to my wonder stick.

They call Maribella—her name for the evening—immediately after me, and she shows me up by making it seven whole seconds.

"Really thought you'd go for thirty," I tell her as we make our way back to our table.

No one's looking at us. Someone else is already up on the bull, and they might make it thirty seconds. Seem to have a good handle on what they're doing in ways that Daph and I—or maybe just I—definitely don't.

"I'm out of practice," she replies with a grin.

"They have a mechanical bull somewhere back home?"

"No, but you know what? I'll tell Bea that if she ever takes her burger bus into a physical location, she should totally add one."

"Is Bea the type to add a mechanical bull?"

Daphne laughs. "Not unless I goad her. Simon would be on my side though. That'll help."

Our burgers and shakes arrive almost as soon as we're seated again, and I'm not exaggerating when I say this is the best burger I've ever had in my life.

"Wait until you try Bea's," Daphne tells me.

Though she's eating her burger like it's the best burger she's ever had in her life too.

I stare at her pointedly.

She rolls her eyes. "Dude. This is me being hungry. Bea's burgers are better. Even though they're not buffalo. They're normal beef. Oh my god. That shake though. Have you tried yours? Wow. Wow, that's good."

Yeah.

This is what I want.

Dinners with Daphne every night.

It's like there's not a single thing in life that she's not enthusiastic about, and I adore that about her.

We spend three hours at dinner, ordering extra milkshakes and fries while we take turns at karaoke, attempting to one-up each other with how bad we can be until Daphne finally admits I win.

And then she whispers that she'd like to go back to our tent and give me my first-place prize.

I can't pay the bill fast enough, and since I'm operating with cash, that makes it pretty fucking fast.

We stumble out into the parking lot, drunk on nothing more than happiness and horniness, my arm looped around her neck, her hand tucked into my back pocket, my throat a tad sore from all of the karaoke, and it hits me.

I'm not paranoid anymore.

Not worried about not having security.

Not worried someone will recognize us.

Not even worried they'll talk about the size of the tip I left on the table inside.

I'm free.

I'm completely, totally, undeniably *free*.

That's exactly what I'm thinking when we reach the little SUV. I've put my hand on the passenger handle to unlock and open it for Daphne when I catch up to the fact that all is not, in fact, well.

There's a man watching us.

And he's not only watching us.

He's *waiting* for us.

Leaning casually against the side of a Mercedes sedan two empty spaces over from us.

Arms folded.

Glaring at us in the light of the moon.

I'm caught between wanting to tell Daph to leave without me and the still-instinctive response of kowtowing to authority, and I don't find my spine fast enough.

Because Daphne's caught sight of who's here.

But her whimpered gasp—yeah.

That does it.

That helps.

"Get in the car," I murmur to her.

"Don't even think of getting in that car," her father replies. "The three of us need to have a talk."

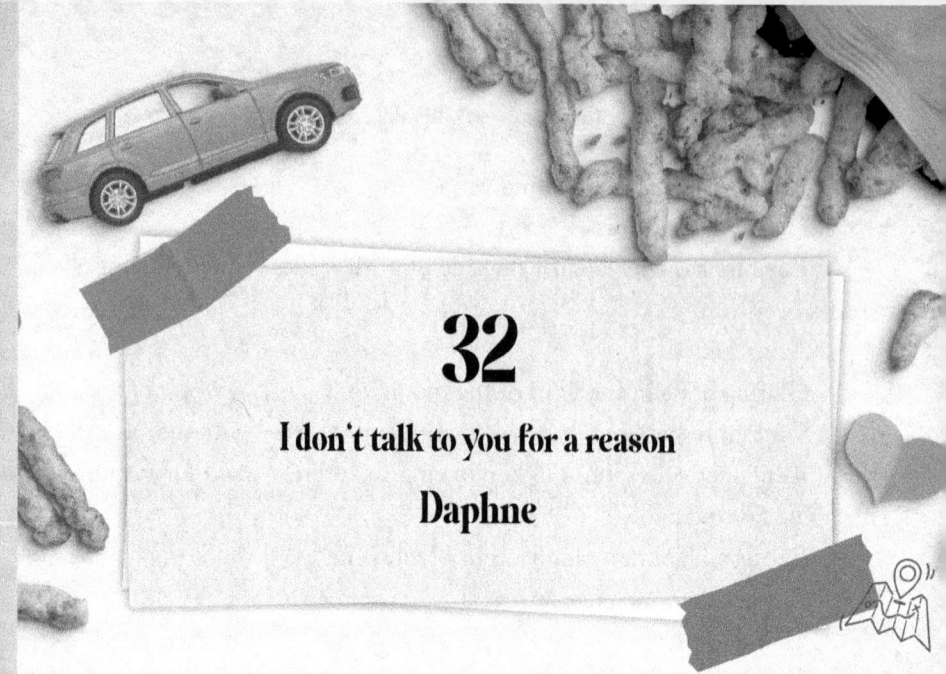

32

I don't talk to you for a reason

Daphne

There aren't many things in life that I can't roll with.

Not after everything I've been through since being disinherited.

But my father showing up in the middle of nowhere, Colorado, all the way across the country from New York, is a punch to the gut that I can't immediately get over.

He hasn't called.

He hasn't come to visit.

So what the hell is he doing here?

"Get in the car," Oliver repeats to me. He's moved so that he's between us, pressing me against the door of the car without direct view to my father.

"I always liked you, Oliver," my father says. "Always thought you were smart. But this…this isn't looking so smart."

Oliver's as tense as an overstretched trampoline. "Frankly, Tobias, this is none of your business."

"You're with my daughter, so you've made it my business."

Oliver snorts. "So *now* you want to claim her? Get lost."

My father growls softly. "She doesn't have to fuck everything up for us here like she usually does."

I flinch.

I don't *want* to, but I do.

"Watch your mouth," Oliver growls.

"And now she can't even face me while she does it," the man who threw me away continues.

"She doesn't owe you a thing. What are you doing here?"

"Negotiating for your future."

"My future's fine."

"But it could be better."

"Not interested." Oliver turns away from him and puts a hand to my lower back. "Let's get in on the other side. I'll drive. You sit in back."

The car's face-first in the spot along the edge of the parking lot. We'll need to back out, and if my father wants something—no doubt he'll stand behind the car and make us run him over to get out.

I look up at Oliver.

He peers down at me, and my breath leaves me.

This man—this man is prepared to protect me at all costs.

Me.

Fuckup Daphne.

He's looking at me as if he's my personal bodyguard and he wants me to know that he has me.

"Find out what he wants so he'll leave," I murmur.

"First smart thing she's said in her entire life," my father says.

Oliver rounds on him. "Shut. Your fucking. Mouth."

Two security agents close in beside my father, but he waves them away. "I've got this. He's harmless."

I grip Oliver's hand and slide halfway out from behind him. "What do you want?" I ask.

He answers Oliver instead of looking at me. "My first choice was Margot to get this deal done, but if you need one of my daughters to go with the merger, then as far as I'm concerned, she'll do."

"*She'll do?*" Oliver repeats.

"It's cleaner when the companies stay in the family. Now, we'll need to have a discussion about why you let her kidnap you—"

"Oh my god, what the fuck is wrong with you?" I yelp.

Yeah.

Me.

Turns out, fear morphs into rage pretty quickly when my father's forcing himself back into my life.

"She did *not* kidnap me," Oliver says, low and tight. "We're both here because we want to be."

"You *want* to be here," my father repeats.

"Said that, didn't I?"

"With *her*."

I tense.

Oliver snorts, but this snort—it's dangerous. "With *Daphne*. Yes. That's her name. And I *like* being with Daphne."

"You *like* this? That's the stupidest thing I've ever—"

And that's the last thing he says before Oliver's fist connects with my father's face.

A *crunch* echoes over the parking lot, even over the sounds of karaoke rolling out of the bar, and then Oliver has my father shoved back against the car. "You don't deserve her, you worthless piece of shit."

My father's security guys grab at him, but Oliver shakes my father again. "You're going to get in this car and go back where you came from and you're going to—let go of me. *Fucking let go of me.*"

I grab at one of the security guys trying to pull Oliver off my father. "Let go of him."

He shoves me away.

So I leap on his back. "*I said let go of him.*"

Oliver's fighting with my father's other security guy.

I'm being thrust back against our SUV.

No idea what my father's doing.

Probably cowering and hiding like the pampered asshole that he is.

I vaguely register that people are starting to spill out of the bar to watch, because I'm struggling to catch my breath.

This isn't the answer.

I know brawling isn't the answer.

But hell if I'll let them do anything bad to Oliver.

"I don't want to hurt you, Daphne," the security guy I'm trying to strangle says.

"Then *let us go.*"

Oliver lands a punch on the other security agent. "Leave us the fuck alone," he barks.

"Police!" my father bellows. "Police, help!"

Fuck.

Fuuuuuck.

Sheriff's deputies are here.

Where did they come from?

Oh, god.

No.

No.

People are filming us.

Bea's going to see this.

Margot's going to see this.

The deputies converge on Oliver and pull him off the security agent while he thrashes about, and I see everything as it's about to happen.

They'll arrest him.

He has a fake ID.

I have no ID.

My father will win.

He'll fucking *win.*

Again.

I'm crying.

I don't even realize I've started crying, but I am.

I'm full-on sobbing.

"Let him go," I say to the deputies who are still trying to get a solid grip on Oliver.

"Daph, get off," the security agent says.

He's familiar.

I think he's traveled with Margot a time or two. I tend to ignore anything that reminds me that she's still supported by our family when she comes to visit, and she's never made a fuss about it.

"Arrest him," my father spits. He's pressing a handkerchief to his nose. "I'm pressing charges."

"*No*," I yelp as I finally slide off the other security guy.

"He assaulted me."

Shit.

Shit.

This is going to get bad.

This is going to get *so* bad.

"Why do you have to ruin everything?" I yell at my father. "Let him go. He didn't do anything. He was defending me. *You* did this. You abusive, narcissistic, fucking asshole of a human being. I am not a fucking pawn in your fucking games. You don't get to throw me away and then use me again when I'm convenient."

"Ma'am, please back up," one of the deputies says to me.

"Don't arrest him," I whisper. "Please, please don't arrest him."

"First time for everything, Daph," Oliver says. He's quit fighting them too. "It's okay."

"It is *not* okay."

Another sheriff's car rolls in, blocking us, and two more deputies spill out.

"Always this bar," one of them mutters.

"Why we patrol it," the second one says back.

"Get him out of my face," my father says. "He abducted my daughter."

"Oh my god, *shut up*," I say. "You disowned me. You disinherited me. You don't give two shits about me."

"Ma'am, did he abduct you?" one of the deputies asks me.

"*No.* I'm with him of my own free will. He didn't do anything wrong. He was defending me."

"Get him out of here," one of the deputies says to another, jerking his head toward Oliver. "We'll sort it at the station."

"*No*," I say again.

Oh my god.

They have him in handcuffs.

"Ma'am, you can come over to the station too," one of the deputies says to me.

"Arrest me," I reply.

"Ma'am?"

I point to the security agent. "I attacked this man. You need to arrest me too."

"I don't need to press charges," the security guy says. "Honest misunderstanding."

"Quit making a fool of yourself, Daphne," my father says.

"Daph, it'll be okay," Oliver says. "Ignore this twatcanoe. He doesn't deserve you."

Twatcanoe.

Oh my god.

I love him.

I love him so much.

"*Arrest me too*," I say to the deputy.

He smirks a little. "Ma'am—"

Fuck it.

Just *fuck it*.

Oliver was defending my honor.

I'm not letting him go to jail by himself.

And you know what else?

I've wanted to do this for *ages*.

And so I do.

I break away from the security guard, away from the deputy, and I charge my father.

And I punch him too.

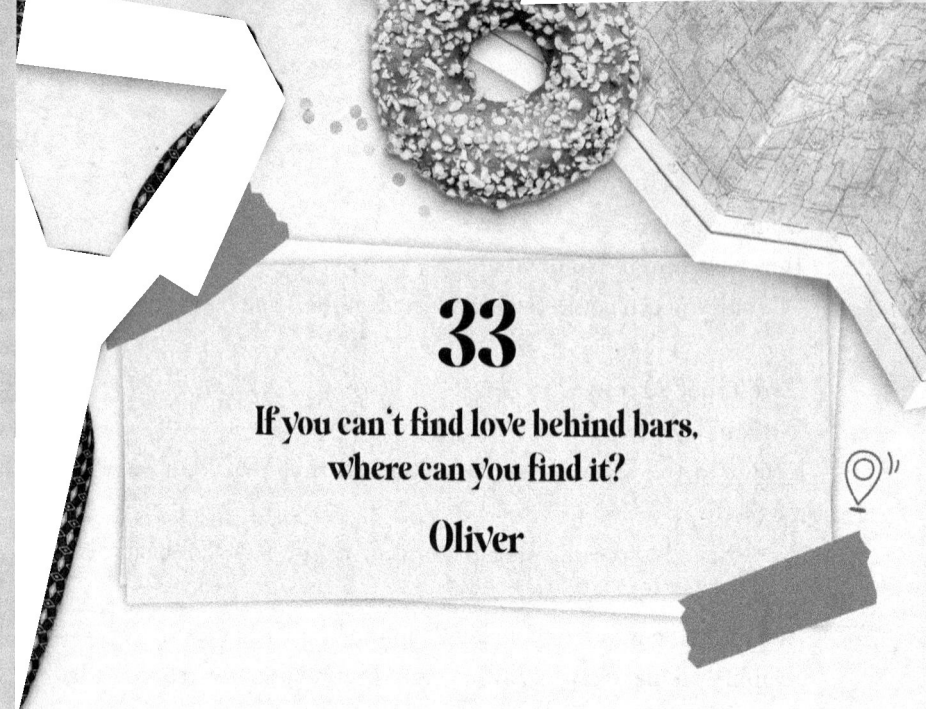

33

If you can't find love behind bars, where can you find it?

Oliver

Jail is both exactly what I expected and nothing at all like what I expected.

There are metal bars to this one.

Daph and I are in separate cells, but I can see her.

It's been hours since her father showed up in the parking lot, and my adrenaline is finally fading. Probably close to sunrise by now, though there aren't any windows or a clock to judge by.

Daphne's pacing.

I'm stretched out on the hard bench.

No toilets in the cells. Maybe that's a prison thing. The deputy who checked us in—so we could calm down while they investigated our stories about our real identities, he said—told us to tell him if we need to use the facilities. He's in a room outside the cells, visible through a large glass window.

I lift my head and glance around, then ask a question I probably should've asked when we were first put in here. "They have video cameras in here?"

"Yes."

We've both been pretty quiet so far.

But not talking to Daph is starting to bother me. "So I shouldn't compliment your form?"

"*Oliver.*"

I smile. "You promised new experiences, and you definitely delivered."

She looks at me, and it's like our roles have been completely reversed.

She is now the adult in our relationship.

She's the one who knew what to say when the deputies started going through my car and found a suitcase of cash. She's the one who knew what to say when they realized my ID was fake and she didn't have any.

And she's the one trying to keep me from making this situation any worse.

Not that I'm overly concerned.

Money can buy its way out of situations like this. Even when money's fighting with money.

But I suspect enough people got my fight with Tobias Merriweather-Brown on video—including all of the things Daphne said to him after the deputies restrained me—that he won't be able to hide from his part in it.

Namely, the parts where he insulted Daphne. Where he tried to cut her to the bone.

The parts where you can see that me punching him was justified.

"Everything will be okay," I tell her.

"We'll be all over the internet. Everyone's going to see."

Yeah. Thought about that.

Gonna make next week harder. The board won't be as inclined to listen to a CEO who got arrested for punching a supposed friend while running away.

And that has another thought cementing more firmly in my head.

"Daph?"

"Yeah?"

"I have to go back. To Manhattan."

Her face drains of color.

"You don't," I say quickly. "You shouldn't go back. You shouldn't *ever* go back. Not where I'm going. You should go home. Be where you're happy. But I—there are things I need to handle myself."

She grips the bar of her cell, which is across the hall from mine, so I can't even touch her. "It's bad for you," she whispers.

"It is," I agree. "But I need to leave it the right way. Not running away. I need to take ownership one last time."

"Oliver—"

"I was going to settle somewhere west of the Mississippi in a flyover state. New name, new identity, pay whatever I had to pay in back-alley channels to get set up in a small town where I could meet my neighbors and get a job mowing grass or popping popcorn behind the ticket counter at a movie theater."

"You didn't know where you were going? At all?"

"Everyone would expect me to disappear to a beach in another country."

She drops her forehead to the bars, a small smile playing on her lips. "I honestly thought you were going to Mexico to pretend to be an Italian banking executive."

"And you wouldn't be the only one. Hence, staying in the US, but in some obscure town I'd never heard of before, because if I'd never heard of it, I never would've mentioned it, and they wouldn't have the first clue where to start looking."

"That's brilliant."

"Thank you. I hope it's the last brilliant thing I ever do."

She laughs a little. "You would love Simon. He'd say the same thing."

"Daph?"

"What?"

"I'm looking forward to meeting him. Bea too. And her brothers."

the grumpiest billionaire

Her eyes blink open, and she stares at me. Her face puckers under all of that glowing red-orange hair with her new dye job, and her eyes go shiny.

She doesn't say a word, but she doesn't have to.

I can *feel* it.

The hope.

The love.

The desire.

"I don't need to keep looking for where I want to live. I already know." My voice is getting thicker.

This isn't how I should do it.

I shouldn't tell her I love her while we're in jail.

But I want her to know—I want her to know I want her in my life.

"My home—it's kinda close to the city," she says. "Comparatively speaking."

"Doesn't mean we ever have to go there."

"But they—they can come to us."

They.

Her family.

My family.

My family that I need to tell, to their faces, that I'm done.

With the company.

With the expectations.

With them, depending on how they take it.

"They're all stupid billionaires," I remind her. "They can go wherever they want. And they won't come to us. They're too caught up in their own lives to care that we're happy living ours."

She sinks into a squat, hands still on the bars, and keeps staring at me. "Falling asleep in your car was the best fuckup of my life."

I swing to sitting, then cross the small cell so I can squat at her level and be as close to her as I can get. "It wasn't a fuckup."

"I don't want this to be a Hindenburg principle either."

The way she can make me laugh while we're in two different jail cells—this is the kind of happiness I've been searching for my whole life. "Only one way to find out."

"What if you hate it?"

"I have my serial—my, ah, hunting lodge in Pennsylvania."

Her eyes nearly cross, and then she's laughing. "You are *not* what I expected."

"I'm not sure I'm what I expected either, but I like this me. And we're only getting started."

"Oliver—changing your entire personality—"

"I'm not changing my personality. I'm letting myself be who I want to be. I've *always* wanted to stick queso in your ear. I've just never been brave enough to do it when I knew it wasn't what a Cumberland is expected to do."

"What else do you want to do?"

"Sleep."

She laughs again, then wrinkles her nose at me. "*After* you sleep."

"No clue. Whatever sounds fun. New. Different. *Normal.* I want to change the oil in a car and plant flowers at a house that has no more than seven rooms in it. I want to sleep in a hammock in my backyard. I want to get a dog. Maybe I'll wash windows. Maybe I'll go to school to learn to be a chef. Maybe I'll watch all of the movies I missed when I get a job as the popcorn maker at a theater. Other than continuing to give away most of my fortune, I don't know what I want to do. I want to try everything until I find what fits. In a place I like. With my favorite people."

"How many favorite people do you have?"

"One so far. But she's pretty fucking iconic. It's like having seven favorite people."

She blinks rapidly, her smile wobbling, and she sucks in a big breath. "Oliver, I—"

"Good news, Ms. Merriweather-Brown." The door to the office area slams behind the deputy. "Your attorney and your sister have both assured us you won't cause any more trouble, and your father is declining to press charges, so you're free to go."

He saunters between us and uses a key to open her door.

She stumbles to her feet, glancing between me and the deputy. "Margot called?"

"Your attorney called. Your sister's here."

She looks at me again. "What about Oliver?" she asks the deputy.

The guy looks between us, then back at the window. "She said she was only here for you."

Shit.

Shit.

"I'm not leaving without—"

"Daphne." I shake my head. "Go home. I'll be okay. I'll see you in a week."

"Oliver—"

"Go home," I repeat. "Go be where you're happy with the family you love best. The road trip's over. We're made. And I have some things I need to clean up when I get out of here."

"I don't want to—"

"Daph. It's okay. I'm okay. I need to know you're okay, and here? This isn't where you deserve to be."

Her brown eyes blink rapidly while she studies me. "Okay. Okay. You've got this. You can survive on your own now."

"One week. I'll come find you."

She glances at the window, and I do too.

Margot's there.

She has her back to us, and she's on her phone, but she's there. That's her hair. Her posture. One of her pantsuits.

"She loves you," I remind Daphne. "Trust her."

"Let's get a move on, Ms. Merriweather-Brown," the deputy says.

Daph looks at me once more, her eyes filling with tears that she blinks away with a forced determination that demonstrates how strong she's had to be and how much her parents always underestimated her.

"A week. I'm holding you to that." She presses a kiss to her fingertips, then brushes it against my knuckles, and then she leaves the jail without another backward glance.

34

Home isn't home when I'm missing my heart

Daphne

"You should've gotten Oliver out too," I say to Margot while her private jet lifts off from a small airfield north of Denver. It's not the first time I've said it.

It likely won't be the last.

But this time, instead of telling me that his own attorneys can handle things for him, that he's in a lot more trouble because our father is refusing to drop the charges against him, or that it's good for him after what he's put his parents through, she squeezes her eyes shut, takes a notebook from the messenger bag beside her, and scribbles a note that she hands to me.

Would you please trust me?

I recline back into the plush seat and eyeball her.

She takes the note back and shreds it, tearing it into strips that she deposits into the water glass on the built-in console beside her.

"Thank you for getting here so fast," I say meekly.

Her face softens, and she looks less like the angry CEO who marched me out of the county jail and more like the sister who comes to visit me on the weekends. "Bea and I have been waiting for the call all week. I've had the plane on standby since Sunday."

I sit straighter. "Oh, god, did she see the footage?"

"It's highly unlikely that anyone you've ever known could've missed it."

I cringe while the plane dips in a bit of turbulence. "Can I call her?"

"If you'd like."

"I didn't mean to get arrested. I mean, in the end, I did, but I didn't think the road trip would end like…this."

"If our father hadn't hired a private detective to verify you two were on a road trip after his staff alerted him to the coverage last weekend, and then decided to do…what he did… you wouldn't have gotten arrested either."

"What the hell was wrong with him? I'm not a pawn in his corporate games. And Oliver—" I suck in a deep breath, then plunge ahead. "Oliver's not going back to Miles2Go."

Margot and I haven't talked about the elephant in the plane.

Not the thing where Margot left Oliver in jail, but the thing where it's obvious she knows how bad I have it for him, and we don't have to speak in code about it and make me wonder if I'm understanding her correctly this time.

And honestly?

If she *is* mad about it…I think I'd pick Oliver.

Because he's picking me.

And that thought has my nose burning and my eyes getting wet.

He says he's picking me.

For the first time in my adult life, I don't know what I'll do if it turns out a man has lied to me.

Because for the first time in my entire life, I am honestly, truly, and completely in love.

It's the scariest thing in the world to know what it feels like to be abandoned and still want someone to love you anyway.

To wonder if he'll get mad that I left him in jail and decide after a few days away from me that I'm not worth it after all.

If I really am just a pawn.

Margot hands me a tissue. "What happened?" she asks softly.

The whole story comes tumbling out.

Me going to tell him to leave her alone. Waking up in his back seat as he drove into Pennsylvania. Realizing he was running away and that he needed more help than he could've possibly understood or anticipated. His first attempt at pumping gas. The way he looked so old and stressed and tired. Him sleeping through the first two days. Us fighting, where he fought back.

Realizing he wasn't who I always thought he was. That he's changed.

His donut apology.

Angelina Juliana Priestly, who's in the car back in Colorado.

Giving away as much cash as we could.

Drinking the Chateau Cheval Blanc with hot dogs and s'mores over a campfire.

Bea's heads-up that we were drawing attention by giving away so much money.

Lying low. Heading to Colorado so he could see the sun rise and set over the mountains, which we won't get to do now. And finally, the saloon.

"I love him," I whisper to Margot as I finish up. "I didn't mean to. I didn't want to. But he's—he's not who I remember. He's fun and he's a little lost and he's a lot like me—he doesn't fit where we always thought we were supposed to fit, but he wants to do good in the world and he recognizes his privilege and it's so irresistibly attractive. And I—please don't hate me."

She doesn't flinch.

She's smiled at times, cringed a little at other times as I've poured it all out, but me telling her that I love her ex-fiancé?

All that gets is another soft smile. "Good," she whispers.

"*Good*? Seriously?"

"Daph, do you have any idea why you're my favorite person in the universe?"

"Because you're a saint?"

"Because you have the biggest heart of anyone I've ever known. You have always—*always*—lived your life with kindness and compassion right beside the chaos and the fun. When you had access to family money, you used it to make other people happy. Remember when you bought a car for the cafeteria lady in your dorm at Vanderbilt? And when you sent a hundred pizzas to that school whose principal had died? And when you funded every pet shelter in the city for two years? While people like Archie Westmore were buying themselves yachts and vacations all over the world?"

I don't mention to her that Oliver and Archie are apparently besties.

I'm too busy trying to see through the waterfall in my eyes.

"And then you put your entire life on hold to help someone you actively disliked when you realized he was in crisis," Margot says. "I have never understood how our parents couldn't adore you the same way I do. You are the easiest person in the world to love, and I'm so, so glad that someone who also has a ridiculously huge heart can see that."

"You—you think Oliver has a big heart?"

"He used to bring extra food on picnics to feed the ants, Daph. The signs were always there. You two fit in a way that he and I never would've. Not long-term."

"But you said you wanted him back."

"Guess I'll have to find another way to help the Aurora Gardens empire branch out beyond hotels. Maybe there's an airline heir who owns fifty-one percent of his family's company somewhere."

I gasp.

She cocks a sardonic grin that tells me she's mostly not serious.

And I dissolve into tears again.

She passes me another tissue.

"Daph—" she starts, then shakes her head.

"What?"

"I don't—I need you to know—I never loved Oliver."

I gasp again. "*How could you not love him?*"

the grumpiest billionaire

"It wasn't his fault. It was all mine. You were right. He was safe. We were boring together. We rarely fought. We agreed about everything, had the same goals, wanted the same kind of life, and he *is* kind, which made it easy to like him. Our relationship was comfortable and compatible, but it wasn't—Daphne, it couldn't have been love, because I don't know *how* to love someone."

Is she serious?

She can't be serious. "*Margot.*"

"You know how to love. You know how to put your whole heart into things in a way that I—that I'm not built for. So you and Oliver? Being this happy together?"

I arch a brow as I blow my nose again, tears drying on my cheeks.

She cracks a half-smile. "If you're this miserable without him, I can only imagine how happy you are with him."

"So happy," I whisper. "But you—you do too know how to love. You love me. You show me all the time."

"Loving you is cheating. It's too easy."

"*You flew across the country to bail me out of jail.*"

"I got an excuse to see you sooner than I would've otherwise. This was entirely selfish."

I scowl at her.

"You being disinherited changed me too," she says softly. "And whatever labels you want to put on it, I never had what you have. How you live your life. The way you feel about Oliver. I thought I loved him at the time, but the kind of love I can give someone—it's not enough. He deserves more. Especially now, after all that he's been through. And you keep saying I should have big, messy, exciting, life-altering love. Daph, you've found it and you'll thrive in it. I never will. And I'm okay with that. My life is good. Amazing, even. Just as it is. Especially with you in it."

"But—"

"What would you tell me if our roles were reversed?"

If Margot had found someone who made her world that much brighter and more perfect, if she found someone who finally made the puzzle pieces of her life make sense, if she found someone she loved so desperately that leaving him behind made her feel like her heart would never work right again?

Even if I'd been with him before?

I'd tell her everything she's telling me.

Because I'd want her to be happy.

That's what you want for the people you love.

My eyes overflow again. "Thank you," I whisper. "I love you so much."

She rubs my knee. "You really are my favorite person on the planet, Daphne. Always."

I need a few minutes before I can talk normally again. "He says he's coming to find me at home in a week."

"If that's what he says, then that's what he'll do."

"What if—what if he doesn't? What if this entire road trip was some big dream? What if he realizes I'm a pain in the ass and he doesn't want me anymore once the road magic wears off?"

She squeezes my hand. "Then you keep the good memories and let me handle the rest. I might be able to appreciate him if he makes you happy, but if he hurts you, well, I hear Bea has a brother with all the resources necessary to hide a body."

I laugh until I'm crying again.

Margot pulls herself out of her seat and joins me in mine, hugging me tight. "I missed you," she tells me while she presses a kiss to my forehead. "You make life the best kind of interesting."

"You're sure you aren't mad at me? Not even the littlest bit?"

"Daph. He's *bossy* and arrogant now. *And* he punches people? You know that'd never work with what I'd accept in a man. If I ever get back in the dating game, I want meek and subservient."

"You are the very best sister in the entire universe."

"Not even close." She nudges my phone. "Call Bea. She's worried, and she needs to hear from you that you're okay."

So I do.

I call my best friend, my bonus sister, and I repeat my story all over again.

And then I somehow sleep the rest of the flight.

Margot's pilot delivers us to Albany instead of the city, and Bea picks me up in Simon's car. Well, the car that his security people have been driving him around in.

Not like she was driving her burger bus out here, and she apparently hasn't replaced her own car yet after an incident with a tree a month or so ago.

She crushes me in a hug, her curly brown hair wild like she's been running her fingers through it. She smells a little like cooking oil and a lot like some new kind of shampoo, and I swear I've never had a better hug from her.

She hugs Margot too, and the two of them have a quick whispered conversation that I don't even attempt to overhear before Margot hugs me one last time and then gets into a car that's waiting for her at the airport.

Bea gets me buckled in like I'm a little kid again, and I can't argue with that either. I'm tired, and I'm worried about Oliver, and I could sleep for four days.

That would make a lot of the next week pass by quicker.

And that's when I realize I don't have Oliver's phone number.

And he doesn't have mine.

We never traded numbers.

We didn't have to.

"Daph?" Bea says softly. "You okay?"

Everything around me is familiar. It's home.

And I feel upside down and inside out. "I forgot to get his phone number," I whisper.

She squeezes my hand as she steers us out of the parking lot of the private airfield. "The guy I saw on that video last night? He won't let something like not having your phone number stop him."

"I left him in jail, Bea."

She grins. "Then you'll *really* know he loves you when he shows up like he said he would next week."

I'm tired of crying.

So tired of crying.

"Tell me everything about you and Simon and the burger bus," I say to her.

"*Everything?*"

"Everything. And please don't get mad if I fall asleep while you're talking. I missed your voice so much, and I miss Oliver, but also—I'm so glad to be home. I'm so glad *you're* my home."

"Do you want me to start at the part where you were right that what he did was a forgivable offense and I'd already decided to see if we could work things out when I found out he bought the drive-in and was showing my favorite movie, or do you need a refresher on why we were temporarily mad at him in the first place?"

I stare at her. "*He bought the drive-in?*"

Her face lights up, and she launches into her story.

I don't fall asleep on the ride home.

It's obvious I missed a ton while I was gone, and I want to soak in every detail.

I want to live my life. And be happy with the family I've chosen.

And trust that Oliver will still want to come find me after he's back in his regular element too.

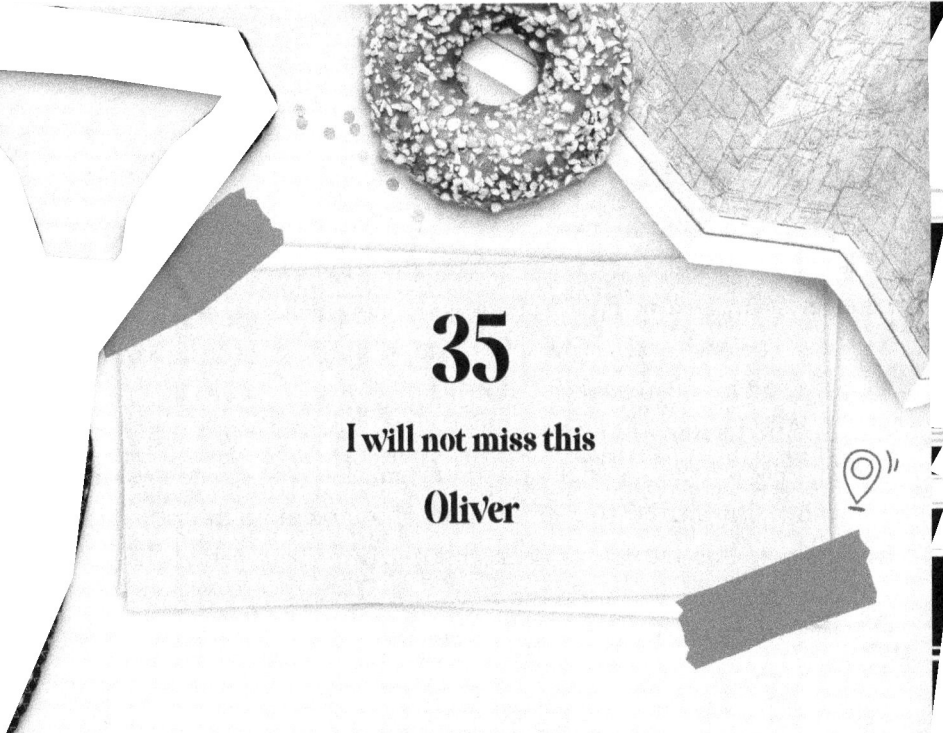

35

I will not miss this

Oliver

When I arrive back in Manhattan late Friday after getting out of jail and driving myself back across the country, there's no one I want to see and nothing I want to do here, yet I'm immediately plunged back into a world where there's too much to do and not enough time to do it in.

Stupid fucking decision to handle leaving the right way.

Even if it's necessary.

Charges were dropped against me back in Colorado, and it's unclear if it was the sheriff's decision or if Tobias Merriweather-Brown saw that he was losing public opinion polls following the videos of our fight going viral.

I'm staying with Archie, and Daphne's right.

He's a dick.

He's a dick who told Margot he was with me when he called to get Daphne's phone number after Margot wouldn't answer my calls.

She hung up on him and won't answer either of our calls now.

I go see my parents on Saturday because time and distance and seeing Daphne's father has given me perspective.

Maybe my parents aren't awful.

Not the way hers are.

But my mother spends the entire thirty-nine minutes—as long as I last there—talking about how relieved she is to finally be able to spend money again, and my father talking about how glad he is that I understand he belongs back in the CEO seat, with neither of them saying a word about my own arrest in Colorado.

And I know.

I know that they might not be the same kind of awful as the Merriweather-Browns, but they're also dicks who are completely disconnected from reality, and I can't be around them for long periods of time without feeling like I can't breathe.

Especially after tasting freedom.

Happiness.

Fun.

With a purpose.

When I'm not practicing with Archie what I'm going to say at the board meeting on Monday, I take some time to seek out the social media and news coverage of the results of all of the money Daph and I gave away, and it gives me a sense of peace that reinforces that I'm doing the right thing.

Mostly.

Possibly I'm also being a dick, considering *how* I'm leaving.

Possibly I don't care on this one.

I get in touch with Carmen, and over a private dinner at Archie's place on Sunday, I tell her my plans for the board meeting tomorrow.

Should've done it sooner, but apparently stress had short-circuited my brains, and it took clearing my head with the trip across the country with Daphne to realize I didn't want to go into the next phase of my life without closing out this phase the right way.

It's a relief to know Carmen's in.

Her feral smile indicates she's going to relish being involved, in fact.

the grumpiest billionaire

And Monday—Monday arrives faster than I think it will, even though every waking minute of the weekend, there's lingering worry over Daphne and a desperate need for me to be done here so that I can go find her again.

Archie's put out that he doesn't get to do this for me, but when I walk into the boardroom, dressed in a suit that feels foreign after the past two weeks of living in clothes Daphne picked for me, I have no doubts.

I have to do this.

I have to finish the job my father made me take.

I stroll into the board of directors meeting as if nothing's wrong.

The same people who have sat there for the past four years, sometimes berating me, sometimes questioning me, sometimes praising me, are all in their spots around the table. The only difference is that my father has rejoined the table, taking the seat I've occupied for the past four years as though reclaiming his former title is a foregone conclusion, even without board and shareholder approval.

A row of windows overlooks the Manhattan skyline, and I pause for a brief moment to recognize the finality of this view for me.

It's majestic in its own way.

And I can't wait to get the ever-loving hell out of here and discover my new life through Daphne's eyes.

"Ladies and gentlemen, if I may, before we begin?" I say as I stop beside my father's chair.

There's an uncomfortable murmur.

The kind that says my father's been schmoozing and has made it known that he's learned some kind of lesson and will be an even better CEO if he takes over.

The kind that says they're anticipating a fight.

Dad looks up at me with a genial grin. "Guess you've been starting this meeting for a while now, haven't you? Go ahead, son. Show me what you've learned. We can give it to you one last time."

More murmurs.

I make eye contact with every last person sitting at the table, then with Carmen, who accompanied me inside and is seated along the wall beside the door with the other executive assistants, and then I begin.

"Four years ago, I walked into this office for my first board meeting, unprepared and ill-equipped to do what you were about to ask me to do," I say. "While no one would say it out loud, every last one of us knew that Miles2Go was in serious financial trouble, and that my ability to do the job that you had little choice in choosing me to do would determine if we survived or if the corporation my great-grandfather founded would become a footnote in history."

"It wasn't *that* bad," my father grouses.

I ignore him. "In the years since, the world has come to regard me as a success, which is one more lie to have come out of this company. Yes, our profit margins are poised for growth. Yes, our franchise owners are the happiest of all major convenience store chains. And yes, this will be the year that shareholders quit holding their breath and see that all of the changes these past few years are paying off."

A few nods happen around the table.

Someone mutters something about me needing to address my arrest last week.

I ignore that too.

"But here's the lie—I haven't been running this company. Every decision I've made, with the exception of two, has been at the guidance of Carmen Miller. I am not the CEO of Miles2Go. I'm the man who insisted we keep selling corn dogs, the man who insisted that all profits be diverted to philanthropic endeavors, and the man who did everything else exactly as Carmen advised me to do. Therefore, I'm tendering my immediate resignation from the company, with my full endorsement behind Carmen for the role of the next CEO of Miles2Go."

Everyone around the table sits straighter.

There are the expected whispers between the people you'd expect to whisper to each other. A broad grin or two from the people who probably suspected this truth all along. Bewilderment from the two or three people who will be loyal to my father forever.

My father bolts to his feet. "Who do you think you are—"

I cut him off. "Following the shareholder vote to confirm Carmen, I will also be distributing my twenty-five percent share of the stockholdings of Miles2Go to the individual franchise owners across the North American continent, putting more control of the company directly into the hands of the people who interact daily with the customers who keep our business running."

The murmurs become a swell of voices.

"Are you mad?" Davinia Kasper, the company's CFO, asks me.

I smile at her. "I was. Very angry, in fact, for most of my tenure here. Happy to report I've found a new purpose in life and will be leaving Manhattan permanently very soon. I trust you'll be in good hands with Carmen."

"He's lost his marbles," someone I can't identify says. Probably Jerry McFee. He's always thought there was something wrong with me.

"Thank you for your belief in me and in the company my great-grandfather founded," I say to the room. "As I'm no longer your CEO, I won't be staying. But if I could ask for one favor—it would be an honor to see the philanthropic efforts continue when I'm gone. I spent the past two weeks traveling the country and seeing for myself the difference we've made, and I believe the company will only benefit from continuing to be a good neighbor to the world."

I nod to the room. "Thank you. Enjoy your meeting."

I don't take questions. I don't address my arrest—public sentiment was so firmly on my side that it wouldn't have been an issue even if I'd wanted to stay.

I don't shake anyone's hand.

Except Carmen. I stop, thank her personally for everything she's done the past four years, shake her hand, and wish her luck.

She's the second person with my new phone number.

She'd be the third, but Archie's a dick who hasn't gotten me Daphne's phone number.

Also, I don't think she'll use it.

She doesn't need me.

Archie's waiting for me in the lobby of the building. "Someone live streamed that," he tells me as we stroll outside to his waiting car.

"Klein's assistant. Figured he would. Might have said the right thing to the right person to make sure it happened."

"Still live streaming. Want to see?"

"No."

"Not at all?"

"Truly don't give a single fuck what else happens there."

"Even if it's—huh. Weird." He pauses and waves his phone at me. Margot's calling him. "This might be for you."

I wince.

The dickhead grins, then answers. "Morning, Margs. What brings you into my ear today after ignoring me all weekend?"

He climbs into his car.

I follow him. He's giving me a lift to my car, so I have to, unless I want to experience New York City taxis.

Could be fun.

But I'd rather have fun with Daphne than do this on my own.

"Uh-huh," he says into his phone. "Sure, sure. Understood... Great. See you then."

He hangs up and grins at me. "Have an extra twenty minutes?"

I drop my head back against the seat. "Gonna have to sooner or later."

We detour on our way to my car, and I'm honestly not sure what to think when Archie's driver takes us into the parking garage beneath a hotel under renovation.

"Are you in cahoots to murder me?" I ask the man I would've called my best friend right up until this exact minute.

He grins, all of the mischief reminding me so much of Daphne that it hurts.

I miss her. I miss her more than I've ever thought I could miss another person.

"Absolutely not," he says. "I don't have any other friends who are nearly as entertaining as you are."

His driver parks us about four levels underground beside a black Rolls-Royce Phantom with tinted windows.

Archie steps out of the car, and Margot slides into his seat.

She looks the same as she did last month, but nothing about this is the same.

"I hear you've been looking for this," she says, handing me a folded note.

I peek at it, see Daphne's name and a phone number, and it takes every ounce of control I have to not hug her. "You couldn't have—I mean, thank you."

"Had to make you earn it." She quirks a half smile that's far more like Daphne's grin than Archie's grin was but quickly sobers. "You're walking away."

"Entirely."

"Saw the live feed. Do me a favor?"

I brace myself.

I don't know if I'm talking to Daphne's sister or to the business shark who's going to one day run half of this city. "Yes?"

"Stall on distributing those stock shares."

"Shareholder meeting's not for three weeks."

"I might need six or seven."

"For...?"

That smile is the shark smile. "Something you'll approve of. Assuming you're headed where I think you're headed?"

"I'm headed where you think I'm headed."

Her eyes narrow.

"And I'm sorry," I add quietly. "If this hurts you. I truly am. That was never my intention."

"Don't apologize to me. Just be good to my sister."

I eye her warily. "Not even a little mad?"

She smiles. Once again, I'm not sure which smile I'm seeing. "So long as she never tells me I need to be. I'm positive I don't need to tell you the hell I would rain down on you to make you pay if you hurt her."

"You do not."

Her smile relaxes. "We'll talk more later. Stall on that distribution. I'll let you know when I'm ready."

And then she's gone.

Archie climbs back into the back seat beside me, and the car immediately shifts into motion.

"Looks like you still have your balls," he says.

I look behind us.

Margot's car is already gone.

"She's somehow the nicest person in the world and also the most terrifying at the same time," I say.

"What's she up to?"

"I have too many guesses to settle on a single one."

He nods to the note in my hand. "That Daphne's phone number?"

"That's what it claims to be."

"Do I need to plug my ears while you call her?"

I glance at the number, and then up at my friend.

And then I'm the one smiling.

"No. I'm doing something way better than calling."

36

Love is always better with burgers

Daphne

Bea's burger bus—now called Spite Burgers, complete with the name graffitied over the old logo and design, and complete with a new placard mounted next to the menu explaining the history of the name—is still open when I leave work early Monday.

"I thought you were selling out every day," I say to her as I slouch at the chef's table in the back of the bus. I haven't eaten much today, but even the scent of her burgers and fries isn't making me hungry like it would've a few weeks ago.

My stomach is twisted in too many knots.

I could go to Manhattan. I could find Oliver. I could get Archie's number and make him give me Oliver's number since Margot refused when I asked her to get it for me.

She actually hasn't taken my calls at all since the day after I got home, but she warned me she'd be busy, and it wouldn't be about me if she couldn't talk for a bit, even if I heard it was, and that I had to trust her.

I do.

I mean, I'm trying to.

But for once in my life, fear is in control.

Fear that Oliver doesn't want me.

Fear that it was all a dream.

Fear that the magic spell we were under has snapped for him, and he's come to his senses and realized I'd be more trouble than I'm worth.

I'm fraidy-cat Daphne, and I hate it, but I can't make myself fix it.

"She's not only selling out, she's having numerous requests for private parties every day," Simon answers for her. "We prepared more food today though. Marvelous solution to such a lovely problem."

He's shirtless and lingering in the window of the bus, drawing people in. His boys are enjoying their last days of summer vacation, playing video games at a friend's house, so he—and one of his security guys—are here with Bea today.

Bea and Oliver have a lot in common—she's not entirely sure what she's supposed to do with her life, much like Oliver's discovering what he wants to do with his.

But Simon's been eager to help Bea with ideas.

The latest is script-writing.

She told me on our drive home from the airport last week that she made suggestions on a script while I was gone, and he's been asking her for more and more ideas and opinions and insisting she'll get cowriter credit when the studio that made him famous produces this show too.

Every time I've heard her tell him she doesn't know what she's doing, he's grinned and told her neither does most of Hollywood.

And honestly?

I think he's right. About all of it.

None of us know what we're doing.

"We're nearly sold out today too," she tells me. She's manning the grill, finishing three hamburgers for late straggler customers. "Even if we don't sell out all the way, we're close. You sure you don't want anything?"

"I'm good, thanks." I glance at my phone.

No missed calls.

No missed texts.

"Daph, he's had a busy day," Bea says gently.

"I know."

the grumpiest billionaire

I was out working with a department of transportation crew all morning—I *do* need to work for a paycheck, and I still love my job and coworkers—and when I glanced at my phone during my normal lunch break, I had several missed texts.

Oliver blew up the internet again. Second—no, third time in a little over a week.

No one's talking about how we were arrested now or even about how we were on a money-donation spree across the country.

They're talking about how he dropped a bomb in the Miles2Go board meeting this morning.

Resigned. Announced he's giving his stock to franchise owners. And endorsed his executive assistant to be the new CEO of the company.

He didn't say he advised against letting his father have a continued role, but the implications were there in his subtle references to how badly Miles2Go was struggling when he took over.

He hasn't simply left the company himself. He's completely taken it out of his family's hands.

They'll no longer have majority control. Or likely even a say on the board of directors.

Some people are framing it as him fucking his family over.

I don't see it that way.

I see it as Oliver being the Oliver that I got to know the past two weeks. Publicly giving credit where credit is due with his nomination for the new CEO and doing some of that trickle-down economics stuff at the same time with his own stock shares.

Putting more control in the hands of the people doing the everyday work.

Preventing his father from destroying what he's built back up.

And it makes me love him even more.

So much so that I couldn't stop crying over my lunch break and had to call my boss and beg for one more afternoon off, which I've sworn to make up for with extra fundraising calls.

She saw the news.

She knows who I was with the past two weeks.

She knows where our funding comes from.

And she told me she's not charging me any vacation days for the past two weeks since I was working with a major donor.

Bea and her family are my family, and my coworkers are a close second.

At the window, Simon flexes his biceps. "Burger and fries and a beefcake show," he calls. "Free autographs too."

Bea smiles and shakes her head. "Sorry, Daph. He is who he is."

I make myself smile back at her. "He makes you happy. And he sells a lot of burgers for you. That makes me happy."

I look down at my phone again and switch over to the family text message.

The one that has Bea and all three of her brothers.

I snap a picture of Simon, then send it to all four of them. *Bet you're sad you're not here to see this*, I text.

Hudson won't answer quickly. He went back to college while I was on my trip.

Griff won't answer quickly. He's getting ready for a game in Atlanta.

Ryker won't answer at all. He stopped by earlier with more vegetables from his farm, saw Simon's flexing for himself, sighed like he's ninety-three instead of twenty-six, and left quickly.

And Bea will eventually answer with something that will make her brothers all respond with throwing-up emojis.

I scroll and pull up my text messages with Margot.

She was one of the people who sent me the livestream with Oliver.

Maybe we can meet halfway between me and you for brunch this weekend?, I text her.

Her response is almost immediate, and she's accurately reading between the lines of my message. *It hasn't been a full week, Daph. Have some faith.*

It's been long enough.

Four days is *forever* when you're in love and don't know if you'll ever see him again.

If he's coming.

If he won't be one more person to abandon me.

I cringe at that thought and switch over to text Lana, Simon's ex. Like, looooong-ago ex. She's the boys' mother, and the four of them have their own unique co-parenting family situation that's surprisingly functional.

Far more functional than my family. Simon keeps talking about Bea adopting him into her family, but he and Lana and the boys have adopted Bea and her brothers and me into their family too.

It's pretty cool.

Plus, Lana let me whine to her about Oliver being bad for Margot before the road trip. It feels like forty-seven years ago that I was telling her how wrong Oliver and Margot were for each other and how boring he was.

And yes, she was one more person texting me this morning.

She heard the story of my road trip at a cookout yesterday at Simon's house.

I need to binge something dark. You in? I text her.

She replies quickly too. *Tomorrow? I have the boys tonight. I'll bring snacks. Hot cheese puffs are your favorite, right?*

Shit.

And now I'm tearing up again.

I have to do something.

I have to get over this fear.

I have to find his phone number, and I have to call him. I need to hear his voice.

"Afternoon, old chap," Simon says out the window. "Would you be interested in trying the best burgers in the entire world? I recommend at least two. One's never enough. And not because they're not big. They're healthy-sized. They're so delicious that one will never be enough."

Bea cracks up. "One is a good-size meal," she tells the new customer.

"Are you Bea?" a familiar voice replies.

I jerk upright at the table. Did I—did I manifest this, or am I imagining it?

I can only see Bea's profile, but I see one of her eyes flaring wide and her jaw going a little slack. "I am," she says.

"And who are you?" Simon says. "And how many burgers would you like?"

"*Simon,*" Bea hisses out of the corner of her mouth, but she's smiling. And I don't think she's smiling simply because Simon's being Simon.

"Where's Daphne?" the customer asks.

His voice—*his voice.*

Oliver's here.

He's here, asking for me, and it hasn't even been a full week, and I need to stand up and get my ass out of this bus and tackle him with a hug and a kiss and tell him that I love him and I never want to leave him behind anywhere again, especially in a jail cell, but my hands and feet are suddenly tingling and my eyes are flooding with tears and I have forgotten how to move.

I can barely make out the sight of Bea leaning into the window beside Simon. "Why?" she asks.

"Because I miss her and I hope she misses me and it's been too long since I saw her, we have a winning lottery ticket from Pennsylvania that we need to put to good use, and also, I have this polar bear for her."

Something thumps onto the counter.

Something that looks suspiciously like Angelina Juliana Priestly would look if I were staring at her through blurry eyes.

"Come inside the back of the bus," she says to Oliver. "Simon only has one security guy with him today, and you're basically the most famous person in the world at the moment, and I've already seen what can happen with that one too many times this summer."

the grumpiest billionaire

Oliver makes a frustrated noise, but he clearly does as he's told because she turns to me with the biggest smile that I can see even through my tears and adds a double thumbs-up to it.

And then I hear, "I don't need any damn secur— *Daphne.*"

It's Oliver.

All of him.

In jeans and a T-shirt, leaping into the back of the bus.

I twist in the seat and try to stand, but I can't make it up.

My legs are too wobbly. It's like every emotion I've ever felt in my entire life is surging through my body and short-circuiting the parts that make me work.

But then I'm being crushed against a solid, dependable, perfect chest while two strong arms engulf me. "Who made you cry? Tell me. They're dead. Absolutely dead."

I somehow make my arms work to hug him back. "You did, you dummy," I sob. "I missed you."

"Ah, Daph." He threads his fingers through my hair and kisses my temple. "I missed you too."

"And I was scared you—you—you wouldn't want me anymore."

"Daphne," he whispers. Just my name, but with tenderness and reverence and empathy and a million little meanings behind it.

"I know you said—you said you'd come—but I left you in—in *jail.*"

"I broke out. Picked the lock. Made a run for the border with the help of an old cowboy and a runaway fairy princess. Totally fine, like I told you I would be."

I laugh, but I'm crying too hard, and instead, I choke and send myself into a coughing fit.

"Ah, young love," Simon says cheerfully. "So marvelous and beautiful."

"Spoken like a man who found it while immensely hungover," Bea murmurs.

"Exactly that, my darling."

I squeeze Oliver tight.

He squeezes me right back. "Archie wouldn't give me your phone number."

"I told you he's an asshole."

He laughs against me, and suddenly everything is right in the world again.

He's here.

He promised he'd be here, and he's here.

Unless he's a mirage.

"Are you real?" I ask him.

"Exactly the same as being drunk," Simon says.

"*Shush.*" Bea laughs.

"Very real," Oliver says. "And glad that you had entertainment the past few days, if the past few minutes are any indication."

"Don't leave again."

"I'm not leaving again."

"Promise?"

"Daph, everything else in my life was chosen for me. I'm not running away from my life. I'm running *to* it. I choose you. I *want* to make a new life with you."

"Oliver," I whisper.

He kisses my forehead, then my hair. "I'm completely done in the city. Any loose ends can be done over email now."

"I was so proud of you today. You did an amazing thing that will be so good for a lot of people."

"I hope you're right." He kisses my forehead again. Strokes my back. Holds me tight while I get a grip on my breathing, just letting me be. Letting me cry it all out until the tears are gone.

He feels so good.

So right.

And for the first time in what feels like forever, I'm safe.

Safe. Home. Loved.

I've had all of those things courtesy of Bea, but now—now, it's *more*.

Oliver makes it all complete.

"I think I'm still a little bit of a disaster," I whisper.

"No, Daph. You're absolutely perfect. God, I missed you."

"She hasn't been sleeping well," Bea says, closer. A bag rustles. "Or eating well. Here. Eat here, take it to go, whatever works for you. But please eat. *Both* of you."

"Thank you," Oliver says.

And I giggle through the threat of more tears.

He's using his manners again.

"Don't think I'm using them with you," he murmurs to me, like he knows what I'm thinking.

"Thank you for making sure she got home safe," Bea replies. "A fortune teller told me a few weeks ago that she wouldn't come home, and I've been a little bit of a wreck waiting for her since she left."

"I would've been too," he tells her. "Don't go see fortune tellers."

"Madame Petty is awesome," I say into his neck. "We are absolutely going to see her. But maybe not for like, a year. Or five years."

Oliver laughs.

Bea laughs.

My tears are drying up, and all I have now—it's all warmth.

Squishy, heart-swelling warmth that comes with a side of glow.

I wipe my face off and sit up, staring into Oliver's hazel eyes, and I start to smile. "You're here."

He smiles back, the worry lines easing in his beautiful face. "I'm here."

"To stay?"

"To find a house with fewer than seven rooms and get a dog and convince this woman who stole my heart to move in with me and help me make the world a better place."

Dammit, he's making me cry again. "You're gonna love it here. We have festivals every weekend—Bea, what's this weekend?"

"Cardboard boat regatta," Bea reports.

Oliver squints one eye at me, then at her, then back at me. "You enter every year, don't you?"

"Not since the first year when my boat sank before they blew the whistle to start the race."

"I have pictures," Bea says. "And video."

"First goal—build Daphne a better cardboard boat," he murmurs.

The scent of hamburger tickles my nose again, and for the first time in days, I'm hungry. I grab the bag of burgers Bea made us, then dig into my pocket for my car keys. "Bea?"

She catches them with a smile. "We'll get it home by morning."

"Thank you. You're the best."

"Only most of the time."

I rise and pull Oliver to his feet too. "Wanna go hide from the world for a few days in a place with running water and every streaming subscription known to man?"

He shakes his head. "No. But I do want to go hide from the world for a few days with you, whether there's running water and streaming subscriptions or not. And then plan another road trip. And some camping. New adventures and fun every day."

And there go my eyeballs getting leaky again. "I love you," I whisper.

His face erupts in the biggest smile I've ever seen as he grabs me and swings me in a circle in the back of my best friend's burger bus, ending with a kiss so thorough that I drop the burger bag.

"Good," he says. "Because I love you too."

37

And just like that, our life finally fits

Oliver

Daphne holds my hand, our fingers interlaced, on our way to the SUV that I've now registered properly in my own name here in New York, and then she challenges me to a game of rock-paper-scissors for the right to drive.

Watching her expression dance as the redness and puffiness clear away, both from her eyes and from her cheeks, the way she's bouncing on her toes like we're about to go on another epic road trip—*this*.

This is what I want.

I've lived in financial luxury my entire life. Slept on the world's most expensive sheets. Eaten the world's most expensive food. Traveled by private jet and visited resorts that most people don't even know exist.

None of it compares to being someone's favorite person.

To being *Daphne's* favorite person.

"Tell me what you're playing so I can lose," I tell her.

She laughs. "Nuh-uh. You have to lose all on your own. Ready? One, two, three, *go!*"

She plays rock.

I switch my paper to scissors, and get the joy of hearing her laugh bounce across the parking lot.

"Cheater," she says as I gesture her into the driver's seat.

I kiss her because I can. "Damn. You've figured out my secrets."

She drives me all over Athena's Rest, pointing out her favorite diner—Hudson's home crush apparently works there on the weekends—and the restaurant that Bea's ex stole from her—with a mostly-empty parking lot and a few protesters outside, which makes Daphne cackle in glee—and the entrance to a walking-only street called the Secret Alley—we're going back later for the cheese shop—and the place in town where she led the protest against the university's emotional support animal policy.

We eat in the car as she drives.

She gets fries as I hand them to her.

I eat both burgers, because she's right.

Even smashed after the way she dropped them, these *are* even better than the burgers we had at the saloon.

And I would've said that even if we hadn't been arrested at the saloon.

Finally, she pulls into the parking lot of a four-story apartment building. "Tomorrow, I would love for you to meet my boss, and also, I'll show you where Simon and Ryker live, but *this*," she announces, "is home."

I study the rectangular building, which seems very boring for someone like Daphne. "I like it."

She cracks up.

It's music.

The sound I want to hear every day—every waking hour—for the rest of my life.

I lean over the center console and kiss her again.

Her hands flutter to my cheeks as she holds me there, kissing me back with a desperation that I feel in my bones.

"I missed you," I tell her.

"Never leaving you in jail ever *ever* again," she whispers back, which sends both of us into a fit of laughter.

"God, I love you," I say as I pop my door open.

the grumpiest billionaire

I need to get her inside.

Inside and naked.

I can't keep my hands off her in the elevator. I don't know how we get through the door.

I couldn't tell you if her apartment has carpet or wood floors or rainbows on the walls or photos of every animal Daphne's ever saved.

How we make it down the hallway.

When my clothes all fell off me. Shoes too.

I just know I'm finally where I've desperately needed to be—in her arms, kissing her rough and hard and desperately while I thrust my cock inside her until we're both coming so hard that I might never walk again.

She curls into me afterward, drawing little designs across my chest while we both catch our breath.

"You shaved," she whispers.

"Last time," I murmur back.

"Good. I like you scruffy."

"I like you."

She reaches around me and tugs at something under my shoulder, then plops a stuffed lobster down on my chest. "Oliver, meet Lolly the Lobster. She's staying in the bed until I'm sure you're an adequate substitute."

I laugh. "You're not sure I'm an adequate substitute yet?"

"Lolly's never kidnapped me and gotten me thrown in jail."

I roll with energy I don't have, smiling so hard my cheeks already ache.

Daphne grins back at me and touches my cheek. "I love your face. Even when it's grumpy and scowly. But especially when you're happy."

I shake my head at her. "I never expected you to be my happiness."

"*Right?*" She kisses me again. "I can't stop doing this."

"Then don't."

She doesn't.

Freaking Daphne Merriweather-Brown.

The most amazing woman in the world.

She's my future. My dreams. And my forever love.

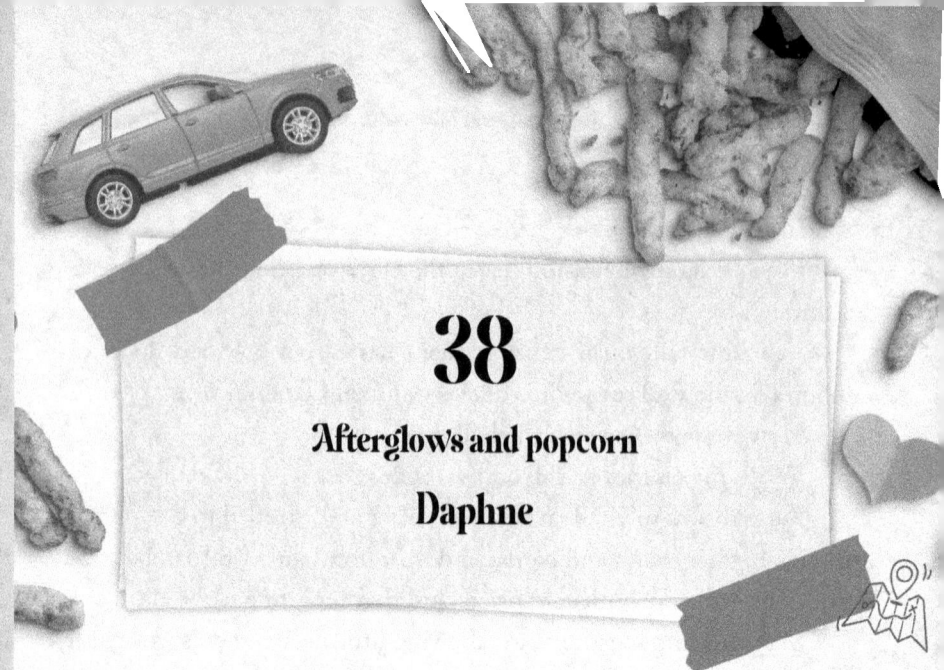

38

Afterglow's and popcorn

Daphne

We're on the couch after a leisurely and orgasm-filled shower, Oliver stretched out with his head in my lap, a cooking show playing softly while I peruse houses on my phone—truly, apartment living won't fit Oliver, not when he needs a backyard for both himself and the dog he's definitely getting to play in—when the door clicks open softly.

Bea pokes her head in, Angelina Juliana Priestly in her hands, and she's about to set the polar bear on my favorite giraffe end table when she spots me.

Her face telegraphs what she doesn't say out loud—*I thought you'd be naked in the bedroom*—and I give her a brow wiggle of *been there, done that a few times already.*

She tries to stifle a snort of laughter and fails.

"Can I borrow your computer?" I wave my phone at her. "Better for seeing pictures."

"Of course."

"I won't go on your socials."

"I didn't think you would."

"I would've gone on Hudson's socials after the way he used all of the hot water all summer, so I wanted you to know I wouldn't do it to you."

"I mean, fair." She heads into the kitchen, which is on the other side of the entry door, then returns with her computer while Simon slips in the door too. She nods to Oliver. "Asleep?"

"Happy," he mumbles, tightening his grip on my leg.

Bea smiles at me.

My eyes go misty as I smile back at her. "Turns out he's not so boring after all," I say.

Zero reaction from Oliver, but it wouldn't surprise me if he's smiling.

"Well, enjoy him not being boring. I'm staying with Simon tonight."

"Whenever we get there," Simon grouses, which is unusual enough that I lift my brows at him.

"Is someone holding your time ransom?" I ask. He's pretty free to go and do as he likes when he doesn't have the boys, and I know Lana has them tonight.

"There's no one else to run the drive-in tonight, so we're up," Bea tells me.

Oliver lifts his head. "Drive-in?" he says.

"Simon bought and reopened the old drive-in theater a few weeks ago," I tell him. "I'll show you tomorrow. Or the next day."

He looks at Simon. "You're short-staffed? At a movie theater?"

Oh my god.

I start to laugh, then try to squelch it while Oliver sits all the way up.

"Yes?" Simon replies.

He and Bea are both looking at us like we've lost our minds.

Understandable. I'm laughing my ass off, and Oliver looks like a puppy being teased with a bone.

"What's the job?" Oliver asks. "I'm unemployed. Looks bad on loan applications for houses."

Simon and Bea share a look.

"I'm not sure it pays well enough for the kind of house you're probably looking for," Bea says.

"Whatever. I don't need a loan to buy a house. What do you need? Someone to pop popcorn? Run the reels? How many shows a night? How many shows a week? Any benefits?"

"*Oliver*," I say between peals of laughter. "I work during the day. When will we see each other if you work every night?"

He stares at me, dead serious, without blinking. "Popcorn maker at a movie theater is on my bucket list."

"Show starts in two hours," Bea tells us. "Wanna ride along and learn the ropes? See if it's for you?"

He grins. "Hell, yes. But I have to have Daph home before eleven. She has a boring day job."

"I hear she's dating a guy who needs help putting a massive fortune to good use," Bea replies.

"Heard she's pretty good at giving money away to good causes," Oliver agrees, like they've planned this.

Like I'm not already halfway to agreeing to quit my job and help Oliver manage a charitable foundation.

I'm not afraid I'll depend on his money and then lose it someday.

He's Oliver. Not my family. He wouldn't rip the rug out from under me.

And even if the very, very worst happened, if someday, somehow, we ran completely out of money—I've survived before. I'd survive again. Especially with him by my side.

But I'll miss my coworkers at Beeslieve.

That's the hesitation.

"Make her take you out for pizza and show you the video game with its own trust fund for upkeep sometime soon," Bea says.

I look between them, then at Simon. "You gonna join in this pile on too?"

"Certainly not. I can't take notes while I'm participating in the conversation. By the way, could Bea and I write a screenplay loosely based on your life? Very loosely. You won't recognize yourself in the final product."

"*Dude.*" I glare at him.

"Or not," he says hastily. "Learned my lesson. That's why I'm asking. I know no means no. I'll find my inspiration elsewhere."

"If you're going to make a screenplay based on my life, I want *everyone* to know it's about me," I tell him. "Do *not* mask a single thing if you want me to say yes."

"Our parents would despise it," Oliver agrees. "You definitely have to make it obvious."

"But you have to make Margot look good."

Oliver nods. "Nonnegotiable."

"And I'm only in if Bea thinks it's a good idea."

"I wouldn't argue with that even if I wanted to. Which I don't. Daph's favorite people are my favorite people. Our favorite people should be happy."

My stomach growls.

Oliver winces.

And Simon starts to laugh. "You ate both burgers, didn't you?" he says to Oliver. Then he grins at Bea. "May I use an *I told you so*, my darling?"

She kisses his cheek. "Yes, you may."

"Forget later this week. Who wants pizza?" I say.

I do.

I want pizza with all of my favorite people.

My best friend.

Her boyfriend.

My boyfriend.

The man I'm going to marry someday. The man I'll probably even have kids with someday.

Because this Oliver?

He's everything I never knew I wanted, and so much more.

Epilogue

Plot twist

Oliver

My new job is fucking awesome. Roughly a week and a half after I arrived in Athena's Rest, I'm fully in charge of the drive-in theater. Tonight, at the vote of the community, we're playing *Sharknado*. It's utterly ridiculous. But everyone has their popcorn, and Daphne and I are in the little building that doubles as control booth and popcorn hub, debating what we should list for choices for the next few weekends of movies.

With school starting, daily showings are going down to weekends only.

Less time to sneak kisses with my girlfriend in the booth, but more time for kissing my girlfriend at home.

Archie's been a huge help with moving my money around to give me a large enough nest egg that Daph and I will never want for anything, while putting everything else—except my Miles2Go shares—into a new foundation.

And Daphne's giving her notice at Beeslieve.

It won't be without tears, but she says that's a good thing.

That being so sad to leave means both it's an amazing place and also that helping me give away the rest of my fortune is an even more amazing opportunity.

Carmen—who will definitely be the next CEO at Miles2Go—has confirmed for me that the M2G Foundation will keep up the charitable work I started, so my money can go toward other things.

Like saving the polar bears.

And as an added bonus to this arrangement—we can set our own hours. Which means more time for exploring the area, for working at the drive-in to see all of the movies I've missed, for camping, for road trips and lazy afternoons at home.

For fun.

For living.

For loving Daphne.

"I can't believe you've never seen *Barbie*," she says to me as she leans over the movie list.

She's sitting in my lap, pulling my hand farther and farther up her thigh.

"You can't?" I say on a laugh. I haven't seen anything for years. Not until this past week or so.

She grins at me. "Fine, I can believe it. But you *have* to watch it. And I'm not saying that to torture you. I'm saying it because it's a masterpiece. But we have to warn Bea. After raising her brothers, that one monologue always makes her completely lose it. Maybe we can show it with a tissue break after the monologue?"

"A masterpiece?"

"Mock all you want. You'll see."

"Daphne?"

"Yes, Oliver?"

"I'd rather kiss you than mock you."

Her smile softens as she lowers her mouth to mine. "Like this?"

I slide my hand the rest of the way up her thigh and dip my thumb under the hem of her jean shorts. "And this," I murmur against her mouth.

"You have the best job ever."

I'm smiling as I kiss her and inch my thumb closer and closer to her pussy. She threads her fingers through my hair, her tongue touching mine and sending electric jolts through my body, straight to my cock.

Definitely the best job ever. Probably not a long-term job, or even close to long-term, but for now—for now, it's awesome.

I'm reaching around her with my other arm to tease her nipple when the door clicks behind us.

"We're closed," Daph gasps at the same time I say, "Go ring at the popcorn window."

"Kissing, ew," a familiar voice replies.

Daph straightens so fast she almost falls out of my lap. "*Margot?*"

"Hate to interrupt," Margot says dryly, "but I need to give both of you a heads-up in a place no one would see me."

I breathe in deep and tell my cock to stand down while I spin the chair so that we're looking at Daphne's sister.

Who's smirking.

"God, you two are stupidly cute," she says.

"We know," Daph replies cheerfully. "We're annoying *everyone*."

She slides off my lap and hugs Margot, who squeezes her back tightly, then releases her. "I can't stay long. Dad thinks I'm on a plane headed to the Caribbean."

Daphne rolls her eyes at both of us. "What's with billionaire heirs lying to their parents about where they're going?"

"Our parents are awful," I reply.

"Exactly that," Margot agrees. "Listen, you're going to hear chatter that I'm having a nervous breakdown over you two getting together. Don't listen to it. I love you both—in the sibling way, don't get weird, Oliver, I definitely love you less—but I do love seeing both of you happy, and I'm glad you have each other. But I needed a cover story, and this one's about as convenient as they come."

"Cover story for what?" Daphne asks.

"You should sit down."

Daph lifts her brows. "Seriously?"

"Yes."

Daph slides back into my lap. "Better?"

Margot blows out a breath. "Everything I'm about to say doesn't leave this room. Understood?"

"Understood," I murmur.

"What's going on?" Daphne whispers.

"You can't even tell Bea," Margot says.

"Whoa."

"Promise, Daph?"

"Holy shit, but yeah, I promise."

"Thank you. I know she's trustworthy, but the fewer people who know, the better, always. I don't want to pull you into this, but I might need you, so I want you to be prepared." Margot pauses, heads to the door, locks it, and then comes closer, squatting in front of us. "You know how Dad's cheated on Mom our entire lives?"

Daph makes a face. "I mean, I suspected, but I kinda didn't want to know."

"Most of his affairs are covered with NDAs and payoffs, but he missed one."

I straighten, seeing where this is going. "You're taking him down."

Margot waves a hand. "You and your imagination."

That wasn't a denial. "Long game?" I ask her.

"There are things you don't need to know yet, and I shouldn't even tell you this, but like I said, I think I'm going to need help, and you need time to absorb this. Daph, it turns out…we have triplet half-brothers in a little town in Colorado."

Daphne squeaks.

Understandable.

That's not something I saw coming.

I grip Daph tighter because she is, indeed, at risk of falling on the floor if I don't. "Triplet half-brothers?" I repeat to Margot.

"I did a DNA test a few months ago—fake name, don't worry—and we matched as sharing a parent. Clearly not our mothers, so by default... And honestly, who's surprised? The triplet part aside. That part was more than I was expecting."

"Oh my god," Daphne whispers.

"I've had...something...in the works for a while, and I've needed one last *thing*, and I think they're it," Margot says, which I suspect is as close as I'm going to get to confirmation that she's been plotting to destroy her father since he disinherited Daphne. "So I'm headed to Colorado to get to know them and see if they want to...help."

"You should probably never be around a tornado," I tell Margot while soft screams carry through the speaker Daphne and I have set up to listen in on the movie behind us.

"Was that a *Sharknado* joke?" Margot asks.

"Yes. Was it good?"

She smiles at me. "It was awful."

"Oh my god, I get it." Daphne tips her head back and laughs. "She'd be the shark in the tornado."

"Do *not* tell anyone," Margot says.

"*Triplets*," Daphne breathes.

"Identical, in fact. And from what I can tell so far through email conversations with one of them, they're definitely related to you."

"*Oh my god*, Margot, *we're sisters*. They're related to *you too*. As *the DNA says*."

Margot smiles again. "Yeah, but you got some genes I didn't. The fun ones."

"You have your own kind of fun," I tell her.

The shark smile makes an appearance. "I'm certainly about to. Oh, also—they think I'm a housekeeper. I got a job at some retreat center. Starting Monday. I'm flying into Nebraska tomorrow, getting a car, dyeing my hair, getting fake glasses, and showing up as Margie Johnson."

I clear my throat.

Daph squeaks again. "Maybe don't stop at any small towns with saloons that have karaoke and mechanical bulls?"

Margot cracks up. "I will not be visiting any towns where you've been arrested. Unless there are more somewhere in Colorado that I don't know about?"

"Nope, that's my only one," Daphne says.

"Same," I agree.

Margot nods. "Good."

"You taking security?" I ask her.

"One man. He'll be lying low and keeping an eye on things."

"Glad to hear it. Check the back seat and trunk of the car for stowaways every time you get in it."

She rolls her eyes, but she's smiling. "Not a word from either of you, please. But I couldn't leave without telling you this part. And to not worry about anything you hear. I needed to tell you in person that I mean it—you two have my full support. Provided you don't do anything stupid, Oliver. Ryker's on standby to dispose of your body if necessary."

"*Oh my god*, you're not going to need Ryker," Daphne says on a laugh. "Will you call while you're gone?"

"I have a feeling I won't be able to *not* call. Not if they're what I'm expecting."

She straightens and hugs Daphne and pecks her on the cheek, then hugs me too. "Take care of each other. Trust me. Don't listen to anything anyone says about me not supporting you. And I wasn't here, okay?"

"Be safe and call," Daphne says.

Margot blows her a kiss, and then she's gone.

We both stare at the door for a minute, and then Daph looks at me. "I'm glad she told me to sit down. Holy shit. *Triplets*?"

I look at the door once more. "She's gonna destroy your father. And if she's been prepping this for four years...she hasn't left anything to chance."

Daphne frowns. "I don't need her to do that for me."

"I think she needs to do it for herself. Even if she's telling herself it's for you."

She snuggles closer. "I can understand that. Telling him off—it felt good. Like I was letting go of the last bits of my relationship that I hadn't realized I was holding on to. I needed that, and I didn't even know it."

I kiss her forehead again. "And now you're free."

"We're both free."

"And happy. Very, very happy."

She smiles at me. I smile back at her.

I miss when the movie ends.

I'm too busy loving my unexpected favorite woman in the world.

Bonus Epilogue
Didn't see that coming either
Daphne

This life is my favorite.

It's a rare warm day in mid-October, and I'm curled up against Oliver in the hammock in his backyard.

Our backyard.

The house he bought for us is a little bigger than what he originally wanted, but the trade-off was the privacy that comes with a gated estate. We're essentially neighbors with Bea and Simon, and we see them all the time.

Bea more often—Simon's travel schedule this fall has been a little brutal—but both of them together as regularly as possible.

The sun is dipping low in the sky, and Feather, the timid rescue mutt that Oliver won over at the shelter after three straight weeks of visits, is snoring softly on the grass beneath us.

I'd say I helped with Feather, but mostly I watched Oliver coax her out of her shell.

He's the best.

The absolute best.

We've gone camping a couple times. We're planning a road trip to go visit his cabin in Pennsylvania before the snow sets in—we do, after all, have a lottery ticket that we have to do something with. We're also going with Bea to see one of Griff's games soon since he's in the playoffs.

Oliver's learning to cook, and he's started doing the work himself to restore the gardens around the house—both vegetable and flower—and he's napping a lot.

Like now.

Here in the hammock.

Which is where I found him when I got home from one of my last days at Beeslieve.

Leaving is bittersweet, so I've been dragging it out, working as much as I can through the days while I can be outside. I'm staying on a little into the winter too, but more so I can train the new staff on best fundraising practices.

The wind rustles above us, a slight chill in it that makes me snuggle closer to Oliver, which makes the hammock sway gently.

"I love this life," he murmurs against my hair.

"I was just thinking that."

It's odd to be happy while I'm still, but I am.

Fully happy. At peace, as Oliver likes to say.

Feather whimpers a little beneath us.

"All good, girl," Oliver says.

But all is not entirely good.

The backyard gate swings shut with a clank, and then—

"*Oliver!* You are *on my shit list.*"

I barely move as I start to smile. "Oliver."

"Yes, my beautiful chaos fairy?" he replies.

"Did you leave a stupid tip at Bea's burger bus today?"

"Would I do that?" I feel him smile against my hair, but it's the giggle that fully gives him away.

"Where are you, you asshole?" Bea says. "Oh, hell. Sorry, Feather. It's okay. I'll quit yelling. But I'm still mad at your dad."

I lift an arm and wave, making the hammock sway a little more. "Hey, Bea. How much did he leave?"

"Oh, good. Witnesses," she replies.

"I attempted to talk her out of this," Simon says, which has me perking my ears up too. I didn't know he was back in town. This is awesome. "But I'm also rather curious to see her full temper play out."

Bea's face pops into view. She's scowling, but Simon's smiling widely behind her.

He gives us a thumbs-up behind her back.

"I saw that," she says.

"I knew you would, darling," he replies. "If not me, at least Daphne's reaction to me. Though possibly she's merely happy to see me?"

I grin back at him. "I'm definitely happy to see you. And I'd hug you, but I've tipped Oliver out of this hammock four times already, and I don't want to land on our dog."

"You don't have to keep the money," Oliver says to Bea. "You could redistribute it."

"How the *fuck*—sorry, Feather. Sorry, girl." She drops her voice lower as she squats out of view, likely getting a treat for the dog. "How am I supposed to redistribute *fifty thousand dollars?*"

"Oh, that was a good one," I tell Oliver. "How'd you get that much into her tip jar?"

"I blackmailed Archie into procuring a few thousand-dollar bills for me."

"High-five." I shift to hold up a hand.

He slaps it. "Fun is my favorite."

Bea sighs.

Simon grins.

Feather crunches on a dog treat.

"That was completely unnecessary," Bea tells Oliver. "You should've tipped the taco truck."

"Oh, I did that too."

She should know by now.

She really should.

Her exasperated sigh echoes across the backyard.

"Consider it practice for when Griff retires," I tell her. "You know he's going to find ways to pay for all kinds of crazy things for you once he starts spending some of his cash."

"Griff has ten or fifteen years, and *someone* got me a *producer* credit on that screenplay I helped him finish, so *I don't need everyone giving me money.*"

"She sounds like you," Oliver murmurs.

"We're two peas in a pod."

He cracks up.

Bea and I might be besties, but we are *very* different people.

"I have a solution," Simon announces.

"I sneak it back into their house while they're on their next camping trip?" Bea says.

"We jointly purchase the cheese shop and convert it into a bar with a mechanical bull."

"Whoa, hands off the cheese shop," Oliver says. "Build a bar at your drive-in."

I don't know why that makes my brain squirrel where it goes, but it does, and suddenly, Oliver and I are on the ground.

Flipped right out of the hammock.

Because I sat up too fast without thinking, because—"*Oliver.*"

He rolls to his side, reaches out a hand to give Feather a light ruffle on her head, and deadeyes me. "Again?"

"No, no, *listen.*"

He shakes his head, the smile starting at the corners of his mouth. "I can't even be mad. You have a look, and I love those looks. Okay, Daphne. I'm listening."

"Do you remember when your father went to prison?"

He blinks one long, slow blink while Bea stifles a laugh behind a cough.

"I think he remembers that, Daph," she says in a strangled voice.

Simon's clearing his throat like he too is trying not to laugh.

"I do recall that," Oliver says patiently, his lips fighting with themselves over whether he wants to be annoyed or amused.

I twist on the ground, land my face in the side of the hammock, bat it away, and then climb to my feet.

"You told me you sold a bunch of your mother's artwork."

"All of her favorites. Yes. It was delightful fun."

"Which artwork? Paintings?"

"So many paintings."

"Who did them?"

Simon makes a noise I've never heard him make before.

Bea sucks in a breath too.

Oliver gives Feather one last rub on the head, and then he rises too, looking at the three of us like we've lost our marbles. "You want me to name all of the artists?"

"Was one of them Naomi Luckwood?"

"Oh, god, yes. That was the biggest—"

He cuts himself off and looks at Simon, eyes round, clearly connecting the dots on the last name.

"Oh, fuck," he whispers.

"*Simon.*" I bounce on my toes. "Why did your parents go broke?"

"Daph, you need to stop," Bea says. "There's budding bromance, and then there's the two of them leaving us for each other."

"Someone sold a vast quantity of my mother's paintings and made the market value of them drop significantly," Simon says reverently.

Oliver's going pink in the cheeks. "I didn't—" he starts, but he cuts himself off as Simon throws himself at him.

"You beautiful bastard," Simon says. "I could kiss you."

And he does.

He plants a smacker right on Oliver's cheek.

"He *hates* his parents," I murmur to Oliver. I lift a hand. "High-five again. You're a superhero to him right now."

"Bea! *Beatrice*! I get to be friends with someone who helped destroy my parents," Simon crows. He lets Oliver go and spins Bea into a hug. "This is possibly the third or fourth best day of my life."

Oliver stares at me, then at Bea and Simon, and then back to me. "Plot twist," he mutters, a real smile spreading across his face again. His scruffy, beautiful, wonderful face.

He slips an arm around my shoulder, probably using me as a shield so Simon won't hug and kiss him again.

"Well worth falling out of the hammock again," I say.

He laughs. "Can we maybe *not* do that again though?"

"Only if you haven't secretly participated in some other revenge scheme I'm unaware of."

He winces.

The man freaking winces.

And then he grins broader. "There *is* something I haven't told you about what Margot asked me to do..."

I stare at him, contemplate everything that's happened since Margot left for Colorado, and then I'm cracking up too.

"I freaking love this life," I say as he hugs me.

He laughs against my hair. "It's the very best."

ABOUT THE AUTHOR

Pippa Grant wanted to write books, so she did.

Before she became a *USA Today* and #1 Amazon bestselling romantic comedy author, she was a young military spouse who got into writing as self-therapy. That happened around the time she discovered reading romance novels, and the two eventually merged into a career. Today, she has more than 50 knee-slapping Pippa Grant titles.

When she's not writing romantic comedies, she's fumbling through being a mom, wife, and mountain woman, and sometimes tries to find hobbies. Her crowning achievement? Having impeccable timing for telling stories that will make people snort beverages out of their noses. Consider yourself warned.

FIND PIPPA AT...
www.pippagrant.com

www.ingramcontent.com/pod-product-compliance
Lightning Source LLC
LaVergne TN
LVHW021055100526
838202LV00083B/6274